ENEMY IN THE DARK

ALSO BY JAY ALLAN

FAR STARS

Shadow of Empire

Enemy in the Dark

Funeral Games (January 2016)

CRIMSON WORLDS

Marines

The Cost of Victory

A Little Rebellion

The First Imperium

The Line Must Hold

To Hell's Heart

The Shadow Legions

Even Legends Die

The Fall

War Stories (Crimson Worlds Prequels)

MERCS (Crimson Worlds Successors I)

PORTAL WARS

Gehenna Dawn

The Ten Thousand

PENDRAGON CHRONICLES

The Dragon's Banner

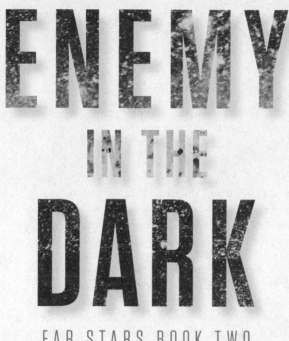

ENEMY
IN THE
DARK

FAR STARS BOOK TWO

JAY ALLAN

HARPER Voyager
An Imprint of HarperCollins Publishers

ENEMY IN THE DARK. Copyright © 2015 by Jay Allan Books. All rights reserved. Printed in the United States of America. No part of this book may be used or reproduced in any manner whatsoever without written permission except in the case of brief quotations embodied in critical articles and reviews. For information address HarperCollins Publishers, 195 Broadway, New York, NY 10007.

HarperCollins books may be purchased for educational, business, or sales promotional use. For information please e-mail the Special Markets Department at SPsales@harpercollins.com.

FIRST EDITION

Harper Voyager and design is a trademark of HarperCollins Publishers L.L.C.

Designed by Shannon Plunkett

Library of Congress Cataloging-in-Publication Data has been applied for.

ISBN 978-0-06-238892-6

15 16 17 18 19 OV/RRD 10 9 8 7 6 5 4 3 2 1

ENEMY IN THE DARK

CHAPTER 1

"I'LL SEE YOUR THOUSAND AND RAISE YOU . . . FIVE THOUSAND."

Ace stared across the table, through the dim light and swirling haze of cigar smoke. His opponent wasn't half the poker player he fancied himself, and Ace would have been licking his chops anywhere else, ready to pounce. A pompous fool, whose arrogance greatly exceeded his skill, was tailor-made for a shark like Ace Graythorn. But today he had a job to do, and that was to keep the sucker at the table—something he would hardly accomplish by cleaning him out early.

Ace looked at his hand for the third time, part of his carefully orchestrated act, and he exhaled loudly. Finally, he pushed his cards facedown into the center of the table with a groan that was only half playacting. Granted, he was sighing because he was laying down a winning hand—he figured his kings were a 90 percent favorite to win—but the sigh went over well. No matter what, the mission came first.

The mission *always* came first.

Alejandro Jose de Cordoba reached out and pulled the chips across the table with pudgy hands festooned with gaudy rings. He wore the elaborate dress of a Castillan nobleman, though Ace knew there was nothing but peasant blood coursing through his veins. Cordoba had earned his position the old-fashioned way. He'd killed for it.

"Ah, Lord Suvarov, now you find yourself in a real game. One hopes you are not easily intimidated." Cordoba's voice was pleasant enough, despite the slightly mocking tone, but there was something else there, a menace only another killer would have noticed. Cordoba was a loud and boisterous man, but just like Ace, it was all an act. *This is definitely not a man to be trifled with.*

"Indeed no, Lord Cordoba. I find the challenge . . . stimulating."

Ace had been gambling almost around the clock for five days, waiting for Cordoba to notice him and invite him to a game. Cordoba was well known at the Grand Palais as a high-stakes gambler . . . and more important, as the top henchman of Lord Aragona, the venerable establishment's notorious owner.

It was easy enough to play the buffoon, but much more difficult to strike the balance Ace had managed most of the last week: that of a reasonably capable player, but one with inadequate control over his emotions. Just the sort of opponent an arrogant shark like Cordoba would seek. Strong enough to feed his ego, but weak enough to fleece.

Ace had vacillated between winning and losing, managing

to stay about even despite making some wild and foolish bets. Of course, that was exactly his job, but it still hurt the gambler inside to give it all away just to play a role. And it wasn't easy, either. He wanted to appear as a gambler who was reckless, but he wasn't looking to actually lose money. Anything he left at the tables would just ramp up the costs of the mission, and that would come right off the bottom line.

"I am delighted to hear that, Lord Suvarov." Cordoba stared across the table, looking into Ace's eyes.

He's trying to get a read on me, Ace thought, *see how far he can push me. Good luck with that, you arrogant ass. It will take a better man than you.*

"Perhaps you'd care to up the stakes, Lord Cordoba?" Ace slipped his hand under the table and pulled a large purse from his belt. He dumped it on the table, and an avalanche of platinum coins poured out. "I need a chance to win my money back, and I am prepared to wager my imperial crowns against your Castillan florins. Shall we say fifty florins to the crown?"

Ace knew it was an attractive trade for Cordoba. Imperial coinage was illegal for use on Castilla, and although the official exchange rate at the planet's central bank was twenty-five to one, that was a ludicrous example of wishful thinking that only supported a flourishing underground economy where a crown could fetch at least sixty florins, and often eighty or more.

"Very well, Lord Suvarov." Cordoba nodded, his eyes barely betraying him. *He's good,* Ace admitted.

Just not better than me.

He'd put it about fifty-fifty Cordoba would try and bargain him down, but he'd picked just the right number, an attractive deal that wouldn't look suspicious. "Then, by all means, Lord Cordoba . . . deal." Ace looked out over the table. He was down about fifteen hundred florins, nothing he couldn't manage. And the big pile of platinum crowns was occupying Cordoba's attention.

Ace wondered how the others were doing. His "wife," Katarina, would be in the restaurant, hopefully making a fool out of him by now. And Blackhawk and Sarge would be approaching the target location soon. In another few hours, the crew of *Wolf's Claw* would be blasting off Castilla after another successful mission—or they'd be in deep shit.

Just like every other mission, he thought.

"Lady Suvarov, what a delight to see you again." Arragonzo Francisco de Aragona stood next to the table, smiling. He wore a magnificent suit, perfectly tailored and trimmed in gold and silver lace. His neatly arranged hair was pulled back and fastened behind his head with a jeweled clasp.

Unlike Cordoba, Aragona *was* a Castillan nobleman. He was also a renowned ladies' man, one who preferred his women as beautiful—and married—as possible. His noble pedigree was modest, something that would normally have placed a ceiling on how high a Castillan could rise. But Aragona was smart. And ruthless. His willingness to use whatever means were necessary to clear rivals from his way had taken him far, and now he was one of the Oligarchs Council, a board of twenty men who ruled the planet.

His interests included most of the hotels and all the gambling on Castilla and, less formally, almost the entirety of the planet's underworld. He was the most junior member of the council by lineage, but he'd made up for that with fear. The other oligarchs, members of proud and ancient families, held their arrogance in check around Aragona. It was well known how he'd dealt with his rivals on his rise and, although he'd never made a hostile move against any in the highest ranks of the nobility, none of them wanted to risk being the first.

"Lord Aragona, what a delight to see you." Her voice was haughty, but there was something else there too for anyone truly listening, a hint of seduction. Katarina Venturi had played many roles, and she slipped effortlessly into the guise of an exiled Saragossan noblewoman. She glanced up with a smile. "Won't you join me for dinner? I'm afraid my husband's attention is consumed by the gaming tables." She sighed, a passing hint of sadness on her face.

Aragona bowed slightly. "By all means, Lady Suvarov. It would be my great pleasure. If I may say, your husband is a fool."

Katarina's smile broadened, and she looked across the table to her dining companion. "Natasha, do get up and make room for Lord Aragona. You may retire." She glanced back at Aragona, a playful glint in her eye. "I don't believe I will be needing you any further this evening."

Sam Sparks stood up and bowed her head toward Katarina. "As you wish, my lady." Samantha was doing her best to look comfortable in the elaborate dress she was wearing, but Katarina could see how much difficulty she was having trying to keep the long skirts in place.

"Lord Aragona." Sam bowed again, but Aragona didn't acknowledge her. *I'm not surprised, given the neckline of this dress,* Katarina thought. Indeed, his attention was focused on Katarina, who was leaning forward slightly, giving him a better view. Sam turned and quietly slipped out of the restaurant.

"Now, won't you keep me company?" Katarina smiled again, more mischievous this time, turning up the seduction just a bit.

Aragona glided around the table and slid into Sam's chair.

"This is an unexpected pleasure." He raised his hand, just a few centimeters above the table. The waiter rushed over, clearly trying to hide his nervousness. "Yes, Lord Aragona? What can I get for you?"

"Have you ordered yet?" He glanced over at Katarina.

"No, Lord Aragona. I have not."

"May I?" He smiled across the table.

"Of course."

Aragona turned his head slightly. "Bring us a bottle of the Antillean Black Château. And we'll start with the chilled Paru melon, followed by the fire-roasted dragonfish."

Katarina suppressed a grin. She was an expert in aphrodisiacs, and she knew most of them were either frauds or only marginally effective, Castillan Paru melons among them. She had a few truly effective elixirs in her own bag of tricks, but she was confident she wouldn't need them. Aragona's mind was already where she wanted it.

"I have heard much of the legendary Castillan dragonfish, Lord Aragona, though I have never had the pleasure." The large fish was from the extreme arctic regions of the planet, and it was considered one of the finest—and most expensive— delicacies in the Far Stars.

"I am certain you will enjoy it." He looked across the table and smiled. "And please, no more Lord Aragona, I beg you. I am Arra."

Katarina returned the stare with a smoldering sensuality. "And I am Irina."

Arkarin Blackhawk crept through the thickets on the outskirts of the estate, knee deep in the warm waters of the estuary. Aragona's home was a vast compound, built along the sandy lowlands just south of Madrassa. The lights of the city were visible in the distance, along the ridge behind the great château.

Blackhawk held his hand up behind him, a reminder to Sarge to move slowly, cautiously. Aragona's residence looked like the opulent seaside home of a wealthy nobleman and, indeed, it was that. But it was much more, and Blackhawk knew it. Arragonzo Aragona was more than a businessman and a politician. He was the undisputed leader of most of the Castillan underworld. Blackhawk didn't have the kind of scouting data on the compound he'd have liked, but he was sure the place was a veritable fortress.

But every fortress has its weakness . . . and sometimes that's someone inside.

He was confident Katarina would manage do the job. He almost pitied any man who was the target of her seductions. No, it wasn't getting her in that worried him. It was getting her out with the prisoner that gave him the cold sweat on his palms.

Blackhawk suspected Aragona was neck deep in a wide variety of unsavory enterprises, but the Castillan mastermind had made one crucial mistake. He'd included the Far Stars Bank among the targets of his frauds, defaulting on a loan for more than ten million crowns. The bank was not an entity to accept such a loss without consequences, and it had hired Blackhawk and his people to capture Aragona and bring him to its headquarters on Vanderon.

It's so easy to see power on one world as being universal. Aragona probably thought he was secure in his little fiefdom.

Blackhawk knew better. *There is always someone more powerful.*

He reached his hand out again, about to signal to Sarge to move forward, but then he froze. He heard something, far away, his ears picking up the dull roar long before Sarge knew anything was going on. Then, a few seconds later, he saw the lights, moving down the road from the east.

It was some kind of convoy, and it was heading right for the compound. He stared into the darkness, trying to focus on the oncoming vehicles. There was something about them, something troubling, familiar.

The convoy consists of imperial Raider-class ground assault vehicles. Probability 93 percent.

The artificial intelligence implanted in Blackhawk's brain was limited to the same sensory input as his own mind, but it was often able to make more effective use of the data.

Imperial Raiders are armed with dual particle accelerator cannons and can carry up to ten . . .

I am well aware of the specifications of imperial Raiders. There was an edge to the thought, directed toward the AI. Blackhawk had an odd relationship with the computer presence in his mind. He couldn't dispute the fact that the AI, whom he'd nicknamed Hans (for HANDAIS—an acronym for "heuristic algorithmic nanotech dynamic artificial intelligence system"), had been incredibly valuable on many occasions, but there was still some part of him that resented the intrusion. Despite the indisputable usefulness of the intelligence, he frequently found himself sparring with it . . . pointlessly he realized, but he did it anyway.

What the hell are imperial fighting vehicles doing on Castilla? More to the point, what are they doing on the way to Aragona's estate?

He wondered for a few minutes if Aragona's château was about to be attacked by his enemies, but as soon as the lead vehicle reached the gate it was apparent they were expected.

He stood stone still, watching the scene unfold. His grip tightened around his assault rifle, but that was pure reflex. He knew fighting wasn't going to solve his problem, especially not a suicidal assault on Aragona's villa.

Blackhawk had no idea what was going on, but this was the second time in six months he'd run into imperial involvement in the affairs of backwater worlds, and he didn't like it one bit. He wasn't a great believer in coincidence.

There's no time to worry about that now, he thought, setting the topic aside. He knew immediately he had to change the plan. Katarina was planning to seduce Aragona and lure him back to his estate, where Blackhawk and Sarge's crew were positioned to get them both out. But the château was going to look like an armed camp in a few minutes. There was no way they'd manage to sneak anyone in or out.

"We're going to have to go with the backup plan, Sarge." That meant getting back into the city—fast. And he'd have to break communications silence, at least briefly, to let Katarina know. Hopefully, he'd get to her before she and Aragona were on their way to the compound.

He reached into his pocket and pulled out a small controller, pushing one of the buttons with his index finger. The communication was short, just a microburst to a small receiver in Katarina's ring. She wouldn't get any details, just a prearranged signal telling her to move to the backup plan.

Just let it be in time . . .

"Let's go, Sarge," Blackhawk whispered. "We need to round

up your boys and get back to Madrassa." He took one last look at the château. The convoy was still coming, with no end in sight to the line of armored vehicles. *That's trouble. Big trouble.*

"C'mon, Sarge. We're already late."

Katarina felt a tingle on her finger, a small electrical discharge from her ring. It was a signal from Blackhawk, and it meant one thing: *trouble.* She had intended to seduce Aragona and get him to take her back to his château, where Blackhawk and Sarge's crew would help her get him out. Indeed, Aragona had already propositioned her twice. She'd been playing along, making sure he was truly hooked, but now that plan was scrubbed. Which meant she was down to the backup.

"I would love to accompany you back to your estate, Arra, but what of my husband?" Katarina glanced across the table, rocking slowly in her chair. She was pretending to be drunker than she was. She and Aragona had finished off a second bottle of the dry Black Château vintage, more than enough of the strong red wine to inebriate most women her size. Women who hadn't been through the years of hard training at the Assassins' Guild on Sebastiani, that is. Who hadn't done the rigorous survival training and the deep body control exercises she had. It took a considerable amount of alcohol to get Katarina Venturi truly drunk, and even then she maintained impressive control of her wits and reflexes.

"He is quite engrossed in his poker game, from what I am told. It will likely be dawn before he tears himself away." Aragona's voice was distracted, his eyes glancing down at Katarina's bare leg. She'd shifted, moving to the side, and the Castillan lord had just noticed how high the slit ran in her dress. "We can slip away, and my men can have you back here long before morning."

She stared at Aragona. She knew he was dangerous, far more so than his charming demeanor suggested. But she'd also heard his weakness for women was profound, and his devious intelligence at times took a backseat to another body part. She suspected it was ego that made him so intent to bed the beautiful wives of other rich and powerful men, another cold-blooded killer undone by hidden insecurities. He was tailor-made for her manipulations—which was why she had accepted the mission in the first place. Sex was a weapon, and one she was uniquely qualified to wield with deadly effect.

"I am sorry, Arra, but it is too much of a risk. Pavel can be a very jealous man, and he controls our fortune. If he should come looking for me and I am . . ."

"I assure you, my dear, your husband will remain at the tables, even if I must order my people to let him win." Aragona's voice was tense, his urgency apparent. She knew she had gotten to him. Lust was doing its work for her, as it had so many times before.

"I want to, Arra," she purred. "But I cannot take the chance. Without Pavel, I will be penniless, trapped on a foreign world." She ran her hand playfully through her mane of shimmering black hair, her dark brown eyes locked on his as she did. "Perhaps—" She paused abruptly.

"Perhaps what, Irina?" He reached across the table, placing his hand on her arm.

She moved her fingers slowly, her polished red nails gently teasing his extended arm. "Perhaps we could sneak off to one of the suites in the hotel for a few hours." Getting Aragona upstairs was the fallback plan, but she didn't like it any more than she had when they'd originally discussed it. *I'm sure I can lure him up there. But how are we going to get him out of the hotel? The château is out in the countryside, but the Grand Palais is right in the middle of the city, full of guests and guards, and kilometers away from the* Claw. *I guess we'll just have to make it work. Somehow.*

Aragona paused, a troubled look momentarily passing over his face. Katarina smiled. "Of course . . ." he finally said. "If you will excuse me, I shall have a suite prepared at once."

He smiled and stood up, walking toward one of the stewards standing nearby. "Go and tell the manager I want the royal suite prepared at once. Flowers, candles, bowls of burning jasmina. And I am in a hurry, so I want it ready in ten minutes."

"Yes, Lord Aragona."

"And I want another bottle of the Black Château in the suite. Lightly chilled."

"Yes, my lord."

Katarina was sitting quietly, listening to Aragona's seduction preparations. *No doubt, he thinks I cannot hear him.* Katarina's hearing was quite acute, though, and her mental discipline allowed her to tune out background distractions. She couldn't match Blackhawk's uncanny senses, but she was the closest of the crew to matching the *Claw*'s enigmatic captain.

Katarina had also heard the fear in the steward's voice. It was another reminder not to underestimate this man. She'd seen terrified servants before, and she'd met a hundred variations of the brutal masters who had instilled them with that fear. She hadn't killed them all, but she'd wanted to. She was a cold-blooded killer herself, but she directed her attentions toward the powerful and dangerous, not the poor and weak, and she despised bullies who brutalized those who couldn't fight back.

No doubt, for all his arts of seduction, he'd kill a lover too. Because she displeased him. Or simply because he felt the urge.

Aragona walked back, smiling. "I am having them open the

royal suite for us, my beautiful Irina. It will be ready in ten minutes." He smiled, but she could see through it, to the monster below the surface. "Just enough time to finish our drinks."

Katarina reached for her glass and returned the smile. "I look forward to a memorable evening." She took a sip of her wine and set it down, still smiling sweetly. But inside she was regretting that this was a snatch-and-grab job.

She suspected she would have enjoyed killing the son of a bitch.

Lucas Lancaster sat in his usual place, the pilot's chair on the *Claw's* bridge. The *Claw* was quiet, too quiet. It was just him and the Twins. He was in charge of the ship, as usual, and the Twins were in reserve, in case anyone got into trouble. Everybody else was out on the op, even Sam.

The brothers were monsters, gargantuan human beings well over two meters tall and weighing at least 150 kilos. They were great in a fight, but a bit too noticeable for undercover work—and a little too stupid, too. For all their blind loyalty and astonishing strength in a fight, Tarq and Tarnan were what Ace liked to call dull blades.

Lucas was monitoring the operation, and as far as he could see, everything was going according to plan. Unfortunately, he couldn't see much, because Blackhawk had mandated near-total communications silence.

But Lucas wasn't without resources. He'd managed to hack into the Castillan Orbital Command before the op and commandeer one of its surveillance satellites. He was scanning the entire area, looking for anything out of the ordinary, any kind of problem that might interfere with the operation. Things had been quiet so far, but if his experiences on *Wolf's Claw* had taught him anything, it was that the situation could go to crap in a heartbeat.

Like now.

His eyes caught something on the scanner, movement around the Aragona villa. "What the fuck?" he muttered to himself. He stared at the screen closely, trying to discern what it was he saw. He thought about sending an instruction to the commandeered satellite, retasking it slightly to give a closer view, but that would require a high-energy communications burst, and Blackhawk had forbidden him from taking that kind of risk—unless the situation was dire. Lucas wasn't shy about massaging the meaning of a word, but he couldn't stretch all the way to "dire." Not yet.

His eye caught a flashing red light on the board. A signal from Blackhawk—and a step closer to dire. The mission was compromised, and they were moving to the backup plan.

Lucas let out a long sigh. That was bad news. The backup plan sucked. Trying to snatch a paranoid psychotic from his villa in the countryside was bad enough, but grabbing him from his own hotel in the center of one of Castilla's biggest cities—that was downright suicidal.

And yet, just another day's work on the Claw.

"Tarq, Tarnan, I need you guys to suit up. We might have some work to do." He wasn't going to rush in and blow everyone's covers. Not yet, at least. But he was damned well going to be ready, because the shit was sure as hell going to hit the fan . . . it always did. And when that happened, he wanted the Twins ready to go.

Ace looked at his cards again. It was one of the false tells he'd invented, a way he'd been controlling the game, allowing Cordoba to win often enough to feel he was getting the better of his adversary, despite the fact that the money had remained fairly even. Ace had left Cordoba feeling he'd outplayed his opponent, and that his own losses had been due to dumb luck. It was the perfect enticement to keep the Castillan at the table. Every gambler knew luck could only last so long.

"Lord Suvarov, I am sorry to interrupt."

Ace turned abruptly, an angry look on his face.

Shira stood behind him, clad in a sleekly tailored white suit. Her short hair was combed straight back, and she was wearing heels that made her already significant height even more impressive. She held a small tablet in her hands.

"What is it, Felice? What was so important it compelled you to interrupt my recreation?" His voice was haughty, dripping with arrogance. Sure, he was playing a part for the mission, but nothing said he couldn't enjoy it, too.

"I am sorry to disturb you, Lord Suvarov," she apologized again, "but we just received news about the shipment. The initial freighter has had to cancel the contract due to mechanical problems. We need to utilize our secondary alternative."

Ace stared at her with a sour expression on his face. "Well, if there is no alternative, then proceed. And don't disturb me again unless it is important." It *was* bad news. Shira was relaying Blackhawk's order to go to Plan B. Beyond the problems that the captain would encounter, Ace's whole purpose had been to keep Cordoba occupied and in town while the abduction went down in the villa. Now, though, all that had achieved was to keep the psychopathic son of a bitch in the same building where they were going to snatch Aragona. Ace wasn't the prime mover in this plan, but he hated being counterproductive.

I'm not a big fan of the plan going straight to shit immediately, either.

Although I should be used to it by now . . .

"A problem, Lord Suvarov?" Cordoba glanced across the table, a hint of concern in his voice, but no real suspicion Ace could detect.

"Nothing a better staff wouldn't solve, Lord Cordoba." He glared up at Shira. "Go. See to it, now."

She looked back down at him and nodded respectfully. "As you command, my lord."

Ace watched her hurry from the room, and he noticed Cordoba doing the same. He had to admit she looked good in the form-fitting suit, but he felt like he was watching his sister. He knew Shira preferred women, at least when she defrosted enough to want anyone, but she had no difficulty attracting attention from either sex. No one could match Katarina for raw seductiveness, but Ace suspected Shira could have done the job, too.

He held back a sigh. Things were going to hell, and the next few hours were likely to be extremely dangerous. Still, he enjoyed treating Shira like a servant, a small perk of the op. He suspected he'd pay for it later, assuming they all made it out, but it was still worth it.

"Indeed, Lord Suvarov. It is a constant challenge to find competent servants." Cordoba paused a few seconds before asking the question Ace knew was coming. "Pardon my curiosity, but perhaps I can assist you with whatever business you are conducting."

Ace reached over and grabbed his glass, taking a sip before answering. "As you know, many of my brethren from Saragossa were dispossessed these last eight years by the revolution there. However, recent news suggests that our cause has taken a turn for the better, and the revolutionary armies are on the retreat. Let us just say I have been safeguarding some . . . special holdings for some of my fellow nobles, items they wanted to keep out of the hands of the rebels." He paused for a few seconds, glancing through the arches separating the VIP area from the main casino. "It is a delicate matter, Lord Cordoba, perhaps one best discussed elsewhere." He gestured toward the table. "Besides, the cards await us now, do they not?"

"Indeed they do, Lord Suvarov. Indeed they do."

Ace watched the pudgy Castillan deal slowly. *Now there's something else for you to think about: how you will manage to cheat me out of a ship full of Saragossan treasures.* He smiled. There was nothing Ace liked better than dealing with greedy men. And he could see by the look in Cordoba's eyes, his reputation was well deserved. That was good, because Ace expected he was going to need every distraction possible if he was going to get back to the *Claw.*

CHAPTER 2

"LET'S GO, BOYS. WE DON'T HAVE MUCH TIME."

Really, we don't have any fucking time. Blackhawk knew Katarina couldn't stall Aragona all night. Sooner or later, she'd end up in one of the hotel suites with him. He knew she didn't need help subduing him, but she was damned sure going to need backup getting him the hell out of there and back to the *Claw*.

"Right behind you, Captain."

Blackhawk could hear the exhaustion in Sarge's voice, and a quick glance over his shoulder told him the rest of the crew was in even worse shape. Blackhawk knew his lung capacity was at least half again theirs, and probably more. He'd been driven by urgency, though, and his concern for Katarina and Ace and the rest of his people in Madrassa. But the others just couldn't maintain his pace. He was going to have to make a choice: go on ahead by himself or slow down enough for them to keep up. He hated the idea of splitting up, but the thought of leaving Katarina on her own was worse.

He stopped and spun around, his eyes focusing briefly on each of them. "Sarge, I'm going to go on ahead. You guys follow as quickly as you can." He stared at the hulking soldier. "You remember the layout of the city, right?" He hadn't expected Sarge's people to get anywhere near Madrassa, but they'd gone over the backup plan anyway.

Once.

"Yes, sir. I remember." Blackhawk wasn't sure he believed the grizzled warrior, but he figured they would manage. Sarge was staring back, a troubled expression on his face. "Captain, we can run faster. We can keep up with you."

"No, Sarge. You can't." It was a little harder than he usually put things for the crew, but he didn't have time to waste. And there was no point in explaining that he'd been holding back so they could keep up. "I need you guys in shape to fight . . . assuming we end up in a battle." *And when the hell don't we?* "Stay as close behind as you can." He gave them all a quick wave, then took off, practically sprinting toward the looming buildings of the city.

He figured they were still ten klicks out, but alone he could cover that in thirty minutes. "Half an hour, Kat," he whispered as he raced down the darkened street, his keen eyes making do with the dim moonlight.

"I'll be there in half an hour. Just hang on."

Katarina looked around the room. The suite was palatial, with an antique grand piano and a sweeping view of the city and the shoreline beyond. The walls were covered with hand-carved wainscoting, and she suspected the art on the walls was among the best on Castilla.

Though that isn't saying much.

Logs were crackling in the fireplace, and the room was full of flowers. There were candles on the tables flanking the bed, and small bowls of fiery liquid. Jasmina was a plant from the Castillan tropics, the fragrant vapors from its burning extract another supposed local aphrodisiac. Katarina suppressed her amusement. She was astonished at the cheap theatrics that worked for men like Aragona. Though she expected his wealth was more of a factor in his success with women, or, when that failed, coercion.

She wondered how much a high roller had to gamble in the Grand Palais's casino to see the inside of this place. Five hundred thousand florins? A million? So much simpler just to flash a little leg . . .

"Here you are, my dear." Aragona stepped up with two crystal goblets in his hand. He stood close behind, handing her one of the glasses. "It is quite a view, isn't it?"

Katarina felt the warmth of his breath on her neck. She was sure she could disable him at will, but she was wondering if she should wait—to give Blackhawk and the others a little more time to get in position.

She'd managed to get him up to the suite without any of his guards in tow. Her pleas for discretion and privacy might have aroused some suspicion if Aragona wasn't already so focused on getting her into bed. But even alone—and that assumed there were no active surveillance devices in the suite—she knew once she disabled him they were on a rigid time clock. They had to get him out before he came to, or she'd have to kill him and make a break for it. She figured she had a decent chance of getting away if she had to, but the mission would be a disaster. And Katarina hated failure.

The bank wanted a live captive, and the price Blackhawk negotiated reflected the increased difficulty over a simple assassination. A dead Aragona meant the crew wouldn't get paid at all—this wasn't a dead or alive contract—and they'd have wasted time and resources on a pointless excursion. And that assumed everyone else made it out. Katarina had lived most of her life embracing a coldly calculating mentality, to consider the people around her as assets, expendable if it helped the mission succeed. But she knew she'd lost some of that keen edge, the almost inhuman coldness that marked a Sebastiani assassin. Against all her training and discipline, she'd become quite fond of her shipmates, and the thought of any of them dying on a blown mission was not something she wanted to contemplate.

Ace was in the worst danger. Despite her efforts at discretion, Aragona's men knew she'd gone upstairs with their boss. They believed she was Ace's wife, sneaking off behind her husband's back. If they found their boss dead in the hotel suite . . .

No, she had to get Aragona out of here, and do it quietly, so Ace had a chance to slip away. When she first bought passage on *Wolf's Claw*, she couldn't understand why someone as coldly competent as Blackhawk had such a loudmouth fool as his sidekick. Her first impressions of people were usually spot-on, but she eventually realized she'd misjudged Ace. Despite his loud—and often annoying—theatrics, she'd found him to be keenly intelligent and enormously reliable. And, if she was being totally objective, not completely unattractive . . .

No—she couldn't leave him at the mercy of Aragona's enraged retainers. She wouldn't. Whatever it took.

"Why, Arra, are you trying to get me drunk?" she purred softly, turning and running her hand down his face. "Because, I assure you, that is not necessary." She leaned back into him.

"Your husband is a fool to neglect a woman like you."

She felt his hands on her shoulders, his fingers slipping under the thin straps of her dress. She moaned softly at his touch and leaned her head back, her silky hair pressed against his face.

We'll see who the fool is. It's only a matter of when . . .

Blackhawk slipped through the dark streets, moving as quickly as he could without attracting notice. It was late, but Madrassa was known for its nightlife, so the restaurants, casinos, and clubs would be crowded until dawn.

He tried to stay in the shadows and on backstreets. He'd expected to be infiltrating the villa, and he was wearing combat fatigues and boots. He was filthy, too, his legs covered with half-dried mud from tramping around in the tidal estuaries. He'd managed to avoid any undue notice so far, but the minute he walked into the Grand Palais, every eye would be on him. The hotel was the finest establishment in Madrassa, and its patrons would be impeccably dressed.

He looked around, his eyes scanning the late-night revelers walking by. He needed clothes, and he could only think of one way to get them. He watched and waited, looking for an appropriately dressed partier . . . preferably one around his size.

Finally, he saw a man approaching. He was alone, and he looked to be a good physical match. And he was swaying back and forth, clearly drunk. *Even better.*

Blackhawk waited for the man to walk by, and then he struck. He lunged forward, striking the back of the man's neck.

His victim crumbled instantly, and Blackhawk caught him and slid his limp form into an alley.

He put his fingers to the man's throat, feeling for a pulse. A look of relief slipped onto his face. He hadn't used a killing strike, but he'd been worried he'd hit too hard. Blackhawk had fought an astonishing array of cutthroats and killers, but he wasn't used to disabling drunk civilians.

He stripped out of his fatigues and put on his victim's suit. It wasn't a perfect fit, but it would do. He picked up his assault rifle, looking around the alley for a place to stash it. Once again, his equipment for the villa had no place on the floors of the Grand Palais, and there was no way he could conceal it with these clothes.

He walked over and shoved the rifle into a trash bin, carefully pushing it down under the garbage. He paused for a minute and sighed, unbuckling his holster belt and tossing it in after the rifle. He wasn't getting in with a pistol, either.

He turned and took a last glimpse at the man lying on the ground. He pulled a ten-crown platinum coin and placed it in his victim's hand. It was enough to buy a hundred suits, compensation enough, he hoped, for both the clothing and the headache he knew the man would have when he awoke. Arkarin Blackhawk was a lot of things, but a thief wasn't one of them.

Okay, it's time. He didn't know exactly what he was going to do, but he knew he had to do it now. He took a breath and slipped out of the alley, heading swiftly through the streets toward the Grand Palais.

"Lucas, we're at the airlock. Armed and ready." Tarq Bjergen's voice was so deep it rattled the speaker on Lucas's workstation.

"You have the extra weapons with you?" Lucas didn't know

what was happening to the rest of the crew, but he was sure of one thing: if they'd moved the op to the Grand Palais, they weren't waltzing in there with assault rifles. They'd be practically unarmed, and if he had to send the Twins in to rescue them, he suspected some extra guns would come in handy.

"Yes, sir. We each have three extra rifles and pistols and a sack of flash grenades."

Lucas nodded his head. That was a lot of extra crap to carry into battle, but then the Twins weren't average fighters. He'd seen the two gargantuan brothers flip over an armored vehicle once. They could handle a few extra guns, along with the giant autocannons the two normally wielded

"All right. Stand by."

"Yes, sir."

Lucas smiled. He wasn't remotely a "sir." No one on *Wolf's Claw* really was, except Blackhawk. And the captain was the last one to make a big deal out of rank. The crew had a variety of respectful names for their leader, but just as often he was simply "Ark" to them all.

Below Blackhawk, though, there really was no rigid hierarchy on the *Claw*. Lucas and most of the rest of the crew generally thought of Ace as second in command. All except Shira. And Lucas knew that in a crunch she'd swallow her pride and accept Ace's orders, too. Truth was, in the end they were a team, and whatever disagreements or rivalries they had disappeared when any of them was in danger.

He stared at the power readouts. He had the field up at full strength. The *Claw* was as good as invisible to any casual observer, and even to a serious search effort unless it was extremely targeted. The distortion field was another of Blackhawk's mysteries. None of the crew knew where it had come from, but they were well aware how useful a device it was. It had probably saved their lives more than once—a lot like Blackhawk himself.

For the millionth time, Lucas wished he could run the engines and the field at the same time, but the strange artifact drew an enormous amount of power. He'd been planning to test the new reactor Marshal Lucerne had given them to see if it could manage the strain, but that was an experiment for a time when they weren't in the middle of an operation—and when Sam was down in engineering where she belonged.

Still, he was tempted. Castilla wasn't one of the Prime worlds by any means, but it wasn't a backwater shithole like Saragossa or Kalishar, either. It wouldn't take long for the Castillan defense forces to detect a launch after he dropped the field. From then he'd have maybe ten minutes to get to Madrassa and grab everyone—or the *Claw* would end up in a battle with the entire Castillan fleet. Not an attractive prospect.

Lucas stared down at the readouts, but his thoughts were with the rest of the crew. Should he blast off and rush to Madrassa? Or should he sit tight and see what happened?

They may call me sir, but I hate being in command.

"Sam, I need you to go back in there." Blackhawk had linked up with Sam and Shira just outside the Grand Palais, and he was doing something he hated to be forced to when he'd had a perfectly good plan: he was improvising.

"Whatever you need, Captain." Sam Sparks was one of the best engineers in the Far Stars, but she was also incredibly capable in a fight. Her age and introverted nature tended to make people either want to protect her or dismiss her, but that's because they'd never seen her in action. Blackhawk had. And he knew she'd killed a lot of people for a twenty-seven-year-old.

A lot of people.

"We have to get Katarina and Aragona out of there," he continued, "and we need a diversion of some kind to do it. Do you think you can get down to the mechanical level and knock out the building's power?"

She looked back at him for a few seconds before she answered. "I can try, Ark." She paused again. "I'll manage it. Somehow."

"Be careful, Sam." Blackhawk reached out and put his hand on her arm. "I know this is dangerous, but don't take any unnecessary risks. If you can't get down there, back off. We'll manage some other way."

She nodded. "I'll be careful." She smiled and turned to walk back toward the hotel's entrance.

Blackhawk watched her go, a little worried about just how careful she would be. He spent most of his time worrying about Ace doing something insane, but he knew Sam had a little streak of craziness in her too. It put a knot in his gut, but it also made him proud as hell.

"What do you want me to do, Cap?" Shira stood next to Blackhawk, also watching Sam walk toward the hotel.

Blackhawk turned back toward her. "Stay close to Ace. If the shits hits it, he's vulnerable." At this point, the mission was of less concern than his crew. For all his skills and enhancements, Blackhawk knew his people were his greatest weakness. Not that they'd let him down, but that he'd let *them* down. He could face his own death, but the thought of his crew being killed tore at him inside. Other than Augustin Lucerne—and Astra!—they were all he cared about in the universe.

"Don't worry, Ark. I'll make sure he gets out." She turned her head, looking down the street. "But where are Sarge and his boys? You aren't thinking about going up there alone, are you?"

He nodded. "How are half a dozen of us going to sneak up to the top floor of that hotel without being noticed?" He could see the concern taking over her expression. "It'll be okay, Shira. I'll handle it. And Sarge and his boys will be here by the time we're on the way out, in case we need backup.

"Besides—Kat will be there to cover my six."

Shira didn't look convinced, but Blackhawk knew she wouldn't argue with him, not in the middle of an operation.

"Good luck, Ark." Her voice was soft.

"To you too," he responded with a quick smile. "Take care of yourself." And with that, he was gone, slipping through the front door and looking like a wealthy Castillan in his exquisite, if poorly tailored, suit.

Katarina felt Aragona's hands sliding down her back, pulling down the zipper on her dress. He had a gentle touch, something she'd found to be quite rare among the butchers and power-mad politicians who'd found their way into her crosshairs over the years. It made no difference. Skilled lover or brutish lout, Arragonzo Aragona was just a mission to her.

She leaned back and moaned softly, feeding Aragona's ego. She reached back behind her, rubbing a hand on his face as her dress slid down her body to the floor.

She felt another tingle from the ring on her finger. A signal from Blackhawk. He was ready. It was time.

She arched backward and reached up to Aragona's head,

running her fingers through his hair. She let her hands drop slowly toward his neck then she spun around behind him in one swift motion, pulling upward and jamming her left hand into the side of his neck.

His body tensed for an instant, and she could feel him pulling away, but then he went limp and slid to the floor. The nerve pinch was an ancient Sebastiani technique, one she'd learned as a child acolyte. Most of Katarina's moves tended to be fatal. She was a trained assassin, not a kidnapper. But her arsenal included a few nonlethal maneuvers, and this one was more than enough to deal with the likes of Arragonzo Aragona.

She slid off to the side, pressing her ring hard against her finger, sending the expected response to Blackhawk. She reached down and scooped up her dress, just as the *Claw's* captain slipped through the door. His shirt was covered with blood. Her stomach tightened for an instant, before she realized none of it was his. "Guards," he said grimly, as if reading her thoughts. "How long will he be out?"

She could see he was trying not to stare, with mixed success. She paid it no mind. She was used to men's reactions to her wearing a few wispy pieces of silk and nothing else.

That's one of the main reasons I'm in this suite in the first place.

"An hour, perhaps. Possibly a bit less." The nerve pinch worked differently depending on the subject's body chemistry and recovery time, but she was sure he'd be unconscious for at least forty-five minutes, and probably longer. Which was enough to get out—or get killed trying.

She slipped gracefully back into her dress. "So, shall we get out of here, Arkarin?" She was the only one who used Blackhawk's full name. "I have had quite my fill of Castilla, and I suspect you have too."

"I have indeed," he replied, reaching down and hoisting Aragona over his shoulder. "I have indeed."

Sam crept down the concrete hallway, stopping every ten meters or so to listen. She was looking for the Palais's power core, and she was tracking it like a hunter stalks his prey. Finally, she caught a hum in the air, and she knew it was the reactor.

The subbasements of the massive hotel complex were labyrinthine, and the corridors stretched on seemingly forever, taking her past storage areas and conduits bringing fresh water in and taking waste out. Finally, she could see she was moving into the main engineering area.

She'd never get to the reactor itself—she knew it would be too heavily guarded. But if she could find the main conduit, she might be able to shut down the entire complex, at least for a while.

She crept forward, her eyes focusing on the pipes and other mechanicals running along the ceiling. She was moving as much on instinct as anything else. The hum was getting louder, and she was sure she was close to what she wanted.

Suddenly, Sam heard footsteps come around the corner behind her. "Halt. Who are you?" The voice was gruff, suspicious.

She turned slowly, grabbing the tiny gun she always carried in her waistband as she did. They teased her about the miniature weapon, told her it looked like a toy. But it was compact and easy to hide. And it was made entirely of hardened polymer, so it slipped past metal detectors and most other security devices. It only held four projectiles, but that was all she'd ever needed.

"I was on my way to engineering. They called with . . ." She fired as soon as she came around, and the guard fell onto his back, a small round hole in the center of his forehead.

Better get moving in case somebody heard that. She jogged down the hallway, turning at each opportunity in the direction of the reactor's hum. She was close, and she started to see heavy electrical conduits along the walls and on the ceiling. They were major trunk lines leading to various subsystems. The main nest of cables had to be close, then.

She pushed onward, tracing the wires backward toward their origin. Finally, she turned a corner. Two technicians were standing in the middle of the hallway, staring right at the main power conduit. When they saw her, they seemed frozen in surprise. Then, as one, they turned to sound the alarm, but she dropped them with one shot each.

Now, I just need to knock this thing out and get the hell out of here.

Blackhawk raced down the stairs, carrying Aragona wrapped in a sheet and draped over his shoulder. He'd considered trying to take out the surveillance cameras in the hallway, but he knew that was a waste of time. He doubted he could find them all anyway, at least in the amount of time he had available. Besides, knocking out a camera was like flashing a warning sign to anyone watching. All they could do was get the hell out before anyone could respond. With luck, they might shake any pursuit once they were outside. Then he could call Lucas and have the *Claw* meet them somewhere near the city.

He touched his ring again, sending a signal to Ace. It was time for him to make an excuse and get the hell out of the casino. Blackhawk didn't have an overwhelming amount of respect for Aragona's people, but they weren't stupid, either.

When they realized their leader had been kidnapped, they would follow the trail right back to Ace.

"You had to get him to take you to the top floor?" Blackhawk glanced back briefly toward Katarina. "Next time, maybe hold back a little." They were two of the fittest human beings in the Far Stars, but eighty floors was a long way, even going down.

Especially carrying eighty kilos of unconscious Castillan gangster.

"I will keep that in mind, Arkarin. Perhaps next time our target will be a woman, and you can use your own not inconsiderable char—"

Their heads whipped around as one. Someone had opened a door above them. They could hear the sound of boots, first walking, but then running down the stairs. There was shouting too, and more feet.

"I think we're busted." Blackhawk quickened his pace, whipping around each flight of stairs.

"Go, Arkarin. I will be right behind you."

"Katarina . . . no." He knew what she had in mind.

"We need weapons. And unless I am very wrong, those footsteps are bringing some guns closer to us."

Blackhawk wanted to stop and argue with her, but he knew there was no point. Katarina was going to do whatever she thought was best, and all he could do by arguing was make the maneuver even more dangerous.

Besides—she was right.

"Just take out the first group and grab their guns." His voice was firm, commanding, though he didn't know how much good it would do.

"I will be right behind you." She turned and raced back up the stairs, her footsteps silent on the concrete risers.

Blackhawk continued down, listening carefully. He knew he shouldn't slow down, but he did anyway. If it came down to escaping with Aragona or running to Katarina's aid, he knew exactly which he'd choose.

He heard a loud thud and then, a second later, another. No shots went off. There weren't even screams. *Chrono, she's good.* He kept moving down. Eventually, he heard something move up behind him, barely audible. "Well done," he whispered.

"Thank you." Katarina reached around him, pressing a pistol into his hand. "Take this. You should be able to manage it carrying that putrid load."

"Got it. Thanks." Blackhawk moved forward again, down the stairs. "But let's try to get out of here without having to kill anyone else." Blackhawk wasn't going to bet on that prospect though.

"I am sorry to disturb you again, sir, but I am afraid there are matters that require your immediate attention. Several of the nobles are vociferously demanding to speak with you." Shira stood almost at attention, her hair perfectly groomed, not a wrinkle on her suit.

Ace understood. It was time to get out. Now. "It is astonishing that nothing can get done without my direct intervention." He looked across the table at Cordoba. "If you will excuse me, Lord Cordoba, I am afraid I must attend to this at once. If you are amenable to a short break, I would be very interested in continuing our game in, say, one hour."

Cordoba stared back at Ace. He was clearly annoyed at the delay, but he nodded and said, "Of course, Lord Suvarov. We must all attend to our work when it demands."

Ace stood up and stared at Shira with a frustrated scowl.

"Let us go, so that I can finish *your* work and get back to my game." He reached toward the table and started to scoop up his chips and coins.

"There is no need, Lord Suvarov." Cordoba's voice was firm. "I can assure you no one will disturb your stake while you are gone. I will have my people guard the table until we resume."

Fuck, Ace thought. *All that money . . .* But he couldn't risk insulting Cordoba. *Not this close to getting the hell out of here.*

"My thanks, Lord Cordoba." Ace tried to pull his eyes away from the stacks of money on the table, funds that were about to be written off as expenses of the op.

"Come, Lord Suvarov. Your associates are waiting." Ace knew Shira was afraid he'd get himself shot to pieces over a pile of chips—and he knew that fear wasn't entirely ungrounded. But the mission came first for all Blackhawk's people, even Ace Graythorn. Even when he had to walk away from a pile of money and an opponent he knew he could fleece.

"Very well, Felice. Let's finish this as quickly as possible." He turned and followed her back toward the main casino floor. His eyes caught a pair of guards moving from a back room toward Cordoba as he and Shira were crossing the room. He didn't get a good look, but their body language was clear. Something was wrong.

"Fuck, I think we've got trouble," he whispered to Shira. "Just keep walking."

"Lord Suvarov . . ." It was Cordoba, and the change in his tone was obvious. "I'm afraid I must ask you to wait a moment."

"I'm sorry, Lord Cordoba, but I really must attend to my business. I will be back shortly." Ace could hear the guards starting to move toward him. His eyes darted back and forth, looking for something, anything he could use as a weapon.

He saw a waiter walking by, carrying a large metal tray filled with glasses. He turned his head slightly, and he saw the guards moving toward him, reaching into their jackets.

"Now, Shira." He spun around and shoved the waiter down, grabbing the tray. Drinks flew across the room, and the crystal glasses shattered as they hit the ground.

Ace turned, swinging the tray hard and hitting both guards in the face. They dropped the pistols they'd pulled out from their jackets, and Ace dove for one.

He could hear the sounds behind him: more guards rushing forward. He lunged for the pistol, grabbing it and swinging around, bringing it to bear. His reflexes were fast, but not fast enough. He knew in that instant his adversary was going to get the first shot off.

He braced for the impact, his enemy's bullet slamming into his body. But it didn't come. Instead, he saw something whip across his field of vision so quickly it was barely visible. Then another.

He fired his pistol, but his enemy was already stricken, hit by the two tiny throwing stars Shira had hidden in her necklace. Ace pulled himself up and ducked behind an overturned table, motioning for Shira to take cover with him. There were half a dozen guards in the room already, and he had no doubt more were coming. He started firing, dropping two almost immediately before they started shooting back . . .

Then the lights went out.

"Sam," Blackhawk muttered to himself, not at all surprised she'd managed to plunge the enormous Grand Palais into total darkness. *So much for the cameras and alarms,* he thought.

He slowed abruptly, stepping much more carefully in the

total darkness. Blackhawk had an eagle's eyes, but even his uncanny vision couldn't cut through total darkness. He and Katarina could do little but wait. *Can't risk breaking our necks. But shouldn't be much . . .*

The emergency lights flipped on.

"Finally." Blackhawk's voice was heavy with frustration.

"Luckily, we're almost to the ground floor," Katarina said. "This stairwell will exit on the far end of the casino, I believe. We will need to go east to reach the main entrance." Katarina's voice was calm, sure. She had stayed right behind Blackhawk, stopping every few flights to turn back and make sure no one was catching up to them. She'd picked off two more guards already, but there hadn't been any others.

Which means that they're engaged somewhere else.

"Be ready. We don't know what we'll find down here." He ran down the last few steps and turned back toward her with a nod. Then he kicked open the door.

There was pandemonium on the floor, people running and screaming and guards desperately trying to restore order and stop patrons trying to get to the exits with stacks of stolen chips. The light from the emergency lamps was dim, but Blackhawk's vision sliced right through the gloom.

He hugged the wall, trying to move around the edge of the worst chaos. There were guards everywhere. At first they were trying to stop the looters with intimidation, but it wasn't long before they resorted to more persuasive measures.

They started firing into the crowd.

Blackhawk ducked behind a pile of broken chairs, with Katarina close behind. "Ace, where are you?" He spoke into the small comm unit on his wrist. Radio silence didn't seem so important anymore.

"I'm in the high rollers' room, with Shira. We're fine. How are you?" Blackhawk could hear the fire in the background, and he knew immediately Ace and Shira were anything but "fine."

"Stay put. We'll be there in half a minute." He turned back toward Katarina. "Let's go. Everybody gets out of here tonight."

Including this heavy son of a bitch.

They crept around the outside edge of the gaming area, taking whatever cover they could behind the rubble and debris. Aragona was starting to become a real burden, and even Blackhawk's considerable strength was waning. He shifted around, swinging the unconscious hostage to his other shoulder.

Blackhawk moved up to the series of arches that separated the high-end gaming area from the main casino floor. He could see Ace and Shira, pinned down on the far side of the room. They were having a firefight with at least half a dozen guards. They'd already taken out at least that many more, but the survivors were behind hard cover now, and the exchange had turned into a stalemate.

"They're trapped in there, cut off from any exit." Blackhawk looked back at Katarina. "Ready?" She nodded. He took a quick look around, and then he ducked inside the room, firing the pistol as he dove for cover.

He took out two guards before he fell behind an overturned table, dropping Aragona hard as he hit the ground.

I need to get him out alive. No one said he had to be in one piece.

He turned in time to watch Katarina, unhindered by the burden he carried, open up with two pistols, taking down the remaining guards with precision shooting.

"Let's go!" she shouted across the room, waving to Ace and Shira. Kat was standing upright in the center of the room, wearing a slightly disheveled but enormously expensive evening gown and brandishing two smoking pistols.

She still looked like she could seduce any man left alive in the casino.

Blackhawk pulled himself up and looked around. *Too much damage. Too much noise. We're never going to get out of Madrassa on foot. Even if we steal a vehicle, we're screwed.* Which could only mean one thing: he had to risk bringing the *Claw* in to get them. He hated putting the ship on the line, but there was no choice.

He tapped the comm unit. "Lucas, you need to get the *Claw* to Madrassa as soon as you can. As close to the Grand Palais as possible."

"I'm here already, Skip. I just picked up Sam and dropped off the Twins to go in and get you guys. Get up to the fifth-floor roof deck, and I'll bring the ship around there."

Blackhawk heard the sounds of heavy automatic fire coming from the main entrance, the massive autocannons the Twins used as hand weapons. He smiled. Damn, he was proud of his crew.

"Everybody ready? We need to hook up with the Twins and get to the fifth-floor deck. Lucas has the *Claw* flying over the hotel, and he'll get us out of here."

The others nodded. Blackhawk leaned down and scooped up Aragona. Standing, he waved his arm forward. "Let's move."

"They're heading up to the fifth level, Sarge. You guys follow them up there, and I'll pick you all up." Lucas had been following Sarge's crew on the scanners.

Lucas knew the radio traffic was going to mean trouble. He was pretty sure the *Claw* had made it to Madrassa undetected.

He'd taken a huge risk and flown over with the field up and engines blasting away. He was damned sure putting Marshal Lucerne's reactor through its paces. *Thank Chrono Sam is back on board.* Pushing a fusion reactor to the brink was crazy enough, but doing it without the ship's engineer on board was downright insane.

Which pretty much describes everyone on this ship.

"Understood, Lucas. We're on our way."

Lucas glanced at the scanner. Nothing yet. But that was only a matter of time. The comm signals he was sending out were like a beacon, and they led back to the *Claw.* "And hurry it up, before half the Castillan air force gets here and starts shooting at us."

He flipped the comm to the intraship channel. "How are things down there, Sam?"

"Shitty, Lucas. What the hell are you doing to my ship?"

He suppressed a laugh. "Just what I had to do, Sam." She'd still been wearing her costume from the op when he picked her up, and he tried to imagine her down in the *Claw*'s tiny engineering space, shoving the layers of silk out of the way as she worked at her familiar controls. *Now that's a scene I wish I could capture on camera.*

"Just hold her together, Sam. The others are in deep shit, and we've got to pluck them off the roof. Drop the field if you have to, but I need full engine power."

"No problem. I'll just sprinkle some fairy dust on it, Lucas." Sam was very protective of the ship and its systems—and she was pissed. Lucas was sure she realized he'd had no choice, and he knew for a fact she was just as concerned about the others. But that didn't stop her from getting mad at him all the same when he was too hard on the *Claw.* They all loved the ship; it was their home. But Lucas knew it was Sam's baby, and she protected it like a mama carnasoid.

"Let's go, boss. The way to the stairs is open."

Blackhawk nodded with a smile. *It's open because you hosed the whole area down with 12 mm rounds.* Looking at the shattered wreckage of the casino floor, he remembered what a force of nature the Twins truly were in battle.

"All right, everybody, let's get the hell out of here." Blackhawk took a deep breath and hauled Aragona with him.

"I can carry him, boss." Tarnan stood next to Blackhawk, reaching out his arms. "You look tired."

Blackhawk almost laughed. "Yeah, Tarn, I'm pretty fucking tired." The giant reached over and plucked Aragona from Blackhawk, throwing the Castillan over his shoulder like a rag doll.

They ran to the stairs and raced up to the fifth floor, ducking back as a burst of automatic fire shattered the glass wall and raked the landing just outside the stairwell.

"Fuck. There are at least a dozen guards out there, and they're not firing those little popguns they had downstairs." Blackhawk turned back, looking toward the rest of his crew. They all had assault rifles now, courtesy of the Twins.

"We don't have time for a firefight, Ark." Ace was looking all around. "What do you have in those sacks, Tarq?" He'd just noticed the small bags hanging from the Twins' shoulders.

"They're flashers, sir. We got a dozen in each bag."

Ace turned toward Blackhawk. "What do you think? Throw a dozen stunners out there and charge?" He stared at Blackhawk for a few seconds. "I don't see any other options."

Blackhawk took a deep breath and nodded. It was a desperate plan, but Ace was right. They didn't have time. More guards would be coming any minute, and if they screwed around long enough, they'd have Castillan army units on their asses too.

"Let's do it." He turned back toward the crew. "Everybody take two. We throw on my command, and then we charge ahead, firing full. Got it?"

They all nodded, and the Twins handed out the grenades. Blackhawk reached back and took two himself.

"Okay, one right after the other . . . then charge." He took a deep breath. "Now!"

He pulled the pin on the first grenade and threw it out onto the terrace beyond, followed immediately by the second one. Then he lunged forward, firing his assault rifle on full auto as he ran through the shattered picture window and out into the cold Castillan night.

CHAPTER 3

THE EXPLOSIONS LIT THE INKY BLACK SKY, EACH BLAST BRIEFLY turning the moonless night to day. The valley was filled with fire, the growing conflagration of war destroying everything in its path, leaving nothing but charred ruins to attest that men had once lived amid these rolling hills and gentle plains. The battle had been raging for weeks now, without pause, without mercy. Rykara was a planet scourged by the hell of war.

Arias Callisto stared at the nightmare laid out before him. He had not expected the enemy to put up such a fight. Rykara had been a divided planet, ruled by a squabbling class of hereditary lords eternally at war with one another. By the standards of a Prime world like Celtiboria, it was a backwater, its strength and technology no match for the invaders.

Callisto had expected to topple Rykara's petty fiefdoms and secure the planet in a few weeks. It had been four months now, and despite being reinforced twice, he was still battling his stubborn foes. The light casualties he'd expected had grown into catastrophic losses, and many of his lead units were down to 50 percent strength. His soldiers were the hardest veterans in the Far Stars, forged in the furnace of Celtiboria's wars—in the endless, brutal battles it had taken to unite that great world. Now they were dying in the thousands, at the hands of an enemy they had expected to sweep away.

Callisto was shocked by the status of the stalemated campaign—and ashamed. One of Augustin Lucerne's top commanders, Callisto was a man who had fought for almost thirty years at the great marshal's side, and his history was one of victory, his sword among the most reliable serving Lucerne.

Until he arrived on Rykara.

The lords he'd expected to find fractured and struggling against one another were instead united into a single power bloc, prepared for war and focused as one against the invaders. Their old and unreliable weapons had been replaced with modern arms, equipment, and technology far beyond anything Rykaran industry could produce. Indeed, much of the enemy ordnance was more advanced than the equipment used by the Celtiborians. Clearly, someone had aided the natives and prepared them to face the expeditionary force. He'd wondered at first if it could be the empire, but then he put the thought out of his mind. There had been nothing but ineffectual governors on Galvanus Prime since his grandfather had been a boy. And this was serious intervention, not the passing efforts of some imperial peacock sent to the edge of civilization for not bowing low enough in the emperor's presence. Still, he couldn't think of anyone else it could be . . .

His soldiers fought on, ignoring their losses and the superior weapons of their enemies. They were Augustin Lucerne's warriors, the proudest army in the Far Stars. Not many could claim to be their equals. But on Rykara they were outnumbered and dependent on a tenuous supply line stretching back to Celtiboria. When the expected quick victory failed to materialize, the impact of their weak logistics moved from problematic to critical. The longer the battle went on, the worse the situation would become. Celtiborian resources were already stretched thin, supporting wars of liberation—or conquest, depending on point of view—on almost a dozen worlds. Callisto knew time wasn't his ally, and so he did the only thing he could: he pushed his forces even harder.

The people of Rykara might not have liked their lords, but the Celtiborians were still the invaders, and the people were too downtrodden and uneducated to understand that Callisto's soldiers had come not to enslave them but to free them from oppression. And while the Celtiborians had no desire to kill any of the Rykaran peasants, without the ability to convince them they *were* liberators, they were forced to shoot them down in the thousands.

Captain Darius ran up the small hill toward Callisto. "Sir, Brigadier Orestes reports his forces have taken Lusania and now occupy the city and its environs. The surviving enemy forces are retreating toward the Olsyrus Mountains in considerable disorder." The aide's enthusiasm was tempered, understated. Both of them knew just how many casualties Orestes's troops had sustained in their triumph.

"Please send Brigadier Orestes my congratulations." Callisto knew he should call his subordinate himself, but he needed a little time. Time to absorb the magnitude of his army's ordeal—and to convince himself this was a victory. Orestes was a good officer, and he deserved his commander's heartfelt thanks, but Callisto didn't know if he was capable of that. Not yet.

He didn't blame Orestes for the losses. He doubted even Marshal Lucerne himself could have won Lusania at a lower cost. But those were still his soldiers out there, and a lot of them were dead or mangled in the field hospitals. If fighting at the side of Marshal Lucerne for three decades had taught Callisto anything, it was never to forget the common soldiers. Generals were prone to blindness toward the suffering their campaigns caused, to the misery of the men they commanded, seeking only personal glory and justifying any amount of pain and suffering with victory.

Officers like that didn't last long in Lucerne's army.

Callisto knew his first stop. He was going to visit the field hospitals to pay his respects. He owed them nothing less, miserable tribute that it was.

Then he would go to Orestes's headquarters. He'd known Ravenna Orestes for a long time, and he suspected the brigadier would be as uncomfortable accepting accolades now as Callisto would be offering them. If there was one thing Augustin Lucerne had pounded into his officers, it was humility, to appreciate and respect the common soldiers, the ones who fought the battles and died in the trenches and the blood-soaked fields.

Callisto walked slowly down the hillside, his mind focused on the battle now entering its final stages. He knew the fight on Rykara would soon be over, but he felt no satisfaction.

There is no glory here. Only death and the heavy burden of duty.

"Marshal Lucerne, I am sorry to disturb you, sir, but we have new reports from Rykara and Nordlingen." The aide stood in the doorway, clad in the absurd red-and-gold uniform the advisory council had mandated for senior staff. His voice was tentative. Like most of Lucerne's people since the completion of the conquest, he tiptoed around the marshal like a supplicant fearful of offending. He leaned through the open door, peering cautiously toward Lucerne.

The marshal was lying on the simple cot he'd brought in to replace the ornate bed the master of the household had chosen for him. After a lifetime in the field, he couldn't sleep a wink in the plush softness of a nobleman's bedding. His eyes were open, and he was staring up at the ceiling.

"I wasn't asleep, Colonel." *And if I was, it wouldn't matter. I've told you all a hundred times I want to be informed when any news comes in no matter what I am doing. Why do you all act like I'm going to strike you down for waking me up or interrupting a meal?*

Lucerne disliked the subservience of the civilian staff, but he understood it at least. To them he was a bloody conqueror, the man who'd crushed the brutal warlords who had ruled Celtiboria for centuries. Millions had died in Lucerne's wars, and their shadows hung over all he did. He was the unquestioned master of the most populous world in the Far Stars, and all but a scant handful of men and women who breathed the air of that planet were afraid of him.

But Colonel Artemis Cross wasn't a civilian. He wasn't just an adjutant. He was a seasoned combat leader with twenty years' experience in the field. He'd been neck deep in the blood and death of Lucerne's campaigns, and he'd served with valor and distinction. *And now he hovers around me like some ancient priest meekly begging favor from the gods. What have I created?*

Lucerne could tolerate the foolish worship from new recruits if he had to, but since the war on Celtiboria had been won, even the hardened veterans stared at him with that stupid look on their faces. He'd shared foxholes with some of those men, eaten rancid beans in the icy rain with them—and now they acted as if he'd descended from the heavens amid a shower of light. It was driving him mad, but expressing his discontent only threw them into a stronger wave of supplication. His men would face any danger at his command, carry out any order, no matter how difficult or dangerous, but the slightest sign of disapproval from him broke down even the most grizzled veteran.

He'd learned to hold his tongue and try to ignore it all. He wanted to be respected by his men, of course, but he had always thought of himself as one of them. The near worship made him extremely uncomfortable. *Though it has its uses, too.*

"Report, Colonel."

"Sir, General Callisto advises that his forces have broken the last major Rykaran stronghold. They have captured the city of Lusania and pushed the remaining enemy formations into the planet's undeveloped areas."

Cross's voice was upbeat, at least moderately so, and a small smile crept onto his face as he read the report.

Lucerne just sat quietly, and his eyes dropped slowly toward the floor. Rykara had been a far more difficult conquest than he'd expected, and he found it difficult to rejoice at the long delayed triumph. Cross saw the victory itself above all, but Lucerne's first thought was of the cost.

"This is good news, sir. The enemy is cut off from their

sources of supply. It is only a matter of time now before General Callisto secures the entire planet."

"Yes, as you say, it is only a matter of time." Lucerne felt a heaviness in his chest. *Only a matter of time until the Rykaran soldiers starve. Or die in the cold, imagining what horrors the invaders, now enraged by their own losses, were inflicting on their families. Every soldier who dies in the mountains, every story of civilian suffering, of women raped and children murdered, true or not, will make the hatred grow. We came to free a world and instead, we will be its new masters, rulers only by force and fear. They will despise us, and their resistance will push us into harsh reprisals to maintain order, intensifying the hate. There will be passive resistance—and terrorism. The nightmare will grow, and the Rykarans will be resentful slaves of the Far Stars Confederation instead of grateful members.*

This is not what I wanted.

"Casualty reports?" Lucerne stared at his aide expectantly. Arias Callisto was a consummate veteran, and despite his new role as a sycophant, he was a man of few words and no bullshit. Lucerne knew the general's reports would be complete and truthful, and his stomach clenched as he imagined how many of his soldiers lay dead and wounded on the battlefields of a distant world.

Cross reached out, handing over a small tablet without a word. His expression—and his silence—told Lucerne all he needed to know. The marshal glanced down at the columns displayed on the screen, and he felt a cold sensation moving down his spine. He'd expected bad news, but the loss figures he was looking at were beyond even his worst fears. Far from the easy conquest he'd expected, the war on Rykara had been a holocaust. *Is victory still victory when the cost is this high?*

Callisto's forces had run into a superbly equipped local force, armed with weapons far beyond anything they should have possessed. The Rykaran propaganda had been enormously effective as well, and the peasant soldiers fought like devils against an enemy they'd been told were ruthless barbarians, cold-blooded killers who would burn their homes and brutalize their wives and daughters. They'd been told the Celtiborians would butcher them if they yielded or carry them off as slaves to work in the uranium mines.

"This is not what I expected on Rykara." His voice was somber. He'd had similar reports from some of the other worlds: local forces far better equipped than anticipated and whipped up into a frenzy to fight the invaders. It hadn't happened on every world, but it wasn't an isolated incident either. "There is more at work here than meets the eye, Artemis."

The aide nodded respectfully. "Yes, Marshal." He paused, but finally the old veteran colonel pushed aside his subservience and offered an opinion. "Someone is conspiring against us, sir. Supplying our enemies with weapons and financial support."

Lucerne nodded. "But who, Colonel? Who has the resources to interfere on so many worlds at one time?" Lucerne had his own thoughts, but he wanted to hear Cross's opinion, untainted by knowledge of his own view.

"One of the other Primes, sir? Who else is strong enough to stand in our way?" There was a touch of anger in Cross's voice at the thought, and Lucerne didn't blame him. All the Primes had agreed to support Lucerne's confederation, or at least to remain neutral. If one of them was behind the mysterious intervention, it was nothing less than deliberate treachery.

"Who else indeed . . ." Lucerne's voice was soft, troubled. His suspicion was in a similar vein, yet far more sinister. And, despite the audacity of what he was thinking, it wasn't something he could easily discount. It kept coming back, pushing its way into his thoughts.

Galvanus Prime.

The last imperial governor had been a buffoon, even by the standards of the disgraced nobles who usually occupied the chair on Galvanus Prime. But that jackass was two years back in the empire now, recalled for incompetence and folly beyond what the emperor could tolerate, even in the tiny imperial foothold on mankind's frontier. Lucerne didn't have as much information as he'd like on the new governor, and what he did know was far from reassuring. By all indications, Kergen Vos was a man of considerable ability, a commoner who'd come up through imperial intelligence instead of being the black sheep of an inbred noble family. Lucerne knew he was likely far more capable—and dangerous—than those who had preceded him.

More ambitious, too.

Lucerne was trying not to jump to conclusions. There were plenty of other explanations. It could be another Prime, fearful of Celtiborian hegemony in the confederation, or even the Far Stars Bank or the transport guilds, concerned their power would wane if the sector was united. But after Blackhawk's experience on Saragossa, the marshal couldn't get away from the suspicion he was dealing with imperial interference—long before he was ready to face it. He'd pursued the dream of the confederation for thirty years expressly to ensure the Far Stars would never fall under imperial rule. If, against all odds, there was finally a capable governor on Galvanus Prime, he too would surely recognize the implications of a united sector and seek to sabotage the confederation at any opportunity.

"Send word to Admiral Desaix. I want him to dispatch a

dozen ships at once." Lucerne looked over toward Cross, pausing for a few seconds. "He is to find *Wolf's Claw* wherever it is and give Arkarin Blackhawk my request that he return to Celtiboria as quickly as possible."

If anyone could figure out what the empire was up to, it was Blackhawk. The captain of *Wolf's Claw* knew more about the empire than any man in the sector.

And he's the one man in the Far Stars I'm absolutely certain is not an imperial spy.

Astra Lucerne sat at her desk, shaking her head at the data she'd been reviewing. She was determined to make sense of it, but it had frustrated her so far.

Her office was in the great palace, at the end of the sprawling south wing. The massive structure was situated at the geographic center of Celtiboria City, and the vast metropolis extended out in concentric circles ten kilometers in every direction.

Astra lacked a clear title, but she was one of her father's key advisers nevertheless. Augustin Lucerne was well aware his daughter was far more than a pretty face, and he took her counsel to heart. Her concerns had proven to be right far more often than wrong.

The status of women varied enormously on the worlds of the Far Stars. Patriarchal societies were common, especially among the backwater worlds along the Rim. Even on a Prime world like Celtiboria, where there was a rough legal equality between the sexes, women rarely served in the armed forces. It was tradition more than law on Celtiboria, and there were indeed a few women in her father's armies. But they were a tiny minority, and cultural stereotypes remained strong among soldiers in the field.

Astra knew she'd have been more useful to her father if she'd been born a son, and she felt an irrational guilt that her gender complicated his succession plans. Celtiboria might accept a female ruler, but the less developed worlds would only do so under the guns of her soldiers. And she knew that was not the nation her father had struggled to create. Her feelings of guilt didn't make sense, but they were real nevertheless, and they drove her to work even harder, striving to help her father support his enormous burden any way she could.

She sighed and moved her hands to her face, rubbing her burning eyes. She'd worked all day and into the night, and now she could see the light again, dappled rays streaming through the two large windows behind her. It was dawn, and she was as stymied as she'd been the night before. The numbers simply didn't add up.

She had four screens on her workstation, each of them displaying columns of figures, her estimates of the economic cost of the weapons and ordnance her father's armies had faced on four of the planets they had invaded, worlds where the strength of the local resistance had far exceeded expectations. She'd been working on the data for weeks, ever since reports started coming in of surprisingly strong defenses on some of the first wave worlds.

Defenses that cost us too many friends.

She'd grown up around her father's soldiers, and the grizzled warriors had adopted her as one of their own. She'd marched alongside them, eaten with them, held their hands in the field hospitals as the surgeons raced to save their lives. She felt the loss of each of them keenly, and the thought of so many dying as they faced inexplicably strong enemy forces drove her to near madness. She was determined to try and find an answer.

She worked alone, as she usually did. The soldiers knew she was extremely intelligent—and tough as nails, too. But the bureaucrats and political parasites who had gathered since the final victory on Celtiboria viewed her as little more than her father's daughter. They saw her great beauty and imagined she would be bartered off in some marriage contract, destined to secure a crucial alliance, but to serve no other purpose than to bear her new husband children and cement a bond between Celtiboria and one of the other Prime worlds.

Astra didn't care what they thought, and she pitied any hypothetical lord married to her against her will. She detested the politicians and courtiers, and the first one to openly suggest she be traded away like some chattel would likely find an early grave. She was her father's daughter in more ways than one, and she would make her contributions on the battlefield or in the halls of government, not in some useful lord's bedchamber.

She looked up from her work, sliding her chair around to gaze out the window. The sun was rising in a perfect blue sky, but her thoughts were elsewhere. *Where is he?* Arkarin Black-hawk and his crew had left Celtiboria half a year before, and they hadn't been back since. Not that she expected to see Black-hawk again. Not for a long while.

Astra Lucerne was many things, but a whiny princess, sobbing over a lost love, wasn't one of them. She had her own duty, and she would see it done, whatever the cost. But she was human too, and she carried a deep sadness with her. She loved Black-hawk, and she was sure he returned her feelings. But she also knew that hadn't been enough to keep him on Celtiboria—or convince him to take her with him on *Wolf's Claw.*

She knew he hid a painful past, one that haunted him every day, and she was sure that was a major reason he had fled from her embrace. But she'd never been able to find out just what it was that burdened him so. She suspected her father knew the truth, but it was one of the few things she'd never been able to talk out of him. Despite her best efforts, Augustin Lucerne was like a block of granite when Blackhawk's past came up.

She couldn't imagine anything that would change how she felt about Blackhawk, no darkness from his past that could diminish her love for him. She'd tried to convince him, but he was infuriatingly stubborn, and she found herself wanting to strangle him more than once. Deep down, she knew she was his mirror image, and she matched him measure for measure in pigheadedness. But he still made her want to scream.

And maybe that's why we're perfect for each other.

Sighing ruefully, Astra drew her mind back to the work at hand. There would be time for personal pain later. Now, Celtiborian troops were fighting on eleven planets, and that was more important than tormenting herself over Blackhawk.

She leaned over and pressed the small comm button on the desk. It was hours before the start of the workday, and the outer offices would be quiet, with only the evening skeleton crew on duty. But Lys was an early riser, and Astra half expected she'd be at her desk by now.

"Lys, you out there yet?"

The response was almost immediate. "I'm here, Astra."

Astra smiled at her friend's alert voice. "Can you come in for a minute?"

"Be right there."

A few seconds later, the door opened and a young woman in a crisp suit walked in. Allysa Dracon was more than Astra's assistant—more, even, than a friend. Her father had been one of Lucerne's officers, killed at the Battle of Mauritania almost two decades before. Allysa's mother had died in childbirth, and the marshal practically adopted the orphaned eight-year-old girl. She and Astra were the same age, and they grew up almost like sisters.

"You've been here all night, haven't you?" Allysa was looking at Astra with a concerned expression.

Astra glanced down at herself and frowned. "It's that obvious, eh?" She took a deep breath. "I've been looking at these figures, Lys, trying to convince myself we don't have an unseen enemy out there. In the dark somewhere, conspiring against us."

Allysa walked up toward the desk and slid into one of the leather chairs. "You mean on Rykara." She paused, and a frown crept onto her face. "And Megara, Nordlingen, and Etruria." Another pause. "You know, I've been suspecting something for some time now myself. I could never put my finger on what was bothering me, though. I just know that our troops should have cut through those locals like a knife through butter. Those planets should have fallen by now, but instead we've been rushing reinforcements to them all."

"Yes. Exactly."

"So did you come to any conclusions?"

Astra shook her head slowly. "Nothing definitive. Whoever it is has resources. One of the Primes, possibly. Or the guilds. Maybe even the Far Stars Bank. They all stand to lose influence if the confederation really takes hold."

"The marshal has been careful to preserve all their perquisites in the Confederation Treaty. For just this reason." Despite Astra's—and Lucerne's—protestations, Lys insisted on always using his rank, and Astra had long given up trying to convince her friend to do otherwise.

"Yes, he has. And he has reached out individually to every major power in the sector, but that doesn't change the fact that they will still lose power, at least relatively. The Far Stars Bank and the guilds are enormously influential because they operate sectorwide, virtually the only entities that do so. Their strength, and their ability to exert influence, derives from that exclusivity as much as anything else. If the confederation comes to encompass all or most of the Far Stars, it will create a framework for other institutions to compete on an interplanetary level. That will erode their positions."

Lys nodded slowly. "That makes sense. The Far Stars Bank would lose its monopoly power as the financier of interplanetary trade. And commerce between planets joined by the Confederation Treaty will not require guild-bonded ships. Existing grants of landing privileges and mercantile treaties will be voided by the confederation's free trade provisions." She took a deep breath, staring down at the floor for a few seconds before she looked back at Astra. "But the marshal has assured the bank and the guilds of preferential treatment within the Far Stars Confederation. He didn't like it, but he recognized the need, and he held his nose and wrote it into the treaty."

"Yes," Astra said softly. "But don't forget that he had to do that, because they have real power now, unassailable, secured by the fragmentation of the sector. Father's assurances are just that, though: the promises of *one* man. Even if they trusted him completely, which I doubt, he is mortal. One day he will be succeeded, and his promises will die with him. Documents like the Confederation Treaty can be changed. They can be ignored, their meaning twisted. It wouldn't be the first time a governing document was twisted to serve the needs of those in power."

"But the treaty . . ." Lys's voice drifted off to silence. "Right. In the end, the treaty is just words."

"Exactly. Would it shock you if the bank or the guilds—or even one or more of the Primes—decided this was all too big a risk? That Father's fear of the empire one day controlling the Far Stars is less a threat to their positions than a sectorwide governing body?"

"No, I suppose not."

Astra nodded. "We speak of the Far Stars as if it is a single entity. But the truth is, the only trait the different worlds share is they are not part of the empire. Beyond that, what do we have in common? Some planets are united, others fragmented. Some are republics—or at least reasonable facsimiles of electoral governments—others are dictatorships. There are what, a dozen major religions in the Far Stars? Perhaps more. And hundreds of local customs.

"The fear of the empire creates a bond between us, but it has been almost two centuries since the last imperial attempt at conquest, and it has become a theoretical worry for most people of the sector. But a Far Stars Confederation will be real. Even though the treaty goes a long way to preserve autonomy, Father couldn't allow total freedom to local authorities. There are over one hundred planets in the sector with sizable populations, right? At least twenty have legal slavery or serfdom. Half a dozen have officially sanctioned gladiatorial combat, and at least twice that many tacitly allow such practices. Two have subcultures that engage in human sacrifice. There is no escaping the fact that the confederation must—and will—impose real laws on them and force them to abandon some of their ways of life. And they will bear their share of the costs of the fleets and armies protecting the sector, armed forces that exist solely to enforce the laws the confederation imposes on them and protect them from an empire they no longer fear."

"Everything you say may be true, Astra," Lys said, "but it is still folly. The empire is a danger to them all, despite the lack of aggression in recent years. And the consequences of imperial domination are far more terrible than any burdens imposed by the confederation."

"That's easy for us to say, Lys. We grew up with my father's armies. How many times did we listen to him go on about it, how the empire was dangerous? But do you think anyone really fears the empire anymore, Lys? Enough to overlook their own petty positions and make real sacrifices?"

"No, I suppose not too many. Not anymore, at least."

"It's just been too long. Two centuries is a long time, and there's no one alive who remembers the last imperial atrocities. Chrono—no one alive today even knew anyone who *lived* during that time! Sure, everybody pays lip service to the old fears handed down from their great-grandparents, but they aren't *really* afraid anymore, are they?"

Astra sat back and shook her head.

Alyssa wore a troubled expression.

"What is it, Lys?"

"I'm just wondering . . . nobody's afraid of the empire anymore, except the marshal, of course. But people are usually wrong about such things. Do you think . . ." Her voice trailed off.

"Do I think what, Lys?"

"Maybe *we* should be worried about the empire. Not in a generation, or a hundred years, as the marshal does, but *right now*."

"What do you mean?"

"I mean, maybe they're involved in all this. Perhaps the danger is far closer than we imagine."

Astra didn't answer. She'd been thinking the same thing, but she hadn't wanted to say it, to admit the possibility. She felt a shiver move through her body. If the empire was working against them already, the Far Stars just got more dangerous. A lot more dangerous.

The two sat long in silence, each of their minds treading down dark roads.

CHAPTER 4

"ALL RIGHT, LUCAS, GET US THE HELL OUT OF HERE."

"Way ahead of you, Skip." The *Claw*'s pilot was working his board like a virtuoso, increasing power at just the right speed, and charting the best route through the thick Castillan atmosphere.

Blackhawk knew Lucas was on it, so he dropped hard into his command chair, reaching around and clipping his harness in place. The tight strap hurt as it pressed against his midsection. He'd caught a round in the side during the final escape from the Grand Palais. He'd been a warrior for thirty-five years, and he'd known immediately it was nothing serious, just a flesh wound. But that didn't change the fact that it still hurt like hell.

The snugness of the strap tugged at it, ripping open the hasty dressing he'd applied.

Just another scar to add to the collection.

Shira bounded up the ladder and ran across the bridge toward Ace's station. She sat down hard and leaned over the scope.

"How is he?" Blackhawk asked. Ace had been hit too, twice, and one of the wounds was serious. Doc was down in the *Claw*'s tiny sick bay, still working on him.

"He's in rough shape, Ark." Shira was usually as cool as they come, but Blackhawk could tell from her voice she was worried. "He's lost a lot of blood. If we were on Celtiboria, he'd be fine. But as good as he is at patching us back together, Doc's not a real surgeon, and the *Claw*'s infirmary isn't a hospital."

Blackhawk just nodded. He turned away for a few seconds, closing his eyes. He wanted to be down there, standing behind Doc, waiting at Ace's side. But his place was here, making sure they all got out. It wasn't going to help Ace if the *Claw* got blasted out of the sky by the Castillan defense forces.

"I've got bogies on the scope, Captain." Her voice was calm once more. Blackhawk allowed himself a quick smile.

Nothing fazes her.

"Lucas?" Blackhawk shot his eyes over toward the pilot's station.

"I'm pushing as hard as I dare, Skip. This atmosphere is too damned thick." Castilla's air was heavier than Celtiboria's, with an atmospheric pressure 30 percent higher. It made lifting off quickly a hazardous proposition at best. The *Claw* was a solid vessel, but she was still subject to the laws of physics. Friction causes heat. If the hull temperature got hot enough, even the iridium-alloy armor would melt.

We've been in tough scrapes before, and if it hasn't melted yet . . .

"Well, push it harder. I'd rather bet on the *Claw*'s hull holding out than fight the entire Castillan Defense Force." He leaped out of his chair abruptly, grabbing onto one of the support columns as he moved toward Ace's station. "Get down to the turrets, Shira. Just in case. I'll man the scope."

"Yes, sir." She jumped up and moved quickly toward the ladder, her step never once faltering. A planetary takeoff was a rough affair, but she raced across the wildly pitching floor with the grace of a dancer and hopped onto the ladder.

"And take one of the Twins with you," he called out to her. "Tarq." The Twins were alike in so many ways it wasn't hard to think of them as anything but two copies of the same person. But despite their similarities in appearance, voice, temperament, and personality, Tarq was inexplicably a better shot than his brother.

"Got it, Captain." She vanished below the floor.

Blackhawk staggered the rest of the way across the bridge, grabbing hold of Ace's chair and pulling himself around. He sat and bent over the scope immediately. "We've got twenty-plus enemy craft launching, Lucas. And that's only from this hemisphere."

"I'm punching it hard, Skip, but I'm a big fan of having a hull between us and the atmosphere."

You and me both. But I'm not a fan of catching a missile in the nonmelted hull.

Blackhawk could feel the ship bucking as the thrusters pushed it faster into the Castillan sky. He knew Lucas was taking it right to the limit. The *Claw* would be fine once she cleared the atmosphere. The big question was *if* she would clear it. The

Castillans didn't have anything that could catch her in space, at least not in a straight-out chase. Blackhawk sighed, watching the enemy ships moving slowly on the scope. At least the thick air was a factor that limited them both equally. That gave the *Claw* a chance to escape.

I hope.

"Plot us the best course to avoid enemy contacts. Let's see if we can get out of here without a battle. It'd be nice to have someplace we could come back to for a change." He didn't have any real desire to return to Castilla, but the list of places where the *Claw* and its crew had worn out their welcome was getting long.

"Already working on it, Skip. Give me thirty seconds."

Blackhawk dialed up Shira's turret. "You in place yet?"

"Yeah, Cap. Just strapping in and powering up the guns." He could hear her scrambling into position and slamming the hatch behind her. The turrets were tight spaces, and nobody really fit in them, at least not well. He had no idea how Tarq managed to squeeze his massive frame in there, but somehow he did, and never once complained.

Ace, on the other hand, complained every. Single. Time.

I wish I had him complaining right now.

Blackhawk flipped the comm unit, bringing the second turret on the line. He knew Tarq would still be working his way through the narrow hatch. He could hear the giant's uncomfortable grunts through the comm. "Listen to me, both of you: I want you ready, but don't fire unless I give the order. No matter what. Understood?"

They both answered yes.

"We're going to try to get out of here without committing an act of war." He paused for a few seconds, pondering how the Castillans would view kidnapping one of their oligarchs. "Another one, I mean."

The ship shook again, almost knocking Doc off his feet. He was standing over Ace, staring down at his hands, both of which were deep inside the unconscious man's chest, working feverishly. The first shot was a flesh wound, but the second one was bad. Really bad. It had clipped the heart, tearing several holes in the muscle and causing a massive amount of bleeding.

The *Claw*'s sick bay had a decent supply of artificial blood, an expensive luxury that few adventurers' vessels could afford. That had kept Ace alive so far, but Doc still had to repair the damage to save his patient. And regardless of the nickname the crew had given him, Rolf Sandor wasn't a surgeon. At least not one with proper credentials. Medicine had been a hobby for him before he'd hooked up with Blackhawk, just another area of interest for the brilliant scholar, one of many. He'd studied the field, and he had a tremendous storehouse of knowledge. But he'd never practiced medicine, not before the day he'd saved a wounded Blackhawk and found a new home. But an amateur doctor was all Ace Graythorn had, and Sandor wasn't about to give up on his patient. At least the *Claw* had a medical AI. That was a help.

Think, think . . . don't just cut. He'd fused two holes in Ace's heart, but the pool of blood substitute still filling the chest cavity proved there was another leak. He felt around with his fingers, trying to find the remaining wound. There was another bullet in there, and at least one more perforation.

His own heart was pounding in his ears, and he knew he didn't have much time. If he didn't finish up and plug the last hole, and soon, Ace was going to die.

The ship shook again, harder this time, and he reached out with a blood-covered hand and grabbed the edge of the table to stabilize himself. "Fuck," he muttered, as he staggered toward the decon unit to resterilize his hand. *Come on, Ark,* he thought. *Keep this thing steadier than that, or I'm going to lose him.*

"Administer another two units."

The *Claw*'s medical AI was a fairly rudimentary unit, but Sandor was glad to have it. The system was scanning Ace's vitals in real time, and it reported instantly when there were any changes.

"Administering. The supply of artificial blood is nearly depleted. Four additional units remain." The AI had an androgynous human-sounding voice. Doc mentally flipped a coin and decided it was female.

"Keep two additional units on standby." He was running out of time. *Focus. You can do this.*

Doc tried to concentrate on Ace, but he couldn't suppress a passing thought about the odd path his life had taken, from brilliant university professor to exiled loser of a political struggle to rogue mercenary. The part that surprised him the most was how much he preferred his life on the *Claw* to his days in academia. For all the danger and hardship—or maybe because of it—Rolf Sandor couldn't imagine going back to his classroom and his lab.

He probed around, moving his finger slowly, probing for any damage. He felt the frustration rising as he continued without success. The AI was projecting a 3-D image of Ace's chest. Doc knew where the bullet was, but he couldn't find the damaged area of the heart wall. It was somewhere under the pool of blood filling Ace's chest cavity.

Finally, his fingertip felt something. The bullet. He reached out with his other hand, grabbing the extractor. He moved the long, slender tool slowly, carefully, toward the projectile, grabbing it and slowly pulling.

An instant later he dropped the small chunk of metal onto a tray. *Good,* he thought. "Administer two more units."

Now I just have to stop the bleeding and get him patched up before I run out of blood substitute.

Katarina sat on the edge of her cot, staring silently at the wall, replaying the last moments of their escape from the Grand Palais. She was troubled, and a strange expression had taken hold of her face.

They had barely gotten away. Another minute and they would all have been killed or captured. But Lucas had managed to bring the *Claw* down over the large roof deck just in time, somehow wedging the ship into the tight confines next to the hotel's massive tower. He popped the lower hatch and dropped a bunch of lines to the ground, and they had frantically scrambled aboard.

Her agile mind focused hard on every aspect of the operation: the final fight with the guards, the race to climb up before enemy reinforcements arrived, the effort of getting a wounded Blackhawk and unconscious Aragona aboard.

Then Ace went down in hail of enemy fire.

He'd been the last one, the rearguard, standing under the shadow of the *Claw,* guns in both hands. His assault rifles spewed death and held the enemy back while his friends climbed to safety.

Katarina had been staring right at him when he was hit. The first shot took him in the shoulder. He staggered back, but he stayed on his feet and kept on firing without so much as a pause. It was no more than a few seconds, a fleeting instant, before he was hit again. The shot took him full on in the chest, and he dropped instantly, his guns falling to the ground next to him. He lay motionless on the rooftop.

Blackhawk saw it too, and he lunged across the deck, now slick with his own blood. He was reaching for one of the lines, determined to go back down and rescue Ace, ignoring his own wound. But Tarnan grabbed him hard, his massive arms holding the captain like a vise while Tarq slid down the cable toward Ace's still form.

Katarina felt an urge to follow, but she stayed frozen in place, unsure if it was discipline or panic holding her back. She was as cold-blooded and fearless in battle as Blackhawk, but something about seeing Ace sprawled out on the concrete below hit her hard, stripping her of her normal decisiveness.

She stood stone still and watched as Tarq dropped to the roof, certain the big man would never make it back up with Ace through the heavy enemy fire. She was about to rush to one of the cables when a blinding flash ripped through the air, and the shattered remnants of the hotel wall erupted into flame and debris.

Another flash followed, and she stared down where the enemy guards had been a few seconds before. The macabre scene was lit by half a dozen fires. There was nothing visible through the clouds of billowing smoke except wreckage and charred bodies.

She understood right away. It had been Shira. Through all the confusion and chaos of the final escape, Shira Tarkus had kept her wits. She'd run to the needle gun controls and blasted the enemy guards to bits, clearing the way for Tarq to rescue Ace.

Katarina was silent now, her mind confused and uncertain

as she stared at the wall of her cabin. Discipline was second nature to her, almost a religion. She'd been trained in the ways of the Sebastiani Assassins' Guild since childhood. Its tenets and commandments had governed her life as long as she could remember—they made her the person she was. She had earned the gold belt, over a hundred confirmed kills. She'd taken out heads of state and leaders of criminal organizations, and she'd survived mission after mission. She had excelled because of her discipline. But it had failed her during the escape, and she had hesitated when she should have acted.

She knew what it was, at least in part, and it was something she hadn't wanted to face. Sebastiani assassins worked alone. Solitude was part of the life, hand in hand with discipline. Emotions, loyalties, even vendettas—they all interfered with the cold, rational judgment expected of graduates of the Sebastiani school. She had lived her life devoted to these principles, but now she found herself facing growing doubts. She knew she had been on *Wolf's Claw* for too long. She had clearly lost her edge. She'd found friends, a family . . .

And that was a luxury an assassin couldn't afford.

She'd fooled herself with mind games, petty frauds she perpetrated to drive away her doubts. She paid for her passage, insisting she wasn't really one of the crew. But her lies were empty, and only she had been fooled.

She knew she had to leave, to return to the loneliness that made her one of the most gifted practitioners of her trade. And yet, the idea ripped at her heart. She didn't want to abandon those she now realized had become her friends, to leave them to face danger without her blade and skills at their side. And she knew, whatever she did, she couldn't force herself to depart now.

Not until she knew Ace was going to survive.

She'd viewed the *Claw*'s informal first officer as a clownish buffoon when she first arrived on board, but two years of living in close quarters and fighting side by side had shown her a different side. The boisterous loudmouth was as much an alias for Jason Graythorn as her own noblewoman persona was for her. The real man hidden beneath the bluster was far different from what he appeared to be. And she began to realize he was far more important to her than she'd imagined.

She stood up and opened the hatch, walking out into the short corridor. She moved toward the small alcove that housed the *Claw*'s sick bay and stopped, standing at the far end of the room, watching quietly as Doc worked frantically to save Ace's life. She didn't say anything. Even her breath was silent. She just stood with her eyes fixed on Doc and waited to see if Ace Graythorn would survive. As she stood there, she suddenly realized something.

I don't know what I will do if he doesn't.

"Just keep us out of range, Lucas. Those Castillan tubs can't keep up with the *Claw*."

Of course, Blackhawk knew it wasn't that simple. There had been patrol ships on duty in the space around Castilla as well as on the ground, and they too had responded when the alarm went out. There were hostiles heading toward *Wolf's Claw* along four different vectors. But he couldn't give the order to jump, not yet. Entering hyperspace would scrag most of the systems on the ship, including sick bay. And that would kill Ace.

"I'm on it, Ark. But you know they're going to run us down eventually. There's no vector that will get us past them all, at least not without spending some time in weapons range."

He did know all that, but he thought that as long as *he* didn't voice it, maybe a solution could be found. One bit of good news: at least the ship was fully functional this time. That wasn't something they'd been able to take for granted over the years, and Blackhawk knew Lucas would take full advantage of it.

Blackhawk looked down at the comm controls on the armrest of his chair. He was tempted to check in with Doc again, but he resisted the urge. The *Claw*'s resident scholar and part-time doctor was doing everything he could to save Ace. Blackhawk had no doubt of that. There was no point in interrupting him with comm chatter.

"Fifteen minutes, Skip." Lucas was staring at a tangled web of plotting calculations on his screen. "Seventeen tops. Then we'll have to jump or fight."

Blackhawk sighed. Seventeen minutes wasn't a long time, and the decision looming ahead of him was one he dreaded. The *Claw* could take on one or two of the Castillan patrol ships, and maybe even more, with a strong prospect of victory. But there were a lot more than one or two out there, and engaging the first group would slow their escape, allowing more enemy units to converge. Staying in the system was gambling with the lives of everyone on the *Claw*. But jumping now was a death sentence for Ace.

Blackhawk was a coldly decisive man, with an almost inhuman ability to analyze facts and commit to a course of action. But this time he didn't know what to do. The young Arkarin Blackhawk had been calculating—and brutal—capable of doing whatever got the job done without concern for consequences or cost. And his crew was pulled together with people who knew the inherent risks in this line of work. But this would be different than going into a fight together, where one of his commands might lead to a crew member's death. No, this time Blackhawk would be giving the order that killed Ace. He might not actually pull a trigger, but he'd be murdering his friend all the same.

> **Failure to jump prior to engagement reduces the chance of escaping the system from 99.2 percent to less than 50 percent. Each additional minute's delay after entering combat range correlates to a further 0.75 percent reduction in survival probability.**

Yes, Blackhawk thought back, not doubting Hans's predictive capability. *But if we jump now, Ace will die.*

> **Jason Graythorn is one man. There are currently fourteen crew and one prisoner on *Wolf's Claw*. Logic dictates a clear choice.**

Fuck logic and fuck you. Blackhawk knew the computer implanted in his head was right, but he just couldn't accept it. The younger version of himself would have pitied—and loathed—his indecisiveness, but that just made them even, because Blackhawk hated his past self, and he'd sworn never to become that again.

All I can do now is try to buy us all a little more time.

He pressed one of the buttons next to the comm unit. "Shira, Tarq: I want you both sharp. We may have some fighting to do after all."

"We're ready, Ark." Shira's voice was unemotional, as usual, but Blackhawk could hear the relief there, too. Ace and Shira sparred constantly, but Blackhawk knew she'd rather fight the devil himself than run away at the cost of her crewmate's life.

Well, we're about to enter hell . . .

"You are commanded to power down immediately and surrender. Failure to obey will result in immediate attack." The voice on the comm dripped with arrogance. Castillan commanders had the *Claw* bracketed and outnumbered, and they knew it.

Shira sat in her turret, watching the enemy ships approach on the 3-D display projected all around her. Her hands were on the laser controls, ready to fire as soon as the targets moved into range—and the captain gave the word.

She listened quietly, waiting for Blackhawk's response. She knew he'd try to buy time, but she doubted it would do any good. The *Claw*'s captain was a gifted bullshitter when necessity arose, but the crew had snatched one of the Castillans' most powerful lords, shooting up half a major city in the process. They had to be pissed.

"This is the free trader *Wolf's Claw,* on a private flight plan, bound for Vanderon. You have no authority to . . ."

"You are a rogue vessel, and you have kidnapped Oligarch Aragona. You will yield immediately, or we will open fire."

Bullshit. You're nowhere close to being in range with your popguns. On the other hand, the Claw's *laser turrets are effective out to a hundred thousand kilometers.* Shira took a deep breath. If Ark gave the word quickly enough, she'd have maybe two minutes before the enemy could respond to her fire. She had to do as much damage as possible before the fight became two-sided.

She heard a staticky sound as the Castillans cut the connection. They were playing this to the hilt, but she knew they had to be careful. If they wanted Aragona back, they were going to have to disable the *Claw,* not destroy it.

She'd be under no such restrictions.

C'mon, Ark. I know you don't want to fire first, but it's the only option. She gripped the firing controls tightly, watching the plotting display. They'd be in range soon, and if they didn't open up, they'd squander their only advantage. *Ark . . .*

"Shira, Tarq . . ." She could hear the resignation in Blackhawk's voice. He paused and sighed softly. "Open fire as soon as we're in range. Target enemy ships as soon as they come into your firing arcs." Another pause. "And try to disable them, not blast them to atoms."

A feral smile grew on Shira's face. She wasn't as reluctant as the captain to resort to violence. The Castillans shot Ace—she didn't even know if he was going to survive. As far as she was concerned, the crew of the *Claw* had a score to settle.

She watched silently as the closest enemy vessel slipped into range. She closed her eyes, concentrating as the targeting system projected the display directly into her brain. She turned off her other thoughts, focusing, feeling the triple laser turret as if it was part of her, another arm or leg.

She felt her hands tighten, her finger brushing against the firing stud. *Another second or two . . .*

She pulled the trigger, watching a projection of the shot lancing through space, slamming into the image of the enemy vessel. She felt the elation she always did when she scored a hit, and she waited for the AI to complete the damage assessment while her guns recharged. An instant later, the projection disappeared in a bright flash.

"Nice shooting, Shira, but what happened to disabling them?" Blackhawk's voice seemed hollow, distant. Shira had surrendered herself completely to the neural targeting system, and outside stimuli had to fight to penetrate.

"Sorry, Ark." *That's a lie, and he knows it.* "I must have hit their reactor. These Castillan ships are piles of junk."

"Well, try to cool it, Shira. Let's try to cut down on the body count for once."

"Got it, Cap." Her attention snapped back to the tactical display. Her guns would be charged and ready to fire again in ten seconds, and she needed another target.

She fired again, another hit. This time the ship survived, but it stopped accelerating. She must have taken out the engines. There were half a dozen vessels moving into range, and in another minute they'd be firing back. She pulled the trigger again. And again. Two more hits, but the targets kept coming, accelerating toward the *Claw*.

The ship shook hard, and alarms started to sound. The one-sided fight was over.

Shira locked her thoughts on her target, firing again, but the *Claw* shuddered a second time, and her shot went wide.

Fuck.

Four enemy ships were firing on the *Claw* now, approaching from three different trajectories. If they managed to score a solid hit and knock out the hyperdrive, that would be the end. The *Claw* would put up a tremendous fight, but there were almost thirty enemy vessels in the hunt now. Eventually, they'd pound her into a floating hulk. Then they'd come for Aragona. Shira promised herself she'd put a bullet in the fucker before anybody boarded the *Claw*. One last act of defiance before death.

Suddenly, the comm crackled to life. "Ark, it's Doc. I just got Ace all stitched up. He looks like shit, but he's out of danger. You can get us out of here whenever you'd like. Now would be good."

Shira felt a wave of relief. She could hear the exhaustion in Doc's voice, but also the satisfaction. He wasn't the cutting edge of the *Claw*'s combat power by any measure, but Rolf Sandor carried his weight and more. Shira would never admit it, least of all to Ace himself, but she'd been scared to death they were going to lose him. For all the caustic friction that sometimes crackled between them, deep down, she thought of the pompous windbag as an older brother. She owed Doc a big wet kiss.

"All right, everybody. Hang on to something. Shutting down all systems. Hyperjump in one minute. Shira, Tarq, get the hell out of the turrets!"

Shira popped the hatch and shimmied through the access tube. She was halfway back to her chair when the lights went dim, and she felt the familiar feeling, like a hundred small electrical shocks all over her body. The *Claw* had jumped. They were out of the Castilla system.

CHAPTER 5

KERGEN VOS STARED ACROSS THE TABLE AT HIS GUEST. "SO YOU are telling me that the Far Stars Bank has hired Arkarin Blackhawk and his people on multiple occasions. That he is indeed on a mission for the bank even as we speak?" He was calm, his tone pleasant as he spoke. His eyes flitted to the side for an instant, flashing a brief glance toward Mak Wilhelm before returning his gaze to the nervous man sitting across the table.

"Yes, Your Excellency. Blackhawk is extremely reliable. The bank has utilized him for dealing with . . . ah . . . troublesome clients before. Cases of fraud mostly, where the bank felt it was necessary to set an example." The man sitting across from Vos wore a perfectly tailored suit made from Troyan silk. Vos could only guess at its price, but he had a pretty good idea his bribes had paid for it.

Trayn Ballock was an executive at the Far Stars Bank, fairly junior in rank, but fortunate enough to work in the chairman's office. That fortuitous positioning had opened another door, one to an even more lucrative, though dangerous opportunity, and now the banker had another role: informant for Vos.

The governor suspected Chairman Vargas wasn't a pleasant man to those who failed him—that he was cold and unforgiving to those who fell from favor. The politics at an entity as large and powerful as the Far Stars Bank tended to be rough. Still, he wondered if Ballock truly understood how much more serious the game had become for him. Vargas might fire him for a failure, even blacklist him and drive him to one of the backwater worlds along the Rim if he was displeased. But Kergen Vos would feed him to a pack of starving carnasoids a centimeter at a time and consider himself merciful.

Vos had ensnared the fool through greed, an ancient and reliable tool of the trade. The payout had been a hundred thousand platinum crowns to start, with the promise of much more if he proved his worth.

Wilhelm had suggested starting with a lower figure, holding back the truly large sums until Ballock had displayed his usefulness. But Vos knew the easiest way to cultivate an asset's avarice was to give him a true taste of wealth. Most men could only look so far above themselves, and the surest way to make them crave more was to give them all they wanted. Invariably, the taste of luxury and power became the most addictive of drugs and ensnared the target, creating an insatiable lust for more. Possessing all they had once desired, they would take ever greater risks and engage in more blatant treachery to satisfy their new cravings. They would become slaves to their paymaster.

Now it was time to back up bribery with its even stronger cousin: fear. Trayn Ballock needed not only a taste of the rewards to come, but also to understand the cost of failure. "Are you aware that I have placed a price on the head of Arkarin Blackhawk?" Vos's tone was calm, but there was an undercurrent of menace there too.

"No, Lord Governor, I wasn't." Ballock fidgeted nervously. Vos suspected the banker was indeed aware of the bounty.

"It is one million imperial crowns. A substantial sum, wouldn't you say?"

Ballock's eyes widened. "To say the least, Lord Governor. I imagine every bounty hunter and freelance mercenary in the Far Stars is after Blackhawk."

"It is fortunate for you then, is it not?" Vos stared at his guest. He reached under the table and pressed a small button.

"For me, Lord Governor?" Ballock paused, an uncertain look on his face. "I'm afraid I do not understand."

"It is fortuitous that you are in a position to deliver Arkarin Blackhawk to me. I had not imagined our new relationship bearing such fruit so quickly." A door at the far side of the room opened, and a man stepped through and walked toward the table.

Ballock looked briefly behind him at the sound of the door before turning back toward Vos. "Lord Governor . . . I, um, appreciate your confidence, but Blackhawk is on a special mission for the chairman; I'm afraid I do not have the authority to intervene."

"Allow me to introduce my associate, Mr. Ballock." Vos

looked up at the new arrival with a grin. "This is Sebastien Alois de Villeroi, one of my most trusted associates."

Villeroi nodded. "Thank you, Governor." He turned to face the nervous banker. "Mr. Ballock." His tone was devoid of emotion.

Vos smiled. "Lord Villeroi is . . . how shall I put this . . . a specialist. He handles particular situations, often involving those who have failed to follow through on their promises to me." Vos let the smile slip off his face as he watched Ballock. He could see Villeroi was having his usual unsettling effect. The operative's words and expressions were utterly unremarkable, but there was something about the man that made people nervous. And Vos could see Villeroi was definitely getting to Ballock.

The banker fidgeted nervously. "It is a pleasure to meet you, Lord Villeroi." His tone suggested it was anything but.

"You are aware of the recent coup on Kalishar, are you not?" Vos knew Ballock was well aware of what happened at Kalishar. Indeed, the bank had just recognized Rax Florin as ka'al and in return, the new ruler had renewed the existing charters, assuring the bank a continued monopoly on formal financial transactions.

"Yes . . . of course." Ballock's voice was confused, uncertain. "May I ask what that has to do with our topic of discussion?"

Vos smiled. "Nothing directly. I just thought you might be interested in how the transition of power on Kalishar took place—and how the previous ka'al perished." The imperial governor stared across the table. Ballock squirmed.

"You see, Mr. Ballock, the ka'al was an ally of mine, much like yourself. He took my coin and made great promises to me." Vos paused, just for an instant, and then he leaned in across the table, bringing his face closer to Ballock. "But he failed me, Trayn. He failed me badly. I gave him a second chance, but to no avail. Lord Villeroi was compelled to defend my interests." He turned and looked to the side, at the grim-faced man standing at attention next to the table. "Perhaps, Lord Villeroi, you could provide some details on how the ka'al met his . . . ah . . . unfortunate demise."

"Certainly, Excellency." Villeroi turned and focused on the extremely uncomfortable-looking Ballock. "Unfortunately, the ka'al left us no choice in how to proceed. We asked very little of him, yet he spurned our requests. He had approached us in friendship, but he failed to act as a friend. As I'm sure you know, Kalishar is a brutal world in many ways, and the prospects of a peaceful transition were scant. Civil strife would have caused considerable suffering among the populace. We were compelled to take action of greater . . . finality."

Villeroi leaned down and opened a small box sitting on the floor next to Vos. "Meet the former ka'al, Mr. Ballock, so you may understand the price of failure." Villeroi extended his hand.

Ballock gasped. The imperial agent held a skull.

"Sadly, the ka'al's death was not a good one. I fear that years of soft living had drained away the toughness of his pirate days, leaving a rather weak man. His demise was a slow and unpleasant one, and he screamed like a wailing infant the entire time. Unpleasant business all around." Villeroi's expression suggested he considered it anything but.

Ballock stared at the smile on Villeroi's face, and he began to shake uncontrollably. He turned his head toward Vos, his eyes wide with shock and fear.

"So, my good Mr. Ballock . . . shall we discuss Arkarin Black-hawk once again?"

"Do you think we can rely on Trayn Ballock?" Mak Wilhelm asked. He sat across the small table from Kergen Vos. The two were sharing a late dinner as they had most nights during the past few months. Operations were under way throughout the sector, and it seemed there was never enough time to properly manage it all. Vos had secured generous financial resources from the emperor, but he was always short of reliable personnel. And the disaster with the ka'al demonstrated the risk of counting on lesser retainers.

After the unification of Celtiboria and the debacle of Astra Lucerne's kidnapping, Vos had accelerated all plans. What he had hoped to accomplish in five years now had to be done in two. There was little choice. The past six months had seen the Celtiborians begin their wars of unification on a massive scale. The imperial forces were running out of time. If Vos didn't oppose Lucerne's efforts and at least delay his progress, he faced the prospect of dealing with a Far Stars that would be at least partially united. That would make his plans vastly more difficult.

"Certainly not." Vos poked his knife at the slices of white meat on his plate, but didn't eat. The Turanian pheasant was a delicacy. It commanded a king's ransom even within the borders of the empire proper; imported across the hazards of the Void it was almost beyond price. He should have been savoring the delicate flavors, but, of late, Vos found that the mix of incompetent allies and enemies as capable as Marshal Lucerne tended to exert a suppressive effect on his appetite. He'd lost almost ten kilos since he'd taken the governor's scepter, despite his habit of importing the very best foodstuffs the empire had to offer.

He'd been pushing the pheasant around his plate for the last ten minutes, but now he set his utensils down and looked across the table at his closest adviser. "Ballock is a weak man and an unreliable asset. But as before, I am at a loss for options. Our trustworthy personnel are already stretched thin. We must make do with the resources we have available." He paused for a few seconds, relishing the image of Ballock's panic-stricken face as he hurried back to his ship. "But we will no longer hesitate to use fear as a motivator. We coddled the ka'al for far too long, and we suffered the consequences of that tolerance. Had he been sufficiently focused earlier, he might have paid more attention to detail, and Blackhawk and his people would have been killed on Kalishar instead of escaping with Astra Lucerne."

"Well, Ballock is as motivated as fear can make him." Wilhelm was a serious man, but Vos could hear the amusement in his voice. "I suspect he required a change of pants by the time he got back to his ship."

"Ballock is an insect. A valuable one, but not central to our plans to neutralize Blackhawk. If he is able to arrange a trap, that will be a bonus. But the bounty we have offered should bear fruit. The Far Stars sector is full of too many desperate men, and a promise of one million crowns should entice all of them." He looked down at his food and picked up his fork. He paused before spearing a piece of pheasant. "I suspect Blackhawk and his people are more capable than most, but numbers will tell in the end. He and his little band will be hunted down and overcome. There is no other outcome I can foresee."

He raised his fork to his mouth and chewed quickly. "But Blackhawk isn't of as much concern to me as the bank, and that's where Ballock must deliver. He is crucial to our plans to take over the Far Stars Bank—and through that, our other economic targets."

"And you're confident he will succeed?"

"Not at all." Vos laughed. "But I fear we once again have no better options."

"Should we dispatch Villeroi to keep a closer eye on him, then? I am sure we can devise a reasonable cover for him on Vanderon. Indeed, with the Far Stars Bank managing deposits of ten billion crowns for the imperial account, we can simply say he is your representative, there to monitor your financial transactions." Wilhelm hadn't eaten any more than Ballock, but he picked up his glass and drained it.

"I am torn, my old friend. We are short of reliable personnel, and I am loath to dispatch one of our few truly effective operatives on a mission that may be nothing more than watching and waiting." He paused, a faint smile forming on his lips. "And I am not sure this mission aligns with Villeroi's unique . . . skills, shall we say? He would certainly serve to remind our associate Ballock on the stakes of the game, but I wonder if he will be wasted at the rather mundane job of monitoring our investment initiatives."

Alois Villeroi was a sadist of almost incalculable proportions. He derived a pleasure from inflicting pain that transcended all other delights for him. Sex, drugs, alcohol—none of it matched the rapturous intensity he felt from making his victims suffer. It made him very useful in some situations, but the bank wasn't one—at least for the moment. Vos wasn't ready to make an open move against Chairman Vargus. Not yet.

"I guess I just think of Vanderon as the key to all our plans. I would expect you'd want your best man there."

"I agree . . . to a point. The fact is, I'd be concerned about Villeroi being patient enough for such an assignment."

"Villeroi is an odd character, I will grant you that. But I ordered him to refrain from action on Kalishar, and he obeyed me to the letter. He didn't make any significant moves until he was authorized to do so. I believe he is capable of considerable patience despite his rather—volatile—nature."

Vos sat silently for a few seconds, thinking. "Very well," he said finally. "Dispatch Lord Villeroi to Vanderon immediately. But do remind him we want no undue suspicion from banking authorities . . . at least not until our buying program is much further along."

And that was another big part of the plan. Vos had been purchasing shares in the bank for the past six months, using a bewildering array of dummy companies and proxy accounts. He had moved as quickly as possible without raising significant suspicion, and he'd accumulated a 7 percent stake in the massive institution. It would take a combination of legitimacy and . . . the more illicit acts that Villeroi excelled at, to allow Vos to take over the bank.

And from there, to begin to consolidate control of the Far Stars.

"What news from Antilles?" Vos didn't like to waste time, and he tended to move abruptly to a new subject as soon as he had finished with a previous topic.

"The Antillean Senate is debating the Confederation Treaty now, but I am told passage is a foregone conclusion. It would appear that the Lancaster Interests conglomerate is fully supporting ratification. Danellan Lancaster owns half the politicians on Antilles outright, and the others are too afraid to cross him. As long as he supports Antillean membership, it is highly doubtful anyone will oppose it."

Vos already knew most of what Wilhelm was telling him. His

mind was already moving forward. "Perhaps we need to take a look at the Lancaster companies. Economic pain is the way to control a clan like the Lancasters. Their greed is their weakness."

"The Lancasters are extremely wealthy, Your Excellency. It will be a considerable challenge to damage them sufficiently to exert meaningful control over them."

Vos looked across the table at Wilhelm. "Difficult. But not impossible." He paused for a few seconds, thinking. "We need not reduce the Lancasters to poverty to exert meaningful influence. Men like Danellan Lancaster do not accept losses well. If we can bring enough pressure to bear—and offer our own inducements—no doubt we can persuade him to withdraw his support from Marshal Lucerne. His alliance has to be based on the expectation of profits. Augustin Lucerne is a patriot and a man of principle." Vos's tone was a strange combination of admiration and mockery. "Danellan Lancaster is neither. He is motivated solely by financial gain."

"Yes, but our resources are already quite extended, sir. Is it feasible to commit a sufficient sum to mount a meaningful assault on Lancaster Interests? The Far Stars Bank is a daunting target by itself, notwithstanding our intentions toward the transport guilds and our support programs for worlds under attack from the Celtiborians."

Vos nodded. "Which is why I have requested additional financial support from the emperor."

Wilhelm put his fork down and looked across the table. He opened his mouth, but a second later he closed it, without having spoken.

"Yes, I know," Vos said to his friend and subordinate. Both men were well aware that Emperor Valens was a volatile man, one who rarely responded well to such requests.

"But you have to realize that the Far Stars is a unique problem for the empire," Vos continued, "and I believe the emperor understands this in a way his predecessors have not. First, because of imperial unwillingness to risk significant military assets on a crossing of the Void, we are compelled to operate without the strength available in the other provinces. Economic power is all we have. We have money and weapons, but not enough ships and soldiers. So we must rely on proxies. We can bribe them to bring them to our side and equip them with imperial weapons they can barely use, but we lack the strength for direct military action." He made a face. "Other than a few squadrons of old rust buckets, two moth-eaten legions—barely enough to defend Galvanus Prime."

Wilhelm shifted in his chair. "But will the emperor agree the Far Stars are worth the investment? It is a backward sector on the edge of human habitation. There are only a handful of worlds of any real value. And even they shrivel to insignificance next to planets like Optimus Prime or Vaconis."

"But they defy imperial will, Mak. They mock the emperor."

Wilhelm shrugged. "That has been the case for centuries."

"Yes." Vos's tone was firm, confident. "But things are different now. The emperor could tolerate a divided Far Stars full of bandits and primitive societies fighting each other with the same enthusiasm with which they curse imperial edicts." He paused. "A sector united under the leadership of a man as capable as Augustin Lucerne is a different matter entirely."

Vos reached out and took his goblet in his hand, taking a long sip. "Danellan Lancaster is an arrogant man, but that doesn't mean he is a fool. If Lucerne puts him in charge of economic development on pacified planets, we could be looking at an enormous problem. He would no doubt rob those worlds blind, but he—or his people—could also spur unprecedented economic development. The Far Stars is a joke because it is backward and fragmented. If its resources are ever properly exploited, though . . ." He let his words trail off.

Wilhelm didn't say anything, but Vos could tell from his expression he agreed. "It is amazing," Vos said, "is it not? How much difference a single man can make? Marshal Lucerne is capable of building a strong and independent Far Stars if we allow it. Can you imagine the effect of that in the empire itself? The emperor is the anointed ruler of mankind. It is one thing to have a cluster of rogue planets and pirate havens nipping at the imperial feet with their defiance, and quite another to have a strong and successful interstellar nation setting an example to every rebel movement and nest of traitors in the empire."

"I hadn't considered the Far Stars situation on such a macroscopic level, but I see your logic. We seek to take control and bring the Far Stars to heel as an obedient sector within the empire. But whatever happens, we must ensure this confederation is stillborn." Wilhelm paused, staring down at his plate for a few seconds, but making no move toward his utensils. "But will the emperor heed your warnings? Will he supply the immense financial resources your plans require?"

Vos looked back across the table, his expression utterly noncommittal. "I am confident that he will . . ." He paused. "But only time will tell for certain. In the meanwhile, let us put our plans in motion. I will find the resources we require. One way or another."

"I agree, Your Excellency." Wilhelm looked like he still had some doubts, but Vos knew his second in command was on board. Which made this next part easier.

"I am sorry, Mak, but I don't have anyone else to send to Antilles, no one with the capability to direct our efforts against the Lancasters." Vos's regret was evident in his expression. He didn't want to do without Wilhelm's support and counsel for the months he would be on Antilles. But he needed him there.

"I understand, Your Excellency. I will prepare to leave immediately."

CHAPTER 6

"WE CAN MAKE THIS EASY, OR WE CAN MAKE IT HARD. YOUR choice." Blackhawk stared down at the prisoner, his expression devoid of emotion. He was alone, as he preferred when interrogating a prisoner. He didn't like his crew to see his darker side, and he suspected it might come out if Aragona was uncooperative.

"Fuck you, you bounty-hunting scum." The captive stared at Blackhawk with venom in his eyes, the look of an egomaniacal elite staring at someone he viewed as an inferior. "When my people catch up with you, you're going to wish you were never born."

Blackhawk sighed. *If only Aragona knew what I am capable of, what I have done to others in his position. He'd piss himself in those expensive pants.* Blackhawk was ashamed of his past, but there were times it provided an interesting frame of reference. "First of all, if you were aware who was paying that bounty, you wouldn't be so cocky, my friend."

The Far Stars Bank had a fearsome reputation for dealing with those guilty of fraud or theft. It was hard on any who defaulted on its loans, but those who deliberately set out to steal from its coffers could expect the harshest treatment.

"But I'm afraid things have gotten much worse for you. There are more terrible adversaries in the universe than the Far Stars Bank."

Aragona sat quietly, and the *Claw*'s captain could feel his prisoner's arrogance suddenly draining away. The mention of the bank had definitely caught his attention, but there was also something in Blackhawk's voice, a coldness, and it was clear Aragona felt it. Blackhawk watched the prisoner, and he could see the change in the Castillan's expression as he began to realize he was not dealing with some ordinary mercenary or bounty hunter.

And yet, there was a touch of arrogance in Aragona's eyes, because he still didn't understand the monster standing before him.

No, he doesn't understand, but if he forces me, I will show him.

Oh yes, I will show him.

For now, though, Blackhawk would fight down his former self. He sat down on the bench opposite Aragona. "I saw the troop convoy moving toward your villa last night. Now, normally I wouldn't care about bullshit wars and coups among petty wog lordlings, but I am very concerned with how *your* backwards-as-fuck personal army was able to acquire imperial equipment." He leaned forward and stared at Aragona's stunned face with icy eyes. "Yes, I know that equipment is imperial in origin. I'm also well aware you'd never manage to find that much of it on the black market." Blackhawk could see the panic building in his prisoner's face. "Besides, you couldn't afford it even if you did turn it up for sale somewhere—and yes, I know how much you're worth, especially with the money you stole from the bank. I'd wager just the stuff I saw from a distance was worth more than everything on your stinking planet."

Aragona stared back at Blackhawk. The arrogance was finally gone from his face, replaced by a look of astonishment—and fear.

There it is. Now we can start.

"I . . . I insist that you return me immediately. I am a duly appointed member of Castilla's ruling council . . ."

"Yes, and abducting you is an act of war. Your people will hunt us down, wherever we go and rescue you.

"Blah. Blah. Blah."

Aragona could only stare.

"That's what you were going to say, right? More or less?"

"Whatever the bank is paying you, I will double it if you release me." His growing panic was clear in his tone.

Blackhawk suppressed a smile. It was a pretty typical progression. Aragona realized his threats weren't getting anywhere with Blackhawk, so he moved on to bribery.

"Assuming we could get past the fact that I do not trust you in any way, it is laughable to expect that you could match the resources of the Far Stars Bank in some kind of bidding war. Or that I would destroy my relationship with Vanderon and risk retaliation for the miserable coin you could offer me."

Aragona seemed to deflate just a touch more, and Blackhawk finally allowed himself a smile. Of course, it was—along with the mockery—all a part of the interrogation. By stripping Aragona of his pride, Blackhawk established his own dominance, and in turn, demanded compliance. He'd seen far tougher sorts than the Castillan gangster broken by words alone. Blackhawk was prepared to move past the verbal abuse if necessary, but he found himself hoping Aragona would yield and not force him to more extreme measures.

"You have been cloistered on your shithole planet for too long, Lord Aragona. You have a distorted view of your own power, one I suspect has been fed by the obsequious parasites hanging on your every word back on Castilla—the same idiots who had us surrounded and *still* couldn't stop us. You may dispense with such foolish views now. You are nothing, a piece of meat subject to whatever fate I choose to pronounce for you. The men and women on this ship will space you without a second thought." He paused. "No, that's not true. They might think of what a waste of oxygen it was, and maybe ask if they could skin you alive instead.

"Messier, but ultimately less wasteful."

Blackhawk stared at his prisoner, his expression cold, almost inhuman. Fact was, he had no intention of killing this man. But this was the second unexplained imperial intervention he'd encountered in less than a year, and he was determined to find out what was going on before he turned Aragona over to the bank. "The sooner you accept that you are utterly without power and completely at my mercy, the better chance you have of coming out of this alive."

Aragona's eyes widened. The mention of survival had clearly piqued his interest. Because while he wasn't going to execute this petty lordling, Blackhawk knew his captive was well aware of what the bank would do to him. The suggestion of a way out was like music to the miserable Castillan.

Blackhawk leaned forward. "I am going to ask you once again, Lord Aragona." His voice was soft, almost like that of an adult addressing a child. "Do you wish to tell me how your forces obtained imperial weaponry, or would you prefer to continue to lie to me while I set a course for Vanderon?"

Aragona sat silently, looking at Blackhawk for an instant before letting his eyes drop to the floor. It was obvious he was torn between fears. Of the bank, of Blackhawk—and of someone else, too. Blackhawk didn't imagine some imperial agent had just given him a huge cache of high-tech weapons without expecting something in return. He suspected there had also been a discussion of the consequences of treachery and failure, and Aragona's nervous fidgeting only confirmed that.

"Look at it this way." Blackhawk's voice took on an edge, and he grabbed the sides of his captive's face, jerking hard until they were staring at each other with only a few centimeters between them. "You are afraid of them and you are afraid of me." Blackhawk paused, the calm demeanor gone, his angry glare itself a blood-chilling threat. "But you are in *my* brig. They can threaten you"—he pulled out his sword, shoving the point hard against Aragona's neck—"but I can cut you into a pile of chunks right now and feed you to a Delphian battle cat."

Blackhawk held his position. His blade was razor sharp, and a small trickle of blood dripped down the prisoner's neck. "So make your choice, Lord Aragona. And I will make mine. Whether to slice you open and watch you bleed to death or leave you to the tender mercies of the Far Stars Bank. Or to spare you . . . if you can make yourself useful to me."

Aragona was defeated, and he sat trying to hold back tears. Blackhawk stared down at him with disgust in his eyes. He didn't doubt he himself could be broken too. Anyone could. But he knew it would take a lot more than threats and the touch of a blade to his neck. Aragona was like hundreds of local bullies he'd encountered in his life. They were ruthless and cruel—when they were abusing the weak and helpless. But he'd never met one he couldn't turn to a quivering creature begging for his life.

"So what is it going to be, Aragona?" Blackhawk's voice was like death. "Because I don't have any more time to waste with you."

Aragona looked at Blackhawk with moist, red eyes. "I will tell you what you want to know."

Blackhawk turned away and allowed himself a brief smile. "Tell me how you got the imperial weapons," he said, his back still turned. "Every detail. If you are cooperative enough, you may yet make a live prisoner."

"You look like a pile of stegaroid shit." Blackhawk stared down at Ace. His friend was deathly pale, and there were half a dozen tubes connected to his chest and arms. His hair was crusted with dried blood, and his breath was a ragged, raspy affair. "But at least you're alive, you crazy son of a bitch."

"What are you talking about?" Ace's voice was soft, barely a whisper, and he spoke slowly, deliberately, forcing painful words from his parched throat. "Never felt better."

Blackhawk smiled. Ace was full of shit again. That was the last indicator, the sign he'd been looking for. Now he knew the fool was going to pull through. The day his sidekick could stay serious for more than a minute he would know they were in *real* trouble. "So what the hell was that, you moron? You thought you could take all of them on yourself?"

"You got hit, Ark." Ace turned his head slowly, painfully. "I had to take over . . . and I knew what you would do . . ."

Blackhawk hid a wince. He didn't like to think of his friend almost dying trying to emulate him. He knew Ace was right, but he didn't want his people following his example, because they didn't have the advantages he had. Blackhawk had all his enhancements, physical capabilities none of his crew could match. And then there were years of experience doing things they couldn't even dream of. Most important, though, Blackhawk didn't fear death. Indeed, there was a part of him, where the guilt and self-loathing lived, he suspected would welcome it. He could do things because the consequences meant nothing to him.

He never wanted his people to think that way.

"Well," Blackhawk said, changing the subject, "Doc was able to put you back together, so I guess we both owe him a debt of gratitude."

Ace moved his head slightly, the closest he could come to a nod. "It feels like he smashed my chest with a sledgehammer." His tone changed slightly, a bit of disbelief creeping in. "I'm surprised you're not in a bed next to me. I know you got hit."

Blackhawk nodded. "Yes, I caught a round. It was just a flesh wound. Doc patched it up after he finished with you." It had been considerably more than a flesh wound, but it hadn't hit anything vital. It was still a little tender, but his recuperative powers had already begun their magic, and he was half healed. "You'll feel better soon, Ace. Doc told me you're past the worst."

"Easy for him to say," Ace croaked. "It feels like he did a little dance inside my chest."

"I'm sure it does, but I promise you'll feel better soon," he repeated. "He told me you'll be up and around in a couple days . . . and causing trouble not long after."

"Me? Cause trouble. Never." He forced a smile. "Are we on the way to Vanderon? Kat told me we got Aragona out. So mission completed. Again." His voice was still weak, but there was satisfaction there too. Ace liked to win. At cards, in the field—anywhere.

"Well . . . we do have him. He's sitting in the brig now, no doubt pondering just how dark his future looks." Blackhawk allowed himself a grin. "I worked him over pretty well. I think he'll feel lucky if we don't sell him for parts on the black market."

"But . . . ?"

"What?"

Ace simply raised an eyebrow. Blackhawk sighed.

"Fine." He paused. He hadn't intended to get into anything this serious until Ace had gotten some more rest, but he realized his inquisitive friend wasn't about to let the subject drop, so he reluctantly decided to bring him up to date. "You were in the Grand Palais, so you don't know why we changed the plan at the last minute. We were outside Aragona's estate, and we saw a troop convoy pull up to the grounds."

Ace took a raspy breath. "Too much firepower to break in? Is that why you went with the backup plan?"

"Partially. Maybe. But there's more to it than that. The convoy had some serious firepower, yes. High-tech armored vehicles, top-of-the-line weapons." He paused. "Imperial ordnance."

Ace turned his head abruptly, wincing at the pain as he did. "Imperial? You're sure?"

"Yes. I'm sure."

Ace just nodded silently. Finally, he said, "First Saragossa. Then Castilla." Ace paused, struggling to take in another deep breath. "What's going on, Ark?"

"I don't know. Once could be a freak event. Twice is something else. If the empire is starting some kind of move against the Far Stars, we have some dark days ahead, my friend." He sighed softly. "Aragona didn't know much. He had a contact, a man he knew only as Tiger. This Tiger offered him enough support to effect a coup and to assume the sole rule of Castilla. Aragona was suspicious at first. He's not smart, but he's not an imbecile, either. But Tiger delivered a shipment of high-tech weapons, stuff so advanced Aragona's greed overcame his caution. He was hooked."

"You think this Tiger was an imperial agent?" Ace looked exhausted, but he was focused like a laser on Blackhawk.

"Yes, I do. This is *exactly* how the imperials would begin a move against the sector: by backing local warlords, establishing puppet regimes through clandestine support."

Ace closed his eyes for a few seconds. Blackhawk wanted to let him rest, but he knew Ace wouldn't let him until he had brought him up to date.

"Maybe he's just a smuggler who managed to get some imperial stuff across the Void," Ace suggested.

Blackhawk shook his head. "No, that doesn't make any more sense than it did on Saragossa. Do you have any idea what that ordnance is worth? Imagine what Marshal Lucerne would have paid for it, even to keep it out of an enemy's hands. Castilla isn't quite the forgotten backwater Saragossa is, but there must be fifty planets that could have paid more for a weapons cache like that. What smuggler turns his back on a fortune to sell to some middling racketeer on an unimportant planet?

"No, it has to be *from* the imperials themselves. And in a way, it makes sense. If Lucerne has to scramble all over the periphery planets to maintain order, when will he have time to consolidate the core?"

Ace lay quietly for a few seconds. Finally, he turned his head slowly and said, "You're right, Ark. But what do we do now? The bank's expecting us to deliver Aragona. We have a reputation for getting the job done."

"I don't know if Aragona's going to be any use to us or not in tracking down whatever imperials are operating in the sector. He says he didn't know anything and that his contact did not ask anything of him except to move quickly to seize power. The coup was scheduled for two days after we snatched him. So the oligarchs on Castilla owe us a favor, though they don't know it. I doubt Aragona's lieutenants were able to pull off the coup without him. And I don't imagine they could hide the preparations forever, either. I suspect things are about to get a little hairy on Castilla. If they haven't already."

"Hopefully that pompous shit who thought he'd fleece me at cards while Aragona screwed my wife is sitting in a Castillan prison cell. Or worse."

"Probably." Blackhawk smiled. Ace always put priorities first, but the *Claw's* captain knew letting Cordoba win at poker was still gnawing at his friend.

"So what are we going to do, Ark?"

Blackhawk took a deep breath. "Well, you're going to get some rest now." He paused. "And we're going to find out exactly what is going on . . . somehow."

"Launch the drone." Blackhawk leaned back in his chair. His side still hurt, but it was more soreness than serious pain.

"Launching." Lucas pressed a button on his workstation. "It's away."

The hypercomm drone was a sophisticated piece of equipment, a communications device with its own miniature hyperdrive. Such drones were enormously expensive and very difficult to acquire. Blackhawk had a small supply of them, mostly for emergencies, but he was expending this one to pull off a bit of subterfuge. Arragonzo Aragona was safely stowed in the *Claw*'s brig, but Blackhawk wanted to keep that a secret for now. The drone was en route to Vanderon, carrying a communiqué to the Far Stars Bank Executive Directorate, a report stating that Aragona had slipped through Blackhawk's trap and disappeared.

It was a gamble lying to the bank, but it was a chance Blackhawk was prepared to take. His people had done a number of jobs for the massive institution, all of them highly successful. He expected them to take the report in stride and to accept his assurance that he was still on the job and confident of ultimate success. That would buy some time, at least, though he couldn't be sure how much. Castilla had been two days from a planned coup d'état when the *Claw* blasted off and made a run for it. They'd been three days in space since, and he had no idea what had happened since they'd made their run for it. If the bank had spies on Castilla, they might report back that Aragona was missing. Still, that wouldn't contradict his story, not directly at least. It was reasonable to assume a scared Aragona might go into hiding after a botched kidnapping attempt.

"I don't know if Aragona is worth anything to us anyway. I'm inclined to believe he doesn't know anything more." He wondered again if he should just turn the Castillan over to the bank. If he didn't know anything, there was no real reason to keep him. He might report Blackhawk and the *Claw* to his imperial contact, but there was very little chance Aragona would ever leave Vanderon anyway. He'd stolen millions, a blatant fraud that made the bank look foolish. The Far Stars Bank could afford a few losses here and there, but its directors could never tolerate a scam that sapped their reputation for skillful finance—and brutal toughness. Aragona was as good as dead if he set foot on Vanderon.

No, we will hold on to him for now. He may yet prove useful.

"The drone's course checks out, Skip. It should get to Vanderon in about a week." Lucas spun around on his chair and looked over at Blackhawk. "So where to now, Skip?"

Blackhawk opened his mouth . . . then closed it again. He had no idea. He was sure the empire was involved, but Aragona's lack of knowledge left them with no direct leads.

"I don't know, Lucas. Maybe I should work Aragona over again. Maybe he knows something more than what he told me." Unfortunately, he didn't actually believe that.

The Klaxon sounded and Lucas's head whipped back to his board. "Contact, Skip. Emerging from hyperspace at 120,000 kilometers, coordinates 201.332.181."

Blackhawk tapped the comm unit. "Shira, Tarq . . . get to the turrets. We've got an unidentified contact." He had no idea if the incoming vessel was hostile, but he'd found it to be much healthier to assume everything was an enemy until it proved otherwise.

"Got it, Cap." Shira's voice was crisp, alert. She never sounded tired or distracted. Blackhawk used to wonder when she rested, but he'd long ago decided she didn't sleep any more than he did. An hour here, an hour there. It was all the ghosts allowed him. And apparently Shira, too.

Tarq's response came half a minute later, and it was clear he'd awakened the giant. The Twins didn't have any trouble sleeping. Waking up was definitely more of a challenge.

"Lucas, got an ID yet?"

"No, Skip. Their identification beacons aren't broadcasting."

Blackhawk exhaled. That wasn't a good sign. "Shira, you in yet?" They weren't in laser range, but Blackhawk wanted to be ready for whatever was going to happen.

"Climbing in now, Cap. We'll be charged and ready before they're in range." Shira's voice was harsh, predatory. Blackhawk knew, as always, she was ready to fight.

"It looks like a frigate, Skip." Lucas's voice was subdued. The *Claw* was a tough ship, and its weapons had a hell of a bite, but a frigate was a tough opponent. Probably more than they could handle, even with Lucas at the controls and Shira manning the guns.

I'd give us maybe one in four odds.

One in five is more accurate.

Thanks.

"We've got communications incoming." Lucas was staring at the screen as he spoke.

"Put it on speaker, Lucas."

" . . . repeat, please identify yourselves. This is the Celtiborian frigate *Aquillus*. Are you *Wolf's Claw*?"

Blackhawk felt a wave of relief, but it was short-lived. He was glad the ship was not an enemy, but he couldn't think of any good news that would have caused Marshal Lucerne to send his ships out looking for the *Claw*.

The captain nodded over toward Lucas, who flipped a switch and nodded back.

"This is Arkarin Blackhawk on the vessel *Wolf's Claw*. Greetings, *Aquillus*." He paused for an instant. "What can we do for you?"

"*Wolf's Claw* just jumped, sir. It appears to be following the Celtiborian vessel."

Cedric Kandros turned and stared at the pilot. His greasy hair was long and gray, and it hung about his timeworn face in large tangled hanks. He was a grizzled fighter, and he bore the scars of many battles, including the mark of one old wound that ran down his face, all the way to the side of his neck.

Kandros was a smuggler and a mercenary, just like Blackhawk and his people. Indeed, he was one of Blackhawk's rivals among that curious breed of disreputable but highly sought after adventurers. But this time he wasn't competing with *Wolf's Claw* to run guns or smuggle supplies to a redlined world. No, this time the competition with Blackhawk was far more direct—and personal.

"Prepare to jump." Kandros and his people had gotten to Castilla half a day too late. They'd found the planet in an uproar and martial law in effect. They'd had to shoot their way out of the spaceport to take off after Blackhawk.

Cutting the red tape was how Kandros had referred to it.

Kandros had managed to track down the *Claw* without being detected, no small feat considering the skill of Blackhawk's people. He had no idea where Blackhawk had been planning to go next. He'd considered attacking the *Claw* in space, but he put that thought out of his mind almost immediately. He'd run into Blackhawk and his ship too many times, and he was well aware that the *Claw* was a hell of a lot more than she appeared to be. The pockmarked and peeling hull didn't tell the whole story, and everybody knew Lucas Lancaster was damned near the best pilot in the Far Stars. No, Kandros knew his *Iron Wind* couldn't take Blackhawk in space. He'd have to follow the *Claw* and make his move on the ground somewhere.

"The hyperdrive will be powered up in three minutes, sir." Starn Quintus was a good pilot, with decades of experience at the helm of ships like *Iron Wind*. He'd signed on with Kandros three years before, but he'd only been up against *Wolf's Claw* once in that time.

It wasn't even close.

The two ships had been racing with several others to get arms to the rebels on Persepon. There was a bonus for the first ship to deliver, double the normal rate, and it came down to *Iron Wind* and the *Claw*. But Lucas Lancaster flew circles around Quintus, and Blackhawk's people won easily. Quintus had been angry at his defeat, but when Kandros told him that Lucas Lancaster was only twenty-five years old, the veteran pilot flew into an apoplectic rage. From that day on, Quintus hated the *Claw*'s pilot with an irrational passion, which was all the more inflamed by the fact that Lancaster didn't even know who he was.

For some reason, this always made Kandros smile.

"Where are we going?" The pilot hadn't even tried to get a tracer on the *Claw*. It was hard enough to avoid detection just sitting dead in space.

"I didn't know, Starn. I was trying to think like Blackhawk, to reason out where he would go. But I couldn't come up with anything. Not until that Celtiborian frigate showed up." He turned toward the pilot. "Set a course for Celtiboria's system."

"Celtiboria?" Quintus's voice was heavy with concern. "But there's a death sentence on us on Celtiboria. And Lucerne's navy will be all over the place."

"I know that, Starn." Kandros's voice was deep, and his determination came through clearly. "But that's where Blackhawk is going, and we're going to get that bounty before someone else does." A million imperial crowns was a king's ransom, and Kandros couldn't imagine why anyone would pay that much for the likes of Arkarin Blackhawk. But he was glad to take it—and settle a few old scores at the same time.

"Bring us out of hyperspace in the outer system. We'll lie low while Blackhawk does whatever business he has on Celtiboria, and then we'll follow him when he leaves."

Quintus nodded. "Yes, Captain." He didn't sound completely convinced, but he laid in the plot anyway. "All hands, we're jumping in twenty seconds."

CHAPTER 7

THE SOLDIERS MOVED STEADILY THROUGH THE SMOLDERING wreckage, chasing the last of the Rykaran defenders, gunning them down in the streets and in the dark holes where they ran to hide. They took no prisoners, showed no mercy. The Celtiborian soldiers were well trained, but discipline had failed them amid the carnage and their desire for vengeance.

Arias Callisto stood in the middle of a street covered with shattered glass and masonry. He wore a plain gray uniform, devoid of all insignia save the four stars on his shoulder. Augustin Lucerne had set the example for his commanders, and fancy uniforms and silver lace were reserved for parades and propaganda. In the field, a Celtiborian general dressed like the men he commanded, and he served in the blood-soaked mud alongside them.

There were half a dozen vehicles along the sides of the street, two of them still burning, the others charred hulks. The city had been virtually destroyed in the fighting, and at least half its buildings were empty shells, the residences and work-spaces they had once housed consumed by the fires. Callisto wondered how many of the former occupants had been inside when the flames ravaged the dying buildings. He hadn't even begun to try to count the civilian casualties, but he knew they were heavy.

It would be winter soon in the northern hemisphere, where most of the people lived. The Celtiborians had no shelters and barely enough food for themselves. He'd sent a request to Lucerne for humanitarian supplies, but he doubted they would arrive in time. He had no idea how he was going to manage, but he knew if he didn't do something, millions of Rykarans would die. And that would cement their hatred for the Celtiborians and the Far Stars Confederation for generations to come.

Callisto held a gun in his hands, an assault rifle of some kind. His men had been bringing them in, hundreds of them stripped from the enemy dead. Its stock was made from some strange carbonite material, but he'd never seen its like before. The weapon was superior to those his troops carried, with a higher rate of fire and a faster muzzle velocity. It fired strange projectiles, darts that flattened and spun wildly inside the tar-get, doing massive tissue damage anywhere they struck. Despite the excellent medical services of his army, he'd had twice the rate of KIAs he'd expected.

He walked down the street toward Ravenna Orestes's command post. Orestes was technically fourth in command, but Callisto knew the brigadier was the most gifted officer in the expeditionary force, and he included himself in that calculus. Orestes commanded the elite Black Flag regiments of the army, units consisting only of veterans of five years or longer and intended to serve as the sharp edge of any attack. His units had served with great distinction, and they had paid the heaviest price.

Callisto moved to the side, avoiding the spray of water from a severed main. The city was without water or power, and its infrastructure was in ruins. He wondered if it was even possible to repair the damage.

It's probably just easier to start again somewhere else.

He saw the cluster of portable shelters just ahead, and he quickened his pace. He needed to speak with Brigadier Orestes, but he wanted to talk to the officer in person. And alone.

The guards at the perimeter of the command post snapped to attention when they saw him approach. He was impressed how quickly they had recognized him, bedraggled as he was. But it didn't surprise him: his men were the best. Being observant had kept them alive for many years.

"At ease." He waved his hand downward as he spoke. "Where is Brigadier Orestes?"

"Straight ahead, sir. Third shelter on the right." The soldier's voice was sharp, crisp. He sounded as if he was on duty back on Celtiboria, not like a man who'd just come out of a nightmare. But Callisto knew the man had been in the line. All of Orestes's men fought. Sentries, aides—everyone rotated in and out of the forward units. Marshal Lucerne's armies had always had a high ratio of tooth to tail, but Orestes took the concept to an almost absurd extreme, embracing the notion that a combat soldier couldn't truly respect a comrade who didn't share at least some of the hardship and danger.

"Very well." Callisto snapped the sentry a salute. It wasn't really appropriate since they were still technically in a combat zone. But Callisto knew the area had been swept for snipers, and he felt the trooper deserved the respect from his commanding officer.

The startled soldier returned the gesture. The crispness of the guard's salute created an amusing contrast with his filthy and battleworn appearance.

Callisto walked briskly down the street, pausing in front of a pair of sentries standing outside a large shelter. The guards snapped to attention, and one of them turned to open the door. "General Callisto to see you, sir."

Callisto nodded and walked through the door. Ravenna Orestes was standing in the middle of the structure's single room. There were half a dozen other officers engaged in various tasks.

"Greetings, General." Orestes bowed his head slightly. "We were not expecting you. This area is not entirely secure yet, sir. I don't think you should be out by yourself without an esc—"

"I'm fine, Brigadier. I'd like to speak with you about something." Callisto panned his head around the room as he spoke. "Alone."

"Out. All of you. Now." Orestes's voice was firm, insistent, and everyone else in the room jumped to their feet and raced for the door.

The brigadier watched as the last of his aides left, closing the door behind them. "Can I offer you something, sir? I'm afraid we don't have much. Water? We may have some coffee left."

"No, thank you, Ravenna." Callisto's tone relaxed a bit now

that they were alone. "I wanted to talk to you about something. I need your help."

"Of course, sir. Anything." Orestes pulled a chair around from behind one of the desks, moving it toward Callisto. "What can I do?"

Callisto tossed the assault rifle on the desk. It landed with a thud. "I'm worried about these, Ravenna. And the other high-tech weapons your people encountered." He paused, sitting slowly. "We were up against more here than just the Rykarans, and we need to know what. Or, more accurately, who."

Orestes nodded, pulling around another chair and sitting down. "Yes, that is an important question, sir. Someone armed these people with some serious stuff . . . millions of crowns' worth of very high-tech weapons."

"We need to know who." Callisto's tone was matter-of-fact. "And soon. So that's your new mission: finding out how the Rykarans got these weapons."

Orestes sat quietly for a few seconds. "We need to find some of the Rykaran nobles, then. We've taken a lot of prisoners, but no one of consequence in their command structure. They must be hiding somewhere, if they haven't managed to escape off-planet."

Castillo sighed. "That's possible, but not likely." The Celtiborian forces did not have a complete satellite network, so it wasn't inconceivable that a few ships could have gotten off-planet undetected. But Admiral Suchet was blockading the system, so any escaping Rykaran lords would have had to launch undetected and also slip past Suchet's ships. Again, not impossible, but not likely, either.

"No, Orestes," he concluded, "we have to go with the assumption that they're still on Rykara somewhere, hiding. Find them.

At least some of them. It's the only way we're going to find out where they got those weapons."

Orestes took a deep breath. "You're right, sir." He paused. "Unless someone has already gotten to them. I imagine who-ever supplied the Rykarans wants to keep their identity a secret."

"I'm inclined to agree, Ravenna. Which is one reason I want you on this immediately."

"I will do all I can, sir."

"I know you will." Callisto got up slowly and turned toward the door. He paused and looked back. "And, Ravenna . . . do whatever you feel is necessary. It is crucial that we discover who is behind this, so use any means to get the information you need." His eyes locked on his subordinate's. "Any means at all."

"Yes, sir." There was a coldness in Ravenna Orestes's voice, and Callisto knew the officer understood him perfectly.

"Thank you for coming, Ark." Augustin Lucerne walked up and threw his arms around Blackhawk. "It is good to see you, my old friend."

Blackhawk returned the embrace. "Of course, Augustin. When would I ever not come?"

"I knew you would answer my call, but that doesn't mean I can't—and shouldn't—appreciate it." He turned and gestured toward a small table with two chairs. "Come, let's sit and talk."

The orbital station was the new headquarters of Celtiboria's space-based defense grid. It was a massive structure, over a kilo-meter in length, and its exterior bristled with weaponry. The levels above where they stood housed dozens of technicians, constantly monitoring scanner and communications panels, directing the operations of Lucerne's spacefleets and standing guard over Celtiboria itself. Below were magazines and power plants and a series of launch bays housing four squadrons of interceptors, one of which was on alert at any given time.

Newly operational, the station's construction had been one of the first major projects implemented by Marshal Lucerne as he undertook the duties of Celtiboria's head of state, and he'd poured enormous resources into it and its companion satellite arrays.

It's certainly impressive, Blackhawk thought.

He nodded to his friend and walked toward the table, sliding into one of the black leather chairs. This level contained Lucerne's offices and the reception rooms used to greet visiting dignitaries. The furnishings were lavish, the specifications for the public areas the work of Lucerne's civilian staff and not his rough and rugged soldiers.

"So what is troubling you, Augustin? Why did you wish to speak with me?" Blackhawk was concerned himself, and his mind was on Aragona and the situation on Castilla. But he had decided not to trouble Lucerne with that. The founding father of the Far Stars Confederation had his plate full already, and, besides, Blackhawk didn't really *know* anything. He just had suspicions. He'd decided to focus on whatever Lucerne needed.

"I remember you speaking of imperial weapons on Saragossa. Indeed, of a ship from the empire that delivered them."

Blackhawk shifted in his seat. Perhaps they *were* worried about the same thing. "Yes. It was definitely an imperial spy ship." He glanced around the room, confirming they were alone. "You know I know, Augustin."

"Yes, Ark." There was a deep weariness to Lucerne's voice. "I know. That is why you are here. Because I know of no one with greater insight on such matters."

"Have you encountered such weapons? Elsewhere, I mean?"

Blackhawk felt the tension in his knotted stomach. *Saragossa, Castilla—and now Lucerne has encountered imperial weapons?* The odds of coincidence were rapidly dwindling to zero.

Lucerne reached behind him and opened a box. He pulled a dark shape out and dropped it on the table. "Is this familiar to you?"

Blackhawk felt as if someone had punched him in the gut. "Yes. That's an imperial Hellfire assault rifle. Standard issue to shock cohorts in their frontline legions." His eyes drifted up toward Lucerne. "Where did you get it?"

"Rykara. General Callisto sent it. It was one of maybe a hundred thousand used against my men."

Blackhawk could hear the anger in Lucerne's voice. The marshal rarely lost his temper, at least openly. But Blackhawk had seen his rage once or twice, and he knew that the thought of thousands of his men dying because of weapons like this had Lucerne livid. Blackhawk had a good idea of how his friend would deal with whoever was behind supplying his enemies with the guns.

"Imperial tech on Rykara." Blackhawk's voice was grim. "I just ran into weapons like this somewhere else, Augustin. On Castilla."

"It's what I've feared." Lucerne took a deep breath. "My people have run into stronger than expected resistance elsewhere, too. I don't have the level of confirmation I do from Rykara, but my gut tells me we've run into these weapons on at least four worlds. That would be six planets in less than a year with highly advanced weapons that have no place on any of them." He paused and stared at Blackhawk. "I need your input, Ark. What the hell is going on?"

Blackhawk knew. He didn't have any proof, but he was as

sure as he'd ever been about anything. "This isn't a case of the weapons being smuggled in by some sort of entrepreneur—it's just too big, too widespread, and too *directed*. So it's got to be the empire itself behind this, Augustin. Or at least this new imperial governor acting on his own."

Lucerne blinked and held his eyes closed for a beat. Blackhawk could see his friend had suspected the same thing. It was the worst possible answer. One of the other Primes—or even the guilds—would have been a problem, but the empire . . .

"I need proof." Lucerne opened his eyes and took a deep breath. "Real proof. Whatever is going on, whomever the empire is supporting, if we can bring it to light, they'll all have to run for cover. The people of the Far Stars have lost their fear, but if they knew the empire was manipulating the affairs of free worlds, they'd get it back in a hurry. Anyone caught dealing with imperial agents would be dragged into the streets and slaughtered by the mobs."

Blackhawk was silent. He knew Lucerne was right. Any imperial plots would have to remain secretive, at least until they'd progressed much further. The inhabitants of the Far Stars might not regard the empire as a threat the way their ancestors had, but they couldn't escape the fact that it was there, just across the Void. Imperial power and brutality was the stuff of legend, and it was only by virtue of the great starless dark that separated them that they'd been free for a millennium while the rest of humankind lived in servitude.

"You want to expose their involvement." It was a statement, not a question. "But that might be difficult. I know how imperial intelligence operates, Augustin, and by all accounts, this Kergen Vos was one of the agency's best. It's not going to be easy to catch one of his agents or tie him publicly to any of this."

"I know, Ark." Lucerne had a sad look on his face, as if he regretted drawing his friend into the whole affair. "I also know this won't be an easy path for you to tread. I fear it will reopen old wounds. But there is no one better prepared for it."

Blackhawk looked down at the floor and sighed. No one would ever call him a coward, but he was afraid now, dreading to dig too deeply into imperial affairs.

As Lucerne noted, Arkarin Blackhawk was no stranger to the ways of the empire. Indeed, he had served it for many years, with a zeal and cold efficiency that he still remembered like it had been yesterday. Blackhawk had blood on his hands from those days, and he knew he always would. His crew knew nothing of his past, no specifics at least. In fact, no one in the Far Stars knew what he'd done. No one save the man sitting across the table from him.

And now he was asking him to face the evil he had once served.

"I'll do it, Augustin." Blackhawk's voice was somber. "I will get you proof, whatever it takes."

Lucerne looked back at his friend and his eyes were soft with empathy. "This is your penance, Arkarin." He leaned forward and put his hand on Blackhawk's arm. "Promise me, my friend . . . if you do this, you will forgive yourself, and accept that you arc a good man, whatever you may have done twenty-five years ago."

Blackhawk stared at his friend and forced a small nod. "I will," he croaked. But he wondered if he really would. If he *ever* could. Some guilt was incurable; some crimes unforgivable. In his heart he knew he'd just lied to Augustin Lucerne for the first time since they'd met almost a quarter century before.

Blackhawk paused. Lucerne hadn't mentioned Astra. *She's*

okay. He'd have told me if anything had happened to her. He leaned slightly forward, almost asking the question that was at the front of his mind, but he pulled back before a word escaped. *Forget about Astra, you fool. She can take care of herself, and you are the last thing she needs.*

"I will leave immediately. I suspect time is not on our side."

"You have to get us out of here, Mr. Bartholomew." The Rykaran lord spoke with a heavy accent, and his words were tinged with fear. "The war is lost, and the Celtiborians are infuriated at the losses they have suffered." He looked over at the finely dressed man sitting quietly across from him, becoming even more agitated at the calm expression staring back at him.

Lucius Bartholomew sat still for a few seconds, watching his companion. He let the Rykaran stew for a few seconds. Finally, he smiled and said, "Please, Lord Saka, do not lose your composure. I have arranged transport off Rykara for your nobles and their families."

The shelter was sparse, utterly devoid of the luxurious surroundings these former lords of Rykara had enjoyed before the war. These nobles had been enemies for years, but imperial bribery and coercion had forged them into an alliance. Now they were drawn together by fear and vulnerability. Their world was lost, and the viciousness of the battle had removed all chance of a negotiated peace. The enraged Celtiborians might spare the people of Rykara, but there was little doubt the leaders would face summary execution.

Bartholomew looked at the disheveled nobleman with a pleasant expression, but inside he felt nothing but contempt for the miserable creature. He had used the Rykarans, that much was inarguable, though he doubted they realized how thoroughly they'd been duped. It was amazing what a minor display of power and a hoard of imperial gold could achieve. The Rykarans had never had a chance to defeat Marshal Lucerne's Celtiborian veterans, regardless of the weapons Bartholomew gave them. But they had turned a likely two-week victory into a four-month bloodbath, and seventy-five thousand of Lucerne's hardened troops were dead in the filth and broken cities of Rykara.

The Celtiborian army was two million strong, and the losses in the fighting here weren't decisive. But Bartholomew's efforts were only part of a larger operation, and he had exceeded his goals. If the other operatives did as well, Lucerne's magnificent army would dash itself to pieces in a dozen bloody campaigns, and the people they'd come to liberate would learn to hate and despise them. The confederation that had been conceived to bring freedom and advancement to backward planets would instead become a brutal conqueror.

And all of a sudden, the empire wouldn't look quite so bad to these "free" planets.

Bartholomew's thoughts were interrupted by the lordling sitting across from him. "How will you get us off Rykara?" There was a touch of doubt in Saka's voice, but mostly impatience. And fear.

"I have a squadron of ships arriving tomorrow. Stealth vessels able to penetrate the Celtiborian blockade without detection." He was making up every word, but he managed to sound entirely sincere. "They will get your people off Rykara and to safety. Then you can decide where you want to go permanently."

"We have lost all our power, Mr. Bartholomew." There was exhaustion in Saka's tone. He'd been distraught over the loss of his position, but fear for his life had gradually pushed that aside. Now, he thought only of escape, and renewed physical comfort. He turned and looked down at the row of chests at his feet. They were filled with neat rows of stamped gold and platinum bars, a fortune in imperial currency. "At least we will have the wealth to live comfortably. Perhaps we will assume new identities and relocate to Antilles or perhaps Palladia."

"I'm sure that can be arranged." Bartholomew stood up and turned toward the tunnel leading to the surface. "If you will excuse me, Lord Saka. I must go to the surface and contact my ship to arrange the departure for tomorrow."

Saka nodded. "Please. It is past time for us to leave."

Bartholomew walked down a short corridor that dead-ended at a metal door. He put his hands on a small wheel and turned it, popping the hatch and swinging it open. He slipped out into a small cave, closing and sealing the portal behind him.

"Are we ready, sir?" A man was standing next to the hatch, holding a small tablet. There was an image of the inside on the screen, displaying a feed from a hidden camera inside the shelter.

"Yes, Hiltes, we are ready." *Past ready . . . if I had to listen to that insipid fool for another minute, I would have lost my mind.*

"You may proceed." Bartholomew nodded.

Hiltes pulled a small control pad from his pocket and pressed a button. He held the tablet so they could both see the screen.

For a few seconds, the lords inside the shelter looked the same as they had when Bartholomew had left them moments before. Then they started moving around quickly, panicking, grasping at their throats, at their faces.

The shelter wasn't wired for sound, so Bartholomew had to imagine the screams, the cries of terror as the Rykaran nobles realized what was happening. One by one they dropped to the ground, some of them twitching for a few more seconds before they fell motionless. It was over in less than a minute. Every one of Rykara's former lords was dead, along with their families and senior advisers. Bartholomew had completed his mission, and now he was cleaning up.

"Clear out the gas, and get a crew in there as soon as possible. I want those bodies gone, disintegrated, and that entire chamber dismantled without a trace. And retrieve the chests of money. Leave nothing for Lucerne's people to find, no trace at all of the Rykaran lords. Let the Celtiborians think the nobles escaped to the wilderness to continue the resistance."

"Yes, sir."

"And, Hiltes?"

"Sir?"

"Get it all done today. I want to be off this shithole for good by tonight."

CHAPTER 8

THE CITY OF CHARONEA WAS A HUGE METROPOLIS, THE LARGEST city in the Far Stars by a considerable margin. It had been founded on an island just off the coast of Antilles's southern continent, but over ten centuries of continued growth it had sprawled onto the mainland, and now a series of bridges and transport tubes connected the two sections, and people and goods moved back and forth night and day over the two-kilometer-wide strait.

Since its unification Celtiboria was widely regarded by most as the strongest of the Primes, and Marshal Lucerne's veteran army inspired respect—and not a little fear—throughout the Far Stars. But Antilles was unquestionably the center of finance in the sector. Indeed, even the mighty Far Stars Bank had begun its long and storied existence as an Antillean institution, and it had been headquartered in Charonea for five centuries before it took control of Vanderon and made that planet its home.

The Old City, as the island portion had come to be called, was home to the wealthiest residential sections as well as the financial center, the home of the Antilles Stock and Commodities Exchange, and the symbolic manifestation of Antillean industrial might.

The middle and lower classes lived in the New City, stretching across two hundred square kilometers of coastal lowlands. Most of the industry was also located on the mainland, and seemingly endless rows of factories and assembly plants ringed the inland periphery. This center of industrial power was connected to the planet's spaceport and other metropolitan areas by a series of high-speed rail lines, with trains running around the clock, carrying the lifeblood of the planet's vibrant capitalism.

In the center of the financial district, surrounded by the headquarters of the old merchant banking families, rose Lancaster Tower, a kilometer-tall behemoth, dwarfing everything around it. Its singularity and enormous scale communicated a stark reality: On a planet devoted to economic prosperity, in a city housing some of the richest and most profitable financial firms in the sector, all stood in the shadow of the legendary Lancaster Interests, an immense conglomcrate, centuries old, whose tentacles extended through space to half the worlds of the Far Stars.

Danellan Lancaster sat in his palatial office atop the tower that bore his family name. The eldest of the family's main branch, Danellan was the patriarch of the Lancaster clan and the custodian of the massive family business. A hundred Lancasters—his wife and daughter and a vast array of siblings and cousins, nieces and nephews—relied on him to maintain the family's almost incalculable wealth . . . and to ensure the continuation of their princely lifestyles.

He'd had a son once, too, though he rarely allowed himself to think of his lost prodigy. Lucas had been his greatest disappointment, a defiant and rebellious child who'd shown no interest in accepting his responsibility for the family business, preferring instead to become a lowly pilot. And even that hadn't been the final blow. No, Lucas Lancaster had been a reprobate and a hopeless drug addict, a self-destructive hell-raiser who'd managed to get himself thrown out of the Antilles Naval Academy, despite Danellan's repeated interventions.

The Lancaster patriarch had ultimately disowned his only son and banished him from the family home. He'd lost track of the boy shortly after, and he had assumed for years now that Lucas had managed to get himself killed, probably brawling in some dive bar or overdosing in a cheap hotel room somewhere.

But this was no time to wallow in old pain and festering wounds. Not now, when he was planning a series of moves that would propel Lancaster Interests to a level of dominance his forefathers could have barely conceived. His alliance with Marshal Lucerne was designed to pave the way to complete economic supremacy in the Far Stars, exceeding even the power of the Far Stars Bank itself. He would allow nothing to distract him now.

"I am concerned, Mr. Lancaster. Our new capital issues have been massively oversubscribed. We very carefully compiled projections on demand for the securities, but the actual transactions have exceeded these figures by more than 100 percent."

Silas Grosvenor was a cautious man by nature, a trait that befitted his position as Danellan Lancaster's chief financial adviser. The Lancasters were enormously wealthy, and after eighteen generations, there was just one overriding purpose for the family: preserving—and expanding—that wealth. Silas adhered to this to the letter . . . too often with emphasis on preservation, and not as much on expanding.

Much to Danellan's consternation.

"What has you worried, Silas? I know you tend to the paranoid, but you can't possibly imagine anyone is making a move on us."

Lancaster sat behind his massive Tanglewood desk. The material alone had cost enough to pay a thousand laborers for a year. He'd had to hire a band of mercenaries to retrieve it from the swamps of Gessenia. The planet was one of the most primitive backwaters in the Far Stars, and the swamp dwellers prayed to the great trees, revering them as avatars of their gods. Lancaster's thugs had been forced to shoot at least a dozen of them before they'd been able to cut down even a sapling. But the wood was among the greatest treasures in the sector, and Danellan Lancaster had decreed he would have it at whatever cost. And so he did.

Just as I'll have this deal.

"I don't know, Mr. Lancaster. There is something about it that is . . . unsettling. We have never misjudged the demand for an issue by such a wide margin. Indeed, we left considerable money on the table by not pricing the securities higher."

"Perhaps word leaked of our pending alliance with Celtiboria and their new confederation. Our . . . ah . . . development . . . of the worlds Marshal Lucerne is bringing into the confederation will be enormously profitable, beyond anything we have ever achieved. My position as head of economic development for the confederation will effectively cut out all competitors."

Danellan Lancaster had readily agreed to accept a post heading up the economic council of the Far Stars Confederation. He wasn't so naive as to be convinced Lucerne had come to him for his economic prowess and not just to help deliver Antilles into the new entity. But whatever the reason, the posting would put him in an incomparable position to pillage the resources of the underdeveloped planets. By the time he'd brought their backward economies into the present, Lancaster Interests would be entrenched. He couldn't even guess at the profits that would flow back to Charonea . . . which is not to say he hadn't tried.

"I do not doubt our potential profits, sir. However, I am also aware that the investment required to spur development on so many planets simultaneously is almost incalculably large. Your decision to forgo the formation of a cartel and to finance the entire cost ourselves is compelling us to dilute our control over current Lancaster Interests. We will have a large number of new shareholders, and some of the existing ones will substantially enlarge their stakes."

"You fear a takeover attempt?" Lancaster's voice was shrill, his tone displaying both surprise and incredulity. "Who could possibly finance such an enormous project? Who would dare move against us?"

"The Far Stars Bank, for one."

"Are you serious, Silas? The bank directors have never made a hostile takeover of one of the bank's customers in good standing. It would be a fatal move. No one would trust them. Their other business partners would run away as quickly as they could, throw their support behind any competitor. Besides, we own almost 10 percent of the bank. Do you imagine we could fail to discover such a plot? Or that Chairman Vargus wants me as an enemy?" There was a touch of darkness in his tone when he spoke the last sentence. He didn't think for an instant Vargus was involved, but even the thought stirred his anger.

"You are right, of course, sir. My point is simply that we cannot take for granted that we are too big to be vulnerable. Especially when we are about to become so extended. We may not be exposed to many entities individually, but our rivals could form a cartel, pool resources . . ." Grosvenor's voice trailed off, and he paused. "But, of course, you are correct, sir. I am sure I am simply being paranoid."

The adviser exhaled softly and looked across the desk, at the sweeping view behind Lancaster, a panorama stretching across the small strait between the Old City and the mainland. There were more than a dozen bridges and tubes extending over the water, connecting the two halves of the city. The mainland waterfront was highly developed, a commercial zone beginning to rival the Old City itself, and beyond that, kilometers of homes and offices and factories. Past the city limits lay a vast rolling plain, rising slowly as far as the eye could see. But Grosvenor turned away, a deepening frown on his face.

"But if it isn't the bank . . . then who is bidding up our stock so aggressively?"

Lancaster stared back at his aide. His arrogance made it difficult to even imagine that someone would dare to challenge the Lancasters. But the thought still nagged at him. *Who was buying so much stock?*

"Did you obtain what I requested?" Sebastien Alois de Villeroi spoke softly, but his tone conveyed considerable menace nevertheless.

Trayn Ballock stood in front of the imperial agent, calling on all his self-control to fight back his fear. Governor Vos had recruited Ballock personally, and he'd been a perfect gentleman in the process . . . at least initially. *We just wish to establish friendly economic ties with the worlds of the Far Stars,* he had said, and Ballock, dazzled by the rewards dangled in front of him, had believed it all.

What a fool I was.

Now he was inextricably involved in something far worse, though he still didn't understand the scope of what was happening. He wanted out, but he knew that wasn't an option. He doubted Vos would hesitate to have him killed if he moved from useful ally to dangerous loose end, and he was sure the psychopath in the room with him now would not only carry out that order—he would enjoy it.

"Yes." Ballock hesitated. The information he was about to provide was highly secret. If Chairman Vargas found out he had divulged it, he would be in deep trouble.

"Well, give it to me. We don't have time to waste on nonsense."

Ballock felt his stomach clench. Villeroi was not a patient man; that much was clear. The terrified banker understood the only thing keeping the imperial agent from roasting him over a spit was Vos's protection. And the only way to keep that was to do whatever the imperial governor demanded.

He'd thought about going to Vargus, telling him everything, and seeking his aid in escaping his situation. But he doubted the chairman, for all his power, could best Vos. The imperial governor was the smarter of the two. That much was obvious. And Vos had even greater resources at his disposal than the bank. The empire was vastly larger than the Far Stars, and it was far more developed. The Far Stars Bank was legendary for its reach and power in the sector, but it was nothing next to the might of the empire.

No, he thought. *Vargus is going to lose this struggle, whether I warn him or not. Besides, even if I'm wrong and the chairman can best Governor Vos, he'd never trust me again anyway. After he defeated Vos, he'd get rid of me too.* Ballock knew a life as a penniless exile on some shithole like Kalishar or Ventos would be the best he could hope for. As for the worst, that was something he wasn't ready to think about.

He held out his hand. There was a small data crystal in his palm. "As Governor Vos requested, the complete shareholder list of the Far Stars Bank."

The bank was the largest and most important institution in the Far Stars, and the names of the individuals and firms that owned it had been a closely held secret for centuries. Holding a near monopoly on interplanetary trade finance, the bank was a natural target for terrorists and industrial combines alike, any of which might seek to influence the bank by threatening the shareholders who owned it.

"Well done, Ballock." Villeroi spat out the praise like he'd tasted something rotten. "I will have this data transmitted to Galvanus Prime at once."

And I've given Governor Vos what he needs to begin to accumulate a controlling interest in the Far Stars Bank.

"I want to thank you for meeting with me on such short notice, Mr. Lancaster. I am sure you are a very busy man." Mak Wilhelm smiled and extended his hand.

"Not at all, Lord Halford." Danellan Lancaster returned the smile and gripped Wilhelm's hand firmly. "It is my pleasure to meet with such an honored guest. Please, have a seat. May I offer you anything? Something to drink, perhaps? We on Antilles pride ourselves on producing the best wines and brandies in the Far Stars."

Wilhelm shook his head, allowing a slightly disdainful

expression to briefly cross his face. "No, thank you, Mr. Lancaster." He hadn't done undercover work in a long time, but he was pleased to see his skills were still fresh. And any imperial lord visiting the Far Stars would surely look down on the sector's vintages and delicacies. On the other side of the Void, the Far Stars was considered a barely civilized wasteland—certainly no place that would produce a brandy suitable for a lord of the empire.

He moved toward the table and took the seat Lancaster had offered, remaining silent as his host sat on the other side of the table. He was focused, cautious. By all accounts, Danellan Lancaster was a man ruled by his greed, which sometimes overrode his judgment. But he wasn't a fool, not by any means. If Wilhelm wasn't careful, he might trigger undue suspicion.

"I must say, I am intrigued. I am not often contacted by industrialists from the empire, Lord Halford."

Wilhelm's face was impassive. *You mean never, my pompous friend. No one in the empire even thinks about the Far Stars. No one but the emperor—and that is simply because your resistance offends him.* Indeed, Wilhelm knew Lancaster would have been suspicious under normal circumstances. But Vos had arranged for Chairman Vargus of the Far Stars Bank to make the introduction. The tacit endorsement of the bank virtually eliminated suspicion. Vargus hadn't asked any questions; he'd just agreed to Vos's request. Of course, the imperial governor had just deposited ten billion crowns with the bank. Vargus probably harbored some old suspicions about the empire, but he was too rapacious a banker to risk his relationship with his newest and biggest depositor.

"No, I would think not." Again, Wilhelm allowed a hint of derision to slip into his tone. "I like to think Halford Transport is one of the more forward-thinking companies in the empire. When Governor Vos told us of his plans to establish trade agreements and move toward full diplomatic recognition, I immediately expressed an interest in participating. His plan to insure trans-Void shipping is nothing short of revolutionary, and I wanted to be part of it from the start."

Halford Transport was a real firm, and Lord Janus Halford was its chairman. Both were inventions of the imperial intelligence service, which controlled every aspect of the firm's operations. Other than that, though, no one but Vos was aware of this duplicity at the moment.

"I admire your boldness, Lord Halford. Indeed, Lancaster Interests will be at the forefront of establishing peaceful trade with the empire."

Wilhelm smiled. "I am thrilled to hear that, Mr. Lancaster." He paused and cleared his throat. "Because I have a project in mind, and I believe Halford Transport needs a partner, one with far greater experience and presence in the Far Stars."

"What kind of partnership do you have in mind?"

Was that suspicion in his tone? Go slowly . . .

"Just as you plan on being at the forefront of normalizing relations, we plan to be at the forefront of trans-Void shipping. However, I'm afraid we have no experience with freight-hauling operations in the Far Stars. We have no landing rights on any worlds of the sector outside the imperial holding, nor any relationships with vendors and manufacturers."

Lancaster nodded. "It sounds like you need a shipping partner." He paused. "Unfortunately, that is not one of Lancaster's areas of business. I may be able to arrange some introductions, however, if . . ."

"Indeed, Mr. Lancaster, it is precisely *because* your firm is not currently involved in transport that I chose you as my first contact."

Lancaster looked back across the table, clearly trying to hide a surprised look. "I'm afraid I don't understand, Lord Halford."

Wilhelm took a breath. "I am not looking for a transport relationship, Mr. Lancaster. We are already such a company. No, what I am seeking is a partner to acquire an existing shipping firm in the Far Stars, so we can eliminate the red tape and begin immediately. Such a venture would be an equal partnership, and it occurred to me this might be an attractive proposition for Lancaster, since you do not have a significant presence in that industry yet." He paused for a few seconds. "You certainly realize how important shipping will become once relations are normalized. I assumed you would be planning your own entry, and I thought we might be able to work together."

Lancaster sat silently for a moment. "Lord Halford, I am most flattered that you have come to me. Indeed, I agree with you on all points." He hesitated.

Here comes the but. Wilhelm remained silent, waiting. He knew what Lancaster was going to say.

"Unfortunately, Lancaster Interests is committed to a very large project that is set to commence shortly. I am afraid we will not have the discretionary capital to invest in such a large acquisition, at least not for some time."

And there it is. Wilhelm refrained from smiling, but he couldn't help but admire how much of this Vos had anticipated.

"I'm sorry, Mr. Lancaster, but I don't believe I explained my intention fully. We are seeking a partner in the Far Stars for expertise and facilitation, not funding. If Lancaster Interests is able to identify a substantial guild-certified transport firm that can be acquired, we are prepared to provide *all* the financing as our contribution to the partnership." He looked across the table at Lancaster. "Of course, we would want to see some investment on your part as a show of good faith, but nothing that should threaten your other expansion plans. Just a bit of skin in the game, so to speak."

Now he could only wait. He'd offered a great deal, and he was aware it might seem almost too good to be true—which, in fact, it was. But they had done their homework on Danellan Lancaster, and Wilhelm was confident he could assuage any concerns the capitalist might have. Sensing a bit too much hesitation, though, he added, "I can assure you, we are not willing to offer such terms to just any partner, and Lancaster Interests was by far and away our first choice. And yet, I cannot wait indefinitely for you to accept. I do wish to move quickly on this . . ."

Wilhelm eyed Lancaster as he sat quietly across the table for perhaps half a minute.

"Your proposal is a very generous one, Lord Halford . . . and I must say, a very intelligent one as well. There is no one who can aid your integration into the business of the Far Stars like Lancaster."

Wilhelm felt a surge of relief.

"I even have a firm in mind. It is not the biggest transport company in the Far Stars, but with the right investment and support, I believe it can become the largest. And the family that owns it is fractured and feuding. I believe they might accept a generous enough offer."

Wilhelm nodded. "My firm has placed three and a half billion imperial crowns on deposit with the Far Stars Bank. I can provide you with a letter of credit immediately upon our negotiating a satisfactory partnership agreement."

Lancaster looked back with surprise. "So quickly?"

"As I said, speed is essential, Mr. Lancaster. Once Governor Vos's intentions are widely known, every major concern in the empire will be looking for Far Stars partners. It is my intention to be first . . . and well established before the competition arrives."

The concern faded from Lancaster's expression. "I couldn't agree more, Lord Halford. I am certain our teams will have no difficulty drafting a mutually agreeable partnership document. Meanwhile, I will put out feelers to the target company immediately."

"That would be extremely satisfactory, Mr. Lancaster." Wilhelm smiled, and then he let it slowly slip from his face. "There is one other thing."

"Yes?"

"There is one disadvantage to moving so early on this. There is still significant bad feeling and distrust in the Far Stars toward imperial concerns." He took a breath and stared right at Lancaster. "I believe it might be advantageous to keep our partnership a secret . . . and for Lancaster to be the public face of the operation. At least at first. Your firm and family have such a powerful reputation throughout the sector. Indeed, this is one of the primary reasons I reached out to you first."

Lancaster sat still for a few seconds. Then he nodded. "I agree entirely, Lord Halford. The faster we are able to complete the proposed acquisition, the bigger our lead will be on the other companies. And I believe that things will be simpler if it appears Lancaster is moving alone."

"Then we are agreed?" Wilhelm stood up and extended his hand across the table.

Danellan Lancaster rose slowly and grasped the imperial

general's hand. "We are agreed, Lord Halford. Would you reconsider that drink now? A toast to our partnership, perhaps."

"Indeed, Mr. Lancaster. I have heard that your red wines are actually quite good. Perhaps you will be kind enough to select a vintage."

"I would be most happy to do so. And please, I am Danellan to my closest friends and partners."

"And I am Janus."

CHAPTER 9

"ARKARIN BLACKHAWK, YOU OLD DOG. BY THE STARS, IT'S BEEN a long time!" Blackhawk had extended his hand, but Arias Callisto walked right past it and embraced his friend.

"It has, Arias. Far too long." Blackhawk returned the hug. "So, you had quite a battle here, I'm told," he said, releasing the embrace and stepping back half a meter. He peered over Callisto's shoulder at the wreckage of war strewn all around and realized his error. Blackhawk had seen his share of war and knew this wasn't a battle.

It was annihilation.

He paused and took a good look at the Celtiborian general.

Callisto's expression changed, the joy at seeing an old friend slipping away, replaced by the gloom that had shrouded him since the struggle on Rykara had come to its bloody finish. "It was a bloodbath, Ark. My losses were . . ." His voice trailed off.

Blackhawk understood Callisto's pain, and he moved the subject along. There was no reason to dwell on the casualties. It wouldn't change anything. "Still, at least it is over. Marshal Lucerne has asked me to try and trace the source of the imperial weapons that were employed against your forces, but so far I've come up with almost nothing."

"So you're positive they were imperial?"

"I'm positive—and pretty sure the source is the empire itself. There were far too many of them to have been contraband."

"What makes you think that?"

"Just the fact that even if some black marketer had been fortunate enough to find a large cache of imperial weapons, why would he choose to sell them here when there are other worlds that would pay ten times what the Rykarans could?"

Callisto nodded, weary. "Are you saying we were fighting against the empire here?"

"Not exactly, Arias. But I'm almost certain that the imperial governor was involved in this struggle, at least indirectly—that he wanted to give the Rykarans a chance to defeat you, or more likely to inflict heavy losses on your forces before you secured the planet." Blackhawk panned his head around, surveying the wreckage. "That's what I'm trying to find out. Were you able to capture any of their commanders or nobles?"

"No," Callisto said with frustration. "Not one. The closest we found of them at all was a shelter of sorts in the mountains. We almost missed it entirely. It had been destroyed, wiped clean of any hint of its former use. But we found traces of nerve gas. Someone apparently executed a large group of people there, though we couldn't find a clue as to who it was."

"It was your missing nobles, Arias," Blackhawk said without hesitation.

"How can you be so sure? You haven't even seen the cave."

"I'm sure, Arias," Blackhawk said sadly. It was standard imperial procedure. The Rykaran lords had served their purpose, and once they'd become extraneous, termination was inevitable. Imperial operatives did not get emotional about their obsolete tools, nor did they leave live security risks behind. "You're just going to have to take my word."

Callisto stood silently for a few seconds. Finally he said, "Well, Ark, if you're right, I doubt there are any leads here. We've got a pile of captured weapons, but that's about it. We haven't managed to take any prisoners higher up than battalion commander, and none of them seem to know anything."

"You're probably right, but if you don't mind, I'll take a look at that cave. I probably won't find anything you didn't, but it's a place to start."

"What about on Nordlingen?" Callisto looked up at Blackhawk. "From what I've heard, they're up against the same kind of thing we ran into here. I don't have any details, but I know they've been bogged down for weeks now. Rafaelus DeMark is in command there, and if he was only facing the Nordlingen militias, he'd have secured the planet in a week, two at most. But his people have been there almost three months, and they're still grinding it out, at least per the last report I saw. In fact, I just got orders to ship out four of my regiments to reinforce the units already there."

"Good call, Arias. I'm better off trying to get there while the fighting is still in progress. Before the imperials cover up their involvement."

"If DeMark is truly facing the same thing we did here. That's just a guess for now."

Blackhawk nodded politely, but he didn't share Callisto's doubts. The more he learned about these weapons—the more he thought about what Lucerne had said, and what Callisto was telling him now—the more he doubted coincidence when similar stories popped up on other planets in the Far Stars.

Now I just need proof.

"I'm going to have a quick look around here before I leave. In the meantime, I need you to do two things for me, Arias."

"Of course, Ark. What can I do?"

"First, I want to get a message to the marshal."

Callisto nodded. "No problem. I can send it with double encryption in the regular dispatch traffic. What else?"

"Contact the *Claw* for me, and tell my pilot to warm up the ship. We're lifting off for Nordlingen in two hours."

"No problem, Ark." He turned and waved his arms toward one of his aides. "If you're going to wander around, let me send a squad with you. We're not completely secure yet."

Blackhawk waved his hand. "That's not necessary, Arias. I'll be right around here; I won't go far." He saw the doubt in his friend's face. "I promise."

"How's the reactor looking, Sam?" Lucas was staring at the monitors on his board. Everything looked right, but he wanted to double-check. The *Claw* had had a new reactor installed during the layover on Celtiboria, courtesy of Marshal Lucerne. It had almost twice the power of the old one, and it was a perfect match for the advanced hyperdrive they'd stolen from the imperial ship on Saragossa. The *Claw* had always been something far different than she looked, but now Blackhawk's ship was truly extraordinary. She was the fastest thing in hyperspace now that her reactor could properly power the new hyperdrive.

"Yeah, Lucas. Like I told you, since I rerouted the secondary conduits she's running like a dream." Sam sounded a little miffed. Lucas didn't blame her—he knew how much *he* hated being questioned. He was just excited to see what the *Claw* could do now.

"All right, everything checks out. Keep the reactor at 50 percent, and we'll be ready to go as soon as Ark gets back."

"Already done," she said. "Everything's secured and ready for launch. Let me know when we're ready to go."

"Will—"

Lucas heard a soft click when Sam cut the line. "—do," he finished. She'd been acclimating to the new systems since they left Celtiboria, trying to reestablish her "connection" with the *Claw*, and clearly wanted to get back at it. He'd hardly seen her since they'd blasted off from Castilla, and—now that he thought about it—this was the longest conversation he'd had with her since then, too.

He decided to recheck his navigation. The message from General Callisto had directed him to prepare for a "best time" trip to Nordlingen. The system wasn't that far from Rykara, only about fourteen light-years, but it was an area of the Far Stars with heavy cosmic storm activity and other navigational hazards. The direct course went right into the worst of it, but Lucas wasn't overly concerned. He'd driven the *Claw* through much worse more than once, but it didn't hurt to have the course firmly in mind.

He was just about to pull up the plot and see if he could shave any time when . . .

"Lucas, can you reach Ark?"

He jumped, almost falling out of his chair. Katarina was standing at the top of the ladder. Lucas had never gotten used to how quietly the *Claw*'s resident assassin moved.

No wonder she's so good. No one ever hears her coming.

"No, Katarina. Sorry. But he sent us a message, so everything is okay." He suddenly realized her voice was nervous, concerned. He couldn't remember ever hearing her sound anything but cool and confident. "Why? What's wrong?"

"I just got a message from my old master at the guild on Sebastiani."

"And?" Lucas felt his stomach tighten. If Katarina was nervous, there was something very wrong.

"There is a contract out on Arkarin. An assassination warrant. One million imperial crowns."

"A *million* crowns? Who?" His throat had gone dry, and his voice was a hoarse croak.

"I don't know. It is anonymous. But it is definitely real—I checked. The funds are on deposit in a numbered account at the Far Stars Bank."

Lucas sat staring at Katarina for a few more stunned seconds, and then he burst into action. "Sarge," he shouted into the comm, "get your boys ready. I need you to go find the captain immediately, and make sure he gets back here safely."

"Is he in trouble?" There was concern in Sarge's voice.

"Isn't he always? Seriously, I don't know. Maybe. Just get ready now. Everyone fully armed."

"We'll be in the airlock in two minutes, Lucas," Sarge replied, and then he was gone.

Katarina turned toward the ladder. Something about the way she was moving told Lucas she was going out herself. He knew there was no point in trying to stop her, so he just watched her slip down to the lower deck.

"Be careful, Katarina," he finally yelled after her. "And remember Sarge and his guys will be right behind you."

Tyrn Mox crouched low in the shattered wreckage of the building, completely still, waiting. He'd been cautious. The city was a ruin, its inhabitants either dead or long gone. But there were soldiers everywhere, routine patrols and larger formations repositioning themselves as the Celtiborian forces swept the city for any remaining enemy troops or civilians who had managed to survive the hellish battle.

Mox was a patient man, and he would wait as long as it took. He'd killed over a hundred men and women, and he'd never failed an assignment. This wasn't a contract job, but the reward was simply too much to pass up. *Call it freelance,* he thought.

Mox was a graduate of the school on Sebastiani, a guild assassin with a long and distinguished track record. But this, he'd resolved, would be his last job. The reward was a million imperial crowns, a king's ransom by any measure. He would collect it and retire to his villa and his stable of mistresses and lose himself in an unending series of hedonistic delights.

Sebastiani doctrine required moral justification for taking a life, but Mox had long skirted the edge of that philosophy, accepting contracts most guild assassins would have rejected. In his days as an acolyte, the guildmasters had been very strict, and they'd adhered firmly to the old ways. They'd beaten into his head the bizarre morality of the Assassins' Guild, an institution that prided itself on a strict code of ethics, even as it trained a new class of expert killers.

The indoctrination had worked on Mox as well as it had on

his classmates . . . but only for a while. He'd always been a greedy man, fond of luxury, and those old passions returned. Soon, he began to stray from the teachings. He cast a doubtful eye on the ascetic lifestyle of his fellow Sebastiani assassins, opting more and more for debauchery and excess in his personal life. He was a brilliant killer, and that provided the means to fund a lavish existence, one he enjoyed to the fullest between contracts.

Mox was good, one of the best the guild had ever produced, and he was certain he would finish this final job and claim the reward. Still, for all his experience and confidence, he felt a strange tension. By all accounts, Arkarin Blackhawk was not a typical smuggler, despite appearances. Mox had studied his target, at least as much as possible with the limited amount of information available. Indeed, the lack of accounts of Blackhawk's many exploits was itself a warning sign. The captain of *Wolf's Claw* was extraordinarily adept at keeping his activities secret. Mox's instincts told him not to underestimate this target, and he'd moved cautiously, studying Blackhawk's moves for weeks, only now making his own.

He had listening devices planted all around the area. It hadn't been easy to keep them hidden, but so far none of Callisto's soldiers had discovered his network. That luck wouldn't hold forever, though, another reason to get this taken care of today.

He'd listened in on Blackhawk's conversation with the Celtiborian commander, and he hadn't been able to believe his good fortune. Blackhawk was heading his way alone, having refused the escort Callisto had offered.

That was a mistake, Blackhawk, a bit of uncharacteristic hubris at just the right time. Now come to me, and I will finish this.

He reached down slowly, silently, taking hold of the sniper rifle he had set to the side. He crouched down and extended the weapon in front of him, resting it on the remnants of the stone wall.

Now all he had to do was wait. His listening posts had confirmed Blackhawk was coming his way. In a few seconds, perhaps a minute, it would all be over.

Blackhawk walked down the street, stopping occasionally to take a closer look. *Some of the heaviest fighting was here,* he thought, looking around at the masonry walls torn and blasted to chunks by the heavy fire. There had been forces battling at close range along this street. Callisto's men had cleared away the dead, leaving only broken weapons and equipment, and the bone fragments and shattered remains of the dead, bits and pieces too small to be noticed by the overworked burial details.

The distribution of the detritus of war told the tale. The Rykarans had been on the side of the street to his right, and Callisto's men on the left. Blackhawk tried to imagine the carnage of a firefight at such close range. *Hundreds of men died here. Maybe thousands.*

His mind drifted back across the years, to other battlefields, other destroyed cities, but he forced himself back to the present. *There are enough nightmares now to worry about nightmares from the past.*

He looked straight down the street. For an instant, he thought he saw something, a dim flash of some kind.

That was a reflection off some type of glass or hyperplastic. A lens, 57 percent chance. Caution is highly recommended.

Blackhawk frowned and started to direct a scathing thought

back to the AI when his instinct took over. He let his legs go limp, falling hard to the ground, just as a muffled shot rang out.

> Sound analysis suggests a high muzzle velocity,
> nonautomatic weapon with silencing device attached.
> Probability: a sniper's rifle of modern design.

Blackhawk scrambled behind a pile of broken rubble lying between him and the direction of the firer.

Thanks, he thought back at the computer in his head. *You saved my life right there.*

> No thanks are necessary. Assisting you is my
> purpose. And this is not the first time my counsel has
> saved your life.
>
> It is the fourteenth.

Blackhawk went back to ignoring the AI. He knew on some level he enjoyed sparring with Hans, but now wasn't the time—the warning was quite welcome, though. He scrambled around, looking for a weapon. His hand dropped to his side. There was nothing there but his sword. *What the hell am I doing out here with no gun and no comm unit? You're an arrogant fool, Blackhawk. You should know better after all these years.*

He crawled into the remains of a building, trying to keep hard cover between him and the sniper as he worked his way forward. He pulled his sword slowly from its worn sheath. The blade had been with him in many difficult spots, and it had seen him out of more than one. But now he was pinned down by a sniper. He doubted his adversary would let him get close enough to use the deadly blade.

He crouched low, crawling behind the collapsed wall of what looked like it had been a small apartment building. He was trying to stay focused, but he couldn't help but notice the debris lying about: charred clothing, wrecked furniture, a little girl's toy doll. The remains of war often painted the truest picture of its cost.

It was then he noticed something: it was too quiet.

No more shots. This is a professional I'm dealing with.

An amateur would keep firing, even without a clear target. But that would only give away the firer's position. The silence was ominous. Far from being a sign of safety, it told Blackhawk there was someone out there good enough to win this exchange.

He crept forward, listening for any sounds, trying to zero in on his adversary. He knew the AI could make better use of his senses than his own brain, but Hans was silent. And that meant his enemy wasn't moving. He was staying put, waiting for Blackhawk to make a mistake.

He thought about calling out. Callisto's men weren't far away. He doubted the single silenced shot had been heard, but if he screamed, someone might hear.

And then they'll come running down the street, and the sniper will drop them in a heartbeat.

Blackhawk knew that would give him a chance to locate his adversary, but he refused to put Callisto's soldiers at risk. Once, he would have done whatever was necessary, but never again. If he was fated to die here, so be it, but he would not sacrifice innocent Celtiborian soldiers to escape from his own folly.

He crept along, heading toward his best guess of the sniper's location. The single shot hadn't given him a good fix, but where he lacked knowledge he decided he would go on instinct.

Where would I be if I was trying to ambush someone?

He peered carefully through a small hole in the wall, his eyes darting back and forth, looking for a good position for a sniper. He tried to anticipate his enemy's moves. Once again he thought, *Where would I be?*

His eyes fixed on a semicollapsed building. It was strong cover, and it was an excellent vantage point overlooking the entire street. *That's it,* he thought, tightening his grip on his trusty blade.

> I concur. It is your best option. However, assigning above-median skills to your assailant, I project the odds of a satisfactory outcome at less than one chance in six. Satisfactory being defined by your survival for the next hour.

Your survival, too, smart-ass.

It was less than ten meters away. He had a good chance of making it across the street, at least if his enemy hadn't heard him approaching. He didn't like it, but he couldn't think of a better option. He took a deep breath and . . .

"Captain . . . are you here, sir?"

He spun around. The call was coming from down the street. "Sarge, get down! Sniper!"

The area all around him was hosed down with automatic fire. He dove to the ground, wincing as he felt a round graze his back. *Fuck, he's got an assault rifle, too.*

He'd given his position away, but he'd probably saved Sarge in doing so. Of course, this meant getting across the street now was going to be next to impossible.

He scrambled around, frantically looking for a working gun. There was nothing, just a bunch of bits and pieces. Callisto's men must have collected all the functional imperial weapons after the battle.

His back hurt like fire, but he put it out of his mind. *That's twice you caught a round in less than two weeks, Blackhawk. You're getting slow, old man. And stupid, too.* He knew he was in trouble. He'd been a damned fool to wander out into a half-secured combat zone by himself. It had been a stupid thing to do, and arrogant. He'd have torn any of his crew a new asshole for doing something as idiotic. But there was no time for that. Sarge and the boys were here now too, and he needed to hold out. He was exposed and facing a dangerous enemy. The fight was still his and his alone. At least for another minute or so, until his people could get to him. And a minute was far longer than it would take to die.

He felt the tension in his arm as his hand tightened on the hilt of his sword. He knew he'd put it to good use at close quarters, but how the hell was he going to get across the street now?

CHAPTER 10

"HIS EXCELLENCY, GENERAL DRACO EUDUROVAN TRAGONIS, Count of Helos, Baron of Saraman and Thebes, Lord of Westorland, Neustria, and Veland . . ."

Vos sat back, hiding his amusement as the chamberlain rattled off Tragonis's titles. Draco Tragonis was a soldier of the empire and one of its most proficient spies. Like Vos, he had clawed his way up the imperial hierarchy, and also like the governor, he had left a trail of bodies to mark his ascent. The two were remarkably similar, though Tragonis was rather more interested in the titles he had gained than Vos, an affectation that tended to make the announcement of his arrival a long and drawn-out affair.

Indeed, few men in the empire held as many titles as Tragonis. His collection of noble patents owed much to his pacifi-cation of the rebellion on Thuringia. The planet's loyal lords had proven themselves incapable of crushing the revolution-aries, so the emperor sent Tragonis with a legion of imperial guards and the enticement that, as his reward, he would have the title of every rebellious noble whose head he brought back to Optimus Prime. Even the emperor was startled when that number turned out to be sixty-three, but he honored his word and bestowed all of them on Tragonis.

" . . . Knight of Vicarus and Besenzia, and Constable of the Graylands." The chamberlain nodded, trying to hide his gasps for breath. He rapped his staff on the ground twice and stood at attention as the nobleman he'd just announced with such formality walked through the massive doors and into the recep-tion hall.

"You may leave us." Vos watched as the chamberlain hesi-tated. He knew it wasn't proper form for the attendants to leave before Tragonis had at least crossed the floor and greeted the governor, but he was sick to death of the cloying court formality so heavily ingrained in life on Galvanus Prime.

"Go!" He grabbed a heavy goblet and hurled it across the room. It landed about halfway to the door and skittered another five or six meters before coming to a stop, still well short of its target. "Out, I said!"

The guards scurried out into the anteroom, but the door wardens still hesitated, holding the great portal half open while the ancient chamberlain hobbled slowly out.

Vos watched with amusement. The former inhabitants of the capitol had been noble-born and vain. Disgraced and exiled to rule the tiny scrap of imperial territory in the Far Stars, they'd indulged in every manner of hedonism and temper tantrum.

Vos was normally much more reserved, like a viper silently waiting for its prey. He was far deadlier than the fops who had preceded him, but sometimes he thought the members of the staff were too dull witted to realize that—so he occasionally threw a dinner plate or smashed a work of art for their benefit. If that was what they understood, he could give it to them, though he thought the whole thing seemed rather foolish.

He waited for the loud clang as the metal-plated doors slammed shut then he bounded up out of his chair. "Draco, you Drusanian serpent!" He moved swiftly toward the new arrival.

Draco quickened his own pace, and the two men met in the center of the room and embraced. They had been allies for years, and each had aided the other in their many endeavors. They were different in temperament and behaviors, but they shared an overwhelming thirst for power. Too, both men had crawled up from the lowest levels of the empire's peasantry, and they had risen on the strength of their own abilities. As much as it was possible for men like them—cold-blooded and madly ambitious—they were friends.

"It is good to see you, Kergen my friend. It has been what? Three years?"

"Nearly. Far too long. I have been here for almost two and a half already. It took me most of the first year to clean the place up. It had the stink of centuries of failure and incompetence." He glanced back toward the doors, where the wardens and chamberlain had fled. "I still have a few things to bring up to standards, but I couldn't delay my plans any longer. I do not intend to spend the rest of my life on this forsaken frontier. Once I break these people and bring them back into the empire, I shall turn over the acting governorship to one of my lieutenants and return to Optimus Prime."

"To accept your rewards?" Tragonis laughed. "Indeed, the first governor in a millennium to tame the firebrands of the Far Stars? No doubt his Imperial Highness will shower you with rewards."

"No doubt." *And that's all you'll get from me about this subject, Tragonis.* "But for now, come, let us sit and drink. Believe it or not, a few of these backwater planets actually produce some palatable vintages. Particularly Antilles."

Tragonis returned his friend's nod. "By all means, Kergen." He followed Vos toward a small table with two chairs. "Antilles is well known in the empire, among the educated classes, at least. It is said an Antillean would sell his grandmother to a Rutarian slaver if the price was right."

"It is an extremely mercantile world for certain. The richest world in the sector, though not the most powerful, I would venture." Vos reached out for a large decanter and poured two glasses full of the deep red wine, holding one out toward his visitor.

"That would be Celtiboria." Tragonis extended his hand, taking the offered glass.

"Indeed. Certainly since Marshal Lucerne has unified the planet." Vos sat, motioning for Tragonis to do the same. "There is still some disorder while he continues to reorganize the economy, but Celtiboria is the most populous planet, and one of the most advanced as well. And its army is unmatched in the sector."

"Even by yours." It wasn't a question, and there was definitely the hint of an insult. But Vos knew it was bait not worth taking.

"Exactly."

"So, Lucerne is your biggest obstacle then?" Tragonis asked, disappointment touching his eyes briefly.

"Yes." Vos hesitated for a few seconds. "Certainly he is the most obvious, and the most powerful, too."

"But?" Tragonis set down his glass and stared at Vos. "There is something else. I can feel your concern. Something unexpected, no?"

"It is probably nothing. Just an adventurer, a mercenary—name of Arkarin Blackhawk. He interfered with one of my plans, by coincidence it seems, but then he went on to wreck another operation. In a few weeks, he cost me a very valuable hostage and control of an entire planet."

Tragonis took another drink from his glass. "Coincidence? Or something deeper?" He looked at his glass as he set it down. "You are right, by the way. I had no idea such excellent wines were produced all the way out here."

Vos pushed the decanter toward Tragonis. "Please," he said, gesturing toward the wine. As Tragonis poured, Vos continued. "I had thought coincidence at first, but then I discovered this Blackhawk has some kind of connection to Marshal Lucerne. I have had him thoroughly researched, and it appears he is more capable than a typical mercenary or smuggler. Vastly so."

"Perhaps he is one of Lucerne's people."

"I thought that, but most of his past operations seem to have no connection to Lucerne. Indeed, the marshal fought a long and bloody war to unite Celtiboria. I have uncovered a few instances of this Blackhawk assisting him, but for the most part, he and his crew have operated elsewhere. But that is not the strangest thing."

Tragonis took the wine and refilled his glass again. "What is?"

"There is no trace of him, none at all, prior to approximately twenty years ago."

"Perhaps he was simply unknown back then. If he hadn't yet

achieved a sufficient level of notoriety, you wouldn't necessarily find any . . ."

"No, my friend. You do not understand. I have found *nothing*. No hints about his past. No information about what planet he came from, the names of his parents . . . not even anecdotal references to anything at all." He paused for a few seconds. "It's almost as if he'd been . . ."

"Been what?"

"Erased."

Tragonis had been reaching for his glass, but he stopped suddenly and focused on Vos. "You mean you think he had another identity? That he was someone of consequence before he became Blackhawk?"

Vos exhaled hard. "I don't know, Draco. Yet it's the only thing I can think of that makes any kind of sense. I can't find a trace of him further back than twenty years, either as Blackhawk or as anyone I can tie to him."

The two sat silently for a moment before Vos slapped his hand on the table. "But enough about Blackhawk. He is hardly my only problem. You are not out here on holiday, I imagine, so tell me. What brings you to the Far Stars?"

Tragonis's face became serious. "I have brought you several things. First, a warning. As you know, you have enemies at court, and they have not been idle. Your operations to date have been enormously expensive, and there are those who have not hesitated to suggest they have been *too* costly. Some have whispered that you have been embezzling the funds. I even heard one rumor that you are planning to make yourself king of the Far Stars, using imperial resources to do it."

Vos made a face. "It is impossible to avoid such nonsense. I cannot be there and here simultaneously, and there are always those who will maneuver behind my back." He looked across the table at Tragonis. "Do I still have the emperor's support?"

Tragonis smiled. "You do. The emperor finds it refreshing that a governor in the Far Stars is actually *doing something*. You have not yet exhausted your pool of imperial patience. Indeed, I have done all I could to add to it. To an extent, I have bet my own position on your success. Which is one reason, beyond simple friendship, that I have come out here to help you."

"My thanks to you, Draco. There are few men upon whom one can rely. And you are one of those." Vos bowed his head slightly. Tragonis was full of shit, and Vos knew it. Draco was a friend, of a sort, but he would only have come to Vos's aid if he saw potential gain in it—and he'd abandon him in an instant if things fell apart. But if he was going to help for the time being, there was no harm in the open display of gratitude.

"I would say we have two more years to achieve some significant results. Not total victory, but something noteworthy—perhaps half a dozen worlds brought under imperial control. After that, I fear the emperor will weaken in his resolve and begin to listen to some of the whisperings of your enemies."

"I thank you for your insights, my friend. It is invaluable to know what trustworthy ears have heard." Vos held his glass to his lips and drained it. "What other counsel do you bring?"

"I trust you know me better than that, old friend. Would I join this venture and bring nothing more than words? I bring more than advice and gossip, Kergen." He gestured upward. "There is a fleet even now entering this system—mostly transports and a few light warships, mostly older frigates. I have brought you more coin, as well as new caches of advanced weapons." A self-satisfied grin came over his face. "And more than that, I bring you an imperial legion. A veteran line formation, not the rabble you have out here. Most of a legion, at least. We lost two ships in the crossing."

Vos was rarely surprised, but his expression was one of pure shock. "I requested military support half a dozen times before I left, but the emperor wouldn't budge."

"I think it had more to do with your operations reports—proof that he finally had a governor out here trying to accomplish something. I was able to obtain a private audience, and I pled the case that without any military power your plans were at great risk. It was difficult, but I finally convinced him to detach a legion under my command. He wouldn't risk any of the imperial guard, but he didn't send me raw recruits, either."

Vos held up his glass. "To your persistence, and your skill in bending the imperial ear."

Draco clinked his own glass against Vos's. "I tried for naval support too, but he was adamant on not risking any battleships in the Void."

"Still, a legion will be enormously useful." Vos sat silently for a few seconds, deep in thought. "I have been planning something, but I have held back for lack of resources." He lifted his head and looked at Draco. "I may have a use for your legion, one with far more impact than its military might alone."

"I'm intrigued."

"It is a less glorious mission perhaps than assaulting an enemy planet, but one that will do more toward attaining ultimate victory." He leaned back in his chair. "I have made efforts at recruiting a force of native soldiers, but they are little more than rabble. But if you will deploy your veterans as a cadre to train and lead the new recruits, we should be able to build a truly effective army, one that can face most of the other forces in the Far Stars."

"Is that what you need most?" Tragonis's tone was inquisitive, with the slightest hint of doubt. "A legion could likely conquer a few of these worlds outright. It's the easy way to show progress to the emperor. That's why I fought so hard for direct military resources."

Vos looked across the table, nodding toward his companion. "Of course, you are right, at least conventionally. We could pick out a few planets and occupy them—and send glowing reports back to Optimus Prime." A strange smile crept onto his face. "But the progress will be false, and in the end take us no closer to true victory. My plan is to subjugate the Far Stars. *All of it*. Anything less will be defeat. I know I could go back to the court—we could go back—and wave a few captured planets before the emperor, the first worlds of the sector to come under imperial control in two hundred years. We would receive a reward, no doubt. A measured prize for a modest goal.

"But I came here for one thing. Total victory. I will return in triumph, having brought the whole of the Far Stars into the empire . . . or not at all. These arrogant frontiersmen will learn to bend their knees, and I—and you, if you will join with me on this quest—will ride victory to the highest levels of the imperial service."

Tragonis's eyes narrowed with understanding. "You have your eyes on the chancellorship." Vos could hear the respect in his friend's voice. Ambitious men respected ambition, and Vos understood Tragonis had just realized how high the governor of the Far Stars had set his sights.

"I do." It was a direct question, and Vos saw no reason not to give an equally straightforward answer. "I did not come out to this forsaken shithole to get a medal and a meaningless title. I came to achieve a level of advancement not possible through anything accomplished in the empire proper. And now that you're here, I think I can do just that. So," he asked, "will you support me on this, Draco? Will you cast aside ambitions for petty rewards and the crumbs left after the noble-born feast on the cake?

"Will you reach for the heights of power with me?"

Vos looked across the table as Tragonis opened his mouth to reply. But he could already see from his friend's expression, his words had done their work. Draco Tragonis was with him.

"I knew there was a reason I came out here . . . besides friendship, that is. This is a once-in-a-lifetime opportunity, Kergen. If you have the courage and determination to reach for it, I will join you, and together we will conquer the Far Stars." He paused and picked up his full glass, downing it in a single gulp. "So about building this army?"

Draco Tragonis sat in his cramped quarters on the cruiser *Vandaris*. He held fiefs and manors on a dozen planets, and he was used to considerably more comfort than an imperial warship offered. But he was a longtime operative as well, the veteran of countless missions, and he'd been in far worse places, too.

That said, he was particularly averse to space travel, and crossing the Void had been like a nightmare become real. The thought of disappearing without a trace in the depths of that starless expanse struck at his deepest fears. It was only his ambition trumping this dread that allowed him to make the journey, but make it he did.

And now he was very glad to have done so.

He'd come to help Governor Vos, because they were friends, but mostly because he recognized his ally's genius and he wanted to attach himself to the victory he anticipated. It had taken almost three months to reach Galvanus Prime, and he'd expected to remain on the firm ground of the sector capital for a good long time. Instead, he was back aboard *Vandaris* after less than a week—and willingly. He'd agreed immediately with Vos's plan to utilize his legion as a cadre to train a large army. He'd assumed that would take place on Galvanus Prime, but Vos had a different idea in mind.

Kalishar.

Tragonis had heard the name before, at least he thought it was vaguely familiar. It was way out on the periphery, a backwater even by the standards of the Far Stars. But he hadn't realized what a shithole it was until he scanned the library computer entry.

He'd almost backed out, or at least insisted the recruitment and training program be carried out on Galvanus Prime. But again, he realized Vos was right. There were probably spies all over the imperial capital, operatives working for the Far Stars Bank, the guilds, Marshal Lucerne—even the other Prime worlds. Tragonis didn't think they could raise an army anywhere without someone noticing, but they'd come a lot closer in a place like Kalishar.

The pirate haven was also a likelier spot for recruiting. Galvanus was populated mostly by imperial bureaucrats supported by a native servant class. There was very little raw material to build an army of effective soldiers. And it was in the middle of the sector, close to the Primes. The citizens of the Prime worlds had the closest thing in the Far Stars to a sense of patriotism, and besides, there was no way any of the governments of those planets would tolerate imperial agents recruiting their citizens.

The worlds along the Rim had weaker governments. They

were poor planets, offering few opportunities to the lowliest among their populations. Several were in a state of near anarchy, and many of the rest were fractured into warring factions constantly at each other's throats. It was an ideal recruiting ground.

Finally, the local monarch—an ex-pirate named Rax Florin—was one of Vos's allies, and he owed his throne to imperial support. By all accounts, the ka'al—*where do these wogs come up with these names?*—had an independent streak. But he'd sworn loyalty to Vos, and he'd seen in his own rise to the throne and the demise of his predecessor just what happened to those who failed the governor.

He will cooperate . . . or I will have his head removed from his body. Tragonis had agreed to go to Kalishar and see to the training of the new army, but he'd demanded—and received—Vos's permission to handle the ka'al any way he saw fit. *I didn't come all the way out to this miserable corner of space to prance around some barbarian playing at kingship.*

He'd been shocked by the true extent of Vos's ambitions since their first conversation in the capitol. His ally had always been aggressive and fearless, but his plans exceeded even Tragonis's wildest aspirations. The Far Stars had resisted imperial control for nearly a millennium. If Vos's plan succeeded—if he brought the entire sector under imperial rule—it would be the greatest victory in five centuries. And he would have achieved it without any substantial military support.

Tragonis had brought his legion to the Far Stars to act as a spearhead, to lead the invasion of a key world, possibly two or three. But now he would disband it instead. His common soldiers would become corporals and sergeants, and his existing noncoms would see themselves promoted to junior officer ranks.

They would command the vast numbers of new troops he would raise, and train them until they were up to imperial standards.

His senior officers, cohort leaders and above, would have their own legions to command. And when the new units were ready, Marshal Lucerne wouldn't be the only one in the Far Stars with a large and formidable army. The struggle for dominance in the sector would change radically, and he and Vos would squeeze the defiance out of these arrogant frontier folk.

CHAPTER 11

SARGE WAS LYING ON THE GROUND, HIS RIFLE POINTING AHEAD.
"Everybody okay? Sound off."

One by one, his four troopers responded. Nobody was hit, but that hadn't been because of their skill or their fast reactions, or even luck. There was heavy fire farther down the road. Whoever was out there was ignoring them—and shooting at Blackhawk.

"We need to get to the captain." Sarge turned his head, looking down the rubble-strewn road. "Drake, Ringo, to the right. It sounded like the captain's voice came from that side of the street. Get to his position as quickly as you can."

"Got it, Sarge." The two men responded almost as one, and they crawled off into the wrecked building to the right.

"Von, Buck, with me. We need to take out whoever is out there shooting at the captain."

"With you, Sarge."

He flipped his comm unit to the ship's frequency. "Sarge to *Wolf's Claw*."

"*Wolf's Claw* here." It was Lucas. "Did you find the skipper?"

"We've run into hostile fire, but yes, I think we found him. Unfortunately, I believe the captain is pinned down by a sniper approximately sixty meters ahead of my position. I do not know his condition or if he has been hit. Moving forward now."

"Don't waste time with me, Sarge. Go get him."

A veteran of many combat situations, he didn't need to be reminded about the task at hand, and his mind was now focused like a laser. "Von, get up to that pile of debris twenty meters forward and get yourself set. That's a strong position to support our advance."

"Yes, Sarge." The soldier crept forward, trying to stay low. There was another burst of fire, but it was directed at a spot up ahead. The sniper firing at Blackhawk again. There was no return fire.

Sarge put the thought out of his mind. *Captain Blackhawk is a survivor. We'll get him out.*

He waited half a minute for Von to get into position. "All right, Buck, let's get down that street. Stay low. You ain't gonna save the captain by getting yourself scragged."

The two moved slowly down the street, rifles at the ready.

"Remember, Buck, the captain's out there, too," he said quietly. "So we don't just blast away at any sound. You make damned sure it's a hostile before you pull that trigger."

"Got it, Sarge."

He took another step forward, Buck following on his heels.

We're coming, Captain. Just stay low, and we'll be there in a minute.

Blackhawk was definitely staying low. He was on his stomach, practically holding his breath as he listened for any sounds from across the street. There was nothing but silence. Whoever was over there was good. Really good.

The sniper had given his location away with all that fire, so that meant he moved. Staying in place was a rookie mistake, and this shooter was no raw cherry. He'd never hold in a compromised position. So that begged the question: *Where'd he go?*

Blackhawk crawled forward toward the wall. The wound on his back hurt, but he knew it was nothing. The bullet had barely clipped him. It was his side that really hurt. The hit he'd taken on Castilla had healed considerably, but it was still tender, and he'd slammed it hard into the ground when he took cover.

None of it mattered. Blackhawk slipped into his battle trance, and the pain moved to the back of his mind. He'd fought on in far worse shape many times, though he'd usually been better armed and equipped.

He pulled himself up to the front edge of the building, now no more than a meter-high wall surrounded by chunks of debris. He crept up toward a small gap, trying to get an idea on the sniper's location.

Suddenly, he heard something. It was coming from above—a dull roar. A few seconds later, a light gunship came into view, moving roughly toward him, hovering over the street. *Callisto's men!*

Blackhawk stared across the street, looking for any trace of movement. There was nothing. His attacker had simply disappeared.

"Patience, Blackhawk," he whispered to himself. *He could be out there anywhere, just waiting for you to make a stupid mistake.*

There would be Celtiborian troops behind the gunship. In a few minutes, Callisto's men would be all over this area. Blackhawk was grateful for the aid, but he was determined to catch his would-be assassin. The Celtiborians were good troops, veterans of Lucerne's great battles. But they were soldiers, and they were out of their league tracking a top-level assassin.

And even if they do, they're more likely going to kill him, rather than capture him . . . and Blackhawk wanted answers.

The odds seemed more and more to be in his favor, but he was worried his attacker might escape. The next time they met, Blackhawk might not be as fortunate. He fought the temptation to run across the street, to frantically look for the man who was trying to kill him, knowing it was reckless. To be honest, his enemy was probably gone already, but if he wasn't . . .

It's been a long time since I've been suicidal.

So he stayed behind the shattered wall, watching and listening until he heard someone scrambling up behind him. He swung around, knife at the ready, but he relaxed immediately as he saw Drake sliding down a pile of rubble, followed by Ringo.

"You guys are a sight for sore eyes," he said gratefully, but his frowning face was turned away from them, staring vainly across the street for a sign he knew wouldn't come.

Mox slipped between two twisted girders and continued on to the south. He'd had Blackhawk in his sights. He'd been half a second from taking him out when the bastard ducked. He knew enough about his target to realize that Blackhawk had a history of escaping close calls. *Well,* he thought, *here's one more for his record.*

Mox was confident, even cocky, but he was still a Sebastiani-trained assassin, and he knew when to pull back—to escape and try again another day. Only fools, rookies, and brainless thugs stayed in a fight when the odds had shifted. Mox was none of those things. He didn't miss many opportunities, but when he did, he was smart enough to abandon the effort and flee.

He raced from one shattered building to the next, avoiding the open streets whenever possible. The Celtiborian troops would be out in force by now and on full alert. He could handle a few if he absolutely had to, but he preferred to avoid a pointless fight. A couple dead soldiers meant nothing to him one way or another, but he was far better off just slipping away. He'd get another chance at Blackhawk. He'd make sure of that.

He leaped across piles of rubble and slipped through narrow openings, all without a sound. This was where the training was most valuable. Not in the kill itself, but in the maneuver, the gracefulness. Anyone could learn to shoot, but to do so and then evade capture—that's what separated the Sebastiani from everyone else. He could hear the Celtiborians stumbling down the streets looking for him from a kilometer away. But they wouldn't find him. There was no one on this godforsaken rock with the skills to track him.

He swung around the corner, catching a shadow in the corner of his eye. He froze. It held still for an instant, and then he caught the motion. He dove to the side, but not quickly enough. A knife bit deeply into his side.

There's no way . . .

He rolled over a large chunk of twisted steel, putting distance between him and his new enemy. He flipped over onto his feet, turning to face his attacker.

There was blood pouring down his side. The blow had been a deep one, but not mortal. It was serious nevertheless. He replayed the meditative chant in his head, using the Sebastiani art of discipline to banish the pain.

He stared back at the spot where he'd been hit. His assailant stood there, blood dripping from the knife she still held at her side.

"Hello, Mox." Her voice was frigid and there was death in her eyes.

"Venturi," he spat. "Why? We have no quarrel."

"We do. You have forsaken our way, Mox. But more important, you attacked my friend. Now it is time for you to die."

"Your friend?" Mox's voice was thick with derision. "We of the guild do not have friends. We are solitary hunters, alone, focused solely on our purpose." He was stalling for time. He knew Katarina Venturi was one of the most gifted assassins who'd ever graduated from the guild school. He'd always rated himself the best, but now he felt the clammy grip of fear on his spine.

"Perhaps I too have strayed from the path. Because I do have friends. Indeed they are family. And you tried to kill the head of that family. For that, I claim the Askarizan, the death oath. Only your blood shall sate my vengeance."

She crouched down, holding the knife in front of her. He opened his mouth to speak, to try to convince her this was not her fight, but her gaze told him all he needed to know. Only one of them would leave this place.

He pulled his own blade from its sheath. His wound hurt like fire, but he pushed back against the pain, directing it inward. Mox had become somewhat of a sybarite, defensive of his comfortable lifestyle, but in his heart he remained a disciple of the Sebastiani school. The toughness was still there. This was a fight to the death, and in mind and body he treated it as such.

The two combatants eyed each other warily. Katarina had drawn first blood, but Mox was standing firm, knowing he showed no weakness from his wound. He feigned an attack, then another, carefully watching his opponent's responses. This was a struggle between two natural killers, not a brawl in a tavern. The first one to let discipline fail, to make an ill-considered move, would be the one to die.

Mox could feel the tension in his muscles, the energy streaming through his body. It had been many years since he'd faced an opponent he knew could best him, and he found it exhilarating.

He watched as Katarina moved slowly to the side, her eyes fixed on his, her bloodstained blade held tightly in her hand. Her face showed no anger, no fear—no emotion at all.

Mox had managed the pain, but he knew he was losing blood from his wound. Time was not his ally in this fight. He would grow weaker with each passing second while Katarina waited for her first strike to take its toll.

I have to make a move. His eyes darted back and forth, looking vainly for an opening to attack. But Katarina stood firm, her defenses solid. She stared back warily, but made no offensive move.

Mox felt the tension in his stomach, the fear growing—a new sensation for him. His options were few. Waiting for Katarina Venturi to make a mistake was a fool's game, a bet stacked heavily against him. He felt the darkness creeping from the back of his mind, the growing realization that he stood in death's shadow.

His hand tightened around his knife, and he lunged forward, twisting to the side, moving to get around Katarina's expected counterstrike. He jerked his upper body downward and thrust his blade toward his opponent. He felt resistance as the tip of his knife bit into her flesh, but she pulled away from his blow before he could drive it home, leaving a spray of blood behind her rapid move.

He saw her response out of the corner of his eye, her body swinging around, the glint of her blade as she slashed at him. He tried to curb his momentum, to angle his body to avoid the attack he saw coming, but there was no time. He felt the pain as her knife struck home and sliced through his shoulder and up the side of his neck and face.

He stumbled back, his blade snapping upward in a defensive motion. He could feel the blood pouring from the ghastly wound, covering his shoulder and dripping down his arm. He called on all his discipline, willing away the terrible pain, struggling to stay focused, to remain in the fight . . .

He backed away slowly, regrouping, locking his gaze on his adversary. He felt weakness, and his sight was beginning to fail. If he didn't strike a death blow in the next few seconds, he knew he never would.

Venturi was staring at him with cold focus in her eyes. She held her knife firmly, her grip so tight her fingers were white. He could see his own attack had hurt her. There was a growing patch of red on her shirt, blood soaking through. She was leaning at an angle, favoring her injured side. But he knew she was as disciplined as he, that she had compartmentalized the pain and fear.

Mox moved slowly forward. He had the more serious injury, and he could hear the sounds of the Celtiborian troops approaching. Time was not his ally.

He took a deep breath, wincing at the pain as air flowed through his severed cheek . . . and threw himself forward with all the strength that remained to him. He thrust his arm out, blocking Katarina's attack. Her blade bit deeply into his hand, severing two fingers, but it didn't stop his momentum. He crashed into her and they both fell hard to the ground.

He brought his knife around, swinging the point of the blade to her side, but her own hand grabbed his arm, turning the strike aside. He felt her knee against his stomach, and he gasped for air.

She kicked again, and a third time, and then she pushed with all her strength, sending him rolling off her and down the gentle hill. She scrambled to her feet, her hand dropping to her side, pulling a smaller blade from its sheath.

Mox took a painful breath. His body was weak, wracked with pain, but he channeled pure discipline and forced himself to rise. His blade was on the ground, two meters away, so he raised his hands in front of him, adopting a defensive stance.

He saw Katarina's arm, moving quickly, almost a blur. He didn't see the slim blade in her hand, or even during the fraction of a second it took to reach him. He did feel the impact on his chest. For an instant, he didn't know what had happened. Then he looked down and saw the slender throwing knife, its blade buried in his chest to the hilt.

He staggered back, his mental discipline finally failing him. He felt a rush of emotions. Shock, fear, surprise. In an instant he knew she had won, that she had killed him. Then he fell to the ground, and the darkness took him.

"I want every building searched. Every hole in the ground, every pile of fucking garbage lying against a wall." Blackhawk could hear Callisto's voice through the walls of the med tent. The Celtiborian general was furious, and he was holding back nothing as he barked orders at his soldiers. "If anyone else penetrates our security cordon, I'm going to start lining people up against a wall. You understand me?"

Callisto burst through the door. "Thank Chrono you are both alive." His eyes snapped to Blackhawk then to Katarina. The two were sitting on adjacent cots while Celtiborian medics treated their wounds. "I have no words to excuse the sloppiness of my soldiers in allowing an assassin to penetrate our defenses like that."

"Please, Arias, do not blame your personnel." Blackhawk was sitting shirtless, leaning forward as a med tech fused the wound on his back. His voice was slightly strained. He'd refused any anesthetic, insisting he had to remain completely lucid. "From what Katarina told me, the man in question was one of the most accomplished killers in the Far Stars. It is unlikely that any security cordon could have kept him out."

"And my gratitude to you, Lady Venturi, for saving Arkarin."

"No thanks are necessary, General Callisto." Katarina was leaning at an angle, partially covered by a sheet as a medic finished applying a dressing to her wound. "I am just happy that I was able to reach Mox in time to neutralize him." She paused for a few seconds, adding, "He was a very dangerous man."

"I don't think you need to conduct the exhaustive search I heard you order, Arias." Blackhawk straightened up as the medic finished working on his back. "Sebastiani assassins work alone." He looked over toward Katarina with a small smile on his face. "Most of the time, that is. I doubt you'll find anyone else."

"We won't be taking any chances, Ark." Callisto's voice was deep with anger. "And if there are any more would-be assassins out there, we will find them, if we have to tear down every structure on Rykara to do it." He looked back at Blackhawk. "Is it true that a price has been placed on your life?"

Blackhawk sighed. "It would seem so. A million crowns . . . a flattering sum if nothing else. I can't imagine who wants me dead so badly." He chuckled softly. "I can think of plenty who'd love to put a bullet in my head, but none who'd pay so much for the pleasure."

Katarina stared over at Blackhawk. "Arkarin, this is nothing to be taken lightly. Tyrn Mox was a very successful assassin, one of the best ever to graduate from the Sebastiani school. If he was willing to cast aside his ethical obligations as a member of the guild, we should not underestimate the enormous incentive effect of so large a reward." Her eyes locked on his. "You are in tremendous danger. We must get you back to the *Claw* now and take you somewhere safe."

"Forget *Wolf's Claw*." Callisto looked at Katarina then back to Blackhawk. "I will detach a heavy frigate from the blockade fleet . . . and a company of veterans. We will keep you safe."

Blackhawk frowned. "I appreciate your sentiments, both of you. But the day I run and hide because someone threatens me is the day I'll put a fucking bullet in my own head." He turned toward Callisto. "Thank you for your kind offers, Arias, but I will be perfectly fine on the *Claw* with my own people. This isn't the first time someone has taken a few shots at me."

Callisto looked like he was going to argue, but Blackhawk put up his hand. "I am serious. Your friendship and concern mean a great deal to me, but I cannot be who I am not. I will not hide, and certainly not when I have work to do. I promised Marshal Lucerne I would track down the source of the imperial weapons, and I intend to do just that."

He looked across the room. Sarge and his men were standing silently at attention. They'd refused to leave him, even once they were safely back in Callisto's camp. "Let's go, Sarge. It's time to get back to the *Claw*. We've got a job to do." He reached down and grabbed his torn, bloodstained shirt, easing his arm painfully into the sleeve. He turned back toward the other cot. "Katarina, my savior . . . are you ready?"

She slipped down to the ground and walked over toward Blackhawk. "I am ready." She clearly had something more to say, but Blackhawk knew she wouldn't utter a word until they were alone. Callisto and his soldiers were allies, but she was still going to be cautious around them.

"Let me go first, Captain." Sarge hurried over to the door, waving for Ringo to follow. "The rest of you cover the flanks and rear."

Blackhawk watched the noncom slip through the door, his hands gripping his assault rifle. He appreciated his crew's loyalty, but he had a feeling they would be driving him crazy in the days to come. He had never allowed his life to be ruled by fear, and he wasn't about to let some unseen enemy with a deep bankroll change that.

He turned back and extended a hand to Callisto. "Arias, thank you again. And please send a message to Augustin to let him know we are on the way to Nordlingen."

"I will see to it myself, Ark. Double encrypted. No one will learn your destination from us." The soldier stepped forward and clasped Blackhawk's hand with both of his. "Fortune go with you, my friend."

"And with you, Arias." Blackhawk nodded once and pulled his hand back, turning and slipping out the door.

CHAPTER 12

DAMIAN VARGUS SAT AT HIS DESK, STARING AT THE THREE MEN standing in front of him. There was a neat row of guest chairs facing him, but he hadn't invited them to sit. And all of them knew better than to presume to take a chair unbidden.

The office was a massive room, its walls covered in centuries-old wood paneling. There was a large fireplace to the side of Vargus's desk, and a pair of huge logs were burning robustly. The crackling of the fire was relaxing, but its effect was overwhelmed by the tension hanging heavily in the room.

"So let me understand this, gentlemen." Vargus's voice was soft, but his anger was clear. "The last Vanderon month has seen transfers of our stock representing 9 percent of the total

shares outstanding. And none of you have any idea who purchased this stock?"

Trayn Ballock stood silently, almost at attention, looking
very much like he wished he was almost anywhere else in the
Far Stars. Vargus's anger—and his question—was not really
directed at him, but the aide looked like he was on the verge of
panic anyway.

For now, though, Vargus's attention was aimed at another:
Philon Jarnevon.

Jarnevon was the president of the Far Stars Bank, a man of
almost unimaginable power and prestige throughout the Far
Stars. But now he stood before the one man who outranked
him, and he silently endured the questioning of the enraged
chairman.

"Nothing? No one has anything to say?" Vargus's voice had
been steadily rising in volume, and his face was red with indignation. "Do you know how infrequently our shares change
hands in such quantity?" He moved his head from side to side,
briefly locking eyes with each of them. "No? Would it surprise
any of you to know that it has been more than a century since
an amount greater than 2 percent of our stock has traded in an
entire year? A year! And now nearly 10 percent has been sold in
a single month!"

Jarnevon cleared his throat. "With all due respect, sir, nearly
3 percent was sold by the Vestron family. As far as we can tell,
they have liquidated all holdings, including their shipping firm.
There has been considerable strife in the family from what we
have seen, and it is . . ."

"Three percent? Actually it is 2.67 percent, but that is irrelevant. What about the other 6 percent? And the twelve separate

owners of that stock? Do you have any thoughts to offer on that? Any suggestion on who is *buying* these shares?"

"Sir, there have been rumors that Lancaster Interests has purchased Vestron Shipping. The Lancaster conglomerate is already our largest shareholder; perhaps it is increasing its stake. It seems likely that the Lancasters were the buyers of the Vestron stocks, at least. Perhaps they also purchased the other shares."

"And why would the Lancasters acquire our stock so aggressively? Particularly when they are raising funds themselves in anticipation of making major new investments on confederation worlds?"

"Perhaps they see it as a good investment. Our dividends have increased without fail for 211 years." Jarnevon shifted his weight back and forth nervously, but he managed to hold Vargus's gaze.

"A good investment? Well, that hypothesis would certainly discount some market rumor suggesting a problem with the bank, wouldn't it? You understand what I mean. The kind of thing that might encourage a longtime shareholder to sell a position, feeling he is getting out just in time. You and I both know things are going very well. Profits are up, and the new accounts we have signed recently suggest more good things to come. So you will all forgive me if I am at a loss to explain why so many stockholders would feel compelled to liquidate their positions all at once."

Vargus slammed his open hand down on the table, and the other three men jumped. "Many of these sellers have held shares for more than a century and, in several cases, considerably longer. They are business entities and families with a long history of owning our stock. And besides the Vestron clan, none of them are experiencing any known financial pressure to sell. So the only thing I can think of is they are being offered amounts well above market value for their shares." He turned his head and stared at Jarnevon. "And that would blow your investment theory to hell, wouldn't it? Who wants to dramatically overpay for shares they are buying solely as an investment?"

Jarnevon's eyes widened with surprise. "Are you suggesting someone is attempting to take control of the bank?" The executive was incredulous. "Is that even possible? Who could possibly finance such a venture? Even the Lancasters lack the resources required."

Vargus leaned back in his chair. Who indeed? he wondered. It had to be a cartel, but could something of that scale be kept hidden? No one in the Far Stars could assemble such a sum without drawing it from accounts on the bank itself. But he'd already checked, and there had been no unusual activity, at least nothing large enough to account for the stock purchases. Unless . . .

"We have recently opened a series of accounts for the imperial governor." He paused, hesitant to say what he was thinking.

"You believe the empire is involved in this, sir?" Jarnevon sounded skeptical, but his expression was thoughtful. He was too shrewd to not at least consider the prospect.

"I find it difficult to believe, too, but I am without other theories at present." Vargus rubbed his hand across his face. "The problem with this theory, though, is that the governor made a massive deposit, and he hasn't made any significant withdrawals. He drew a single letter of credit secured by the account, but as substantial a sum as it was, it was not nearly enough to finance stock purchases on this scale."

Jarnevon nodded. "Well, we will know soon enough. The buyer or buyers will have to register their stock within thirty Vanderon days of purchase."

Vargus shot a withering stare at his second in command. "Is that what you think, Philon?" The chairman shook his head in disgust. "Has it occurred to you that anyone with resources north of fifteen billion crowns to buy our stock might also be aware of the registration period? Either they have a plan to hide their true identity, or they don't think it will matter by then. Neither of those things is good for us."

He waved his arm. "Out. Leave me alone."

Jarnevon paused, but one more look at Vargus's expression sent him scurrying toward the door, followed closely by the others.

"Not you, Trayn."

Ballock froze in place, turning slowly to face Vargus. "Yes, sir?"

"Close the door and come sit down. I want to speak with you."

The banker moved slowly, nervously toward Vargus. He stopped and stood about a meter from the desk.

"What the hell is wrong with you, Trayn?" Vargus motioned toward one of the chairs. "Sit."

Ballock stepped forward and sat down. "Yes, sir." He paused. "What can I do for you?"

"I want you to do a bit of . . . research for me. Kergen Vos has a representative on Vanderon, ostensibly to serve as liaison with regard to his pending business transactions."

Ballock was fidgeting in the chair, but he kept his eyes focused on the chairman's. "Yes, Mr. Vargus . . . I seem to recall something to that effect."

"I want you to serve as *our* liaison to Governor Vos. Meet with his representative. Tell him you have been assigned to aid him any way possible. Get as close as you can, and report anything you learn back to me."

"Of course, sir," Ballock croaked.

"That will be all." Vargus's head dropped to stare at his screen.

Ballock stood and walked toward the door.

"And, Trayn?"

The aide stopped abruptly. "Sir?"

"I do appreciate this. Do a good job for me on this assignment, and I will see that you are rewarded with a significant promotion."

"Thank you, sir."

"There is nothing more important than loyalty, Trayn. Always remember that."

"I will, Mr. Vargus." He nodded and hurried out the door.

"Mr. Lancaster, please. You must listen to me. There is something very wrong here. We have done hundreds of offerings of both debt and securities, but over half the purchasers of our recent stock sale are firms I have never heard of before. Now we are seeing unusual activity in the daily trading of our outstanding shares." He paused a few seconds, staring across the desk with an agitated expression on his face. "Someone is making a move against us. Not a takeover attempt, perhaps, but something." Silas Grosvenor was upset, but Danellan Lancaster wasn't listening to him, not really. He'd been brushing off the adviser's warnings for days now.

"You are too paranoid, Silas. No one but the Far Stars Bank is large enough to make a takeover attempt on Lancaster Interests, and even in the exceedingly unlikely event they would choose to do so, we would have ample warning from our contacts within the bank." The Lancasters paid millions a year in bribes, precisely so they would obtain crucial information about their partners and business associates.

"Mr. Lancaster, please . . ."

"Enough of this foolishness, Silas. I appreciate your concern, but you are simply being paranoid. We are about to begin the Far Stars Confederation development program. From what I've been able to glean from Marshal Lucerne's communiqué, Rykara is in rather worse shape than he'd expected it to be. And the people are more . . . resentful than might be ideal." He leaned back in his chair and spun around, staring out over the Topaz Sea.

"That might be to our advantage though, Silas, don't you think? Our development teams will have ample protection from Lucerne's troops, so local resentment should be no more than a minor inconvenience. And the widespread destruction should provide us with additional opportunities to increase profits. The Lancaster Construction Consortium will handle the entire rebuilding effort planetwide. We will skip any competitive bidding on humanitarian grounds due to the urgent need of the people for rebuilt shelter and infrastructure. Advise Conrad Koln to increase markups by 50 percent on all building projects." He paused for a few seconds. "No, make that 75 percent. Augustin Lucerne is a military genius, not an economist."

"Yes, Mr. Lancaster." Grosvenor's voice was soft, his face downcast. The Lancaster patriarch was so fixated on the massive profits to be made in the wake of Lucerne's conquests, he was completely ignoring everything else.

Lancaster turned back around, and his eyes caught Grosvenor's expression. He sighed loudly. "Okay, Silas, you're so sure something is going on . . . what is it? Who is coming after us? A bunch of dummy corporations? The Far Stars Bank? Tell me. I'm listening."

"I don't know, sir. Whoever is behind the recent activity

has covered their tracks well. But that doesn't mean there isn't something going on."

Lancaster took a deep breath. "Some invisible enemy? Then tell me one thing. Who could it conceiv—"

The intercom buzzed. "Mr. Lancaster, I have—"

"I told you I didn't want to be disturbed, Mya."

"I'm sorry sir, but Lord Halford is here, and he says it is urgent that he see you at once."

"Very well, Mya, send him in." Lancaster's voice was calmer, but there was still a touch of annoyance. He reached over and flipped a small switch, and his screen went dark. The confederation development program was none of Halford's business.

The door opened and Mak Wilhelm walked into the room. "Good day, Mr. Lancaster, Mr. Grosvenor."

"And to you, Lord Halford." Lancaster rose and extended his hand across the desk.

Wilhelm walked the rest of the way and shook hands with Lancaster. He sat down abruptly in one of the chairs, before Lancaster could offer him a seat.

Lancaster sat down himself. "So what can I do for you, Lord Halford? As you know, we closed the purchase of Vestron Shipping two days ago. My people have been sitting with yours around the clock, working to integrate the company's shipping routes with your proposed ingress points for trans-Void deliveries."

"Yes, Mr. Lancaster, I am aware of all that. But there is something else I'd like to discuss now, if that is acceptable with you."

Lancaster nodded. "Certainly." His voice was clipped, as if he was biting down on a flash of anger. "What would you like to discuss?"

Wilhelm leaned back in the chair and took a deep breath.

"Perhaps we should start with the 31 percent stake of Lancaster Interests my associates and I now control."

Lancaster was silent, staring across the table with a stunned look on his face. "Excuse me?"

"I'm sure you noticed the heavy trading in your stock in recent weeks. Our purchases, coupled with the 57 percent of your new issue we were able to accumulate, give us just under a one-third interest in your holding company." Wilhelm's expression was neutral, his voice cool, businesslike. He could have been reading a quarterly report to Lancaster as much as telling the man his company was under assault.

"What the hell do you think you are doing?" Lancaster's tone became angry. "I think you'd better get the hell out of my office, Lord Halford. In fact, I strongly suggest you leave Antilles while you still can."

"Threats are pointless, Danellan." He glanced up at Lancaster. "If I may call you Danellan."

Lancaster was silent, staring at his visitor with eyes filled with rage.

"As I was saying, threats are so nonproductive. First, I do not want your company, though I do want considerable cooperation from you. If you behave and do as you're told, I will arrange for the stock to be sold to your family trust at a very reasonable price."

"What *do* you want, Lord Halford?"

"Well, to begin, allow me to introduce myself. My *real* self. I am afraid the esteemed Lord Halford is an alias. I am General Mak Wilhelm, special envoy of His Excellency, Governor Vos."

Lancaster turned pale. "You are an imperial general?" His mouth had gone dry, and his words were a scratchy whisper.

"Indeed I am, though you should find it at least somewhat

reassuring to know that I am not here in a military capacity. I wish only to discuss closer cooperation between your firm and the governor."

Lancaster sat still, frozen in his chair staring across the table. "But I am in charge of economic development for the confederation. There is no way I could also conduct business with the empire. Marshal Lucerne would . . ."

"Yes, we understand the motivations of the good marshal, and I am afraid we cannot allow this confederation of his to take form. At least not as currently conceived." He smiled and stared across the table, his eyes boring into Lancaster's. "You may work with us and maintain control of your company. Or you may oppose us, even run to Marshal Lucerne and disclose what I have told you. In which case, another thousand years will go by before a Lancaster heads up this firm again."

Lancaster slammed his fist on the desk. "By Chrono, I will not be pushed around in my own building. You may have acquired 31 percent of Lancaster, but my family controls—"

"Thirty-five percent. Yes, I know. That would leave us on opposite sides of a war for control. I am motivated by factors other than profit potential, and I am prepared to issue a tender offer at three times the last closing price for additional shares." He paused and smiled again. "Are you able to match that, Danellan? Perhaps you can mortgage the family silver. I suspect there is a lot of it lying around."

Lancaster had opened his mouth, but he didn't say anything. He just let his body slide back into his chair. He was clearly trying to remain defiant, but Wilhelm could see the realization setting in. Danellan Lancaster had been a colossal fool, and he stood on the verge of losing his family's legacy.

"I assure you, there is no reason for such a downcast look.

You can come out of this stronger—and wealthier—than ever. As long as you work with us. Kergen Vos is well known for the ferocity with which he dispatches enemies. But he is also a man who knows how to treat an ally. One with the good sense to choose the winning side."

Lancaster sat quietly, staring at his desk. Finally, he lifted his head and spoke with resignation. "Very well, General Wilhelm. What do you propose?"

"I have been ordered to stay close to you. I am to report back directly to Chairman Vargus with any information that may be useful to him."

Villeroi was lying on a large chaise longue, stripped to the waist and staring sideways across the room toward Ballock. There was a young woman perched behind him on the settee. She wore a tiny costume that appeared to be made entirely of white silk, and she was massaging his shoulders.

"Don't mind my . . . assistant, Trayn. Please continue." His words were polite, but there was always something in his tone, an undercurrent of menace that made Ballock shiver.

"He suspects the governor is behind the recent accumulation of the bank's stock."

"But he doesn't know?"

"No. I don't believe so. But who else could it be? Who in the Far Stars could afford such an investment?"

"Who indeed, Trayn? And what do you propose to tell our good friend the chairman?"

Ballock felt himself taking a step back, an involuntary response. He hated even being in the room with Villeroi. The entire affair had turned him into a nervous wreck, but dealing with this sick . . . animal. It was too much to handle.

He'd wanted to tell Vargus when he'd been in the office. To spill his guts about Vos and the imperial plan to take control of the bank. But something had stopped him. He was in too deep already, and he knew it. Telling Vargus would have been suicide, whether the chairman decided to send him to his death or Vos retaliated and took the handcuffs off his pet psychopath.

"I have no idea. What does the governor want me to say?"

Villeroi smiled, but on him it was more unsettling than his normal scowl. "A little lower, my dear." He leaned back, flashing a glance to his masseuse.

He turned his head back toward Ballock. "Well, there is no way to achieve control of an entity the size of the Far Stars Bank without arousing some suspicion. Indeed, when the stock transfer reports are completed, Chairman Vargus will have no more information than he does now. He will be faced with a nearly impenetrable maze of dummy corporations and false identities. Nevertheless, it might be in our best interests to lead the good chairman on, to nurture his suspicions without confirming them."

"You don't want me to try to convince him it is not the governor behind the stock purchases?" Ballock was surprised. He'd expected Villeroi to threaten him and send him back to tell the chairman the governor was not involved.

"That would be ideal, Trayn, if it were a possibility. However, I doubt you are capable of carrying it off. Indeed, it is unlikely anyone could. There are few entities capable of threatening the Far Stars Bank. None, in fact, in the Far Stars, save some kind of large consortium, which would be nearly impossible to hide without imperial resources. In truth, the governor and empire are the only likely suspects. I see no way to completely convince the chairman that Governor Vos is not involved. So our best option is to cultivate that suspicion . . . *slowly*. Vargus will not dare challenge the governor openly until he has proof. We must allow him to think he is moving toward such evidence, though. If he feels you are on the trail of what he needs, we may divert him from other means of investigation—and buy the time the governor needs to complete the accumulation of a controlling interest."

"So what do you want me to tell him?"

Villeroi sighed. "Must I put the words into your mouth?" He rolled his eyes. "Yes, of course I must. I wonder what it would be like to work with truly intelligent assets one day instead of imbecilic meat puppets."

"I—"

"It wasn't a question, you idiot." Villeroi sighed. "Just tell the chairman that you spoke with me, that I assured you the empire has no involvement in the accumulation of the bank's stock. Say that I was convincing, but you still have suspicions. Inform him that you have arranged to monitor my communications and to have my rooms placed under constant surveillance. He will applaud your initiative, and he will wait to see if you discover anything useful. Meanwhile, Governor Vos will move toward completion of his plan. In another month it won't matter what Vargus discovers."

He stared at Ballock, and a perverse smile crept across his face. "It will be too late for him to do anything about it."

CHAPTER 13

"RAFAELUS, IT IS GOOD OF YOU TO MAKE TIME. I REALIZE YOU are extremely busy."

"When Arkarin Blackhawk calls," General DeMark said, "one makes the time. I'm just sorry we had to keep you in orbit so long. They made a real push to take out our LZ. It was touch and go there for a while. But we finally forced them back, and we could reopen for landings." The Celtiborian general threw his arm around Blackhawk's neck, greeting him with a one-sided hug. His other arm was bound up in a sling under his jacket. "Besides, you bear the Silver Seal if I am not mistaken, so I would be compelled to shine your shoes if that was why you have come."

Lucerne had indeed given Blackhawk the Seal, the Celtiborian badge of vice-regal authority. It compelled all Celtiborians, military or civilian, to accede to any request the holder might make. But Blackhawk had left it on the *Claw*. He hadn't needed it with Castillo, and he wouldn't need it with Rafaelus DeMark.

"So, tell me, my friend, what is the situation here?" He gestured toward the general's arm. "You're wounded?"

"It is nothing, just a scratch. I'd like to say I was hit while leading a charge. That sounds very gallant, no? But sadly, it was an enemy bombing run. I was caught out in the open and took a piece of shrapnel." He raised the injured arm, wincing as he did. "I've had worse."

Blackhawk smiled. DeMark had a bit of the swashbuckler in him, but he was one of Lucerne's most gifted commanders, which was why he had been given command of a planetary expedition. "So I take it things have been tougher here than you expected?"

"That's an understatement. Nordlingen was supposed to be a second-tier world—with a second-tier army. But these sons of bitches have been hitting us with particle accelerators, for Chrono's sake! And they pounded us for weeks with their fighter-bombers. They weren't even supposed to have an air force. We were badly equipped to deal with all of it. My initial force was forty-five thousand strong. I lost a third of them the first day."

"You are not alone, Rafaelus. Arias Callisto ran into something similar. And so did my people. On two different worlds." He paused. "It's the imperials. I don't know what is going on, but they are intervening in struggles across the Far Stars."

DeMark exhaled loudly. "The empire? That's just about the worst news you could have brought. I know the confederation is intended to be strong enough to ward off imperial threats, but it still only exists in theory for the most part. If they're hitting us now . . ."

"Fortunately, I don't think they have the resources in the Far Stars for an up-front fight, at least not yet. The empire has always been wary of risking major military units in crossings of the Void. I suspect they plan to intervene wherever they can make things most difficult. Any way they can slow the growth of the confederation and keep the Far Stars fractured. Their ability to provide advanced weapons and financial support should not be underestimated."

"I underestimate nothing. Not anymore. I came here to round up a few local troops and garrison this planet, and I almost had my beachhead pinched out. Those first few days were unreal, Ark. We barely held on until the marshal got reinforcements out to us. We expected defenders armed with gunpowder rifles, and we ran into an entrenched force equipped with energy weapons and coilguns."

"That's why I'm here, Rafaelus. The marshal asked me to try and figure out what is going on. If we can find proof that the empire is behind all this, Lucerne can rally the rest of the Far Stars behind his banner. Evidence of imperial involvement is worth a hundred divisions of veterans in terms of bringing the sector in line behind the confederation."

"I've got captured weapons, Ark, but that's it. Nothing that proves the empire is involved."

"Any prisoners?"

"A few. But no one of any rank. We haven't managed to break their main defensive line yet. If we're able to push through, we might round up a few senior officers at least." The exhaustion was obvious in DeMark's tone . . . and it was clear he was unsure if his people could manage a climactic breakthrough.

I don't think I've ever heard him so defeated. Blackhawk tried another tack. "Any sign of the king? Gustav XXIII, right?"

"Right. But no, we haven't even caught any comm chatter from him. Which is strange, considering the ferocity of the defense." DeMark shook his head. "He was the last person we thought would order this kind of suicidal resistance. We half expected him to yield without a fight. I was authorized to reaffirm his monarchy if he agreed to join the confederation and accept the rights guarantees in the treaty." An angry look crossed his face. "Now, he can rot in hell. Assuming the soldiers don't just blow him to bits when they find him. Or something more creative."

Blackhawk nodded. *This is worse than I thought.* DeMark had always been one of Lucerne's calmest and most rational commanders, but now his anger was driving him. *He wants vengeance, not justice. And from what I saw on Rykara, it was much the same for Callisto's troops. This imperial involvement is not just attriting the Celtiborian forces. It's wearing away at their devotion to the cause.*

Which means I need to expose the empire now. Before all Augustin has worked for becomes just another brutal trail of conquest.

"So what is the plan? We sneak behind enemy lines, break into the palace, and snatch the king?" Ace was standing at the end of the corridor that led to the *Claw's* sick bay. He was leaning against the wall and looking out over the rest of the crew assembled in the main gallery.

Blackhawk turned around to face his friend. He was surprised at first, but he thought about it for a few seconds then realized he wasn't really. This was vintage Ace, and he respected the courage and loyalty of his informal second in command. But that wasn't going to stop him from sending Ace back to his bed—and carrying him there if he had to.

"What the hell are you doing up?" Blackhawk made eye contact with Shira. He could see the amusement in her expression. He suspected she felt as he did—glad to see Ace strong enough to be up and around, but firm that he would sit this op out. "This time, I'm afraid 'we' doesn't include you, my friend. Next time. When you are fully recovered."

Ace waved his hand, a dismissive gesture aimed at all the concerned glances directed his way. "Bah! I'm fine. Never felt better."

Blackhawk tried to suppress a laugh. Ace *did* seem better than he had when he stood at death's door, but he was still hardly the picture of health. He was white as a sheet, and he looked like he'd fall over if he hadn't had the wall to lean on. He was thin and haggard, and his voice, for all his efforts to enunciate, was weak and thin.

"Nice bluff attempt, Ace, but you're not fit for duty yet, and you know that well."

"You're making a move on the king of Nordlingen, aren't you? You're planning on slipping through their defensive perimeter using the field—and then pulling a quick snatch and grab. Am I right?"

"Yeah, Ace, you're right. But you're still going back to bed. Now."

Ace wobbled a bit, but he caught himself. "Look, I'm not saying I'm ready to hit the ground, but I can still help."

"Ace . . ."

"C'mon, Ark. I'm on board anyway. I can at least make myself useful."

"I was going to leave you with General DeMark. It will be a lot safer in his main field hospital than here on the *Claw*."

"Leave me *behind*?"

"Ace, you're still recovering. We almost lost you, and we want you to be safe."

Ace looked up. So did Blackhawk. It wasn't his voice.

It was Katarina's.

"The wife is worried about me," Ace said. He winked at her. "It was a pleasure playing your husband, my dear, even if you were in the next room seducing some local gangster. But I'm afraid now that our little fiction is over, you don't need to pretend so much concern for me." He looked right at Katarina and smiled—but then he saw something in her eyes, a look he'd never seen before. Was it hurt feelings?

Ace paused, distracted by Katarina's reaction. He'd been infatuated with the cold, beautiful assassin since the day she'd boarded the *Claw*—he suspected most men reacted to her that way. But he hadn't imagined she'd felt anything for him beyond basic camaraderie.

"I may be a little worse for wear, but I'm not useless," he finally said. He turned his head, looking out over the whole group. "And I'm damned sure not going to sit in some field hospital while you all go into action." His voice strengthened, and he pulled his hand away from the wall, standing without support. He looked a little unsteady, but he stayed on his feet.

"All right, Ace," Blackhawk said. There was amusement in his voice, but concern as well. "You can stay on the *Claw*. But you're not seriously suggesting we hand you a rifle and drop you into the palace, are you?"

Ace let out a short laugh, followed by a wince. "Of course not. Do I look crazy?" He smiled, holding back the laugh this time. "Okay, don't answer that. But Lucas will be at the controls, and Sam will be in engineering trying to keep the field and the engines running at the same time. And the rest of you are going to hit the ground, right? You've got to get in, secure the route back out, and find the king, taking out any guards you run into along the way. So the way I see it, you're going to need all the firepower you can get."

Blackhawk nodded. "True enough, Ace. But I've got half a crown that says you couldn't even *lift* an assault rifle now. So what do you propose?"

"The needle gun, Ark. Lucas and Sam will be too busy to man it, and everybody else is going to be in the palace. Don't you think it would be a good idea to have the *Claw* on standby, for when—sorry, *if*—things go to hell?"

"You sure you can manage it, Ace?"

"What's to manage? Just strap me in my chair before you go."

Blackhawk nodded. "All right, Ace. You're back in the game. But just the needle gun. I don't want to get back here and find out you moved from your seat on the bridge. Agreed?" He stared right at Ace, and his expression was clear. He wasn't kidding around.

"You have my word, Ark." Ace was always joking, but everyone could tell from his tone he was dead serious. "Who knows? Maybe things will go to shit like they usually do, and I'll get the chance to pay you guys back for saving my ass on Castilla."

"Maybe so, Ace. It wouldn't be that unusual for us, would it?"

"Ark, have I told you how insane this plan is?" DeMark was shaking his head, as he had been almost since Blackhawk had laid out the plan for him. "It's not too late to call it off."

Blackhawk shook his head. "We can't, Rafaelus. I promised the marshal I'd expose imperial involvement. And I can't think of another way to do that. If we wait until your people win the battle, it will be too late, just like on Rykara. Imperial agents don't leave loose ends behind. If the Nordlingeners fall, I guarantee you the king, and anyone else in his court who knows anything about the empire's part in all this, will disappear. You won't even find the bodies."

"But can your people do this? It sounds almost impossible."

Blackhawk smiled. "Almost impossible we can do. As long as it doesn't slip over into plain old impossible. I'm just sorry your men have to bear so much of the burden, Rafaelus." Blackhawk had asked DeMark to launch a major offensive, a diversion to keep enemy attention away from the daring raid. It was an essential part of the plan, but it pained him to basically use the Celtiborian soldiers as cannon fodder. And yet, without the distraction, this mission wouldn't have a chance.

DeMark probably knew he felt this way, but he was a veteran commander, and he understood what was at stake. "We would be attacking soon anyway. Moving the op up a couple days is no big deal." This was Blackhawk's one consolation: DeMark had to hit those lines eventually anyway. His army was too far from home, his supply line too long and tenuous for a protracted campaign. He had to end the war on Nordlingen soon one way or another. If attacking now helped Blackhawk expose the empire's interference, all the better. The cost was going to be heavy no matter when he made his move.

DeMark reached out and put his hand on Blackhawk's shoulder. "Don't worry about our attack, Ark. This fight's a bloody mess no matter what we do. If you can get the evidence you need, you might save some of the other invasion forces from facing what we have."

"I hope so."

"So we are agreed, then?" DeMark's voice was deep, firm. "I will launch my attack tomorrow at dawn, all across the line.

We will hit them hard at every point and do all we can to fix their attention. Then, just after nightfall, you and your people will go."

Blackhawk nodded. He stepped forward and embraced DeMark. "Fortune be with you, my friend, and the brave soldiers you lead."

The Celtiborian general threw his good arm around Blackhawk. "And fortune go with you and your crew as well . . . and bring you safely back."

"All right, Sam, just be careful with those power feeds." Blackhawk was standing on the bridge holding on to the back of his chair as the *Claw* raced toward the target. It was a windy and rainy night, and that wasn't making the ride any smoother as the ship zipped by, barely above the tree line. Not many pilots could fly a vessel the size of *Wolf's Claw* through an atmosphere with such a light touch. But fortunately, Blackhawk and the *Claw* didn't have just any pilot. They had Lucas Lancaster.

"Yes, Captain. I *know*." Sam tended toward a touch of petulance, especially in any discussion involving the ship's engines and reactor. But not usually with Blackhawk. Sam was a master at what she did, and if she was nervous, he knew they all had something to worry about.

"Okay, Sam. You run your engineering section."

"Thanks, Captain." The line cut off.

"Lucas . . . ETA?"

"About four minutes, Skip. You better get down to the hold."

"Okay, hold the ship at the designated position, and keep the field up no matter what." He flashed a glance over toward Ace. "Unless I order you to open fire . . . or you decide it is absolutely necessary. Understood?"

"Got it, Ark." Ace paused for an instant. "Be careful, Ark. You all make it back, you hear me?"

Blackhawk smiled and nodded. "Don't we always?"

He turned and walked halfway toward the ladder, stopping to look back across the bridge. "You sure you're up to this, Ace?"

"Damn straight, Cap. Hell, I might just hop over there and take the stick from our young friend and see what this ship can really do." He looked up at Blackhawk, and the smile slipped off his face. "Seriously, Ark. I'll be fine. You worry about the mission, not me or the *Claw*."

"Roger that." Blackhawk turned and slid down the ladder, his boots slapping hard onto the metal floor of the lower level as he landed. He walked down the corridor toward the hold.

He opened the hatch and stepped through, closing it behind him. The rest of the crew was standing along the wall, gripping the handholds as the *Claw* bounced around in the heavy air. Everyone but Katarina. She stood in the middle of the hold, her balance perfect as always. She wore the form-fitting jumpsuit she favored for operations like this. It looked like a little scrap of nothing, but Blackhawk knew better. The high-tech material was infused with tiny tubes of polymer. A blow of sufficient force ruptured them, causing the suit to instantly harden at the point of impact. The result was a highly effective defensive system. He'd seen her suits stop bullets.

Her throwing knives were lined up on a thin strap wrapped over one shoulder and stretching diagonally across her midsection. Everyone on the *Claw* knew how deadly she was with those tiny weapons. She'd killed dozens of enemies each with a single, blindingly quick throw.

She had her pistols too, one on each side of her waist, and

a light carbine strapped across her back. Blackhawk suspected she had a few other lethal surprises hidden on her somewhere.

The Twins looked almost identical, as usual. They each wore a heavy carapace of body armor, and a matching pair of massive blades hung from their belts. Blackhawk had watched the immense brothers virtually cut adversaries in half with the heavy claymores. He smiled as he saw the autocannons in their hands. The heavy guns weighed almost forty kilos, and they were designed for use with a tripod.

Tarq and Tarnan held them like rifles.

Shira stood next to the Twins, gripping one of the handholds but looking like she didn't really need it. She had an assault rifle slung over each shoulder, and a massive pistol in a holster at her side. A long knife hung down from her belt, and she had half a dozen grenades hanging from a shoulder strap.

Sarge and his boys were on the other side of the hold. They were gripping the rail tightly, and a few of them looked a little green. They were foot soldiers to their very core, and years of Lucas's wild maneuverings hadn't done much to change that.

The men were outfitted with identical gear. Their fatigues were dark gray, and they wore heavy body armor. They were holding their assault rifles, and each of them had a bandolier full of spare cartridges and, on a strap slung in the opposite direction, a complement of grenades identical to Shira's. They had heavy knives—almost shortswords—and pistols on their belts.

Sarge was equipped the same as his men, but he had a large weapon slung over his shoulder, one of the particle accelerators they had captured on Saragossa.

Blackhawk tried to hide a smile. This op was indoors. They were about to infiltrate the palace, and Sarge was packing a gun that could blow half the building to debris with a single shot. *There's a lot you can say about Sarge and his men, but no one's going to call them subtle.*

"You guys ready?" he asked, but he knew they were.

They gave him a round of nods and yeses anyway.

Blackhawk reached down to a small pile of equipment next to the door. He strapped on the belt with his pistol and his shortsword. The blade had been with him for years, the only vestige from a past he tried hard to forget. Its leather hilt was worn smooth, and he'd forgotten how many people he'd killed with it.

Twenty-seven killed, nineteen wounded. That covers the period from my activation to the present. You already possessed the weapon when I was implanted, so I can only estimate prior numbers based on an assessment of accessible memories. Do you wish me to do so?

God, no. Blackhawk tried to remember what it was like to just forget something, without some know-it-all in your head answering rhetorical questions.

He reached down and scooped up the small pack lying at his feet, and he slung it over his shoulder. There was an assault rifle strapped to the side, and he pulled it off, taking a cartridge from his belt and sliding it home.

He took one last look around, his eyes fixing for a second on each of his people. Then he slapped the comm unit on the wall.

"All ready, Lucas. Take us in."

CHAPTER 14

RAX FLORIN SAT IN THE THRONE ROOM, STARING OUT AT THE petitioners. Kalishar was a frontier world, a dusty planet with little industry and few resources. Its lifeblood was its reputation as a pirate refuge. The thieves and pirates spent their coin freely, overpaying for all manner of debauchery and recreation, and in return, Kalishar's code of laws protected them from extradition to any other planet and ignored whatever acts they may have committed elsewhere.

Despite the significant sums of ill-gotten gains flowing through its taverns and brothels and gambling halls, the natives themselves had always existed in considerable poverty. Originally desert nomads, most of them now lived in the ramshackle cities, seeking work in the establishments catering to off-worlders.

And because of their miserable existences, they streamed into Florin's daily levee, seeking the closest thing to justice in their oppressed lives. There was nothing new about this—the ka'al's palace had always had its line of those pleading a case. The difference was, the latest ruler had proven to be more attentive to the plight of the people than any previous ka'al.

Rax Florin had been a pirate just as Tarn Belgaren before him, and he'd amassed a considerable fortune from his dishonest gains. He'd retired to Kalishar, having left himself few other worlds where he could show his face.

His retirement had been pleasant and comfortable, but he'd lived under the shadow of the ka'al. Florin hadn't coveted the throne, but he knew Belgaren viewed him as a potential rival, and as Kalishar's ruler became increasingly paranoid and unstable, the danger of Florin's own situation pushed him to launch his coup. He was uncomfortable being indebted to the imperial governor, but he'd decided that course was the lesser of two evils, at least in terms of his own longevity.

Belgaren had been a fool, a reckless sybarite who'd passed his days in the pursuit of idle pleasure while his corrupt ministers siphoned off the lifeblood of the economy, and the planet slipped closer to a peasant rebellion.

Florin had seen what was going on for years. And while he'd treated his own servants well, striving to create a reputation for kindness to the natives, he'd always kept a small ship ready on his estate as a last-ditch escape option for him—along with his closest retainers and favorite mistresses—in the event things ever went completely to hell.

When the imperials contacted him about replacing the ka'al,

he'd driven a hard bargain. He'd had no intention of stepping into Belgaren's shoes just to reap the bitter fruits of his predecessor's mistakes. Florin was willing to take the power, but not at the risk of being crucified outside his palace, overthrown by those who hated and despised the previous ruler.

So he'd demanded an enormous sum as the price of his participation, and the imperials had granted it. He had taken a portion of the payoff himself, of course, hiding it along with his existing fortune—reserves for a rainy day he hoped would never come. The rest of the money, though, went to securing his position.

For buying the throne had cost a significant amount, payoffs to Belgaren's allies mostly, bribes to ensure they would stand on the sidelines while their old ally was murdered and Florin took his place.

Florin had always been amused by the strange workings of loyalty. The real thing was vanishingly rare and enormously precious. It was something that most people were incapable of providing, and even in those who had the potential, it took years of cultivation. But a reasonable short-term facsimile was often available for purchase.

He had been surprised at how low the going rate was.

In all, it had taken less than a million crowns to secure the superficial allegiance of almost all of Belgaren's allies and retainers. And because of that, almost no one raised a hand to save their old patron. Even Belgaren's old shipmates had abandoned him in the end—again for a shockingly small amount of Florin's imperial coin.

Florin knew that men like Belgaren—indeed, like most of the adventurers and cutthroats who had made Kalishar their home—would have claimed the vast hoard of imperial gold for themselves. But Florin, as greedy as any of them, was also smarter. He looked to his own future, to the security of his rule, and he poured funds into the development of Kalishar. He still welcomed the renegades and their free-spending crews, but now there were factories under construction and distributions of free food to the poorest of the planet's inhabitants. None of it came from Florin's altruism or his concern for the people. Rather, he saw prosperity as a way to cement his power, and feeding the poor as a cheap insurance policy against rebellion.

Better petitions than knives in the back, I suppose.

"Your Majesty, the imperial envoy has arrived." The attendant was clad in the white-and-gold livery Florin had decreed for the palace staff. He was determined to make Kalishar a prosperous world, but that was a long-term goal, and in the meanwhile he felt there was no reason not to at least look the part. He'd allowed his favorite mistress to design the uniforms, and he'd been delighted to see how well they turned out. Now, at least, visitors to Kalishar would see the kind of court finery they witnessed on their own worlds. The old Kalishar was changing, and slowly—very slowly—a more cosmopolitan feeling was replacing primitive barbarism.

"Clear the petitioners, and then you may bid him enter the hall."

The attendant bowed low and turned to walk back to the entry.

The guards moved swiftly to get the Kalishari peasants out of the room, and Florin was pleased that only a few shouted their indignation. *Progress. A year ago, that could have turned into a riot.*

A moment later the hall was empty and the attendant swung open the doors and spoke loudly, reading from an embossed card. "Announcing General Draco Eudurovan Tragonis, Count of Helos, Baron of Saraman and Thebes . . ."

The ka'al sat quietly as the attendant worked his way through several dozen titles. He suspected court chamberlains in the empire were accustomed to such long and absurd announcements and were able to quickly memorize a visiting dignitary's ranks and perquisites. *Kalishar is a long way from that,* he thought without regret. *Such nonsense.*

He stared out from his throne as the imperial walked slowly forward, past the pool and fountain that tinkled elegantly where Belgaren's pit of carnasoids had once stood. Florin wasn't above throwing an enemy to a pack of wild beasts, but he had enough class to do it more privately. He had no intention of adding to Kalishar's reputation for primitive barbarism.

I prefer cultured barbarism. A thought seemingly echoed by the sight of the man walking toward him.

"Greetings, General Tragonis. Welcome to Kalishar."

Tragonis nodded slowly. "And my greetings to you, Lord Ka'al." He glanced around the room. "This is my first time on your world, but from what I have been told, it is evident that you have made some . . . improvements."

"Indeed, General Tragonis. I am sure such is typical on any world. Each new monarch steps up to the throne eager to place his own mark on the world he rules."

"No doubt that is the case. Still, I must say, I find your . . . modifications . . . commendable. I believe you will prove to be a far more capable ally than your predecessor."

A subtle reminder. We own you. He may not be that psychopath Villeroi, but Florin was no fool, and he knew this Tragonis was more than capable of carrying out any threat he said . . . or left unsaid.

But I can be subtle, too. "I am indeed grateful for the aid the governor has provided. His largesse has done much to improve the state of the Kalishari people, and we are eager to assist him in whatever way we can." *Because I am an ally, not a slave.*

"I have come with a request from His Excellency," Tragonis said. "We would like to lease a section of your deep desert for a new program. I am authorized to offer you a hundred thousand platinum crowns per year for the use of this wilderness area—and for unlimited shipping rights to supply and support our operation there."

The ka'al leaned back and took a deep breath. "My reports indicate you have a sizable fleet in orbit already. It seems you have presumed my agreement to your proposal." *I don't really have a choice here, not with imperial warships in orbit. But I won't give in too easily. I plan to get all I can.*

"Not at all. I just wanted to be prepared in the event you do grant our very reasonable request. After all, we are friends, are we not? And what we ask is to our mutual benefit."

Tragonis spoke softly, respectfully. But out here, the diplomatic game always had a hint of violence to it. And while the new ka'al was smart and capable, he knew he couldn't oppose the governor outright, not with any real hope of success. Kalishar's fleet had been almost destroyed in the previous ruler's desperate attempt to recapture Astra Lucerne, and it would be several years before the ka'al could finish building it back to strength. The planet had no friends among the other worlds, and the pirates who'd made it a second home were untrustworthy, very unlikely to fight in its defense without considerable expenditure on his part . . . and even then, he couldn't count on them. All of this meant Kalishar—and thus Florin—was vulnerable and exposed.

But Florin didn't get to where he was by giving in to bullies. And for all the danger imperial meddling brought with it, this Tragonis was still nothing but a bully.

"I am always delighted to aid an ally, Count Tragonis. Yet I would be remiss in my duties if I did not inquire into your proposed use for the territory. What operation do you propose establishing on Kalishar?"

Tragonis looked around the room. "Lord Ka'al, security concerns prevent me from discussing this further in open court."

"Out!" Florin roared, almost shaking the structural supports with the volume and power of his voice. "All of you. Petitioners, guards, advisers. I would speak alone with the imperial envoy. Now!"

There had been a brief pause, the occupants of the room staring toward the throne in stunned surprise. But that lasted only an instant, and it was followed by a general stampede to the door. The old ka'al had screamed and yelled constantly, but Florin's demeanor had been much calmer during his ten months of rule. And that made his intensity now all the more terrifying.

"Close the door and wait outside." He stared across the now empty room toward the two doormen, waving with his hand to emphasize his command.

"Please, Count Tragonis, you may now proceed in private. I assure you, anything you say to me will be held in the strictest confidence." The ka'al sat still and offered his visitor a pleasant smile. He had intentionally shown Tragonis a flash of anger and an example of his decisiveness. He thought about inviting the envoy to his office behind the throne room, but he decided to stay and make the imperial stand. It wasn't a clear act of defiance, but it subtly altered the dynamic at work. Tragonis held most of the cards, and both men knew it, but Florin was playing his weak hand to the hilt.

"Of course, Lord Ka'al." There was a faint look of surprise on Tragonis's face, as if he was surprised by Florin's actions.

Florin's eyes were locked on his visitor's. *You expected a stupid wog, an imbecilic barbarian more interested in watching his pets devour those who upset him. You can control me, that is the bed I made for myself. But you will not walk over me, nor assume I will accede immediately to your every demand.*

"As I was saying," Tragonis said, "we wish to establish a training facility in a remote location, an area where we will not attract undue attention."

Interesting. "Training? For military personnel, I assume?"

"Yes. For military personnel. We will be sending new recruits to the facility. They will be trained, armed, and equipped here and then shipped out to wherever they are needed."

Florin nodded, but he didn't say anything immediately. *My God,* he thought, *they really are planning some kind of move into the Far Stars.* "I am happy to aid my ally, the governor, in any endeavor."

"Excell—"

"But I have several conditions."

"And what conditions would those be, *Lord* Ka'al?"

He's right at the edge. I need to play this carefully.

"First, General, while one hundred thousand platinum crowns is a considerable sum, I must insist upon a higher lease payment. My involvement in this matter brings increased risk to Kalishar. As I am sure you know, our fleet was badly damaged in the course of the last mission undertaken for the governor, and if we are to participate in this new initiative, I will be compelled to step up the effort to replace our losses."

He glanced down for a few seconds then back up to Tragonis. "Shall we say five hundred thousand crowns instead? Payable in advance, on an annual basis?"

Tragonis almost swallowed his tongue, but he maintained

his composure. "And assuming that request is acceptable, what else would you want?"

Florin smiled. "Well, aiding a valued ally is reward enough, but I would also request that you agree to station a hundred thousand of your newly trained soldiers on Kalishar, deployed for the defense of the planet." He locked eyes with the imperial. "We are not enormously popular with our neighbors to begin with, General Tragonis, and I cannot help but think our participation in your program will only serve to inflame the hostility that already exists."

Florin felt his stomach tighten. This was the tough part—he knew he was taking a huge chance demanding the soldiers. The money, he knew, was a drop in the bucket for the imperials, and the fact that Tragonis hadn't even negotiated the sum proved that. Asking for so many foreign troops to stay on the planet, though, seemed reckless. But he knew the governor could overthrow him whether those forces were in place or not—and that's not what he was afraid of. Despite the discomfort of having so many imperial soldiers on Kalishar, he realized it was a level of protection he needed. If his close ties with Galvanus Prime and the governor drew too much attention, he might have to deal with neighboring planets' aggressions—or Chrono forbid, the eyes of Marshal Lucerne or one of the Primes.

The two men stared silently at each other for a long while. Finally, Tragonis spoke. "Very well, Lord Ka'al. The rent will be five hundred thousand crowns annually, calculated on the Galvanus Prime calendar." He paused. "And one hundred thousand soldiers will be permanently deployed on Kalishar to aid in the defense of the planet. The empire will pay these forces, but you shall be responsible for billeting and provisions. Agreed?"

Florin nodded slowly. *It's the best deal I'm going to get. Push harder, and I will begin to make an enemy of this man.*

Or more *of an enemy, that is.*

"We are agreed, Lord Tragonis."

"Maintain position. Minimum power." Kandros was frustrated. He'd been chasing *Wolf's Claw* across half the Far Stars, waiting for the right moment to strike. *Iron Wind* was a good ship, but he doubted she could take the *Claw* in a straight-up fight. Blackhawk did a good job of hiding his vessel's true capabilities, but word still got out, at least among the strange community of smugglers and mercenaries prowling around the fringes of the Far Stars. There weren't a lot of specifics, but the whispered warnings were all the same:

Stay away from the *Claw*.

Kandros would have been happy to steer clear of Blackhawk's ship. He didn't need to be told that Blackhawk was dangerous.

But Blackhawk had finally pissed someone off enough to put a truly huge price on his head—and for a million crowns, Kandros was prepared to match wits with the captain of *Wolf's Claw*.

Starn Quintus turned and looked back toward the command station. "Yes, Captain. We can remain on life support only for another ten hours. Then we'll have to engage the positioning jets to reestablish our orbit." *Iron Wind* was tucked in next to a large asteroid, deep in the fringes of the Nordlingen system. They'd managed to drop a couple scanner buoys closer in toward the planet, and they were waiting to pick up *Wolf's Claw* when it lifted off.

It was a dangerous place to be. The Celtiborians had

invaded Nordlingen, and their naval forces were all over the system. Kandros had intended to follow Blackhawk right down to the planet's surface, but blasting through the Celtiborian fleet wasn't an option. And there were the thousands of soldiers down on the surface. Blackhawk would be right in the middle of the Celtiborian army.

Not an ideal setup for an assassination.

"Just keep a watch on the scanner buoys." The Nordlingener navy had consisted of a few rust buckets, secondhand junkers purchased from other worlds taking them out of service. They were hardly up to the task of protecting the planet's shipping from pirates, and the Celtiborians had destroyed two in the first moments of entering the system, and compelled the others to surrender. Kandros knew he was lucky. If the invaders had been more concerned about the defending navy, they would have conducted a thorough search of the system, and they'd have discovered his scanning devices.

But they hadn't. *And we're far enough out,* Kandros thought, *that even if the Celtiborians discover us, or pick up the scanner buoys, we'll have plenty of time to jump.* That was the last thing he wanted to do, though, because then he'd lose Blackhawk's trail.

"Yes, Captain." Quintus stared back at his scope. "As long as the Celtiborians don't find those scanners, we'll pick up *Wolf's Claw* when she lifts off. Don't worry about that."

"I worry about everything, Starn. Don't underestimate Arkarin Blackhawk, or anyone on his crew. This is the toughest mission we've ever had, and one mistake could send us all to hell in a hurry."

And yet, even as he said it, Kandros stared at the system plot on the main display and his thoughts drifted. *This is the crown-*

ing moment of my career. It will be my greatest achievement. Killing Arkarin Blackhawk.

He got up slowly. "I'm going to my quarters, Starn. Call me if anything changes." He walked slowly across the cramped bridge toward his quarters, his mind racing. *What are you up to, Blackhawk? Where are you going next?*

CHAPTER 15

"THE TWENTY-SEVENTH REGIMENT IS TO ADVANCE." RAFAELUS
DeMark stood in the command post watching the reports
streaming in from the front. The battle had been raging for fourteen hours, and there was fierce fighting along a thirty-kilometer
line. He'd been planning to launch the decisive push in another
week, when the newest group of reinforcements arrived. But four
regiments from Rykara had landed right after *Wolf's Claw*, and
that gave him enough force to push for all-out victory.

At least then my soldiers' lives will be spent for more than just a
distraction.

DeMark was a hardened veteran, and when he made a decision, he stuck with it, whatever it took. Still, when he'd seen the
first casualty reports, he came close to doubting himself. Had

he moved too soon? Were his forces strong enough to attack so aggressively? Perhaps he should have launched smaller spoiling attacks to give Blackhawk his diversion and waited until he had more troops to advance across the line.

Well, we're all in now. No more second-guessing. Now I just need to make sure those boys on the line have what they need to win.

"Colonel Martine reports his forces are in place and moving forward." Captain Varne had been DeMark's aide for almost five years, ever since the then-colonel DeMark had commanded a single regiment in the polar wastes of Celtiboria's deep southern continent.

"Very well." DeMark had nothing else to say. He knew he was sending those troops into a meat grinder. But there was no choice. Lucerne had dispatched him to Nordlingen to bring the planet into the confederation, and that's exactly what he was going to do.

The Twenty-Seventh was a crack unit, but it was under strength. It was one of the four regiments transferred from Rykara, and its soldiers had already been through one brutal campaign. They deserved a trip home and a long rest, but the demands of war were seldom fair.

"Sir, we're receiving a flash signal from *Wolf's Claw*." Varne turned and looked over at his commanding officer. "They're in position over the palace, apparently undetected." He paused, glancing back at his screen. "They're going in now, sir."

DeMark nodded. "Thank you, Captain."

He sat quietly, losing himself in his thoughts. He'd known Blackhawk a long time, and he had memories of the *Claw*'s captain visiting Celtiboria as far back as his days as a junior officer. The mysterious adventurer had been a close friend of Marshal Lucerne for as long as he could remember, and he knew Blackhawk had completed more than a few missions for Celtiboria's leader. Indeed, he was privy to the details of a few of them, and one thing was for sure: Arkarin Blackhawk and his crew were uniquely talented and capable. The operations Blackhawk had conducted for Lucerne had been difficult and dangerous and, as far as DeMark could recall, the captain and his crew had successfully completed them all.

The mission they were on now seemed like the most desperate of them all. Sneaking forty kilometers behind enemy lines and infiltrating the center of their command structure was insane enough. But finding the king of the entire planet and kidnapping him, getting past all his guards and security, both on the way in and out, seemed impossible.

DeMark remembered one night not long ago, when Astra Lucerne was still missing. The marshal had been a wreck, but he made a comment that DeMark still remembered. He said that Blackhawk would bring Astra back, that there was more to him than anyone knew. He wouldn't say anything more, but DeMark remembered feeling a strange confidence that came through the marshal's deep worry, a faith that Blackhawk would indeed bring his daughter safely home. And so he had.

I hope you're as good as Lucerne thinks, Ark. Because you're going to need every bit of it to get out of this one alive.

Katarina slid swiftly down the cable, dropping down to the grassy field behind the palace and landing softly, as always. She pulled the carbine from her back as she hit the ground, and her eyes quickly scanned the area. Nothing. No sign of enemy soldiers. *That's a bit of luck.*

She looked back up, watching the others slide down to the ground. It was an odd sight—half a dozen thin cables stretching up about six meters, and apparently disappearing into thin air. She'd seen the field from outside the ship before, but never in circumstances quite like the current one. She knew the *Claw* was hovering overhead—she could hear the engines—but other than the cables, there was nothing there.

Anyone on the ground watching the crew descend would have thought he was going crazy.

But while the ship was cloaked by the distortion field, Katarina definitely wasn't—she needed to get out of the open in a hurry. So she quickly moved toward the huge stone wall of the palace, her head darting around, eyes scanning for movement in the semidarkness. Blackhawk was down now, too, and the Twins. A few seconds later, Shira dropped on the same cable Katarina had used and ran up behind her.

Katarina turned and nodded, pointing northward, toward what appeared to be a service entrance of some kind. Shira silently returned the nod. She had an assault rifle in each hand, holding the heavy guns like they were pistols. Katarina had seen her wielding the two weapons before, blasting death on her enemies. It struck her as a cumbersome way to fight, and she wondered how Shira managed to aim. But she couldn't argue with results, and Tarkus had a tremendous track record of putting her shots where she needed them.

Katarina and Shira were similar in many ways, at least superficially. They were both cool and unemotional, especially in battle. Katarina had always kept her close relationships to a minimum. Her training stressed the lonely nature of her profession, and she was highly suspicious of those she didn't know well. Her experiences had only reinforced her general sense of distrust. A career as an assassin didn't tend to expose one to the best in people.

And yet, Shira Tarkus was colder still. Her views weren't the result of training and discipline. No, they had developed from her experiences alone—most of them bad. Katarina never let emotions get in the way of her work, but she'd never witnessed a killer as naturally cold-blooded as Shira. As far as Katarina could tell, outside of her shipmates, Tarkus didn't care who lived or died.

She was glad they were shipmates.

One thing Katarina often wondered about was what Shira would have been like if she'd gone through the guild training on Sebastiani. She suppressed a shudder at the thought of what fifteen years of indoctrination would have done to someone so naturally cold. She might have been the greatest assassin ever graduated from the celebrated ranks of the millennia-old school.

Or the most dangerous psychopath ever loosed on humanity . . .

For all her training in human behavior and psychology, Katarina had never been able to completely figure Shira out. But one thing was clear. Like the rest of the odd assortment of characters Blackhawk had assembled, she had found a home on the *Claw* and a family in her shipmates.

Katarina took another look across the wide expanse of grass and leaped out from her position next to the wall. It was probably a risk running across the open ground, but hugging the wall would take a lot longer, and she had a feeling time wasn't their ally.

Shira was close on her heels, though Katarina doubted anyone but she would have heard her companion's soft steps. The two of them had their assigned area. Blackhawk and company were here for the king, but the truth was they had no idea where he was. He could be in his apartments or a throne room—or in a bunker in the subbasement. So despite the likelihood of heavy resistance, they were forced to split up and cover as much of the huge complex as they could.

Katarina put her hands out, stopping her momentum as she ran right up to the wall. She crept along the rough gray stone, moving toward a small door. She took another step and froze.

Shira was just behind her, and she could feel the tension in her companion's body. They'd both heard it. The door creaking slowly open.

Katarina's eyes were focused like lasers, watching the heavy wooden door swing slowly. She was listening, concentrating. Her actions would depend heavily on how many enemies were coming out of the door. Her ears were sensitive, and years of training had taught her to screen out background noise. Footsteps, she was listening for footsteps, and her mind screened everything else out.

Just one, she thought, as her hand moved to the leather strap hanging down her body. Her fingers felt the cold metal of the throwing knife. Her other hand moved back behind her, waving Shira off. She would handle this herself.

She was silent and stone still, waiting like a predator for her enemy to expose himself. Her prey walked slowly, his footsteps loud, clumsy. She saw his shadow in the crack between the doorway and the wall, silhouetted against the light coming from inside.

Her arm moved like a cobra, pulling the knife from its place and throwing it toward her victim in one smooth motion.

He let out a single gasp then he fell hard to the ground. Her blade had found its mark, and it was buried to its hilt through his neck. Blood poured from his severed carotid artery, and one look confirmed he was already dead. His leg was stretched out behind him, holding the door half open.

Shira lunged forward and jumped in front of the door, bringing her rifles to bear in case anyone else was there. "It's clear," she whispered to her comrade. "Goes about ten meters and ends in a T."

Katarina reached down and retrieved her blade, cleaning it off on her victim's coat. "Let's get him inside. There's too much chance someone will see him out here."

Shira hopped over the body and threw her rifles over her shoulder. She grabbed the dead man's legs while Katarina held his shoulders. A small pipe fell from his hands as they moved him. Katarina looked down and shook her head slightly. She'd imagined he was a guard on his rounds, that he'd heard them or seen them on a monitor. But he was just walking outside for a smoke. That's how little it took to get killed sometimes.

The man with the pipe might have been an imperial agent, a mass murderer responsible for incalculable suffering. Or a Nordlingener who worked at the palace to feed his family. She didn't know. She didn't need to know.

She didn't want to know.

In a few seconds, they had the body through, and the door closed behind them. The hallway was lit with small fixtures, placed every three meters or so.

They were in.

"Let's go. Move your asses!" Captain Gregor Zel stood next to the ruins of a large building, urging his men forward. They'd been in the thick of the fighting all day, and now they were pushing into the central zone. After hours of intense combat, the enemy was finally giving ground, falling back slowly through the dying city, and Zel wasn't about to give them time to regroup.

Above the battlefield, the heavy gray of dusk was giving way to the darkness of night. And yet there was plenty of light, the chaotic landscape lit in places by the fires all around the combat zone. It seemed like half the buildings were ablaze, and dense clouds of smoke hung low over the field.

The Celtiborian veterans advanced methodically, half of each squad moving forward while the others stood firm and covered their comrades. They leapfrogged from building to building, dashing across the empty streets.

Zel was moving with one of his squads, on the front edge of the advance. Officers in Marshal Lucerne's army led, they didn't follow their men into battle. He watched the first half of the squad running down the street to the next position. They were halfway there when he heard a shot. One of his men fell forward to the ground. His squadmates halted and looked up, aiming their rifles, looking for the sniper.

"Team two, hold." Zel listened to the squad leader firing out orders. "Scan the area. Find that fucking sniper."

Zel was already looking himself, scanning the buildings across the street. Another shot rang out, and another of his men fell. His head snapped to the origin of the sound.

"Fourth floor, third window from the left," he shouted to the men around him, whipping his assault rifle from his shoulder as he did. He jumped up to his feet, a risk, but one that would give him better positioning to aim, and he cut loose on full auto.

He couldn't see if he'd hit the sniper, but he knew he'd put about thirty rounds into the space the enemy soldier had occupied. A few seconds later, one of his own men leaned out the window and gave a thumbs-up—Zel had gotten the bastard.

The sniper had taken out two of his men, but he was an amateur—no veteran would have stayed in position after firing two shots. The enemy troops on Nordlingen were dug in and equipped with highly advanced weaponry, but they were still novice soldiers. Which was why, in the end, Zel knew he and his Celtiborian comrades would win this war. Whatever the cost.

And it's been a hell of a cost so far.

"All right, looks like the sniper's down. Let's keep moving." Colonel Martine had been clear: Zel was to keep up the intensity of the attack until further notice. *No matter what.* Those had been Martine's exact words, and Zel knew what they meant coming from a veteran like the colonel.

There was something going on, some reason his men were hitting the enemy so hard. He didn't know what it was, but that was no surprise. He was sure it was something well above his pay grade. All he had to know was what he'd been ordered to do.

Attack.

Blackhawk was pressed flat against the wall, creeping closer to the corner. He and the Twins had made it deeper into the palace than he'd dared to expect, but they'd finally run into resistance. There were two guards down the hallway to the right, maybe three. They had Hellfire assault rifles. Blackhawk had run into those terrible weapons too many times, and he knew he'd never forget their distinctive sound.

"Be careful, guys. I know you think nothing can take you down on one shot, but those guns are no joke. Sarge caught one of those rounds in the shoulder on Saragossa, and he came a hairsbreadth from losing his arm."

"Got it, Captain." Tarq was standing right behind Blackhawk, his brother a few meters farther back. Blackhawk was no one's idea of a small man, but the hulking warriors towered over him. It felt comforting knowing that two giants seemingly plucked from some primitive world's mythology had his back.

Blackhawk pulled a grenade from his belt and sighed. "Well, I guess surprise is out the window already anyway." He leaned forward and tossed the weapon around the corner. "Down, boys," he yelled to the Twins, and he hunched lower, putting his hands over his head.

The explosion was loud, and a jet of flame burst down the hallway from the direction of the guards. The fire had stopped.

Blackhawk swung around the corner, whipping his rifle from his back as he did. He was ready to unload on full auto, but he held his fire. The guards were gone, blown to bits by the heavy incendiary grenade. He looked around as he ran down the corridor. *Three,* he thought. *There had been three guards.*

At least that's what it looked like from the body parts.

"Let's go, guys," he yelled back to the Twins. "We've damned sure announced our presence, so we better keep moving."

"DeMark's troops seem to be making serious progress. They've advanced almost twenty kilometers since the attack began." Ace sat at his station on the *Claw,* trying to hold his exhausted body upright. He'd taken half a dozen stims already, and he didn't dare pop another one, not unless things got really hairy. He was pretty sure if Doc knew he'd taken this much, he'd be in trouble. He'd argued so hard that he was capable of manning his post, he'd half convinced himself. But his body was delivering a harsh reminder that he was far from recovered and ready for duty.

None of that mattered, though. His friends were down there, and he was going to stay at the needle gun controls until everyone was back on board.

"I thought they were just mounting a diversion." Lucas was

leaning back in his chair. He'd pulled the *Claw* up a couple of kilometers and engaged the nav AI. The field was keeping them effectively invisible, but it did nothing to mask sound. And the *Claw*'s engines were working hard to keep the ship airborne, not a quiet undertaking by any measure. They'd be a lot harder to detect up here where no one could hear them, and if Blackhawk needed help, they could still be ten meters above the palace in a few seconds.

"That's what I thought, too." Ace leaned over his board, wincing as he did. His chest felt like someone had hit it with a hammer, and the rest of his body wasn't much better. Just about every movement hurt.

He pulled up a series of maps on his screen, superimposing the scanner data on top of them. "This definitely isn't a diversion— it's an all-out attack." He started to turn to glance over at Lucas, but he winced at the pain and decided it wasn't worth it.

"Well, if anything, it will only get more of the enemy's attention. If the Celtiborians are really breaking through, that will give the Nordlingeners something to focus on."

"Let's hope." Ace's voice was edgy. Diversions aside, he knew how dangerous a mission this was. The chance of the others making it back—all of them—was pretty damned poor. He knew he couldn't go along, but sitting on the *Claw,* waiting to see if his friends survived the next few hours, was torture.

They'll make it. Blackhawk will bring them all back. I know he will. Ace tried to convince himself, but the doubt still tugged at him. Visions of the mission on Castilla kept going through his head. He knew they'd barely made it out of there, and ever since he'd been unable to get it out of his mind. He'd been in tough scrapes before, more than he could count, but it was different this time.

Maybe you can only laugh at death so many times . . .

"Where is the king?" Blackhawk wasn't shouting, but his voice was threatening nevertheless. He was pretty sure the man cowering in front of him was some kind of low-level palace staff, a cook or member of the cleaning crew. But this prisoner was what he had to work with. He and the Twins had run into over a dozen guards, but they hadn't managed to take any live prisoners. Until now.

They had managed to find the king's apartments, but the rooms had been empty, and from the layers of dust on the furniture, they hadn't been used for some time.

"I don't know." The man was kneeling on the floor, trying to summon the courage to look up at Blackhawk. "They took him. They took him away."

Blackhawk grabbed the man by the shoulder and jerked him up hard. He felt a small wave of guilt for tormenting the poor servant, but fear—unlike time—was his ally. If he could scare the captive into telling him everything, he wouldn't have to hurt him. *I'd much rather release the poor bastard instead of gutting him like a fish.*

"Took him where?" He stared into the man's eyes, almost melting the miserable captive with his glare. Blackhawk listened to the man whimpering unintelligibly for a few seconds, and then he grabbed harder and yelled, "Where?"

"T-t-to the lower levels, the . . . the old d-dungeon."

"Where is it?" Blackhawk loosened his grip on the man's shoulders. "How do I get there?"

The man cowered miserably, but he didn't say anything.

"How?" Blackhawk pulled his sword from its sheath.

"My people have served the royal family for over a century."

The man was clearly trying to summon his courage, with only moderate success. His eyes locked on Blackhawk's well-worn blade. "No . . . please."

"I am not here to harm your king. And I don't want to hurt you." He glared at the sobbing man. "But I will if I have to. Now tell me how to get to the king."

The man was crying piteously, barely able to speak intelligibly. "G-go down the h-hallway. Turn left. There is . . ." The man slid down slowly, falling into a heap at Blackhawk's feet.

"There is what? Finish." Blackhawk softened his tone slightly.

"A large metal door." He sucked in a deep breath, struggling to hold back his sobs. "It leads down to the sublevels. To the dungeons."

"And where is the king? Those levels must be huge." Blackhawk looked up at the Twins, motioning for them to start down the hallway.

"I don't know."

Blackhawk tightened his grip again and pulled the man's face up toward his.

"I don't know, I really don't know. Please . . ."

Blackhawk raised his blade and brought the hilt down hard on the man's head. He fell backward, unconscious, but very much alive. Blackhawk knew it was a risk leaving anyone alive, but he did it anyway. Murdering a servant in the name of efficiency was something his imperial enemies did, not him. Not anymore.

He stood up and slid the sword back in its sheath. Then he took one last look behind him and trotted off after the Twins.

Katarina slipped through the open door, quickly, silently. She and Shira had managed to remain hidden. They'd dispatched the few guards they'd encountered quickly and quietly. Katarina had taken two of them down with her throwing knives, and Shira had slit the throat of another with the heavy combat knife she carried on her belt.

There was something about the guards that was bothering Katarina. They didn't look much like the other Nordlingeners. The planet's inhabitants tended to be very fair-skinned, with blond or light brown hair and slight of build. But two of the guards were markedly different, stocky with thick black hair. The observation probably meant nothing. Even on a planet with near-universal genetic similarities in the population, there were those who differed from the norm, often significantly. But she'd been trained to notice every detail of a situation and to separate out anomalies.

She looked around the room carefully, her eyes moving across every millimeter. Sebastiani training covered many areas of discipline, but paramount over them all was *irishu,* the sense of awareness. Sight, sound, even the vague sensation of instinct—things like the proverbial bad feeling—were deemed important. A Sebastiani assassin might be bested in battle, but she should never be surprised by an enemy.

The room housed rows of machinery, pumps and conduits that were part of the massive mechanical systems providing water and heat to the many chambers of the palace. There was a faint hum in the background.

She turned and glanced at Shira, then she pointed toward a large metal box on the wall. "I think that is an electrical routing station. We may be able to cut the power to much of the palace, at least temporarily." Unspoken was the question—would that be helpful or not?

Shira walked up to the box and slid the small door open.

It was indeed full of wiring and circuits. "I think you're right. Should we blow it?"

Katarina was silent for a few seconds. She wasn't accustomed to indecisiveness, but now she didn't know what to do. A power failure would alert the guards, though they might attribute it to mechanical problems and not an attack. Regardless, it might put them on a heightened alert. "As long as we're undetected, I think we should leave it alone. Let's see if . . ."

She stopped abruptly and held up her hand. "There. Do you hear that?" It was distant, somewhere far away in the massive structure, but she was sure. Gunfire.

"Yes, I think I just heard it too." She turned to face Katarina. "Ark? Sarge and his people?"

Katarina just nodded. There was no way of knowing, but the odds were it was one of the other teams. "So much for our surprise. Maybe we should rethink this circuit . . ."

They turned simultaneously at the sound of a loud boom, an explosion of some kind. Whatever doubt Katarina had was now gone. The enemy knew they were there.

She turned and glanced at her companion. Shira just nodded. Katarina pulled the carbine from her back, and she smashed the butt of the weapon into the circuit box.

A shower of sparks cascaded around her, but the lights stayed on. She flashed a quick look back toward Shira, and then she hit the circuit board again, harder this time. There was a blinding flash this time, and then the room went dark.

CHAPTER 16

WILHELM SAT IN THE CONFERENCE ROOM, STARING ACROSS THE table at Danellan Lancaster. The patriarch of the wealthiest family in the Far Stars was white as a sheet. He looked like he might be sick at any moment, and Wilhelm realized the enormity of his predicament—and his own hubris—had finally sunk in.

Lancaster had a difficult choice to make. To fight the governor or to yield and succumb to his demands. His choice would be a true test of the man.

Wilhelm had played his hand perfectly, and he could see in his adversary's eyes how deeply the fear ran. Danellan Lancaster was afraid of losing his company, the legacy of his family for twenty-five generations. Wilhelm had understood that all along, and he'd made his moves accordingly. The imperial agent knew Lancaster had the strength to fight back, to resist his demands, but it all depended on Lancaster seeing past the risks. Wilhelm had played up those hazards, a carefully choreographed routine intended to convince Danellan his only choice was to ally himself with Kergen Vos.

The facts were less clear-cut. While Governor Vos had indeed managed to purchase over 30 percent of the outstanding shares of the giant conglomerate—threatening the beleaguered master of Lancaster Interests with a stake almost as large as that controlled by his family—the matter was far from concluded. And if Danellan Lancaster held firm, the contest for control could go either way. Now, Wilhelm would find out for certain if he'd faced down the Lancaster patriarch—or if a brutal fight lay ahead.

Wilhelm knew Lancaster had the tools to mount that fight, to challenge the governor's takeover attempt. The imperial move was half bluff. Yes, the governor could command the resources to outbid the Lancasters for the remaining stock needed for ironclad control. But that didn't mean they could find the shares to buy. The 31 percent Vos had already acquired was the low-hanging fruit, the stock readily available in the market. Much of the rest was held deep in multitiered family trusts or institutional endowments, where any sale involved endless bureaucracy. Purchasing those shares could take months, even years, and if word leaked that the empire was the buyer, the whole scheme would collapse.

Other holdings were owned by close allies of the Lancasters, and Wilhelm was counting on Danellan's fear to blind him to his chances to call on their loyalty, on their willingness to hold their shares with his to form a controlling bloc. While he couldn't match the governor's bids on a purely cash basis, a large percentage of his shareholders did long-term business with Lancaster Interests, relationships that often dated back centuries. There were many permutations and agreements to be made with the right negotiation.

But, for all his wealth and power, Lancaster was proving to be a moral coward. Wilhelm's gut told him his adversary didn't have the strength for a fight with such grand stakes, nor the willingness to risk total defeat in a bid for total victory.

Silas Grosvenor sat at his side. Wilhelm knew the capable aide had tried to warn Lancaster, that he had been suspicious of the mysterious move against the stock long before his arrogant master. There wasn't a doubt in Wilhelm's mind that Grosvenor would have shown him the door by now if it had been his decision.

But it wasn't his choice. Sure, Grosvenor would continue to counsel resistance, but that was all he could do. If Lancaster didn't capitulate soon, he'd have to do something about Grosvenor, something with a significant degree of finality. A well-timed accident might do more than just remove an obstacle—it might make a point to Lancaster. A reminder that Kergen Vos had weapons in his arsenal beyond simple financial maneuvers.

"So, Danellan." Wilhelm's voice was controlled, disciplined. He continued to call Lancaster by his first name, though the terrified industrialist had reverted to calling him General Wilhelm. "What will it be? Profitable cooperation and a bright future together or a proxy fight and financial ruin?" He made sure to sound as if he didn't particularly care, though he was hoping Lancaster would capitulate so he could get back to Galvanus Prime. Antilles was a comfortable enough spot, far preferable to shitholes like Kalishar and Saragossa, where many of the more junior agents had been sent. But he longed to return to Vos's side, to be there as the great plan continued to unfold.

"I have several questions regarding various aspects of your proposal, General Wilhelm." Wilhelm could tell Lancaster was trying to sound resolute, but the weakness behind it was obvious.

He sighed hard. "I have had my people at the disposal of your staff for almost a week now." He paused, deliberately sighing again. "If this is your way of stalling, I can assure you . . ."

"General Wilhelm, I assure you I am not stalling. But if we can just focus on these matters of concern." Lancaster looked across the table at Wilhelm, who nodded for him to go on.

"You wish for me to appear to proceed with the development plans for the worlds conquered by Marshal Lucerne, but in actuality, we will be serving primarily as cover for you to sneak soldiers and weapons onto the planets with the ultimate goal of seizing control from the Far Stars Confederation."

"Yes, in essence that is correct." Wilhelm glared across the table. "Is that a problem?"

"Of course it is! General, the cost of initiating planetwide programs like those proposed are enormous. While I am not above skimming easy profits, if we divert the focus to providing cover for your armies instead of building factories and digging mines, there will be no return. No financial return that is." He paused again. "Lancaster Interests will bleed to death of a thousand cuts. Our investments will be lost, with no income to offset them."

Wilhelm sat for a few seconds. He knew what he was going to say, but he wanted to let Lancaster stew a bit. "I would hate to go back to the governor and tell him your commitment to our plans is halfhearted, Danellan."

"I assure you," Danellan replied, "if we proceed, we will do everything necessary to assist you in achieving success."

Wilhelm felt a wave of amusement. He couldn't help but think that Lancaster's lies weren't even good ones. *I can see what a loyal ally you are right now, you piece of carnasoid dung, watching how easily you sell out Marshal Lucerne. Who, by the way, will crucify you if he finds out about this.*

Lucerne was the part of the whole plan that had Wilhelm worried. If he found out about Vos's moves on Lancaster and the Far Stars Bank, there was no way of knowing what he would do. His reaction might be swift, and extremely violent. Wilhelm had discussed it with Vos before he'd left for Antilles, but the governor seemed less concerned about it. It was one of the few areas where Wilhelm thought Vos himself was being careless. Unless the governor had plans he hadn't yet disclosed to his second in command, that is.

Which I wouldn't put past him.

He stared at Lancaster. "I am gratified to hear what a loyal ally you will be, and I can assure you that we have no desire to bankrupt Lancaster Interests. So let us say that the governor will provide an annual stipend of one billion imperial crowns for Lancaster Interests' services on the worlds in dispute." The words *one billion* seemed to have their effect. Lancaster was interested, but there was still doubt in his eyes.

And here I sweeten the pot—and close the trap.

"Further, once each world is secured as part of the new imperial demense, Lancaster shall have a monopoly hold on the subsequent exploitation of all resources. We will give you what Marshal Lucerne offered, minus the need to pretend to care about the indigenous populations or play at allowing other firms to participate." The doubt in Lancaster's eyes was quickly replaced with a sparkle. "You may squeeze these planets dry, Danellan. Subject to a 25 percent imperial levy, of course."

Wilhelm had to fight to hold back a smile. He'd hit Lancaster right at his greatest dream. The fool would imagine himself becoming a true robber baron, stripping dozens of worlds of their resources, all without having to hide it from the prying eyes of an idealist like Augustin Lucerne. He knew Lancaster was already counting the untold billions in profit his company would reap. Lancaster Interests would achieve total economic domination of the Far Stars.

For as long as Governor Vos thought it was advantageous to allow it, at least.

Wilhelm stared across the table. He knew he'd offered an enormous bribe, one he wasn't sure Governor Vos would sanction. But none of that mattered. When Lancaster had served his purpose, the governor could reevaluate. If he was still useful, he would remain an ally. If not, well, he wouldn't be the first powerful man to disappear without a trace.

"So what will it be, Danellan? The time for a decision is now. This offer is contingent on immediate acceptance."

Wilhelm glanced at Grosvenor. The aide looked to be on the verge of an apoplectic fit, but he sat silently. Lancaster had forgotten his adviser completely, and Wilhelm knew the fool was lost in dreams of untold riches. *Greed. How many men have been ensnared by its siren call?*

"Very well, General Wilhelm. I am with you." He paused. "But first, I want an ironclad guarantee that control of the company will be returned to the Lancaster family. The price of my cooperation is the transfer of your shares to my family's trust. All of them." He paused. "At no cost. Consideration for services rendered."

Wilhelm was impressed at Lancaster's audacity. *Is a traitor's guilt less egregious,* he wondered, *when the price of treason is so incal-*

culably high? How many men could turn down such an astonishing reward? Not many, I suspect. But some. Marshal Lucerne for one. And probably the mysterious Arkarin Blackhawk. They are the true obstacles to victory, the dangerous enemies, not weak men like Lancaster, who can be bought or sold like melons in a marketplace.

"Very well, Danellan. I accept your terms. The shares will be returned. But we shall hold them as your word bond, and they will be released to you only after Augustin Lucerne and his confederation have been destroyed." He allowed a small smile to slip onto his mouth. "And now that we are truly aligned, we have much to gain from Lucerne's defeat, do we not?"

Tragonis stared out over the vast city of tents and portable shelters, stretching across the barren desert. He'd known in theory that his ships were packed with everything needed to build a giant base almost overnight, but seeing it actually come into being was still a sight to see.

One week after setup began, Camp Kalishar was open for business. The eight thousand men of his legion—the ones who had survived the crossing—were divided into cadres, and the first of the recruits were already arriving. They were just a small taste of what was to come, and imperial agents were swarming around the periphery of the Far Stars, seeking every down-on-his-luck criminal or unemployed peasant they could find. Men like Augustin Lucerne chose their soldiers with great care, but the imperial way was different, its methods based on the idea that any man can be broken and rebuilt in the image of a soldier of the empire.

The vermin and outcasts who accepted the imperial bounty would soon discover they were in for an ordeal like nothing they had experienced. The training program was long and brutal,

designed to weed out those without the potential to become disciplined soldiers. And in the imperial military, being "weeded
out" meant dying in training. There would be only two ways out
of Camp Kalishar—as a graduate and a soldier in one of the
new legions, or as a corpse destined for the reclamation center.

Tragonis knew the death rate in imperial training facilities
was about 15 percent, but he suspected it would be far higher
out here in the middle of nowhere. These Far Stars dwellers varied enormously. There were educated Prime worlders and wild
inhabitants of the frontiers, merchant princes and penniless
scavengers. He decided he'd be satisfied if half of them made
it. As for the rest—that was the cost of building an army. And
there were always ways to process excess bodies, even if they just
ended up in the food supply of Kalishar's poor. The Kalisharis
were practically animals anyway, and protein was protein.

"We're starting the basic training regimen for the first class
tomorrow. We have ten thousand recruits ready to go." Hailus
Fuering was an imperial legate and the commander of the Eighty-
Second Legion. His soldiers were dispersed now, his elite combat
unit broken apart, turned into the cadre for an army a hundred
times as large. Fuering would be the field commander of that
force. Like most imperial officers and ministers, his career was
an ongoing exercise in gaining power. And he was about to take
an enormous leap forward. If he led this new army to victory, he
would return to the empire in glory, and leapfrog his peers who
would still be commanding individual legions.

Tragonis nodded. "You have your work cut out for you here,
Legate. I question the quality of the raw material. And the governor's plans call for a much larger force. Your class of ten thousand recruits will be an anomaly. We will be increasing that
tenfold at least for subsequent drafts."

"You needn't worry, General Tragonis. With an entire legion of veterans as cadre and training staff, we can make soldiers out of whatever human debris your recruiters bring us. The ones who do not have what it takes will die in training, and they will serve a purpose in that, instilling fear and motivation in the others. The Eighty-Second is a strong unit, heavy with veterans. I can promise you we will build the army you need."

"I needn't express the rewards for success, Legate, save to say that subjugating the Far Stars will be an enormous accomplishment, one certain to enhance the careers of all involved."

"I thank you for your words, General. But your word of command is sufficient."

Bullshit, Tragonis thought, but protocol still required such protestations. Fuering understood just what was at stake—what he had to gain . . . and lose.

"Very well, Legate. I will remain for the first several days to observe. Then I will go to the capital and stay with the ka'al for a few weeks. I will check back with you before I return to Galvanus Prime." He took a deep breath and stared out over the vast camp, imagining the beehive of activity it would become as more and more recruits were shipped in.

"In any event, Legate, I will be making regular visits, perhaps every three or four months. This project is of the highest priority."

It is the army that will conquer the Far Stars.

CHAPTER 17

BLACKHAWK WAS HALFWAY DOWN THE WINDING CIRCULAR STAIR when the lights went out. For an instant it was pitch-black, and then the emergency lights went on.

The dungeons were an ancient section of the palace, only marginally updated to modern standards. The battery-powered lights were dim, and they were spaced too far apart. It was better than total darkness, but it wasn't much more than a sort of deep inside dusk.

Blackhawk's eyes adjusted immediately. But he stopped for a second and turned back toward the Twins. "Be careful, boys. It's pretty dark, and these stairs are tricky." He didn't want either of them to fall, and he certainly didn't want them tumbling down the stairs on top of him.

"Got it, Captain." Tarq's voice was tense. Blackhawk could tell he was having trouble navigating his way down the staircase in the near darkness.

I wonder what caused the power failure. Coincidence? What's the chance of that? Maybe one of the others? Taking down the power hadn't been part of the plan—but it seemed like a decent way to disrupt the enemy. Blackhawk discounted Sarge immediately. The old noncom was as solid as they came, but he'd never show that kind of initiative. Not without checking in with Blackhawk first. That left Shira and Katarina. *And either of them might do just about anything they thought made sense.*

He reached the bottom of the stairs and stopped in front of a large iron door. They'd searched the other levels already, albeit quickly. They could have missed something, but if the king was down here somewhere there'd be some kind of sign. Servants, guards—something.

"You guys hang back. I'm going to scout the other side of this door. If I don't come back in two minutes, come and get me."

"Yes, sir." Tarnan nodded, but it was clear from his tone he didn't like the idea of Blackhawk going forward alone.

That's a nice thought, old friend, but you don't get a vote.

Blackhawk reached out and pushed the door slowly open. His pistol was out, ready to deal with any enemies he encountered in the hallway. He was listening carefully, but he heard nothing. He leaned through the doorway and looked quickly in both directions. The corridor was dark and dismal, with small lamps positioned every seven or eight meters. The dark stone walls seemed to soak up the light, creating a deep gloom that permeated the place.

He walked out into the hall and stopped again, listening carefully for any sounds at all. There was a small humming noise, probably the building's power plant in the distance. He tried to discern any other sounds, but he wasn't sure. There might be something, but then again . . .

There are voices coming from the north end of the hallway. Estimated distance sixty to eighty meters. Lack of knowledge on layout and composition of walls and doorways accounts for the larger than usual range of values.

Whatever else he thought of the AI that shared his consciousness, Blackhawk had to admit the thing made better use of his senses than his own brain did.

Sixty-plus meters. He'd never get there and back before the Twins came to his aid, no doubt as subtly as an armored division advancing across a battlefield. He'd expected to encounter more resistance, but whoever blew the power had probably drawn away the enemy's attention. He felt a momentary rush of concern for his crew, wherever they were in the building, and his mind flashed with an image of Katarina and Shira surrounded by enemy soldiers. He shook the picture out of his head. There was no point in worrying about that now. They had managed to take some heat off him, whether they realized it or not, and he was going to use it to find the king and get to the bottom of whatever was going on.

Blackhawk ducked back into the stairwell. "You guys sit tight for ten minutes, okay?" He could see from their expressions they wanted to argue. But he knew they'd obey him. The giant brothers were simple creatures at heart, and they didn't have it in them to disobey his orders. He imagined how much more difficult it would have been to get Katarina or Shira to sit tight.

Slipping back out into the hall, he moved quickly down the north passage. He came to an intersection, and he stopped dead. Now he could hear voices, even without the AI's assistance. There were several, four or five. One of them was yelling, and at least two others seemed to be arguing.

He slowly eased his rifle off his back and double-checked the magazine. Once he whipped around the corner he knew things would move quickly. He'd have to make a split-second decision on what he faced and, if they were enemies, take them down before they did the same to him.

Blackhawk wished he had the Twins with him for the fight he suspected was coming, but the two brothers would have been too loud stomping down the corridor. He knew the entire facility had to be on alert already, and he needed to keep whatever shreds of tactical surprise he had left.

He took several deep breaths, exhaling slowly, quietly. He closed his eyes and centered himself, preparing his psyche for the battle trance. He had been bred for fighting and trained to surrender himself to his instincts in combat.

Blackhawk spun around the corner, staring straight ahead. There was a group of men standing around in a small room at the end of the hall. His eyes were focused like lasers, and he saw two of them as they began to react to his presence. He knew immediately they were enemies.

Moving instinctively down and to the side, Blackhawk ducked away from where he knew the guards would target their fire. As he did, his own gun began to spit out death, ten rounds a second ripping through the air toward his targets.

He felt time slow, as it always did when he fell into the trance. He could hear the rounds his rifle fired individually, each tenth of a second slipping by, marked by the crack of another deadly shot.

Blackhawk could feel the bullets of his enemies, too, zipping by into the empty space where he'd been standing an instant before. His eyes were locked on the figures down the hall, and he saw as the first one went down, struck by at least three of his shots.

The guard fell back, and for an instant a spray of blood filled the air where he had stood. He was still dropping backward when Blackhawk's rifle moved to the left, almost cutting another guard in half with its fire.

Two.

Blackhawk dropped to one knee, steadying himself and moving his weapon yet again, taking another guard in the head.

Three.

He let his knee give out, dropping onto his belly as a burst of fire blasted just above him. He shot again, taking his target in the leg. Then another hit in the midsection. The guard had been about to fire, but now his gun slipped from his hands as he crumpled and fell.

Four.

The last guard dove to the side, leaping for cover. Blackhawk saw him disappear behind the wall, out of sight.

"Fuck," he muttered under his breath. He was screwed if his enemy could bring a weapon to bear from behind cover. Blackhawk was in the middle of the corridor, with nowhere to hide.

He dropped his rifle and pushed himself up with his hands, bending his knees and springing himself forward with all his strength. He still felt as if he was operating in slow motion, conscious of every fraction of a second that ticked by. For an instant he didn't know if his push had been strong enough to take him past the corner, where he'd have a shot at his adversary.

His hand reached to his side as he lunged, whipping out his

trustworthy pistol. It was an old piece of imperial tech itself, a tiny coilgun with enough power to fire a dozen rounds at hypersonic velocities between charges.

Blackhawk swung around, bringing the gun to bear as he sailed past the corner. His enemy was turning just as he did, bringing an assault rifle—a Hellfire—around. He ignored it, pushing aside any concern about the gun's deadly projectiles. His eyes locked on his target as his finger squeezed firmly on the trigger.

Feeling the recoil as his pistol fired, he saw his enemy twist hard to the side, his own shot going wide as he did. Blackhawk hit the ground with a thud, despite his instinctive efforts to take the fall in a graceful roll. He felt the pain as his shoulder slammed into the stone floor, but he managed to hold on to his pistol as he spun around and leaped back to his feet. He turned and scanned the room, checking for any remaining threats. He was light-headed from the fall, but he forced himself to focus. He looked over at his last opponent. He was lying on his back, dead. Blackhawk's shot had taken off the top half of his head.

And that's five.

He stumbled around the room, checking the others. Only one was still alive, but he wouldn't be for long. He lay in a pool of his own blood, staring up at Blackhawk in disbelief as he gasped desperately for his last few breaths.

Blackhawk stood still, breathing deeply, regularly, following the battle mantra he'd been taught so long ago. He felt his focus returning, the pain from his injured shoulder receding. He turned and scanned the room again. There was a single large door, reinforced iron with a key lock to the side.

He began searching the guards. The last one he'd killed

had a card in his pocket. Blackhawk turned and walked back to the door. Then he stopped dead.

Did I just hear . . .

Multiple footsteps approaching. Estimate ten plus, approximately fifty meters down the north corridor.

Blackhawk took a deep breath and scooped up his rifle, ducking behind the corner as he ejected the clip and slammed a new one in place.

Ten more. Just great. He paused and took another breath. *That's just fucking great.*

"Captain Rhemus is dead. His company is on your right flank. I want you to take command. With his men added to yours, you should be pretty close to full strength." Colonel Martine's voice was hoarse and the tension obvious in his tone. But he was steady, and it was clear he was firmly in charge, despite the losses his regiment had taken.

"Yes, Colonel." Zel felt a twinge in his gut. Rhemus had been his friend since the two had been junior lieutenants. He was a good officer, and he would be sorely missed—by his peers and by the men he so ably led.

And his wife and two children.

"Your people are to be commended, Captain," Martine was saying. "You are at the forefront of the advance. One more big push and the enemy lines will break." The colonel was a veteran, one who typically addressed a battlefield situation with calm deliberation and not wishful thinking. But now, Zel figured the regiment's commander was halfway between the two.

The vicious attacks had definitely pushed the Nordlingener forces back. But he wasn't sure they were quite on the verge of breaking. Not yet. Still, he couldn't fault Martine for needing to see some payoff for the men he'd lost. Soldiers dealt with the deaths of their comrades in many ways, but no one wanted to think their friends had died for nothing.

"Thank you, sir. The boys have been giving their all." Zel was an enthusiastic follower of Marshal Lucerne's philosophy. Credit for victory begins at the bottom of the organizational chart, and the men in the trenches, fighting it out along the line, deserved the largest share.

"Your men have performed admirably, Captain. They are to be commended." A short pause. "But there is little time for well-deserved rest, I'm afraid. I want you to be ready to move forward again at 1730. The entire regiment will be attacking. We're going to break the enemy lines once and for all and finish this fight."

Zel hesitated. Half an hour wasn't much of a break for his exhausted soldiers, and it didn't give him a lot of time to consolidate his two companies. But he realized Martine was right. It was hard to push his exhausted troops so hard, but time would only benefit the enemy. They were disordered now, on the run. Staying hard on their heels was the right tactical move. And pushing his soldiers now might end the fight sooner—and save a lot of their lives in the longer run.

"Yes, sir. We'll be ready."

"Very well, Captain. Martine out."

Zel turned and looked over toward Sergeant Bella. He almost hit the communicator clipped to his collar to call the noncom, but Bella was only twenty yards away. "Sergeant Bella," he yelled.

The veteran turned and ran over. "Sir!"

"Bella, I need you to go to Captain Rhemus's company command post straightaway. Rhemus is dead, and we're merging what's left of their formation with ours. Figure out who is left over there and tell them to take position on our right, extending our line from Tarik's platoon." Zel could have called over on the comm, but he suspected things were a mess after Rhemus's death. He only had half an hour, and he knew Bella would see his orders carried out. The sergeant was a twenty-year veteran, and Zel was sure he wouldn't let some half-hysterical lieutenant push him around.

"Yes, sir." Bella didn't salute. By all accounts, the enemy had pulled back completely, but the company was still in the battle zone.

"Go, Sergeant. And if anybody gives you shit, call me immediately." Zel nodded. "Dismissed."

Zel turned and looked out over his men. They were sitting on rocks, piles of debris, anything that got them off the wet, muddy ground. Most of them were still eating. It was the first real meal they'd had in two days, and the chance to eat something other than a nutrition bar was something veteran soldiers rarely passed up.

He would have to get them up and organized for the attack soon, but for now he'd let them have another fifteen minutes of rest, miserable reward though it was for what they'd been through. Then he would order them back into the line. And more of them would die.

Blackhawk had his back pressed up against the cold stone wall. He pulled the release on his rifle, sending another spent cartridge flying across the room. He reached around his belt for his last one.

He'd stopped trying to get an accurate count of the enemy soldiers bunched up in the hallway. He'd taken down eight, but more had come, and they were stacked up behind the corners of the passageway. His accurate fire had turned the connecting hallway into a death zone, and he'd managed to keep his attackers at bay. But he was almost out of ammo now, and he knew they'd rush him as soon as he emptied the last magazine.

The captain had almost called the others, but he still didn't know the king was down here. For all he knew, he'd been given misinformation, sent into a trap in the bowels of the palace while the king sat laughing in bed. Maybe the others were closer. There was no point in dragging them down here, especially if it was a trap. He wasn't going to get his friends killed to save himself.

He glanced around the corner, his eyes focusing instantly on one of the enemy doing the same. His hands moved swiftly, and he fired a single shot. The target fell instantly, blood pouring from the between his eyes.

That's nine. But I'd wager there are another ten over there. Maybe more. He glanced down at his rifle. *I need to make these shots count.*

He stood still, listening for any moves. He could hear his enemies talking among themselves, but he couldn't make out what they were saying.

They are discussing an attack with gas grenades. Apparently, they are expecting further reinforcements so armed momentarily.

Blackhawk nodded. He wasn't sure exactly how Hans was able to use his own senses with greater effectiveness than his own brain, but he couldn't question something he'd seen hundreds of times either.

I would suggest that time is not your ally at present.

When has it ever been for me? Any idea what I should do about it?

Your options seem limited at present. If you are
unwilling to call for aid, I am unable to devise an
alternate exit strategy.

*If I call any of the crew they will come. And they'll just get stuck
down here with me. No. We either get out of this ourselves or we don't.*

Your attitude is courageous, at least within the
computational range of my limited understanding of
human emotions and motivations. But your parameters
severely restrict your options. Our options, as you
acknowledge with your use of the pronoun "we."

Blackhawk's head snapped around. There was a burst of
fire, and the sound was coming from a distance.

That is a 50 mm autocannon. Correction: two
autocannons.

The Twins! He hadn't called them, but they were coming
anyway.

Now he could hear return fire. Just a few guns, and the sound
was sporadic. The cracks of the assault rifles sounded almost
like children's toys next to the loud bang of the big automatic
weapons. He felt a rush of adrenaline, and he gave himself up
to instinct again, taking a deep breath and spinning around
the corner, racing down the hallway.

There were bodies all over, the men he'd killed, and another pile at the intersection. The newer corpses were almost torn to shreds by the heavy projectiles from the autocannons.

Tarq came down the hallway, firing as he ran. "Glad to see you in one piece, Cap," he said as he passed by Blackhawk, pursuing the last of the guards as they fled down the hall.

Tarnan came up behind his brother. He'd slung the autocannon back over his shoulder and drawn his massive claymore. The blade was polished steel, over a meter long, and it was thick and heavy. Blackhawk had lifted the thing before, and he'd have bet it weighed fifteen kilos, maybe more. He could see the muscles flexed in Tarnan's massive arm as he held the terrible weapon, ready to strike.

"We figured you could use some backup, Captain." The giant stood in the intersection, surrounded by bodies.

"You figured right, my friend." He hadn't wanted to call the Twins and get them trapped with him, but sometimes he forgot just what a pair of true killing machines they were. They'd cleared the enemy position in less than a minute, obliterating everyone in sight. Tarq returned a few seconds later, having blown the last of the fleeing guards into bloody chunks.

"Thanks for the assist, guys." Blackhawk held his elation in check. He knew more enemy soldiers would come and they were far from out of the woods yet. But things were looking better than they had a few minutes before. "We need to get this door open." He pulled out the card he'd taken earlier, but the plate around the slot was riddled with bullet holes. He slid the card in anyway just to be sure, but nothing happened.

"Shit," he muttered, jamming it in again, as much out of frustration as expectation it would work.

"Step back, sir." He felt Tarq's huge hand on his shoulder, gently pulling him to the side.

The giant aimed the heavy autocannon where the door met the locking mechanism, and he opened fire. The heavy slugs tore the plate apart and pounded huge dents in the metal door itself. After a few seconds of fire, Tarq turned toward his brother and nodded. Then he hurled himself at the stricken door.

The entire room shook as his massive weight slammed into the straining iron. The door rattled and almost gave way, the broken remnants of the lock almost breaking. But it held—barely. He took a deep breath and pulled back, throwing himself once again at the door, even harder than the first time.

The metal groaned for an instant before the lock shattered and the door slammed open. Tarq went tumbling through the now-open portal, landing hard on the stone floor inside the room.

Blackhawk ran in right behind. Tarq's solution wasn't elegant, but Blackhawk couldn't argue with its effectiveness. "Are you okay?" he yelled, as he hurried over to his crewman.

"Yeah, Captain." Tarq was picking himself up slowly. "Shoulder hurts a little, but no big deal."

Tarnan had walked in behind the two, and he was facing to the side, holding his massive blade watchfully over a single man sitting on a bench.

Blackhawk turned to face the prisoner. He was wearing a pair of canvas trousers and a matching tunic, clearly some kind of prison uniform. His blond hair was long and filthy, twisted into large clumps that hung about his face. He looked up at the newcomers, his blue eyes bright and defiant despite his situation.

"Who are you?" Blackhawk demanded, holding up his hand and motioning for Tarnan to pull his blade back. The man did not look threatening, though he bore himself with a certain stature, despite his position.

"I am Gustav Algonquin. The king of Nordlingen."

CHAPTER 18

AUGUSTIN LUCERNE SAT ON THE EDGE OF HIS BED, RUBBING HIS face with his hands. Maximus, the larger of Celtiboria's two moons, was high in the night sky, and his windows glowed with its reflected light. It had been even brighter earlier, but Minimus had since set, leaving its larger sibling to stand watch alone until dawn's first rays.

Lucerne knew morning wasn't far, barely an hour. He'd always struggled to sleep, but things had only gotten worse since his final victory on Celtiboria. So long it had been his goal, the driving force of his existence, yet its attainment had produced so little joy—and no rest, no peace. Only a sharpened focus of all that remained to be done. There were so many wars to fight, so much treachery to counter, endless terms to negotiate.

He'd expected some of it, but other problems had taken him by surprise. When his wars had been restricted to his home world, he'd been close to his officers and men. He'd shared their risks, their deprivations. But now his armies were scattered across light-years of space. Their losses—their pain—were now reduced to words on an endless stream of reports. He hated the pointless luxury of the palace, despised the meetings, loathed the diplomats. He wished he could walk through the door, to lead his men in the field as he had for three decades. But duty was still his master, and it had taken him from the battlefield and cast him into the webs of ambassadors, politicians, and businessmen.

Rest had always been elusive, but now it had become a forgotten dream. He'd slept some, two hours in total perhaps, though as usual it had been fitful and broken into short stretches. He was tired. Indeed, he'd never felt so worn, so used up. So old. Yet sleep still played its frustrating game with him.

The worries weighed on him, more even than usual. His armies had fought with their accustomed courage and success, but some of them had run into greater resistance than expected. He wasn't concerned about the final outcomes of those battles. He had every confidence his people would prevail. But he mourned the extra losses, thousands more dead soldiers than he'd anticipated. And he was troubled by the unknown. Someone was opposing him, interfering with his campaigns. He wasn't sure who it was, but he'd considered every reasonable option, and every one of them was bad news.

Either one of his allies, one of the other Primes, was conspiring against him, dangling support in his face as a distraction, while supporting his opponents secretly—or it was the empire. He found it disillusioning, though not really surprising, that one of the Primes would stab him in the back, despite assurances of solidarity. They were the strongest worlds in the Far Stars, and a successful confederation would foster sectorwide development. The lesser worlds would gain prosperity, and they would lose their dependence on the six great planets that dominated the economy of the Far Stars.

He'd even wondered if it was Antilles. The economic powerhouse had the most to lose in terms of dominating commerce, but Lucerne had addressed that, offering Danellan Lancaster and his planet the lead role in developing the lesser worlds. He'd given them a virtual license to steal, the price of their support. It made him sick to do it, but he'd long ago realized that sacrifices were essential to greater success.

It didn't make it any easier to swallow. He was trying to free the Far Stars, not replace military dictators with economic ones.

Perhaps his one comfort was that, as far as his intelligence had been able to confirm, none of the Primes had the technology to produce the weapons his soldiers had faced. He obviously couldn't be 100 percent sure, but his gut told him it wasn't one of the Primes, or even an alliance of several. Which had his mind drifting back over and over to the same ominous thought: the empire was trying to oppose the confederation before it even took shape. He had always feared that the empire would one day look again to the Far Stars and seek to bring its people under the emperor's heel, and that was why he had started this war in the first place. But if the empire had already begun its campaign, before he was ready to stop it . . .

Blackhawk will discover what is going on. He brought Astra back to me, and he will help me yet again.

Lucerne rose slowly. Sleep was truly over for the night, that much was clear to him. He walked across the room to the large table in the corner. It was the field desk he'd used on campaign, and now it was set up in his room, an odd sight amid the splendor of the great palace.

He had a massive office elsewhere in the building, surrounded by attendants and support staff, but he did much of his work here. He'd acceded to the demands of his position in almost every area of his life, but he'd made one concession to himself. In his inner sanctum, the room where he slept, where he worked when he needed solitude, all but a few close associates were banned. When he toiled in his refuge or took a meal as he worked at the old field desk, only men who had served with him in his wars attended his needs. It was the last special relationship he had with them. Ambassadors and political hacks had claimed much of his time, but he had reserved at least some of his moments for those who truly mattered to him.

He punched a small button on the table, and his screen came to life. Another report from General DeMark. Blackhawk had arrived on Nordlingen. He had been too late on Rykara. Whoever was behind the intervention there had already covered his tracks. Lucerne tried to imagine what his enemies had said to the feuding nobles to convince them to cast aside their arguments and join against the Celtiborians. It was a war they could never have won, even with the advanced weaponry their backers provided.

It doesn't really matter, I guess. They were always pawns in the struggle, useful but expendable, but they'd listened to lies, and they'd paid the price.

The battle on Nordlingen was still raging, though, and those in command would still be there, directing their armies. Perhaps Blackhawk would have more luck there.

He looked back at the report . . . and read about Blackhawk's plan. Lucerne reread the passage three times, and he stared at the screen in disbelief.

I knew Blackhawk was daring, but this . . . it's downright reckless. And yet, if anyone can manage it . . .

"Callas!" he yelled loudly for his aide. He turned and walked across the room, opening a door and walking into his dressing room.

"Sir!" The surprised officer was rushing through the door. He stopped and stood at attention.

Lucerne was pulling on a pair of uniform trousers. The council of advisers had retained a valet for him, a man named Dumont, who had served one of the now deceased warlords for a decade. But Augustin Lucerne had been dressing himself for almost sixty years, and that was not about to change anytime soon. He'd tasked the attendant with keeping his laundry clean and pressed, but that had been the extent of the duties he'd assigned.

"Callas, advise Admiral Desaix to prepare a ship. I am going to Nordlingen. Immediately." He pulled a perfectly pressed shirt from the rack and put it on.

"Marshal, sir, the council will . . ."

"Callas, the day I ask the council for permission to do what I feel I must is the day I blow my brains out. Understood?"

"Yes, Marshal." Callas paused for a few seconds. "Shall I awaken Dumont and have him pack for you, sir?"

"Yes, Callas. Thank you." Lucerne was buttoning his jacket. "And tell the admiral he may assign an escort squadron, but I do not want him dispatching the entire fleet to nursemaid me. There is enough already for them to handle."

"Yes, Marshal."

"And Callas?"

"Yes, sir?"

"I want to leave today. And I'd like to slip out without Astra knowing if possible. She'll insist on coming, and after what happened, I'd really prefer she stay here where it is safer."

"Yes, sir, I will try to keep it quiet. But you know Miss Astra, sir."

An odd smile crept onto Lucerne's face. Astra had been a handful since the days when she'd followed him around his command post, sharing her chocolate bars with him. His daughter was headstrong, and intelligent. And she damned sure didn't take no for an answer. She was a colossal pain in the ass sometimes—and he couldn't be prouder of her.

But he still intended to try and slip away.

"I know the *Repulse* left orbit this morning. And I can't find my father anywhere. Or Callas, either." Astra Lucerne's voice was loud and deadly serious. She didn't carry an official rank, but there were few in the Celtiborian military with the courage to defy her.

The duty officer was entirely out of his depth trying to stand up to the marshal's fiery daughter, but he had his orders and he was doing his best to carry them out.

"I am sorry, Miss Lucerne, but I have no information on that at present." His voice was a little shaky, but he was doing as good a job stonewalling her as any of her father's officers could manage.

Which isn't all that good.

"Then I suggest you log into the network and access the *Repulse*'s flight plan." She stood less than a meter away, staring at him with ice blue eyes. She wore the usual pistol, hanging low on her hip like some gunslinger's weapon, and her hand was on her waist, just a few centimeters above. Everyone in the army knew she was a crack shot.

The officer took a step back, but he just repeated what he had already said. "I am sorry, but I am not authorized to release that information at this time." His nerves were clearly strained. Still, he stood his ground.

Astra held her stare. She wasn't about to shoot one of her father's officers, or even threaten one at gunpoint. She'd done that to Lucas Lancaster on the *Claw,* but that had been an extraordinary circumstance, and Ark's life had been on the line. And even Lucas had been sure she wouldn't really shoot him, just like the officer standing in front of her now knew she wouldn't.

"Aaagh!" she yelled, voicing her frustration. She knew she couldn't get too angry with the officer for following her father's orders, but that didn't mean she couldn't be angry at all. She turned and stormed out of the command center and into the hallway.

Where the hell did he go?

She knew *why* her father had slipped away. He'd been doting on her ever since Blackhawk had brought her home. She couldn't get too angry with him, either. After all, she had been kidnapped and taken away to a lawless backwater on the edge of civilization. If it hadn't been for Blackhawk, she might have died there or spent the rest of her life as a captive. She knew her father loved her, and she couldn't begin to imagine how worried and scared he'd been while she was gone.

I get all that . . . and couldn't care less.

She couldn't live that way. It's just not how she was wired. Astra Lucerne was her father's daughter, in more ways than one. She didn't hide from her enemies; she faced them head-on. And she didn't cower under guard from danger. No matter how much her father—or Blackhawk, for that matter—tried to protect her from the realities of the world.

And that's where the frustration really came from. She had two of the strongest, most dangerous men in the Far Stars trying to protect her and keep her safe. She loved them both, but she had no intention of letting either one of them get away with it. They were both off somewhere again, probably getting themselves into trouble, and she'd be damned if she was going to stay behind under lock and key while the two people she loved most in the world were in danger.

She was walking down the corridor, back toward the suite of offices she shared with Lys. She was going to find out where her father went if she had to hack into the main data system to find out. And then, by Chrono, she was going to follow him if she had to steal a ship to do it.

Because wherever he went, I bet a million crowns I find Blackhawk there, too.

CHAPTER 19

ZEL CROUCHED DOWN, DUCKING BEHIND THE LOW RIDGE. HIS TWO companies, together barely two-thirds the size of a single full-strength unit, were drawn up behind the ridge. They had been advancing all night, and now the first rays of dawn were casting a tentative light across the field.

The enemy capital city stretched out before his position, its battle-scarred skyline standing defiantly, as the enemy soldiers prepared to mount a last-ditch defense.

The Nordlingeners had been trying to break off since the previous night, but Zel's people—and the rest of the Celtiborian army—had been pushing hard, keeping them engaged, staying on their heels all the way back to the city and denying them the chance to regroup. The Celtiborians were exhausted, and their losses had been brutal, but they could taste victory.

"Captain Zel, are your people ready?" It was Colonel Martine on the comm.

"Yes, sir." Zel slipped forward, lying flat on the half-frozen ground and staring cautiously over the ridge. "We've just been resupplied, and we're ready to advance." Ready was a relative term. His people were tired and hungry and cold. But they knew winning battles was mostly a matter of timing. They had the enemy on the run. If they let the Nordlingeners reorganize, thousands more of their comrades would die in attacks against a resupplied and entrenched enemy. If they pushed themselves now, tapped into that inner power that had won them so many battles before, they could end it.

"Okay, Captain. Your people are opposite the royal sector. When we advance, I want you to slice through the enemy lines and head straight for the palace. Don't worry about your flanks. Benz and Altavon are covering your advance."

"Understood, Colonel."

"We'll be attacking in half an hour, Captain, so if you hurry, there should be time to get a quick meal for your men."

"I'll see to it sir." That was the least they deserved.

"And, Captain?" There was a hint of hesitancy in Martine's usually assured voice.

"Sir?"

"Try not to take the palace apart when you attack. I have word from HQ." The colonel paused. "Apparently, Arkarin Blackhawk and his people are in there on some kind of mission for Marshal Lucerne."

Fuck. How am I supposed to take the palace without wasting whoever is in there?

Zel had never met Blackhawk, but he knew the adventurer was one of the marshal's closest comrades. And from what he'd heard, the captain of *Wolf's Claw* had long been a friend to the entire Celtiborian army.

"Understood, sir. We'll be careful. Zel out."

He took a deep breath, and hit the comm unit on his collar. "Sergeant Havers, we've got about half an hour before the attack now. Let's make good use of it. Get a quick breakfast going."

Katarina slipped down the hall swiftly, silently, with Shira right behind. The main power was still out, but the backup systems were engaged. The rooms and corridors all had the same dim light.

They'd explored most of the upper level, and they'd found it to be almost deserted. There had been more shooting, but the sounds had all come from downstairs. Katarina's first reaction had been to head to the sound of the fighting, but the mission was to find the king, and he was as likely to be upstairs as down. Besides, Blackhawk and the Twins—not to mention Sarge and his boys—could take care of themselves.

The two women had stumbled onto a few guards, but they'd gradually come to realize most of the enemy strength was downstairs. The few sentries they'd encountered on the upper floor had been easily—and silently—dispatched. Shira's heavy blade and Katarina's slim and deadly throwing knives had found their marks without fail.

"It's too empty up here," Shira whispered softly. "And not just because everybody rushed downstairs. It doesn't look like it's been used in a long time. It's dusty. It feels almost abandoned."

"I agree. But the king's quarters are up here. If he hasn't been living up here . . ." Katarina stopped and turned back toward Shira. "Do you think he moved his headquarters? That we're wasting our time here?"

"I don't know. But something's not right." Shira's voice was full of concern. "And there's some kind of fight going on. Maybe we should . . ."

Katarina was nodding. "Let's find out what is going on down there." She glanced down the hall. "The main stair was back that way. Do we chance it?"

Shira took a quick look behind her. "Either that or back the way we came." The two had scaled an abandoned old shaft leading up from the service area, an ancient dumbwaiter or laundry chute. It hadn't been fast or pleasant, and it was all the way on the other side of the building. But they hadn't passed another set of steps or an elevator except the main stairway.

Katarina paused a few seconds. Her training told her to find another way, to remain hidden as long as possible. But she wasn't a lone wolf assassin right now. She was part of a team, and the rest of that team—of her family—were likely fighting for their lives right now. She reached around, pulled the carbine from her back. "Let's go. If this is a wild goose chase—or worse, a trap—we need to get everybody out of here."

Shira nodded. She already had her two assault rifles in her hands, and a look of cold death on her face. Her readiness said it all.

The two spun around and moved back the way they had come. Knowing the way had been cleared with their first go-through, their pace had quickened significantly. They had to get to the others, and if that meant fighting their way through half the guards in the city, so be it.

Shira was in the front now, and she slipped out into the broad upper hall. The grand foyer was below, and the main stair was a curved affair, carved from pure marble and at least three meters wide. Two guards were on duty just inside the main door, but she couldn't see anyone else.

She turned back to Katarina, holding up two fingers. The Sebastiani assassin just nodded. Shira slipped one of her rifles onto her back and carefully aimed the other. She paused an instant and then put a bullet in the rightmost guard's head. Half a second later, she dropped the other. Then she sprang to her feet, running down the stairs, whipping the second rifle from her back as she did.

The two women raced down, their heads snapping around, peering into the adjoining rooms, looking for any enemies. There was a man walking through what looked like a reception room. From the angle, Katarina couldn't tell if he was a guard or a household servant. She didn't relish the idea of blowing away some handyman or butler, but there was no time for second-guessing in action. She dropped him with a single shot.

They reached the bottom of the stairs and turned in opposite directions, scouting out the area and supporting each other's blind spots. "Clear," Shira snapped, with all the harsh certainty of a veteran sergeant.

"Clear," came Katarina's reply, somewhat softer, but just as decisive.

"So where do we . . ." The buzz of Shira's comm unit interrupted her question. Her hand darted up and activated the unit. "Shira," she said simply.

"Shira, it's Ark. Listen carefully. We've got the king, but we're trapped in the dungeon level. I need you to hook up with Sarge and get down here and help us bust out. I've activated my transponder. You can follow it to our position. But we can only keep it on for short bursts, because it's a damned road map for every guard in the place, too." She could tell he was distracted, and she could hear the sounds of gunfire in the background. "And call Lucas. Tell him to have the *Claw* ready."

"Got it, Ark. We're on the way." She heard the click as he signed off. "You heard the captain," she said to Katarina.

She turned back toward the main arch leading deeper into the palace. She took one foot forward . . .

And all hell broke loose.

At least a dozen guards were pouring into the corridor ahead of her. They'd been headed somewhere, probably down to the dungeon where Blackhawk was holed up. But they stopped on a dime when they saw two women standing in the foyer, armed to the teeth.

Shira whipped up her arms and started firing both guns on full auto, diving for cover as she did. Katarina had beat her to it, though, and two of the guards were already down, each with small, smooth holes in their heads from the assassin's carbine.

Then the rest of the enemy troops opened fire.

"General DeMark, the enemy forces have retreated back to Nordlingen City. They have assumed defensive positions around the perimeter of the urban area, and Colonel Martine is spearheading the final assault." Varne's voice was hoarse, but it was loud and clear too. The aide had been at his post since the attack began over thirty-six hours before—everyone in the command post had. The soldiers in the field had been fighting that long, and DeMark would be damned if any of his support staff would do less than the troopers advancing against enemy fire. He knew every one of his people agreed.

"Any word from Blackhawk or *Wolf's Claw*?"

Varne sighed softly. "No, sir." He hesitated a few seconds

then added, "But *Wolf's Claw* wouldn't break radio silence until they got Blackhawk's signal anyway."

DeMark knew that was true . . . but he also knew they should have gotten that signal by now. He didn't think it would help anything to say it out loud, though. They'd all expected to hear something from Blackhawk sooner than this, and his hope faded with every passing minute.

"Advise Colonel Martine to exert extreme caution if his people reach the palace." Blackhawk might have taken one risk too many and finally gotten himself killed, but DeMark was damned if it would be his friendly fire that took down the legendary adventurer.

"I already forwarded that directive, sir."

"Well, send it again," DeMark roared. He knew he was just working through his own frustration. He'd heard Varne warn Martine twice already, and he was well aware his men only needed to receive an order once. But he felt helpless being stuck in his command post while his men were fighting and Blackhawk and his people were missing behind enemy lines. Rafaelus DeMark was a combat soldier, and in his heart he longed to be in the field with his men. But he was also the commander of the entire expeditionary force, and his closest replacement was fourteen light-years away.

Rank has its privileges . . . and its shackles.

"Message confirmed, General." Varne's confirmation was crisp.

DeMark's eyes drifted down to the small screen on his workstation. He pulled up the list of units held in reserve. It was a pointless exercise. He knew exactly what the screen would show him, but he confirmed it nevertheless. He'd committed every fresh formation but one: the Forty-Eighth Regiment. It was positioned ten kilometers behind the line, loaded up on the last of his trucks and waiting for the order to move forward.

He'd waited, keeping them back while the men strained at the leash to reinforce their comrades. Marshal Lucerne was the greatest military genius in the Far Stars, and he had taught his officers well. And the number one rule, the paramount maxim for winning battles, was to be the last to commit your final reserve. He was pretty sure the enemy had everything they had in the fight, but he couldn't be sure. And the wisdom of holding something back seemed even more profound on a planet light-years away from home.

But Marshal Lucerne also knew just when to launch the final blow, to throw everything into the fight to win the final victory. And DeMark's gut was screaming, *Now!*

Or never.

"The Forty-Eighth will advance and support Colonel Martine's assault," he ordered. "All units along the line are ordered to attack, and no one is to halt until every square centimeter of Nordlingen City is ours."

"Yes, sir." It was clear from Varne's tone he approved. Then again, it was easy to vote for courage and aggression when you weren't in command. But DeMark suspected a titanic victory and a crushing defeat looked eerily similar to each other at this stage.

Now we just hope I'm right, and that the enemy doesn't have a last trick up his sleeve.

Because I'm completely played out.

"You okay?" Shira yelled across the foyer to Katarina. Katarina wanted to ask her the same thing, considering Shira herself had taken a flesh wound to the arm. It didn't seem too serious, but it had been enough to knock her down to a single rifle.

"I'm fine." Katarina had taken cover behind a heavy marble statue next to the stairs. She glanced across to Shira, who had ducked behind the doorway leading to a small drawing room.

The two had been much quicker to react than the surprised guards, and they'd taken most of them down in the first seconds, before the soldiers regained their composure and reacted. By then, Shira and Katarina had gotten behind cover, firing all the while.

The problem was, while there were only four guards left by the time they too had gotten out of the line of fire—and two of those were down now—another four had arrived since.

"We can't stay here. My ammo's running low, and they'll just get more support," Shira yelled to her comrade, her deep voice loud and clear, even over the din of battle.

"Agreed." Katarina didn't look like the tough customer Shira often did, but that was pure illusion. Katarina Venturi was the most relentless killing machine on the *Claw,* save possibly for Blackhawk. "Be ready in three."

She reached behind her and pulled a grenade from her belt. It wasn't the usual light frag model; it was a high-powered incendiary, normally used on the field, not in the confines of a building.

Screw it.

She was done with being pinned down and helpless.

"Two."

She set the timer for six seconds, and she put her finger in the pin, flashing a last glance across the foyer to Shira.

"One. Get down."

She pulled the pin and threw the grenade hard through the archway. It landed deep into the room, well behind the guards.

"Be ready to go," she shouted to Shira, and she slipped back behind the statue.

She counted down in her head. *Three, two, one.* The explosion shook the entire palace, and a jet of flame billowed into the foyer, blowing the front door out and bringing a chunk of the ceiling down.

The heat was almost unbearable, and the rooms around them were on fire, everything flammable burning fiercely. The oxygen had been sucked out of the room, and it was a few seconds before Katarina could even take a long and tortured breath. "Now. Let's go."

She swung around from behind the statue and ran past the fires and through the archway, her carbine in front of her, the last clip in place. She could see Shira at her side, her shirt ripped and a bright sheen of blood on her upper arm where she'd been hit.

Her eyes darted wildly from left to right, searching for live enemies. But the instant she saw the first body, she knew there were no guards left alive. The twisted, blackened thing still had a vague resemblance to a human being, but only if you really paid attention.

The room was ablaze, and burned bits of moldings and other fixtures were falling to the ground. "Let's get the hell out of here," Shira said, still scanning the area for enemies. "According to the last transponder reading, Ark and the Twins are on the lower level and somewhere to the right of us. We'll have to wait until they signal again to get a more precise reading."

Katarina nodded and turned down the hallway. "All we need to do is find a way down there, then."

"Already on it. Sarge," she said into her comm, "Shira here. Do you read me?"

"I read you. What's going on? It sounded like an asteroid just hit the palace."

"Close. A heavy incendiary. No time for that now. The captain needs us. He's in the dungeon, and we're looking for the way down. Lock into my transponder, and hook up with us as soon as you can."

There was a pause, while Sarge got a fix on her signal. "We're close to you. We should be able to catch up in a few minutes. But how do we get to the captain?"

"I don't know, Sarge," she said, "but it'll be easier to look if we're able to move through the building in force. Just get here ASAP."

"Roger that."

Blackhawk stood just inside the cell door, peering cautiously around the edge. His fire had been deadly accurate, and half a dozen fresh bodies lay in the hallway, guards who had been careless enough to peer around the corner. And yet, it was a standoff, and the enemy would only get stronger, and Blackhawk and the Twins would run out of ammunition. Soon.

A war of attrition definitely *isn't in our favor.*

"Let's get a barricade in front of this opening." There was no way to shut the door. Tarq had torn the hinges from the frame when he smashed through. The door itself lay bent and twisted in the middle of the floor. "When we run out of ammunition, they'll rush us for sure. And we'll be down to blades."

Tarnan leaned down and picked up one end of the door, dragging it slowly toward the opening. He was careful not to expose himself, in case any of the enemy dared look around again.

Blackhawk turned back toward the captive monarch. "So you are King Gustav." It was more a statement than a question. Blackhawk didn't doubt the man was Nordlingen's monarch. "How did you end up in your own dungeon?"

"Treachery," he spat. "How do all such things come to pass?" There was deep resignation in his voice, and below that, a smoldering rage that Blackhawk understood all too well.

There was a loud crash. Tarnan had leaned the door sideways across the entry. He and his brother had moved to the bench on the far wall, the two of them straining to pull its brackets free of the wall. It was a close battle, but the rivets hadn't been enough to withstand the combined strength of the Twins. When it finally came free, though, they both fell back, and the heavy metal plank landed hard on the ground.

Blackhawk had spun around instinctively at the crash, but after a quick glance down the hall he turned back toward the king. He'd seen the awesome power of the Twins before, and he wasn't surprised that they'd pulled the rivets right from the wall. The king was another matter, however, and he stared in astonishment, eyes wide and mouth hanging open.

"Don't worry about them. They are harmless. Unless you piss them off." It was an odd time for a joke, but Blackhawk couldn't help but smile. He turned again. "Cover the door, guys. I'm going to have a talk with the king."

"Got it, Cap."

Blackhawk stared right at Gustav. "Treachery?" he asked, picking up where they had left off. "What kind of treachery."

"We had a visitor. He offered us weapons, money, technology . . . all to fight the Celtiborians. He told us Marshal Lucerne would enslave us if he conquered Nordlingen, that he would sell our children as slaves, take our women to his harem and his soldiers' brothels. That our only hope was resistance to the end."

Half a dozen shots rang out. The king's head snapped around abruptly, but Tarq's voice boomed, "One of the bastards showed his ugly face, boss. All taken care of. It's even uglier now."

"You were saying?" Blackhawk stared at the king. "It's okay," he said, trying to reassure the king. "Tarq and Tarnan can hold the doorway. At least for now." *I shouldn't have added that last bit. It's true, but not very helpful. Too late.* "Please, go on."

Gustav looked terrified, but he managed to keep his composure. "I refused. I had heard other things about the marshal, and I believed we could negotiate with him, that his forces would not attack us if we yielded and agreed to join his Confederation. That his actions were for the good of the entire sector and not bids for conquest and power. One of my aides, Thimolenes, had spent time on Celtiboria. He told me how Lucerne had treated other honorable foes who had yielded. I was prepared to treat with his envoys."

"Your aide was right. Augustin Lucerne is an honest man. One of the few I have ever known." Blackhawk's eyes were boring into the king's, trying to decide if he believed the man. He decided he did, and the familiar feeling of the AI chiming in supported his decision.

Visual analysis suggests 85 percent chance the subject Gustav is speaking honestly.

"Thimolenes is dead now." Gustav's voice increased in volume. "Which left my prime minister, Davanos, to conspire behind my back. He met secretly with the visitor, obtaining the promised support, and when he had received it, he launched a coup against me. The visitor had provided him with soldiers from off-world, and they overwhelmed my loyal guards. I was taken by surprise and imprisoned. They have ruled ever since in my name."

Blackhawk glanced back toward the door. The Twins were

still firing the occasional burst, maintaining the uneasy status quo between the opposing forces. He knew time was running out, but wasn't sure what to do except wait until the others arrived—and hope the ammunition held out long enough. He flipped the switch on the transponder, sending out another burst. *C'mon, Katarina . . . hurry.*

He looked at the king. "Are you saying the population at large does not know you were deposed?"

"No. That is why Davanos did not kill me. They have compelled me to appear for broadcasts to make the people and the army believe I am commanding them to battle." His voice had a sharp edge, and Blackhawk could see that his fists were clenched.

Gustav stared at Blackhawk. "They drugged me, and they used the computers to synthesize my voice." He slammed his fist down onto the bench. "I would never have cooperated with them. *Never.* I would have died first."

Blackhawk was surprised at the king's reactions. He'd seen so many monarchs and dictators in the Far Stars and, other than Lucerne, he'd judged few to be worthy of their positions. Blackhawk almost universally distrusted those in positions of power. He knew from long experience how badly they abused their authority—how brutal he himself had been when the pursuit of power had been his life as well.

Augustin Lucerne was a rare breed of man, and now Blackhawk began to wonder if King Gustav had a spark of the same thing that made the Celtiborian marshal a man worth following.

> **Estimate now 93 percent probability subject is speaking honestly in gross. Analysis based on eye movement, word selection, and emotionality**

> displayed in posture and vocal tone. Increase
> in probability due to wider range of moods now
> displayed by subject.

That, coupled with his own gut, made Blackhawk conclude something he rarely thought: *I think I trust this man.*

"Cap, we're both down to our last belts." Tarnan was slamming the heavy magazine into his autocannon. His brother was on the other side of the open doorway, already halfway through his last reload. "If we're going to make a move, it's got to be now."

Damn. Can we surprise them? Can we make it down the hall to close combat range? He wasn't sure. His gut told him the odds were against it. Still, there wasn't another choice. Once the enemy realized they were out of ammunition, they'd storm the room. They had to do something now, before their guns ran completely dry.

"All right, boys, we charge in one minute. Fire everything you've got on the way down, and then it's hand to hand."

The Twins both nodded. "Yes, Captain," they said, almost in perfect unison.

Blackhawk turned back toward the king. "I'm sorry we couldn't arrange a better rescue, but this is your chance for freedom. You can stay in here too . . . they will probably spare you, at least for now."

Gustav got up slowly. "I am with you."

Blackhawk felt a rush of respect for the monarch. "We haven't been properly introduced. I am Arkarin Blackhawk, commander of the vessel *Wolf's Claw,* and an emissary of Marshal Augustin Lucerne."

"It is my pleasure, Captain Blackhawk." The king extended his hand.

Blackhawk reached out and grasped the king's hand for a few seconds. Then he started walking toward the Twins. He took two steps and turned back. He handed his rifle to Gustav. "You may need this, Your Highness."

Gustav took the rifle and nodded his thanks. Blackhawk reached down to his side and pulled out his heavy pistol. His hand tightened around the well-worn grip.

"All right, men. It is ti—"

He was interrupted by a blast of static. "Ark, we're almost there." It was Shira on the comm. An instant later the sound of gunfire erupted in the corridors.

Blackhawk smiled. "The cavalry is here." He turned his head and glanced at the other three men. Then he looked back through the door. "Let's go, boys.

"Charge!"

CHAPTER 20

"ENTERING NORMAL SPACE, CAPTAIN."

"Very well, Ensign. Proceed." Captain Jonas Flint sat quietly at his station.

He felt the usual feeling, a brief fluttering in his stomach. It was almost nothing. He wouldn't even call it nausea. As symptoms of the hyperbarrier transition went, he could hardly complain. He'd seen far worse among his crew. Indeed, he'd never forget what he saw on his first cruise, a lifetime ago.

He'd joined the merchant service with his childhood friend, Ernesto. They had heard horror stories about bleeding eyes and projectile vomiting—spacers liked to give the rookies a hard time. But when it was over, Flint had hardly noticed the slight feeling in his gut. Then he turned to his friend, and he knew immediately.

Ernesto had been one of the 0.87 percent of space travelers completely unable to adapt to entry into hyperspace. Flint remembered every detail as if it had been yesterday—his friend's cold, dead eyes staring back at him, a constant reminder of the inherent danger of space travel . . .

"The fleet has transited, Captain. All vessels report normal operation."

Flint glanced down at the screen. His ships had held their positions well during the voyage. It wouldn't take more than twenty minutes to get them all in formation. "Proceed with fleet maneuvers. Plot a course in-system."

This was his second run to Nordlingen. There had been rumors flying around back on Buchhara before they'd embarked, tales of invasion and war. He'd half expected the voyage to be canceled, but the loading continued, and when it was done, he got the clearance to set out. He'd assumed the rumors of strife on Nordlingen were just that. If he had an imperial crown for every piece of pure bullshit that flew around in spacers' bars, he'd be as rich as the Lancasters.

The name Lancaster had become synonymous in the Far Stars with wealth, but now Flint had a different perspective. The word had just come down, and it had proven another set of wild rumors to be true. Old man Vestron had finally sold the company, and to the money-grubbing Lancasters of all people.

The Vestron family had started with a single ship, two centuries before, and space travel had been in their blood for generations. Indeed, until forty or fifty years before, it had been the custom for each new generation of Vestrons to put in their time aboard the company's freighters. But like all such things, the fire that drove success waned, and the Vestrons took to wild decadence and feuding with one another while the family business faltered.

A sale had become inevitable, and there were only so many companies large enough to absorb Vestron Shipping. The transport guilds would never allow one of the other big shippers to consolidate so much power, so that left even fewer potential suitors. But Lancaster Interests had a culture utterly foreign to Vestron, at least to Flint's way of thinking. The Lancasters had nothing in their blood but money. To them, shipping was just another product or service, no different than mining or electronics. Nothing more than figures on a spreadsheet.

Flint knew it had been years since the Vestrons had been anything different, but the spirit of past generations still infused the company, at least to the old salts like him. Flint's own father, and his grandfather before, had commanded Vestron freighters, and he'd grown up on tales of family scions manning bridge stations on the company's vast ships. Now this proud old firm was nothing but a single division in the vast monster that was Lancaster Interests.

And everything was already changing.

Flint thought of his son, who was on his second voyage, a milk run from Sebastiani to Antilles. He'd raised his son as he had been brought up, on tradition and old spacers' stories, but he knew his future grandchildren would grow up a different way. The Far Stars were changing, and not for the better in Flint's view. Everything that had once mattered had faded away, and a new, harsher reality had taken hold.

"The fleet is in formation, Captain. Awaiting your orders."

The mate's voice brought Flint out of his aimless musings. Deep philosophy was for others, for academics and wealthy men with too much time on their hands. Flint was a working senior captain, in command not only of his own vessel, but of all six in the fleet.

I'll let others play the politics, and I'll keep my mind on the only thing that's ever mattered about this business: flying through space.

"Proceed to Nordlingen. Approach speed." The only occupied planet in the system was close to the guild transit point. They'd be in orbit in twelve hours if nothing went wrong, and unloaded a day after that. This was a one-sided run, and there was no cargo to load up, so his people would be on their way in two days, three days maximum. Then it would be back to Buchhara, and a well-deserved leave. He closed his eyes and imagined his wife, her thick hair, brown, but with a coppery tint, especially in Buchhara's setting red sun. Spacefarers missing their wives was as old as travel between the stars, but that didn't make it less real. Flint was a creature of space, a man raised from birth to ply the trading lanes. But as he got older he longed more and more for the comforts of home.

That too, he imagined, was as old as space travel itself.

"Contacts, sir. Six vessels inbound, bearing 321.098.145." The officer manning the scope was young. Ensign Harcourt was fresh out of the academy and on her first cruise. She'd conducted herself with admirable calm since joining *Warrington's* crew, but the sighting of six unidentified vessels had pushed her past what a rookie bridge officer could hide, and her tone advertised her excitement.

"Full scan, Ensign." Captain Jeran Nortel's voice was calm itself. Nortel had twenty years of service in space, first for the warlord Carteria, and then for Augustin Lucerne. The transition had been a rough one. Nortel was a loyal sort, and Lucerne had personally beheaded his old master. He'd found it hard to swear allegiance to the man who'd killed his employer, but when Carteria the Younger signed the peace accord with Lucerne, Nortel felt he could follow with at least some degree of honor. It had taken him years to realize he'd served a monster and that fortune had finally smiled on him and brought forth a leader he could respect and obey with all his heart.

"They appear to be freighters, Captain. They are broadcasting Vestron Shipping credentials."

Nortel frowned. *Who doesn't know we've blockaded Nordlingen?* He took a deep breath. "Ensign, report the contacts to Commodore Jardaines immediately. And set up a comm channel with the lead vessel."

"Yes, sir." Harcourt looked down at her controls, forwarding the scanner data to Jardaines's flagship.

Nortel sighed. *Constellation* was almost five light-minutes distant, so it would be at least ten minutes before the fleet commander was able to respond. Until then, Nortel was in command. Of the situation, and of any diplomatic repercussions. For all practical purposes, he was the personal representative of Marshal Lucerne, at least for a few minutes.

Diplomacy isn't really my strong suit. But let's give it a try . . .

"I have an active channel, sir."

He reached down and pressed the button to activate his commlink. "Attention incoming spacecraft. This is Captain Nortel, commanding the Celtiborian naval vessel *Warrington*. The planet Nordlingen has been declared a war zone, and all traffic in and out is forbidden. Vessels entering this system without authorization are subject to search and seizure. You are instructed to cut your engines and prepare to be boarded."

"*Warrington*, this Captain Jonas Flint. Captain Nortel, my

vessels are guild-bonded transports sailing under the flag of Vestron Shipping. We are not hostiles, and we have no involvement in any battles currently taking place. I invoke guild rights and refuse any boarding of my vessels."

Nortel paused. He didn't want to explain to the commodore—or Chrono forbid, the marshal—why he'd picked a fight with the trading guilds. But he wanted even less to explain why he hadn't followed his orders, and those were clear.

"I am sorry, Captain Flint. I understand your position, but your vessels have entered the proscribed zone. Guild protection does not supersede the rights of combatants in a war zone. I have no choice but to conduct a full inspection of your cargo, after which, if no contraband is found, you will be allowed to leave the system freely."

Nortel hit the button, muting the comm line. He looked over at Harcourt. "Bring the ship to General Quarters, Ensign."

"Yes, sir."

Nortel nodded and reactivated the comm. " . . . must object, Captain Nortel," his counterpart was saying. "My personnel have no part in this conflict, and I insist you allow us to proceed with our bonded delivery."

"I'm afraid that is impossible, Captain Flint. The only option is for your vessels to comply with blockade protocols and submit to a full inspection." He paused. "If you refuse, I must advise you that we will regrettably be forced to open fire to prevent either your approach to the planet or any attempt to flee the system."

"This is an outrage, Captain. My vessels are not combatants, and . . ."

"Captain," Nortel interrupted, "you may file a complaint with your guild, or directly with the Celtiborian government if you wish, but the fact remains that I am operating under wartime rules and strict blockade protocols. I do not wish to see any of your personnel needlessly injured, so I will repeat my demand that your vessels cut power and submit to immediate boarding. Any attempt to power up hyperdrives or to evade inspection will result in our opening fire without further notice."

Nortel leaned back in his chair. *Come on, Flint . . . you don't have any choice. Don't make me fire on a bunch of civilian freighters . . .*

"Welcome aboard, Captain Nortel." Commodore Lavare Jardaines had been standing at the door to the shuttle bay, waiting for Nortel to disembark from the shuttle. What had started as a routine blockade enforcement action had quickly escalated, and Jardaines wanted to speak with his captain face-to-face.

"Thank you, sir." Nortel stopped a few meters short of the hatch and snapped the commodore a textbook salute.

It had taken him quite some time to perfect that after joining the Celtiborian forces.

"Come with me, Captain. We will go to my quarters and discuss the situation with a bit more . . . ah . . . discretion than the open landing bay offers."

"Very well, sir." Nortel slipped in alongside Jardaines and followed the commodore down the hall and to the lift.

"I understand you originally served with Carteria before transferring your allegiance to the marshal."

Nortel hesitated, uncertain if his loyalty was being questioned. "It . . . umm . . . it has been some time since I accepted Marshal Lucerne's commission, Commodore."

Jardaines suppressed a small laugh as he punched at the lift controls. "Please, Captain, I meant no offense. Indeed, all of us have served other masters before, or most at least. Marshal Lucerne began his ascent to power from the Northern Highlands, an area not known for its interplanetary dealings. As a practical matter, the veterans in the Celtiborian navy all served one or more of the old warlords."

Nortel felt foolish. He realized Jardaines was making trivial conversation until they were alone, not hurling veiled insults. Nortel knew he still had some sensitivity about his past. He had served an evil man, and he hadn't fully realized that until he'd transferred his allegiance to a worthy leader. Truth be told, he was ashamed of his days in Carteria's navy.

"I understand, sir. Of course. Yes, my prior service was to Carteria. After his final defeat, I swore my service to the marshal along with Carteria the Younger, and I received my commission in his own navy." He glanced up at the commodore. "Might I inquire as to your prior service, sir?"

"Of course, Captain. I was originally commissioned in the fleet of Bellegarin the Red." The commodore offered his subordinate a passing smile. "So you see, my old master was no less a bloodthirsty monster than yours, it would seem." He paused a few seconds. "We choose our masters to the extent fortune allows, Jeran, and even good men serve evil masters. Until Marshal Lucerne managed to break the old system, I'd venture there were few of the warlords who were not fiends in one way or another."

Nortel nodded. "So it would seem, sir. Thank Chrono the fates brought us Marshal Lucerne."

Jardaines walked out of the elevator, turning left into a long hallway. "Thank Chrono, indeed, Jeran. Augustin Lucerne is a noble man, I would wager my last breath on it." He stopped and turned, waving his hand over the entry sensor. The door slid open, and he gestured for Nortel to walk inside.

"Thank you, sir." Nortel tried to focus on his commanding officer, but he'd never been in the quarters of a flag rank officer, and he couldn't help but steal a quick look around.

"Please sit, Jeran." Jardaines gestured toward a large sofa in the middle of the room. "Can I offer you anything? Coffee? Water?"

Nortel was about to decline when he realized how dry his throat was. "Just some water, sir, if it's not too much trouble."

"Not at all, Captain." He reached over and pressed a button on the comm unit. "Hanson, a pitcher of ice water, please."

Nortel couldn't hear the orderly on the other side of the comm, but Jardaines added, "No, nothing else." The commodore moved to close the line, but then he added, "And, Hanson, tell them this time that ice means cold. If they send me another batch of tepid water, so help me I will have the entire kitchen staff on the hull cleaning particulate matter from the scanning array."

Jardaines turned to face his guest, taking a seat in a large chair opposite Nortel. "I wanted to wait until we were alone to discuss this matter." He stared at Nortel. "You know, of course, that the cargo your personnel found on the convoy consisted of contraband weapons." Jardaines paused and gazed over at the captain. "To be specific, *imperial* weapons."

Nortel stared back wordlessly for a few seconds. He knew Marshal Lucerne's Far Stars Confederation was intended to balance out the power of the empire, but throughout his life, imperial strength and brutality had always been somewhat of a theoretical fear, one consisting more of old stories and less of actual guns stacked up in the holds of ships.

"Are you sure, sir? I could tell the weapons were highly advanced, but imperial?"

"So I've been told, Captain. By no less than General DeMark, whose men have been facing enemy soldiers armed with this type of ordnance." Jardaines sat quietly for a few seconds. "Captain, I am going to get right to the point. General DeMark has ordered your ship interned, cut off from all communication with other fleet units." Jardaines could see the confused look on Nortel's face turning quickly toward defensiveness.

"Sir, I can assure you that my entire crew . . ."

"You needn't continue, Captain. General DeMark asked me to meet with you specifically to address the reasons for his decision, though I would have done so on my own, even if he hadn't." He gave Nortel a weak smile. "Captain, your crew behaved with exemplary conduct and efficiency and, indeed, I have put you and your people up for a commendation." He sighed. "However, for reasons I cannot disclose—indeed, to which I myself am not entirely privy—secrecy regarding the contents of the freighters you captured has been deemed of vital importance. Therefore, your ship will proceed immediately to Celtiboria, with the interned freighter crews accompanying you in the transport *Olsyndra*. You will maintain complete communications silence until you arrive home, at which time you will follow the directions provided by fleet command."

"Understood, sir." Nortel was still confused, but he knew how to obey orders. He sat for a few moments, as the door slid open and the steward brought in the water, setting a glass in front of him. He cued off Jardaines and stayed silent until the attendant had walked back through the door.

"Commodore?"

"Yes, Captain?"

"Does this mean the marshal was right all along? That the empire is planning a move against the Far Stars?"

Jardaines let out a long sigh. "I don't know, Jeran, I just don't know." A short pause. "But I'm not willing to bet against Marshal Lucerne being right. Are you?"

CHAPTER 21

BLACKHAWK HAD PULLED OUT HIS SWORD AND WAS MOVING down the corridor even as his shout continued to echo in the king's small cell. The Twins were right behind him, with King Gustav bringing up the rear. There was a wild gun battle raging in the hall running perpendicular to his position. The fire was much heavier from the left, where he knew his people were advancing. The surviving enemy guards were to the right, and the volume of their shooting was rapidly falling off.

"Shira, hold your fire," he shouted. *It's time to finish this*. And to do what he had planned, he needed a live prisoner.

"Got it, Ark." Her response was clipped. Clearly, she knew what Blackhawk had in mind, and she didn't like it.

He whipped around the corner, bending his knees and sinking low to the ground as he did. He could hear the enemy shots ripping by, but they went high, over his head. His eyes quickly scanned the remaining enemy fighters. There were three guards, each with assault rifles in their hands, and a fourth man standing behind, with no apparent weapon. He guessed that was the commander, and he decided to take him alive if possible.

He felt the battle trance taking him, and the strange sensation of time slowing was upon him again. It was as if his enemies moved in slow motion. His pistol recoiled hard as he fired, taking the first guard in the head. The man began to fall, but Blackhawk's attention had already shifted to the second target.

His arm moved, almost involuntarily, whipping his weapon around. The soldier was moving himself, bringing his rifle to bear on Blackhawk, but he was already too late. The deadly pistol fired again. And again. The guard fell back, his chest blown almost to shreds by the heavy rounds.

Two down.

Blackhawk's eyes were on the third guard. He brought his pistol around . . . but now *he* was too late. His enemy's rifle was almost on him. He knew he was finished, that any instant the soldier's weapon would spit out his death.

Then he heard the sound, the loud cracks of two heavy autocannons firing, the massive bullets tearing past him, taking his would-be killer in the neck and chest. The heavy projectiles tore through flesh and bone, and they almost decapitated the guard. He crumpled to the ground in a spray of blood, dropping the weapon that had come so close to ending Blackhawk's long and bizarre career.

He didn't dwell on it. Instead, his eyes snapped back toward the last of the enemy, and he lurched up to his feet, lunging forward. The man was turning hard, trying to flee toward the door behind him, but he froze suddenly and stared at Blackhawk.

"You!" he said, his tone a combination of surprise and fear.

Blackhawk stumbled to a halt. The hazy image in his mind crystallized, and he recognized the man almost immediately, though it had been over twenty years since he'd last seen him. He felt his stomach clench, and suddenly his mind was fighting back a wave of memories, recollections he'd fought for two decades to forget.

"Shira!" he shouted. "Get everybody out of here. NOW!"

"Captain . . . ?

"Get outside, and call Lucas to bring down the *Claw*, and get the king to General DeMark. Don't wait for me. I'll get back myself."

Shira was staring down the hallway, a startled expression on her face. "And leave you behind? Ark, we can't . . ."

"Not now, Shira! Just follow my orders!" He never addressed any of his crew so harshly, but he had no time to explain now.

Shira hesitated, but then she turned to the others. "You heard the captain. Let's move." It was clear she wasn't happy with the course of action.

I can't care what you feel about the order, Shira. Just follow it.

Blackhawk turned back to the mysterious figure, but suddenly, the corridor was filled with a thick gray cloud.

Fuck—smoke grenade! The billowing black cloud spread throughout the hallway. Blackhawk couldn't see more than a few centimeters, but he could feel the movement of the air, and he knew the man had run.

"Get back to the *Claw*, all of you!" Blackhawk screamed once more to his stunned crew, and then he was gone, chasing the mysterious enemy down the corridor.

"DeMark's people are in the city. It looks like the Nordlingener lines are breaking." Lucas was staring into his scope. Between the thrusters and the field, he had little of the *Claw*'s tremendous power available for other uses, but he committed some of the small surplus to running the scanner suite on low power.

Operating in a planet's low atmosphere created a number of challenges—the thrust requirement to offset gravity, the friction from flying in the air, the precision of flying so close to the ground—but there were a few benefits, too. It took a lot less power to scan targets a few kilometers away than it did to track enemy ships in the vast distances of space.

Ace was leaning back in his chair with his eyes closed. He felt like shit, and he was so light-headed, he felt like he'd fall out of his chair any minute. But he wasn't about to admit that to Lucas—or anyone else. If he couldn't be down in the palace with the others, this was where he belonged. And it was where he was going to stay until everyone was safely back aboard.

"I'm not surprised. I wouldn't call the Nordlingeners wogs, not exactly. But they were never going to beat Lucerne's veterans, no matter what kind of weapons they had."

Lucas nodded. "No, I don't . . ."

He was interrupted by Shira's voice blasting through the comm. "Lucas, we're coming out of the palace now, southeast corner. We've picked up more enemy. They're behind us, and it looks like we've got some outside waiting for us too."

Ace shook his head, trying to clear his thoughts. *It's time,* he thought, exerting all his mental energy to focus his foggy mind. He reached into his pocket and grabbed one of the stims he'd stashed there, popping it into his mouth as he activated the needle gun controls. The effect was almost immediate, like a rush of adrenaline. He felt the fatigue pushed back and a new alertness take hold. He knew it wouldn't last long, but hopefully he would only need it for a few minutes.

"We're on the way, Shira. ETA one minute thirty," Lucas said. "Stay alert. Ace is on the needle gun. We'll try to give your reception party something else to think about."

"Acknowledged." Shira cut the line.

"We're heading down, Ace. Make sure you're strapped in."

"I heard you."

The *Claw* pitched almost immediately, as Lucas put her into a steep dive. Seconds counted, and there was no time for a gentle descent.

Ace brought up the needle gun's targeting system. It was simpler than the neural feed units in the two main turrets. Those targeting systems were state of the art, and they provided a unique perspective to the gunner. The smaller needle weapon was fired from Ace's station on the bridge, and it was much lower tech. Then again, his targets here would be meters away, not half a light-second.

"Drop the field, Lucas. I need to charge the gun." With the thrusters and field running, there was no way the *Claw* could power any of its weapons systems, even with its new reactors and conduits.

"Sam," Lucas yelled into the comm. "Dropping the field in ten seconds, activating the needle gun."

"Acknowledged," came the reply. "Diverting power immediately to the needle gun firing system."

Ace sat and listened, but he didn't say anything. Lucas and Sam worked seamlessly as a team, each in their own way coaxing a level of performance out of the *Claw* that astounded everyone else. He knew intellectually *Wolf's Claw* was an inanimate object, though he'd never managed to think of it quite that way. His connection to the old girl had always been a deep one. But that was nothing compared to Sam and Lucas. For them, the *Claw* was an extension of their minds, their bodies. When the ship went into battle, the two of them almost merged with the vessel, becoming an integral part of it. He wished he could understand how they meshed so perfectly with a machine, but while he was a little jealous, he wasn't going to begrudge them in the slightest. Their connection had surely saved the entire crew more than once.

He felt the same rush he always did when the *Claw* went into a fight. But he couldn't help but feel something was missing. He turned around for a second, and his eyes stopped on the command chair. The *Claw* felt empty with most of her crew on the ground. And most of all, she was without her captain, the beating heart of her crew.

Ace realized that put him in command, informally at least. Even Shira tended to accept his role as de facto executive officer, but now all he wanted to do was get Blackhawk back into the command chair as quickly as possible.

"The field is down." It was Sam's voice on the comm. "Ace, you'll have power to the needle gun in eight seconds."

"Got it, Sam." Ace turned and looked across the bridge. "We're detectable, Lucas. Keep an eye on your scope."

"You mean, do my job?"

"Smart-ass."

"Just filling in for you while you're taking on the responsibility of command. All clear so far." A pause. "Better get your targeting online. I've got a cluster of troops out behind the palace. I think we're gonna need to clear a path for the others."

"You think?" Ace growled, and he could hear Lucas laugh. That was all the encouragement Ace needed—he was back in his element. As good-natured as Ace was around his comrades, there was a bloodthirsty side to him. Blackhawk, Katarina, and Shira shared it, and they understood. The others were fighters through and through, but they didn't understand the primal rush from the kill the way their more aggressive comrades did. Ace only fought against those seeking to harm his friends, and against them he had not the slightest shred of mercy.

He stared into the targeting scope. He counted at least thirty-five troops running around. They were taking position, most likely waiting for Shira and the others. They were there to kill his friends. *That's not going to happen, motherfuckers.*

"I've got them," he said to Lucas.

He smiled and pulled the trigger.

"Let's go. Whatever's outside, we're out of time in here." Shira was standing just beyond the door, waving her arms wildly to the others.

Sarge and his men were in the lead. They filed out the door and fanned out, taking position along a narrow berm. They opened up almost immediately, and Shira could hear the return fire—and was not encouraged by what she heard. There were at least several squads shooting.

"Anybody who still has ammo, get in position flanking Sarge's men." She was doing a mental tally, and it kept coming up the same: nobody but Sarge's crew had squat ammo left. The Twins were completely out. *Too damned bad. Those heavy cannons are just what we need right now.* She was also dry. She'd fired her last rounds as they'd fought their way down the final corridor on the way to the exit. Her heavy knife was in her hand, its blade bright with blood.

She was pretty sure Katarina was out as well, though she'd

learned never to discount the wily assassin. She was likely to pull a gun from some unimagined hiding place and drop an enemy in his tracks when you least expected it. Whatever she might be hiding, though, she had no place on a firing line now. If it got to close quarters, that was something entirely different . . .

Shira turned toward Gustav, who was moving toward the left of the line. He still had Blackhawk's rifle and half a magazine. "You . . . get down. Ark wants you out of here alive, so we're going to try to keep you that way." She wasn't about to call this jumped-up Nordlingener king or your highness or any other bullshit like that. Shira didn't grant courtesy respect. If you wanted it from her, you damned well had to prove you deserved it first.

She looked up, trying to get a glimpse of the *Claw*. She couldn't see anything, but then she heard a dull roar in the distance. *There she is!* She'd know those engines anywhere.

"Grab some dirt," Lucas said over the comm. "We're on the way down."

Shira knew exactly what that meant. She could almost see Ace at the needle gun controls, lining up those guards in his sights. She'd never say it to his face, but she was glad Ace Graythorn was up in the *Claw*, ready to waste the bastards out in that field.

She'd barely crouched down when a blinding flash lit the sky, and a blast like a bolt of lightning ripped into the ground. It was a perfect shot, right in the middle of the largest enemy formation. It fried at least half a dozen soldiers, and the rest of the unit broke and fled in every direction.

"Stay down," Shira growled when she saw Gustav look up. She was counting in her head. She knew exactly how long it took the *Claw*'s needle gun to recharge. She gave one last peek before ducking down as the second shot ripped into another cluster of guards.

"You ready, Shira?" It was Lucas again. "They're all running. I'm bringing her down."

"We're ready, Lucas. Way past ready." She turned toward the others. "The *Claw* is landing. Wait until she's completely down, and on my signal, we all make a run for it. Understood?"

She was answered with an assortment of yeses and nods.

She turned and watched for about half a minute, and then she could see a glow on the ground from the *Claw*'s landing thrusters. It was a slow and delicate process to bring a vessel the size of the *Claw* down—unless you had a pilot like Lucas Lancaster at the controls. Shira watched as he brought the ship toward the ground in one perfect, graceful motion. Thirty seconds later *Wolf's Claw* was on the ground, and Shira and the others were heading her way at a dead run.

"Keep moving!" She waved her arms, gesturing toward the open airlock as the others raced aboard.

She turned and looked back the way they had come. "Come on, Ark . . . where are you?" she muttered. More than anything, she wanted to run back into the palace, to go and look for him. She even began leaning forward to make a mad dash to the door. But she couldn't. His orders still echoed in her mind. She'd never heard him issue a command with such anger and intensity before, even when they'd been in combat. Even when it looked like they faced certain death.

Whoever that was in there, Ark knew him. And he was scared.

And that left her feeling cold.

"Shira, come on." It was Katarina, standing on the edge of the airlock. "Ark knows what he is doing. You have to trust him."

Katarina's words took hold of her, and she turned slowly and looked back at the ship. She took a deep breath and took one last look behind her. Shira couldn't remember the last time she'd cried, probably when she was a child. But right now she felt tears fighting to escape her watery eyes.

She moved toward the *Claw*, willing herself to take each step. She saw Katarina ahead, waving, urging her forward. She took another few steps and grabbed onto the handholds, pulling herself up into the ship. She slapped at the controls, closing the hatch. Ten seconds later they were airborne, their mission complete—but without Arkarin Blackhawk.

"We can't leave him behind. What the hell were you thinking, Shira?" Ace leaped out of his seat . . . and he almost fell to the ground. His face was red, and he was covered in sweat. He grabbed hold of his chair and steadied himself. "Lucas, we're going back to that palace now. Turn this ship around."

"No, Lucas." Shira was standing next to the ladder. Her eyes had been on Ace, but she glanced quickly toward the pilot. "These were Ark's orders."

"To leave him behind to die? If that's his order, then I say we disobey him. Let him scream at me when he gets back. Let him cast me out. At least he'll be alive." He stared at Shira with red and watery eyes. "How can you leave him behind, Shira? How can you do it?"

"Shut the hell up, Ace! You weren't there! You didn't see him. Didn't hear his voice . . ." She was shaking with anger and could barely get the last words out.

"But . . ."

"She is right, Ace." It was another voice that interrupted him, calmer, more controlled. Katarina's head appeared as she climbed up to the bridge. "I was there. This is what he wanted.

Arkarin Blackhawk is an extraordinary man, a very intelligent and highly capable one. He did not want us there. His orders were not careless bravado. You are his retainer—and his friend. You must put aside your own feelings and respect his wishes."

Ace looked over at her, but he didn't respond. He grabbed the other side of his chair to steady himself. He stared at Katarina for a few seconds.

Then he collapsed.

Katarina ran across the deck, dropping to her knees and lifting his head from the hard surface. "Lucas, call Doc. Get him up here right away." She lowered herself, sitting on the floor, cradling Ace's head as she listened to Lucas call Sandor to the bridge.

Shira walked over too and leaned down on the other side of Ace. She could see he was still breathing, but she knew he'd pushed himself too hard. He shouldn't have even been out of bed, but none of them would have made it back without him at the needle gun controls. For all their sparring and fighting, Shira loved Ace like a brother. Coupled with leaving Ark behind, it was almost too much to bear. And yet, as she looked across at Katarina, she noticed just how upset the normally emotionless assassin was . . . and was shocked. The Sebastiani was worried about Blackhawk also, no doubt, but there was something else, the way she was cradling Ace's head. Shira had never noticed before, but . . .

"He'll be okay, Kat," she said, her voice soft. "He just needs rest." Her head turned around at the sound of Doc climbing the ladder.

"I told him to get right back to bed after you were on board," he said. "What happened?"

"We had to leave Ark behind. It was his order." Shira was sitting on the floor, looking up at Doc. "Ace got upset." She glanced down again at her nearly unconscious comrade. "Very upset."

"You left Ark behind?"

"Not now, Doc," Shira said between gritted teeth.

Doc just shook his head and strode quickly across the bridge, waving his arm as he did. "Out of my way. Both of you."

Shira slid to the side and got up, but Katarina moved more slowly. She was holding Ace's hand as she rose, and she paused just before her fingers slipped off his.

Doc leaned over Ace. "I told you to get right back to bed, didn't I? Am I going to have to use the restraints?" He was holding a small monitor over his patient, reading the vital signs and other data on a compact screen. He reached into his bag and pulled out a small injector.

"He seems okay," Doc said as he gave Ace a shot. "He's got a small fever, so I'm giving him an antibacterial/antiviral cocktail just to be safe. But he needs rest, so I'm counting on all of you to make sure this man stays in bed for at least another three days. And preferably four. Can I count on you all?"

Katarina glanced up from Ace to Doc. "I will make sure he doesn't move."

Shira had no reason to doubt her.

CHAPTER 22

BLACKHAWK RAN DOWN THE ALMOST-DARK CORRIDOR. HE COULD feel his heart pounding in his chest and sweat pouring down his back. Every sense in his body was fully aware, every muscle tense, ready for battle.

His prey had gotten a jump on him, but he was pretty sure he was on the right track. He was using every tool of his superior genetics—sight, hearing, even the strange gut feeling that had always worked for him in the past. This was life and death, and there was no way he would let himself fail.

He'd run into two guards, and he'd dropped them each with a single shot. Now he stopped abruptly at an intersection and listened carefully. If he chose the wrong direction, it was over. His quarry would escape. He heard something down one of the hallways, and he turned and ran toward the sound. He ejected the empty clip from his pistol, slamming his last cartridge in place as he ran.

His mind was racing, old memories and new fears struggling to distract him from the hunt. He'd known in his heart the empire was up to something, but now he was certain. This was no random assortment of interventions, no unfocused actions by a bored imperial governor. It was a well-coordinated move against Lucerne—and the Far Stars themselves.

There was no other reason for Vagran Calgarus to be here.

And there was no way Blackhawk was allowing that imperial killer to escape, especially not after he'd recognized him. Calgarus knew who Blackhawk really was, the identity he'd abandoned so long before—and that was a secret Blackhawk resolved would die within these walls.

He pushed himself harder, running as quickly as he could manage in the dark, twisting tunnel. He felt something unfamiliar, a sensation he rarely experienced. Fear. A cold, relentless terror that gripped him like a cold hand on his spine. Not fear of death, but of what was happening and how it might affect his friends. And something else, too.

Fear that his past had finally caught him.

This wasn't an abstract thing. He knew better than anyone in the sector just what imperial rule looked like: millions dead, children slaughtered, refugees starving in the wilderness, cities burning like funeral pyres. Arkarin Blackhawk knew precisely the cost of the emperor's unquestioned power—and the fate that awaited those who dared to dream of freedom. He knew because he'd been part of the machine that imposed that brutal rule.

The empire's true power was built on terror, and its continued dominance depended on maintaining that fear. Imperial forces punished disobedience with almost unimaginable ferocity, and the emperor's henchmen knew that with each example, with every group of rebels savagely crushed, the fear that kept the people in line grew. Blackhawk knew no one in the Far Stars, not even Augustin Lucerne, was truly prepared to face an enemy so dark and bloodthirsty.

Blackhawk feared what was coming to the Far Stars, the brutal and costly fight he knew lay ahead. But there was something else too, something worse, a coldness that stripped away all his courage and left him completely exposed. He was afraid of what would happen if his friends found out the truth. They all knew he had a dark past, of course, one he didn't like to discuss, but he doubted any of them had an inkling of just what he had done, of the enormity of his crimes, of how many people he and the troops he had led had massacred. His crew was his family, and he dreaded the thought of seeing the disgust and anger in their eyes when they found out who—what—he really was.

And Astra.

Astra . . .

The thought of her knowing him not as the rogue adventurer she loved, but as a black-hearted butcher, was too much to bear. No, he'd die in this palace if that's what it took. But he would not let Calgarus escape. He would protect his secret, no matter the cost.

Not that it's going to be easy.

Calgarus was one of the deadliest practitioners of imperial brutality, a cold-blooded killer who would stop at nothing in carrying out his mission. Blackhawk was sure of that. He was sure because he had taught the bastard everything he knew. Vagran Calgarus had been his protégé, his pupil. All he was—

the sadism, the viciousness, the deadly persistence—he had learned it all from Blackhawk.

I created this monster . . . and now I will destroy him.

He took a deep breath and continued forward.

This fight has been twenty years in the making, Vagran. But this time, we're going to finish it. And maybe with this, I'll be a little closer to atoning for my sins.

"*Wolf's Claw* just landed, sir."

DeMark had been staring at maps, watching the progress of his forces as they pushed inexorably forward. The Nordlingener capital was about to fall, and with it, he hoped, the last of the significant resistance would collapse. His men were still involved in a block-by-block battle, and slowly but surely they were chipping away at the enemy's position. He prayed this would be the last fight.

At least Blackhawk is back. That's good news by any measure.

"Bring Blackhawk and his people here immediately." He was surprised by the *Claw's* sudden arrival, but then he realized Blackhawk wouldn't have broken radio silence to announce he was coming in, not when he was only a five-minute flight away. And with that strange distortion field device Blackhawk had, DeMark knew his scanners were worse than useless at detecting the *Claw*. No matter what, they were very welcome.

And it meant he could take the leash off Zel.

"The crew is already on the way, sir. They should be here in a few minutes." Varne paused, listening to something on his earpiece. "Actually, they are here now, sir."

DeMark turned, just as Shira Tarkus and Katarina Venturi walked briskly into the control room. Lucas was right behind them, with a man DeMark didn't know alongside him.

"General DeMark"—Venturi bowed her head slightly as she stopped in front of him—"may I present King Gustav XXIII, the ruler of Nordlingen."

The guards flanking the doorway sprang into action, bringing their rifles to bear on the Nordlingener. But DeMark waved them off. He felt his own surge of anger, an almost overwhelming desire to put his hands around the king's neck and squeeze the life from him. Gustav's pointless resistance had cost thousands of him men, and his soul cried out for vengeance.

But DeMark was an intelligent man too, and a wise one as well. His anger subsided quickly as his eyes panned across the *Claw*'s crew and settled on the king. Something was wrong here. Or right. Or at least different from what he'd expected.

"King Gustav," he said firmly, "I am General Rafaelus DeMark. I wish to welcome you to my headquarters." There was no friendliness in his tone. But the hatred had subsided, too.

"General DeMark, I am pleased to meet you. Though I wish it were under different circumstances. I am deeply sorrowful for the losses your soldiers have suffered, as I am for the thousands of my own men who have been killed in this disastrous—and needless—conflict."

DeMark stood and gazed at the king, trying with limited success to mask his confusion. "I appreciate your words, King Gustav, but surely all of this could have been avoided if you had just—"

"General," Katarina interrupted, her voice smooth, calming, "perhaps I can enlighten you." She glanced at Gustav then back to DeMark. "We just rescued the king from a dungeon under the palace. He was deposed on the eve of your arrival, overthrown in a secret coup by his prime minister." She paused and looked directly into DeMark's eyes. "With imperial aid."

The general stared back at her. "You mean all this time, the king was held captive?" His eyes darted over to Gustav, who answered the question with a nod.

The more pressing question burst from his lips. "The empire?" He was looking at Katarina again. "Are you sure?"

"We are sure." There wasn't a hint of doubt in her voice.

DeMark stood silently for a moment. Then he turned back to Katarina. "Where is Ark?"

The assassin stared back silently, her normally cold eyes hard . . . *With concern?*

"He is in the palace, General," she said finally. "He stayed behind to pursue an operative of some kind. If pressed, I would guess it was the imperial contact responsible for this entire situation."

"You mean Ark is alone in that palace, surrounded by enemies?"

"Yes, General. That is precisely the situation. Ark very specifically ordered us to leave at once and to bring the king back here without delay."

DeMark spun around toward Varne's station. "Captain, get me Colonel Martine. He has to break through and get to the palace immediately, whatever the cost."

"General DeMark, if I may?" Gustav took a step forward. The guard tensed as he approached the general, but DeMark shook his head and the soldier backed down. "If you allow me to address the soldiers in the field, perhaps we can end this destructive conflict immediately—and open the way for your soldiers to reach the palace without suffering further losses."

"How?"

"I will order the Nordlingen forces to cease all combat operations and to surrender at once."

DeMark looked at Gustav with a withering stare. "And why would you do that? We have not negotiated yet. I have promised you nothing. Why would you simply surrender your armies now? Even if you were not to blame for the outbreak of fighting, you have no assurance I will not hold you responsible."

The king took a deep breath. "I will do it for Arkarin Blackhawk. Though I barely know him, he freed me from captivity. He trusted me with a weapon, and he ordered his people to get me to safety while he remained in the fight." He paused for a few seconds. "I am your prisoner." He looked back toward Shira and Katarina. "Or at least the captive of Captain Blackhawk's crew." He turned again to face DeMark. "But I never wanted this war. None of this was by my command, and I would have the death and destruction cease and Blackhawk saved at once if such is possible. Even if the cost is my crown.

"Even if it is my life."

DeMark stared at the proud man standing before him. He was surprised by how much he believed this king in such a short amount of time.

"Okay, Your Majesty. I will allow you to contact your troops. But if you say anything to them other than a command to surrender, I will wave my hand." He looked over at the guards. "And these men will kill you without hesitation. Do we understand each other?"

"Indeed, General, we do. I assure you, I intend no treachery."

"Varne, set up the broadcast. Video too." It was important the Nordlingeners be able to see the king if they were to believe it was their ruler addressing them.

"Yes, sir." The aide sounded less than convinced, but he followed the order immediately. "Ready." He gestured toward the workstation, to a small microphone.

Gustav took one last glance at DeMark. The Celtiborian general nodded, and the king walked over to the workstation. Varne hit a switch and nodded for Gustav to begin.

"Attention, all Nordlingener forces, this is King Gustav Magnus, of the house of Kron. I have been held captive for weeks now, the victim of a treacherous coup. I did not issue the orders for this war. I repeat, it was not my wish to fight this war. Prime Minister Davanos is a traitor. He seized power and imprisoned me. The broadcasts you heard from me were false, staged.

"For the tragedies this has caused, for the thousands killed in this needless fighting, I can only express my profound sadness and regret. But this treason ends now. The dying ends now.

"I now command the armed forces of Nordlingen in their entirety to cease all combat operations immediately. Lay down your weapons and surrender to the Celtiborians. If an officer orders you to continue to attack, he is a traitor to our planet, and should be apprehended. All fighting is to end now—there's been far too much pain and death already. I order you all to do what must be done in order to stop this war. The traitors who have caused this catastrophe will be found and dealt with. But first, the killing and dying must stop.

"This is your king's command. Chrono save Nordlingen."

Gustav nodded at Verne, and the aide cut the line. The room was silent.

"Will they follow the command?" Shira asked the king.

"I do not know, Shira Tarkus," the monarch said softly. "I simply do not know." He turned back toward DeMark. "But I suggest you order your forces to advance on the palace regardless. We must get Arkarin Blackhawk out of there whether or not my armies resist."

Blackhawk felt the hollow click as he pulled the trigger. His gun was finally out of ammunition. Enemy soldiers were lying around the room, each of them with one perfectly aimed bullet in their heads.

All of his enemies dead but one.

He stepped forward, slipping the empty pistol back into its holster. "Hello, Vagran," he said softly. "It's been a long time." He stared at the only other person still standing in the room. The imperial agent had a sword hanging at his side, but otherwise he was unarmed.

"Indeed it has," the imperial replied. "Should I address you as Blackhawk? Is that what you call yourself now?"

"It's not what I call myself, it is my name. It is who I am." Blackhawk stepped to the side slowly, his eyes locked on the other man's. "Anything else is the past."

"I remember another name, and a man with different priorities. A great warrior of the empire and dynamic leader. A hero who received his rewards from the hand of the emperor himself. A man I called my mentor."

"That man is gone. He died long ago."

"Did he?" The imperial stared back at Blackhawk. "Or do you just tell yourself that? For twenty-five years I believed him to be dead. Indeed, everyone thought you had been killed. They still think so." His hand was hanging at his side, close to his blade, but he made no overt move to pull it from its sheath. "But here we are now, and not only do I find you alive, I see you lurking among Far Stars filth like a worm crawling through the dirt. What has become of you, my old master . . . my old friend?"

"Indeed, Vagran, that is exactly how I'd expect *you* would see it. Clearly you are no wiser now than you were then." Blackhawk nodded to his adversary. "We were friends of a sort, once. But that time is long past. And it doesn't matter anymore. You know who I am, what I am. I cannot allow that information to leave this room. You have come to the end, Vagran. This is where you die." He pulled his shortsword slowly from the scabbard, his fingers clenched tightly around the worn grip. "You know you cannot defeat me. I am still the teacher, and you the student. Now it is time for the final lesson."

"You *were* my teacher, but that was long ago, and much has changed since then. You abandoned who you were, left your greatness behind to languish here, at the edge of the universe among the detritus of humanity." The imperial pulled out his own blade and held it out in front of him. "We shall see who passes this last test."

Calgarus crouched into a fighting position, his feet moving slowly, his body edging toward Blackhawk. The two men stared into each other's eyes, and they began their deadly dance.

Blackhawk took a deep breath. He was exhausted, and his old wound still ached. Calgarus had always been a dangerous fighter, and Blackhawk reminded himself his old protégé had nearly a quarter-century's experience since last they'd met. The imperial was younger, too, though only by a few years.

As always, Blackhawk felt the adrenaline surging through his body, giving himself over to the part of his mind that always took control in combat.

Let's see what you're made of, Vagran.

He moved suddenly, feinting forward to the left then ducking and slashing with his blade. Calgarus dove backward and lunged out with his sword, parrying Blackhawk's strike just in time. The imperial stumbled, but he caught himself.

"You strike like a snake, just as you always did." Calgarus

nodded his head slightly. "But I am not the green young man you abandoned so long ago." He raised his sword and brought it down hard. Blackhawk extended his own weapon to block the strike, and a loud clang echoed from the walls.

Calgarus increased the intensity of his attacks, swinging his blade at Blackhawk's with as much force as he could manage, but Ark stood firm, parrying every blow.

Then Blackhawk ducked below one of Calgarus's strikes and brought his own blade around in a vicious swing. The imperial jerked backward, but Blackhawk's blade bit into him, barely. It was a flesh wound, but it was the first blood drawn.

Yet Calgarus barely paused, throwing himself toward Blackhawk, his anger feeding his attack. He swung hard at his enemy's sword, pushing it to the side as he reversed the move and slashed at Blackhawk's body. But the older man was the quicker, and he evaded the blow.

The fight went on, the two exchanging strikes all across the room, each seeming to read the other's every attack and responding with the proper defense. Though Blackhawk couldn't manage to land a decisive blow, he was getting the better of the engagement. He'd drawn first blood, and Calgarus was tiring out. Blackhawk had entered the battle exhausted and wounded, but his natural abilities were beyond that of any normal man, however well trained and experienced. Calgarus's skills were a match for his own, but the imperial couldn't overcome the genetic engineering that made Blackhawk such a deadly adversary.

"We don't need to do this." For the first time since they'd encountered each other, there was a hint of desperation in Calgarus's voice. The fact that he was talking at all was the proof

Blackhawk needed to know he was winning. Vagran continued, "I don't know what happened to you so many years ago, but you can come back with me. You can reclaim your position within the empire."

Blackhawk stared at his adversary with pity in his eyes. Calgarus's attempt was laughable. No one knew the ways of the empire better than Blackhawk. There was no going back, no forgiveness for traitors and deserters. Only death awaited him back in the empire—even if he could have brought himself to return to what he'd been.

Which he couldn't.

"That is not the way for me—I left that path long ago. It is you who are lost, Calgarus. Your soul is mired in darkness, and with each step you walk farther past the point of no return. Nothing remains for you but the hope for salvation in death, and that shall take you soon."

Calgarus tested with his blade, probing for a weakness while his old mentor spoke. But Blackhawk parried easily, and then launched his own attack.

The *Claw*'s captain brought his blade down toward Calgarus's neck. The imperial twisted around, holding his sword up to block the killing blow. But it was a diversion, and Blackhawk pulled his arm low, his sword slipping under Calgarus's and biting into his side, sending a spray of blood through the air.

The imperial howled in pain, and he lunged back, holding his sword in front of him with shaking hands. His breath was coarse, and the pain was written on his face.

He stared at Blackhawk with a strange expression. Fear certainly, but also astonishment, as if only now he'd begun to believe his old friend would really kill him.

"We were brothers, comrades. We served side by side, earned the gratitude of an emperor." He stared across the floor, and Blackhawk could see the pain and fear in his eyes.

"I do not want the emperor's gratitude. That is what you will never understand. Those days you view as a time of glory—they are my great shame."

Calgarus staggered, his side soaked with blood. He was badly wounded, but it wasn't mortal. But the fight was over. That was obvious to both of them.

"I . . . I yield to you." He shuffled forward and let his sword arm drop to his side. "I am your prisoner."

Blackhawk was startled by Calgarus's surrender. He'd been ready to kill his opponent in battle, but to murder him in cold blood? To refuse his surrender and summarily execute him?

"I surrender to you, Blackhawk. I beg for your mercy." Calgarus's blade hit the ground with a loud clang. "If you would kill me, my old friend, then strike me down. I am unarmed and helpless."

Blackhawk felt his heart pounding. His mind was racing, old dark memories mixing with newer, lighter ones. His old self could have rationalized killing a captive in cold blood, even an old friend. All he'd known in those days was duty—and the pursuit of power. But now he understood so much more. He had friends, loved ones, attachments he'd never have allowed himself twenty years before, when Vagran Calgarus had been his comrade and pupil.

But none of that mattered now.

An atrocity to hide a nightmare . . .

"I'm sorry, Vagran. I truly am. But you are what you are, and I cannot allow what you know to leave this room. The imperial evil you represent must not spread any further." Blackhawk tried to justify his actions, to himself at least, but it was point-less. He knew just why he was going to kill Calgarus.

He took one last look into his old friend's eyes, and he saw the terror rising inside his old friend, the realization of what was happening. Then he swung his sword, taking off the impe-rial's head in one blindingly quick motion.

He instinctively took a step forward and grabbed the younger man's body, sliding it slowly to the ground instead of letting it fall. He knew Calgarus had been an evil man, and Blackhawk couldn't begin to calculate how much brutality the imperial had probably inflicted over the past twenty years. He didn't have the slightest doubt his old pupil deserved death for his acts, but Blackhawk was still wracked by guilt.

Do I deserve death any less than Calgarus? I walked away from what he was years before, but does that wash away those old sins? Or do the shades of those I killed still wait to petition against my soul for vengeance?

And now I have killed a man to hide those sins.

Blackhawk knew he'd once been no better than his old protégé; indeed, he'd been worse. Now he stood, alive, staring into the dead eyes of Vagran Calgarus. Was redemption just an unattainable dream? A wispy image, always out of reach?

He felt a strange compulsion, a temptation to drop his sword and wait—to wait until more guards came. He'd lived far lon-ger than he deserved, longer than he'd expected when he had fled what he was, with no idea of who he could become. Death here would be but a tithe of the fate he deserved for all his sins, a small measure of justice for those he'd slain.

But he pushed the feeling back, and the strange need for self-preservation kicked in, as it had so many times before. He'd never known if it was some old conditioning deep in his brain or a facet of his carefully engineered genetics, but there was something inside him—an irresistible need to survive, to fight against any odds, to suffer any pain or torment.

To never give up.

He sucked in a deep breath and took one last look at Calgarus's severed head. Then he turned and slipped out into the hallway. It was time to get out of here. Time to leave the past behind, to become Arkarin Blackhawk again.

CHAPTER 23

BLACKHAWK RACED THROUGH THE STONE PASSAGEWAYS, TRYING to find a way out. His wounds hurt like fire, and his fatigue was almost overwhelming, but he pushed himself with single-minded purpose: get out of the palace and slip through the battle lines to get back to his friends. It was all that mattered. Even if only to get them word that the empire was here. It was beyond doubt now, and he had to make sure the news reached Augustin Lucerne.

The palace shook hard—again. It sounded like DeMark's people were bombarding the place. A few chunks of stone from the ceiling hit Blackhawk as he ran, and he heard louder crashing sounds ahead.

Fuck . . . the last thing I need is to get sealed up in these tunnels . . .

He'd made a promise, and by Chrono, he was going to see it done. And that meant getting out of here . . .

Footsteps ahead, estimate two or three contacts, approximately forty meters past this intersection.

Blackhawk didn't respond to Hans, but he lunged to the side, taking cover just down the passage on the right. He was out of ammunition, so he needed a close-range fight. He'd tried to get a gun from one of the dead guards, but the cave-ins had made that difficult. Some of the bodies were covered with debris, and he'd come across several guns damaged by the falling rock. But he hadn't found anything useful.

He'd have to hide from these approaching guards, or sucker them in. Otherwise, they'd just blast him to pieces.

He stood quietly, his shortsword in his hand. A few seconds later, he heard the enemy himself, without the AI's assistance. He listened, closing his eyes, locking out everything else, getting a feel for the distance.

Twenty meters? He flashed the thought to Hans.

I estimate sixteen. Project enemy will reach the intersection in nine seconds.

Blackhawk's hand tightened on the sword's hilt.

Six seconds.

He took a deep breath, inhaling slowly, quietly. He felt the muscles in his arm flex as he tightened his grip on the blade.

Four seconds.

He imagined his enemies, walking down the hallway, just around the corner.

Two seconds.

He held still for another beat then he leaped around the corner, his blade already swinging. His eyes focused as his body moved in front of the enemy troopers, and he subtly adjusted the trajectory of his strike. The razor edge of the blade sliced across the throat of one of the soldiers, and he fell back immediately, hands on his neck, trying in vain to hold back the arterial flow of blood.

Blackhawk let his momentum take him forward, and he thrust hard with the sword, taking the second guard under the ribs. He gritted his teeth and thrust with all his strength, feeling the blade drive through his victim's chest cavity. He pulled back, trying to extricate the blade, but the dying man twisted to the side, and the momentum of his fall pulled the sword from Blackhawk's hand.

His head swung around, and his eyes focused on the third enemy. The man was still surprised. He had dropped his assault rifle when his comrade's body crashed into him, and his hand was down on his belt, pulling his pistol from its holster.

Blackhawk's eyes were on the weapon, watching as it moved slowly up toward him. He lunged hard, bringing his leg around in a backward roundhouse kick. The battle trance made each second seem an eternity. He felt his leg moving through the air as he watched his enemy's gun moving toward him.

It's going to be close . . .

His boot slammed into the side of the guard's face, and he felt his victim's head snap wildly to the side, heard the sickening sound of his neck breaking. The pistol cracked loudly, but Blackhawk's strike had hit first, and the shot went wide. The guard fell to the floor, landing with a thud that implied utter finality.

Blackhawk took two steps to regain his balance and checked to make sure all three of his adversaries were dead. Then he pulled his sword free and grabbed one of the pistols before he continued down the hall.

"We're approaching the target now, sir. The regular Nordlingener forces appear to have obeyed the surrender order, but we're encountering resistance at the outer defenses of the palace." Martine's voice was hollow and tinny on the comm.

"Push ahead with all speed, Colonel. If Blackhawk is . . ." General DeMark paused, and his eyes drifted to the right, where half the crew of *Wolf's Claw* was standing next to King Gustav. "I want Blackhawk found immediately," he said into the microphone.

"Yes, General. Captain Zel's people are assaulting the perimeter as we speak."

"Keep me updated. I mean every detail, Colonel."

"Yes, sir. Martine out."

"Thank you for your efforts, General. We are extremely grateful." Katarina stepped forward and nodded to DeMark.

"Of course, Lady Venturi." DeMark smiled. Katarina's charms were rarely ineffective, even when she wasn't attempting to employ them and the subject was as disciplined as the Celtiborian general. "I am certain that Ark will make it back."

DeMark was a poor liar, and his tone implied he was anything but sure.

"Arkarin is an extremely capable man, General. He has escaped from some very difficult situations."

Katarina wanted to believe he would make it out of the palace. Indeed, in most situations, she would have believed it. But she could still see the expression on his face before he took off in pursuit of the strange man who had accompanied the guards. Blackhawk had gone pale, as if he'd seen a ghost. The man was an agent of some sort, she'd guessed that immediately, and clearly one he'd encountered before. But she'd never seen Blackhawk so rattled.

And, in turn, that rattled her. In fact, these last few days had her unsure of herself, and that was a feeling she didn't like. But the lie of convenience that had been her life aboard *Wolf's Claw* was crumbling around her, for even *she* no longer thought of herself as just a passenger. And while she wouldn't yet admit she had affection—in some cases, *more* than affection—for the crew members of the *Claw,* she knew with certainty that these people meant more to her than anyone in the Far Stars.

And Blackhawk was the core of all that. Without Arkarin Blackhawk, the unlikely family of the *Claw*'s crew couldn't exist. He had assembled them—he was the glue that held them together.

She turned and walked to the side of the room. The others were restless too. "What is it, Ark?" she whispered to herself. "What darkness has come out of your past?"

"Odds, we're going in. Evens, stay in position and provide covering fire." Gregor Zel's voice was a harsh growl, and his parched throat burned like fire. His men had been fighting for two days with nothing more than a few thirty-minute breaks. They were exhausted and hungry, and their canteens had been dry for the last twelve hours.

They'd moved quickly through the city, slowed only by the need to accept the surrenders of various enemy units and send details to the rear with the prisoners. Zel had begun to wonder if the fighting was truly over. Then his people reached the palace, and they were pinned down almost immediately by heavy fire.

The enemy had positioned heavy autocannons around the perimeter of their defenses, and the massive firepower of the weapons threatened to turn any attempt to storm the palace into a bloody fiasco. Finally, Zel brought up his two mortar teams with orders to silence the autocannons. It had taken half an hour of sustained bombardment, but they'd finally taken out the last of the heavy guns, opening the way for the company to storm the palace.

"Let's move." He lunged forward, leaping over the small stone wall in front of him and rushing toward the palace. The enemy fire was light. With the autocannons silenced, there were just a few sporadic bursts from different locations around the building. The shooting from behind was heavier, his own men immediately targeting the sources of the enemy fire.

He ran hard over the manicured lawn, trying to reach the relative safety of the stone wall of the palace. The enemy fire was light, but it didn't matter. Gregor Zel had seen hundreds of comrades fall, guilty of no greater error than being in the wrong place at the wrong moment.

I will never get used to running across an open battlefield.

He threw his hands out, cushioning the impact as he ran up to the wall. He looked quickly side to side. Everything looked clear. Then he snapped his head around, checking on his men.

It looked like a couple were down, but fewer than he'd feared. So far, so good. Now he had to get inside. And find Blackhawk.

He moved around the perimeter of the building, working his way to the main entrance. "First and Second Platoon with me. Everyone else, around back."

He peered around the corner, toward the front of the building. The massive double doors had been blown apart, and the shattered remnants were lying in front of the entryway. Zel ducked back just as someone opened up from inside, and he heard the bullets impacting right around the corner, sending shards of broken stone flying all around. It was two assault rifles, he figured, three at most. That was a lot less resistance than he'd expected.

"Plessey, Bevern . . . you guys set up here, right behind the corner."

The two men moved forward, each holding one of the grips of the heavy autocannon. They moved swiftly, and in less than a minute they were ready to fire. They pushed the massive gun to the side, bringing its muzzle just past the corner.

Zel took one last glimpse then he pulled back again. "The front entry, guys. We've got two or three bogies in there. Blast it to hell."

A couple seconds later, the gun was firing on full auto, sending hundreds of heavy rounds into the doorway. Zel leaned over his firing crew to get a look. The enemy shooting had ceased.

Just as the door had ceased to be. As well as much of the wall surrounding it.

"That's enough. Squad A, take the entrance."

Zel watched as his men ran across the open ground toward the shattered doorway. There were sounds of sporadic fire around the field, but the advancing troops made it all the way without losing anybody. He watched as half took up position around the exterior while the others slipped inside.

A few seconds later, his comm unit crackled to life. "Entry secured, Captain." A few seconds passed. "I don't know what the hell happened, sir, but it looks like a nuke went off in here."

"Hold your position. I'm sending the rest of the platoon in." He turned and blasted out his orders. "Squads B and C, to the door."

The eighteen survivors of the two units dashed across the open space and linked up with Squad A. Zel was about to order the other platoon to advance when he heard the sounds of fighting behind his position.

He whipped his head around and he could see figures silhouetted against the intermittent light of a series of fires.

"Lieutenant Quarrel, take D and E squads in, and assume command at the entryway. Proceed with caution and occupy the palace." He turned his head and yelled, "F squad, with me." He pressed the release on his rifle, sending the half-empty magazine flying through the air as he slammed a full one in place. "Let's move!"

Blackhawk shoved hard, and he felt his sword push past the resistance and slide into his opponent's chest. The man's face was right in front of his, and Blackhawk saw the life drain out of his eyes. There were at least ten of them on him, and he knew in his current condition he wasn't going to be able to beat them all. He'd emptied the pistol he'd taken from the last set of guards, and he was back down to his trusty blade.

He made sure to stay close to his enemies. As soon as he gave them a clear shot—or they decided this enemy was too dangerous and they'd blow away a couple of their own men to take him down—Blackhawk knew he'd be dead.

Until then . . .

He pulled hard, freeing the blade and swinging it in a quick motion, drawing the razor-sharp edge across the throat of another attacker. Blood sprayed everywhere, and from the warmth on his face, he knew he looked like he was covered with warpaint.

Blackhawk's eye caught the glint of a blade coming at him, and he ducked just in time, punching hard with his left hand into the gut of his attacker. The man dropped his sword and fell to the ground and, an instant later, Blackhawk's blade pierced him from behind.

The *Claw*'s captain was deep in the battle trance. There was no pain, no fear, only the exhilaration of combat. His blood boiled with the lust for battle, and he relished the victory over each dispatched enemy. It was always easy during the calm moments of his life to convince himself he didn't enjoy killing. But when he was actually in a fight to the death and struggling with every bit of energy and strength remaining to him, he knew the truth. He'd been bred for this, and it would always be a part of him. The feeling of his blade piercing a foe, the surge of excitement as he dispatched attacker after attacker—it touched him on some primal level. It energized him. It felt . . . natural, like he was one with his true purpose.

It was the conditioning, he knew that. He'd broken much of it years before, forced it from its control over him. But it was still there, and every time he went into battle he felt it. It was no longer his master, but rather a prisoner instead. And, sometimes, an uncomfortable ally. Yet even that was tenuous. Because while it would rush to his aid in combat, the caged monster also longed to escape, to claim him again.

It took all of his iron will to hold it back, to keep it in its place.

He spun around again, and he saw more men approaching, ten or twelve, moving quickly. They were armed with assault rifles, and there was something about them.

I know those uniforms . . . he thought, fighting through the battle trance.

Which is about the moment they began firing at the soldiers surrounding him.

Thank Chrono—Celtiborian soldiers!

"Hold your fire!" Zel's men were halfway toward the strange melee. He'd ordered his best shots to pick off the soldiers around the perimeter. They were clad in the uniforms of the palace guard, the same livery worn by the soldiers who'd fired on his people earlier. But this wasn't an enemy position, it was a fight. And whoever these men were attacking was probably an ally.

"Arkarin Blackhawk," he shouted as his men moved forward. "This is Captain Zel of the Celtiborian Expeditionary Force. If you are there, identify yourself."

"I am Arkarin Blackhawk," a voice cried from the center of the deadly scrum.

Zel kept running toward the surging mass of struggling bodies. He threw his rifle over his shoulder as he approached and drew his blade. "Swords," he shouted to his men. He could hear the sound behind him, hard metal ringing as ten blades were pulled from their sheaths, almost as one. "Strike with care. There is an ally in there."

His force crashed into the mass of enemy soldiers, and battle was joined. Swords swung through the air, clanging loudly as they struck their counterparts. The mass of men surged and flowed around the area. The two forces were similar in number, but the Celtiborians were veteran soldiers, and Marshal Lucerne had always insisted his men train with their blades as seriously as they did with their guns. And they were attacking the guards' rear, which made it even less of a contest.

And in the center of the bloody mass, Arkarin Blackhawk dispatched foe after foe, fighting his way grimly toward his rescuers.

When it was over, Blackhawk stood before Zel. He was wounded in half a dozen places, but nowhere severely. He was covered head to toe in blood, though little of it, Zel suspected, was his own. The Celtiborian didn't even want to guess how many men Arkarin Blackhawk had killed during his escape from the palace.

"You're safe now, Captain Blackhawk. General DeMark sent us to find you."

Blackhawk stared back for a few seconds, and it looked like he was about to say something. But he just fell forward and collapsed into Zel's arms.

The Celtiborian stood firm, holding the exhausted man while he turned toward the squad leader. "Sergeant Avanari, contact headquarters at once. Tell them we found Captain Blackhawk. Alive."

CHAPTER 24

"IT IS GOOD TO SEE YOU, MAK. IT HAS BEEN TOO LONG." VOS stood up from his chair and walked toward his second in command. "Out," he said, smiling as the door wardens and the chamberlain scrambled to leave the room. He didn't have to shout anymore or throw things. He'd finally gotten them trained to jump at his commands. *Still, I may toss something every now and again, just to keep them on their toes.*

"And you, Governor." Wilhelm was resplendent in his dress uniform. Vos thought he had broken him of the practice of dressing formally every time they met to discuss things, but the long separation had apparently caused a minor relapse to old habits.

"You are to be commended on your work on Antilles, my old

friend." Vos's voice was cheerful. Things were going well—very well indeed. "I am sorry to have missed Danellan Lancaster's expression when you informed him we had purchased nearly a third of his company."

"He was quite surprised. And very rattled. I think whatever capacity the fool has for rational thought slipped away in the blink of an eye."

Vos gestured toward the table as he walked over and took a seat. "No doubt. He is—was, perhaps—an arrogant man. I doubt he ever gave a second thought to anyone challenging his control of Lancaster Interests, much less so quickly."

Wilhelm followed Vos, taking a seat across from the governor. "That speed came at a cost, Governor. We paid double what it was worth. An enormous commitment of resources."

Vos held back a smile. Wilhelm had always been conservative, and it was difficult for the general to embrace a strategy so aggressive. Vos knew, however, that cost was irrelevant if it led to victory. Once the Far Stars was firmly under imperial control, the emperor's tax farmers would squeeze these Rim-worlders in ways they'd never imagined possible. The cost of subjugation, however enormous, would be paid by the conquered, as it had been from the dawn of time.

"A necessary commitment, Mak. If we'd offered less, our purchases would have been far slower, and eventually, even a fool like Danellan Lancaster would have been in a position to do something about our actions. Speed was the overriding factor."

"In any event, it appears to have worked. He agreed to all our demands. He didn't even offer much of a struggle, just a few face-saving changes that altered nothing." Despite the good news, though, Wilhelm didn't seem happy.

"What is it, Mak?"

"Well, sir, Lancaster has acceded to our demands, but what is to stop him from changing his mind? Perhaps once we have halted our share purchases, he will take steps to shore up his control."

"A reasonable concern . . . but who ever said we are going to stop our share purchases?" Vos smiled. "Danellan Lancaster isn't the only one who can disregard an agreement, is he?"

"So we are going to resume buying? What if he finds out? Won't he back away from his own obligations under the agreement?"

"Perhaps, Mak, but our current purchase efforts are much slower and less noticeable now. As you know, most of the remaining shares are held in trusts and institutional accounts, and we face a cumbersome approval process from potential sellers. Our activity will be much more difficult to notice than our previous open market buying."

Wilhelm nodded, but he still looked skeptical.

"But more important, Mak, Danellan Lancaster will soon have no option but to beg us for our friendship. Indeed, he will soon be committed to us irrevocably, for reasons even more dear to his cowardly hide than money."

"I don't understand, sir. We threaten his company, but as you just explained, we do not have the capacity to obtain 51 percent ownership of Lancaster Interests, at least not in the short term. We are playing off Lancaster's fear, but should he rethink things, he could turn on us at any time."

"Yes, except for one new piece of intel: Marshal Augustin Lucerne is about to be very, very angry at Danellan Lancaster."

"What makes you think that?"

"Do you recall seeing a report about a weapons convoy intercepted as it was attempting to deliver a shipment to Nordlingen?"

"Yes, it was in the security briefing I received when I returned. An unfortunate turn of events."

"You think so? Perhaps you have not considered it from all angles . . ."

"You mean . . . it was *intentional*? You set the convoy up to be captured? But why? What gain was there in handing over a huge weapons cache to the enemy?"

"The weapons are inconsequential. A means to an end and nothing more."

"You fed them information? False information?"

Vos leaned back in his chair. "Information? Yes. But false? Certainly not, Mak. I only lie when I cannot obtain the desired result telling the truth. In some ways it is easier dealing with an intelligent adversary like Lucerne. It allows subtlety that is not an option with fools like Lancaster, who are likely to miss the point entirely."

"You want Lucerne to know Lancaster is working with us." Wilhelm was silent, thinking. "You want to provoke a confrontation?" His voice grew stronger, his tone more certain. "No, not just a confrontation." He looked up at Vos.

"You want all-out war between Celtiboria and Antilles."

"Exactly. I arranged for the convoy to be sent unknowingly into the teeth of the Celtiborian blockade, so there was no chance they would avoid interception. And the cache of weapons was particularly large, ensuring it would be brought immediately to Marshal Lucerne's attention."

"And they will tie Vestron Shipping to Lancaster," Wilhelm added. "And *only* Lancaster, since we are silent partners."

"Indeed, Mak."

Wilhelm thought some more. "But that wouldn't be enough . . . there's more . . ."

"Very good," Vos said. "I took it one step further by making sure that the data systems on the Vestron ships detailed deliveries made to all the worlds where our weapons have been discovered . . ."

"Such as Rykara and Castilla . . ."

"And now Lucerne has no choice but to assume the Lancasters were pulling the strings at Vestron even before they purchased the company. He will suspect our involvement too, but he will have direct evidence pointing only to Lancaster."

"He will believe Danellan Lancaster was betraying him from the beginning, even when they met on Celtiboria." A smile crept on to Wilhelm's lips. "And when Lancaster arranges to delay the vote on Antilles entry into the confederation as I instructed him to do, it will confirm Lucerne's belief that his new ally was lying to him all this time." He paused and his smile widened. "He will be furious."

"And as we've seen, Marshal Lucerne is a very dangerous man when he's angry."

Wilhelm laughed.

"So while the two largest Primes of the Far Stars battle each other, we'll be free to secure our positions on the fringe worlds. And though I have no doubt Lucerne will conquer Antilles, the fight will exhaust his forces even more than his recent planetary excursions. He will lose dozens of ships and hundreds of thousands of his precious veterans. And the other Primes will see his aggression against Antilles, and they will resist his entreaties to join the confederation—especially with a bit of . . . shall we say, encouragement. If we are truly fortunate, one or more might actually fight him.

"Then we will simply pick up the pieces."

"Brilliant," Wilhelm murmured. There was a hint of doubt in his voice.

"You have a question . . ." Vos said.

Wilhelm shook his head. "Sorry. I was just wondering what happens if Lucerne defeats the Antilleans more easily than you expect. We should not underestimate his military capabilities. If he doesn't lose enough, he will still be stronger than anything we can oppose him with—and he will have the wealth and resources of Antilles at his disposal . . . whatever is left of it after the war, at least."

Vos smiled again. "And that's the other thing you don't know yet, Mak. Something that happened while you were on Antilles. Do you remember Draco Tragonis?"

"Of course," replied Wilhelm. "We worked with him a number of times. A very ambitious man. And a capable one, if a bit too impressed by titles and puffery."

"That's Draco," said Vos, allowing himself a brief chuckle. "Well, he is here. And he brought a legion with him, a veteran formation."

Wilhelm stared back in surprise. "The emperor finally gave in and released a combat unit for the crossing?"

"Yes, well, Draco was always very persistent. It appears I was correct that the Far Stars is still a considerable burr in the imperial backside. Even the modest amount of progress we have made so far contrasts well with the folly of our predecessors."

"That is good news, certainly, but a single legion cannot hope to meet Lucerne's armies."

"Who said anything about a single legion, Mak? Tragonis is even now on Kalishar, setting up a training facility. His legion will become the cadre for an army recruited from the dispossessed of the Far Stars. We will turn every fringe gutter rat who takes our bounty into an imperial soldier."

Wilhelm sat quietly, a stunned expression on his face.

"Indeed, Mak, we initially designed a plan to seize control of the Far Stars with trickery and manipulation. Now, we will have an army to back that up. And if the two most powerful worlds in the Far Stars fight themselves to exhaustion, the rest will fall in rapid succession." Vos paused and slapped his hand down on the table. "And then these arrogant Rim-worlders will learn obedience. Yes, by the gods, they will learn how to heed the commands of their betters."

He finally let the full laugh out, and his eyes gleamed with self-satisfaction, as he imagined his plans reaching their ultimate fruition.

The Far Stars crushed under his iron boot.

CHAPTER 25

"BY CHRONO, YOU LOOK LIKE HELL, ARK. I KNOW I ASKED YOU TO do me a favor, but what the hell?" Lucerne had walked through the door briskly, his eyes focusing immediately on Blackhawk, who was sitting on the edge of the bed while two med techs worked on him. The *Claw*'s captain had chunks of semidried blood in half a dozen places, and he had a nasty bruise on the side of his face, but he looked a hell of a lot better than he had an hour before, when they had brought him in half conscious and covered in blood.

"You know me, Augustin. I've never known how to do a job half-assed. What reports have you heard?"

"So much for small talk?"

Blackhawk offered him a weak smile, but there wasn't much behind it.

Sighing, Lucerne said, "Only that you walked right into the palace forty kilometers behind enemy lines to grab King Gustav, and then you found him a prisoner and rescued him, almost single-handedly ending the battle for Nordlingen." Lucerne walked across the room. "Did I miss anything?"

"That might be a bit of a dramatization. If I didn't know better, I'd swear that's how Ace told the story."

Blackhawk looked around the room. There were half a dozen medical personnel and two guards at the door. He stared back at Lucerne, but he didn't say anything.

"Out." Lucerne understood Blackhawk's unspoken message. "All of you. Now."

The two old friends stared at each other while everyone left the room, closing the door behind them.

"Okay, Ark. What's going on? I mean really going on?"

"It *is* the empire, Augustin. And it's no small effort. They are systematically intervening in conflicts all over the Far Stars. Saragossa, Castilla, Rykara . . . now Nordlingen. They are all related. Even Astra's abduction, I suspect, had something to do with it." He paused, sighing softly. "This is trouble, Augustin. Big trouble."

Lucerne took a deep breath and exhaled hard. "Are you sure, Ark?" He looked into his friend's eyes. "I mean, really sure. No doubts at all?"

Blackhawk slid off the table and stood in front of Lucerne. He wobbled a bit, but he caught himself and held steady. "Absolutely sure. No doubt. None."

"You know I trust you, Ark, but it's not just us. I need proof. I talked with King Gustav, and he told me everything, but he had no real evidence it was the empire interfering there. How can you be so certain?"

Blackhawk instinctively looked in both directions, reaffirming what he already knew—that they were completely alone. "I just know, Augustin. You'll have to take my word." He paused, wrestling with what else he wanted to say. With anyone else, he'd have stopped there, offering his assurances but no specifics. But Lucerne already knew who he was—who he had been. *He accepted me even after he knew I was a monster. I owe this man my complete trust.*

"Of course I trust you—"

"There was a man in the palace," Blackhawk said, cutting off his friend. "An imperial agent."

"You're positive? It's been a long time since you've been in the empire, Ark."

Blackhawk's voice was somber. "Oh yes. This man wasn't just any agent. He . . ."

He hesitated, swallowing hard before he continued. "He was my protégé. I trained him, instructed him in how to kill in the emperor's name. We did horrific things together, Augustin, inflicted terror on millions. Then I broke my imperial conditioning and I ran—and I left him behind. But I knew him as soon as I saw him. It all came crashing down on me in that dungeon. And not just the horror I inflicted, but the fact that I never tried to reach him, teach him how to flee from that life, how to repent and struggle to save the remnants of his soul. No, I just disappeared."

"Ark, you can't hold yourself responsible for that. You did what you had to do, and for twenty years you have been a good man."

"Am I a good man, Augustin? Am I really? I made Vagran Calgarus into the creature he became, and then I abandoned him. I killed, I made a killer, and then I left that killer free for *twenty* years. Who knows how much blood is on my hands because of him?" He stared down at his palms, then he looked at Lucerne with haunted eyes. "And you know why I killed him? Not to purge the world of a murderer. Not out of some sort of feeling of justice or redemption or even kindness. No, I killed him because I didn't want him to *tell anybody about me.* I killed him because I was selfish. Because I was a *coward.* Scared of what my crew would think. Or Astra . . ."

Lucerne moved closer to Blackhawk, and he threw his arm around his friend. "Ark, I want you to listen to me. You've been running for twenty years. Hiding. It's time for that to stop. Tell your crew. Tell Astra. You are underestimating them. They know who you are now, and that is what matters to them, not who you might have been long ago. They love you, Ark. You talk about not being able to save this agent's soul, but what about the souls of all those men and women on your ship. Are you telling me you didn't give them second chances . . . or third, or fourth?" He paused. "You took a risk on them. And I also remember when you took a chance on me. Remember? When you told me the truth all those years ago. Did anything change between us? Aren't we still friends to this day?

"Ark, there is no one I trust more, my friend."

The two men stood for a long time, neither speaking a word. Finally, Blackhawk said, "Maybe you are right, Augustin. It would be a relief, one way or another. I'm so tired of hiding my past, of wondering what they all imagine when I say nothing."

Lucerne forced a smile. "Tell them, Ark. Trust them."

"I will. I promise. But this isn't the time. Whatever I did, whatever I am, it is immaterial right now. We have a very real problem. The current imperial governor appears to be considerably more capable than his predecessors . . . and he also seems to have substantial resources at his disposal." He paused then added, "This is a grave threat, Augustin. To Celtiboria, to the confederation, to all the Far Stars."

Lucerne nodded. "We still need proof, Ark. Something we can use to rally all the sector. We know it is the empire, you and I. But we still have to find a way to shake the other worlds into action. To make them rediscover their fear of the empire."

"We will find something, Augustin. It is my fault Calgarus is dead instead of in a cell confessing the empire's involvement. So I give you my word, I will get you the proof you need. I will do whatever is necessary." His eyes blazed with resolve. "Whatever it takes."

"Commodore Jardaines, you are to be commended. This is an enormous cache of weapons, and keeping it out of the hands of our enemies has saved thousands of Celtiborian lives."

Lucerne was staring out over the mountain of crates his people had confiscated from the six Vestron freighters. They were full of imperial weapons, all of them. Enough to equip an entire army, or nearly so.

"Thank you, sir. But Captain Nortel of the *Warrington* deserves the credit. He detected the convoy, and by the time I arrived with additional fleet units, he had boarded all six vessels and secured their crews."

"I will see to it that he is suitably decorated, Commodore." He pulled his eyes from the weapons cache and looked at the naval officer. "Have you questioned the crew?"

"Yes, sir. Typical freighter jockeys. They claim to have no knowledge of their cargo."

"They may be telling the truth, Lavare. The men on those

ships may be utterly in the dark, but I want the captains questioned aggressively. They may not know anything, but if anyone does, it will be them."

"Indeed, sir. In the meantime, I've ordered a complete review of the data systems on the vessels, and I believe we have uncovered some disturbing patterns."

Lucerne's eyes widened. "Such as?"

"Well, sir, it appears that two previous Vestron convoys arrived at Nordlingen shortly before our invasion."

"That is interesting, however not necessarily conclusive. It is still possible the firm was duped on the cargoes they were delivering."

"Perhaps it is not conclusive on its own, sir. But there were other Vestron shipments . . . to Rykara. And to Castilla before that. I would say the likelihood of coincidence is falling rapidly."

"Indeed, Commodore." Lucerne's tone darkened. "That is too much contraband to be coincidental. Even if the source of those weapons was external, someone at Vestron would have had to have known what they were carrying. There were too many convoys for them to have been completely in the dark."

"Agreed, sir. The company had to be involved. Deeply, if you want my analysis."

Lucerne turned and walked slowly across the room. "The Vestron family was rumored to be having considerable financial difficulties. They may have been susceptible to a bribe. Perhaps not openly from the governor, but through an intermediary. They may have believed they were dealing with criminal or black market traffic, a risk they might have taken for enough gain." He shook his head. "But that doesn't make sense either. For one shipment, perhaps. But it had to be clear that this kind of volume could only come from one source. Is it possible the

Vestrons took imperial coin and betrayed the entire sector?" Even as he asked it, though, he was incredulous. Augustin Lucerne couldn't imagine anyone in the Far Stars selling out to the empire.

Jardaines shifted his weight uncomfortably. He opened his mouth to speak, but he closed it again without saying anything.

"What is it, Commodore? Speak freely."

"Sir . . . I guess you haven't heard the news, but the Vestron firm has been recently sold. It must have come out while you were in hyperspace."

"Sold? To whom?" Lucerne had a tight feeling in his stomach. He suspected he wouldn't like what he was about to hear.

"Lancaster Interests, sir. Apparently they bought the whole thing, lock, stock, and barrel. For a generous sum too, especially considering that the Vestrons were in distress."

Lucerne looked down at the floor for a few seconds, trying to compose himself.

He failed.

"Danellan Lancaster! In league with the governor?" He felt the wave of anger sweeping across him, and his whole body shook.

Is it possible? Could Lancaster—could all of Antilles—have betrayed me? If they did, I swear to Chrono I will . . .

"Excuse me, sir, but there is more."

Lucerne turned abruptly. "What, Commodore?"

"It was in the morning briefing, sir. The Antillean Senate postponed the vote on formal membership in the Far Stars Confederation. The stated reason was a localized drought that prevented a significant number of senators from attending. But if the Lancasters have . . ."

"Betrayed us," Lucerne finished the statement. He turned

and slammed his fist on the table. *Danellan Lancaster stabbed me in the back. He lied to my face, and he waited for just the right moment to make his move.*

The rage surging through his body was elemental. Lucerne was normally a patient man, one slow to anger. But now he surrendered to it completely. *What arrogance! What greed! I offered Lancaster the lifeblood of a dozen worlds to feed his insatiable lust for money and it wasn't enough!*

"Commodore," he said, barely containing his fury at the news, "send a communications drone to Celtiboria immediately. Admiral Desaix is to assemble the fleet, every ship fit for combat. He is to recall the vessels dispatched to the expeditionary forces. I want every transport that can fly filled to the supports with troops, every freighter commandeered and stuffed with ordnance." He turned and stared at Jardaines, his eyes glittering with rage. "Destination Antilles."

"Yes, sir." The commodore snapped his commander a perfect salute, and he turned and rushed out the door to carry out his orders.

Lucerne stared at the wall, his body shaking, his hands at his sides clenched into tight fists.

You will learn, Danellan Lancaster. You will learn the price of betrayal. You and all of Antilles.

"He's gone mad, Ark." General DeMark sat in a chair looking across the table at Blackhawk. The two were sitting on the lower level of the *Claw,* just outside DeMark's camp. The room was filled with most of the crew. DeMark had intended to speak alone with Blackhawk, but he'd come to trust and respect the rest of them as well.

The Celtiborian general was tense. He was worried about

Lucerne—and uncomfortable speaking behind the marshal's back. "I wouldn't be here, but there is no one as close to Lucerne as you, Ark. I didn't know who else to go to. You need to stop him."

"Stop what, Rafaelus? What has he done?"

"We discovered that Vestron Shipping was behind the weapons deliveries. To Castilla and Rykara as well as Nordlingen."

"Vestron? The Vestrons are headquartered on Buchhara, aren't they?"

"Yes, but the company has been sold." He paused. "To the Lancasters."

The *Claw*'s crew had been watching silently, but now a ripple of murmurs swept through them.

"Are you saying that the Lancasters are working with the governor? With the empire?" Blackhawk's tone was one of disbelief. "That is hard to believe. I know Danellan Lancaster would sell his grandmother for a trading concession, but it never entered my mind he had the guts for a play like this."

"We seized a Vestron convoy entering this system. The ships were stuffed with imperial weapons. And there was other evidence. Records in their computer systems that suggested the Lancasters had effective control of the company even before the acquisition closed. During the time period of all the deliveries."

Blackhawk took a deep breath.

"I still find it hard to believe. Danellan Lancaster is an ambitious—no, a *greedy*—man, but it is quite a leap to sell out all of the Far Stars and become the greatest traitor in five centuries. How could he even trust the governor's word, regardless of what he was promised? He's a fool, but not a complete imbecile. And I can't imagine him having the courage to cross Lucerne."

"I don't know, Ark, but I'm sure the marshal believes Lancaster is in league with the imperials. I've never seen him so angry. And you know Augustin Lucerne is not one to let a problem fester."

"What has he done?" Blackhawk asked in a flat voice.

"He has ordered Admiral Desaix to assemble the entire fleet." He paused. "He is going to Antilles, Ark. He is going to Antilles with the whole fleet and half a million troops."

Blackhawk stared back for a moment, before asking, "You mean he is planning to invade Antilles?"

DeMark just nodded.

"Where is he now, Rafaelus?" Blackhawk said as he leaped up from his seat. "I need to talk to him."

"It's too late, Ark. He's gone. His ship entered hyperspace an hour ago." There was deep resignation in DeMark's tone. He'd tried to dissuade Lucerne himself, but the marshal had ignored his entreaties.

Blackhawk sat back down. "We have to find a way to stop this. A war between Celtiboria and Antilles will be a holocaust. We can't let it happen." He hesitated, clearly thinking, then turned back to his people. "Sam, get down to engineering right away and warm up the reactor. We're going to Antilles, and we've got to get there before Lucerne and the Celtiborian fleet. We have to find out what is going on . . . and if Danellan Lucerne was actually foolish enough to get involved with the empire, we need to put a stop to it. Immediately."

"How are you going to do that, Ark?" DeMark asked. "How will you even get to him? He virtually owns Antilles. The planet is a Prime. You can't just land out in the desert and sneak into town like you can on the Rim."

"*I'll* get to him, General." The voice came from the other side of the room, where the *Claw*'s crew was gathered. There was a chill to the tone. DeMark recognized the pilot, as he stepped forward. He had met him once or twice—Lucas, he believed it was—but he was one of the few members of the *Claw*'s crew he didn't really know.

Lucas was saying, "I will find out what he has done. I will find out everything, every detail. And I will do whatever is necessary to stop this war from happening. Even if I have to put a bullet in Danellan Lancaster's head."

"I appreciate your spirit, Lucas," the general said, "but how are you going to get to Danellan Lancaster? What makes you think he will see you?"

Lucas stared right at the Celtiborian with cold eyes. "Because he is my father, General."

"Get a tracer on that ship before they jump, Starn, or by Chrono, I will slice you open from your neck to your flea-infested sack." Kandros was standing on the bridge, watching *Wolf's Claw* blast out of the Nordlingen orbit like a bullet leaving a gun.

Starn Quintus was staring intently at his screen. The *Claw* was going somewhere in one hell of a hurry. The way they were going, he wouldn't be surprised to see them jump any minute. Normal procedures called for moving at least a light-minute from any planetary body before entering hyperspace, but Quintus had a feeling Blackhawk and his people were about to disregard that. Jumping close to a planet was dangerous, but then again *Wolf's Claw* had Lucas Lancaster at the helm.

"I'm getting strong power readings, Captain." Quintus knew immediately. "They're powering up their jump drive."

"Bring us around into their blind spot, Starn." Kandros looked at the long-range scanner. The blockading ships were all farther out into the system. They might detect *Iron Wind*, but there was nothing they could do about it. By the time any of them were in range, the ship would be in hyperspace, hot on the trail of the *Claw*.

"Coming around behind them, Captain. We should be in their blind spot." His fingers moved over the controls. "Deploying tracer now."

The bridge was silent, every eye on the screen, waiting to see if they managed to get a link to the *Claw* before she jumped.

Easy does it, Quintus thought, his hands moving slowly over his workstation. *Don't let them slip away . . .*

"Is that *Wolf's Claw*?" Astra stared at the yacht's small screen. "They're heading somewhere in one hell of a hurry."

Lys was sitting in the pilot's seat. She looked up at the display, hitting a few keys and bringing up a list of statistics. "It's not broadcasting any identification beacon, but it matches the *Claw*'s mass and dimensions." She was watching the AI display a 3-D model. "Upper and lower turrets too, Astra. If it's not the *Claw*, it's a hell of a coincidence."

"It looks like they're about to enter hyperspace." Astra's hands ran over the controls. "Yes, we're picking up an energy buildup." She paused for a few seconds, her eyes focusing on a small symbol on the edge of the display. "Lys, take a look at this ship. If I didn't know better, I'd say it was following the *Claw*."

"It sure looks like it's tailing, and the way it's maneuvering, I'd guess its crew is trying to get a tracer on the *Claw*."

Astra frowned. "I'm surprised they managed to get that close to *Wolf's Claw*. I've seen Ace on the scope before, and I can't imagine him letting someone get into the ship's shadow."

"Well, I don't know what's going on there, but they are clearly in a rush to get somewhere."

Astra got up and moved forward, sliding into the copilot's chair next to Lys. The yacht normally had a crew of eight, but this time it was just the two of them. Their takeoff hadn't been what would normally be called "authorized," but Astra wasn't about to sit uselessly under guard on Celtiboria. Not while everyone she cared about was in some kind of danger.

"Why is that ship following them?" She spoke softly, mostly to herself. She had no answers, but she was pretty sure it couldn't be good. She punched at the control panel, bringing up the communications interface. "Damn . . . the *Claw*'s jumping. It's too late to warn them."

She turned and looked at her foster sister. "Lys, do you think you can work us behind that ship and get a tracer on *it*?"

Lys sighed. "I don't know, Astra. I'm not a hotshot pilot. I can barely fly this thing as is."

"Try." Astra's voice was tinged with concern. "I don't know what that ship's crew is up to, but if they're following the *Claw* they're up to no good."

"And they're powering up for a jump now. They're definitely following the *Claw*." She gripped the controls tightly. "Okay, Astra, strap yourself in. This may be a rough ride."

"Just stay on them, Lys. We can't lose that ship." She shook her head. "We just can't."

CHAPTER 26

"MARSHAL, ARE YOU SURE ABOUT THIS? DON'T YOU THINK WE should wait until we have a better idea what is actually happening?" Callisto was standing at Lucerne's side on *Glorianus*'s flag bridge. The hulking vessel was the biggest and most powerful instrument of war in the Far Stars, though even its enormous strength failed to match the legendary firepower of an imperial battleship.

"I know enough, General."

There was an anger in Lucerne's voice that shook Callisto. The marshal was always in control. Whether it was in the middle of war or when his daughter was abducted—through whatever pain or difficulty he was enduring—the man was always under control. But now Callisto could tell that legendary hold on discipline was frayed to the breaking point.

"But, Marshal . . ."

"General Callisto, I appreciate your sentiment, but this has nothing to do with anger." *All evidence to the contrary,* Callisto thought, even as the marshal continued. "If Danellan Lancaster—indeed, all of Antilles—is in league with the imperial governor, we have no time to waste. We cannot allow our only true rival in the Far Stars to ally with the empire." He turned toward Callisto and stared into the general's eyes. "Is that the war you want to fight? Do you want to see your sons march off to die in battle with the legions of the empire? Would you have our soldiers—and then our civilians—become the victims of Antillean treachery?"

No, Callisto thought, *but a war with Antilles will be a bloodbath. I know what that means . . . and you used to as well.*

And yet he said nothing.

"We must take decisive action or see all we have fought for for thirty years disappear. I didn't trust Danellan Lancaster, but I never imagined the man would betray the entire sector and bow down to the imperials. Now he will pay the price."

Callisto took a deep breath. His head had been spinning since he'd gotten Lucerne's order to prepare the bulk of his army on Rykara to embark immediately. He knew Lucerne was enraged, but he couldn't argue with the marshal's reasoning either. If Antilles became a puppet of the empire, the rest of the Far Stars would be in mortal danger. Even the great Celtiborian war machine Lucerne and his people had built would be imperiled. If the marshal's suspicions were true, there was no choice. But war with Antilles was as unthinkable as it seemed to be necessary. Perhaps there was no choice, but Callisto was nervous. He'd never seen Lucerne so angry before, never seen him react on pure emotion. Would he try everything to avoid war? Or would he just lash out as soon as the fleet arrived?

"We have to be sure, Marshal. If we are in error . . ."

"It is no error, General. Danellan Lancaster's ships have been providing imperial weapons to our enemies for months now. The thousands of your men dead on Rykara—and all those on Nordlingen as well—that is the blood price of this man's treachery." He glared at Callisto, and the general could see a glint of madness in his master's eyes.

"But perhaps his treachery is his own, and not the whole planet's."

"Perhaps, General. I would like to think that. But don't forget that the Lancasters virtually control Antilles. And, because of that, Danellan Lancaster was able to delay the vote on the planet joining the confederation, which hardly suggests any independence on the part of the other Antillean leaders." Lucerne paused, the anger in his voice dropping slightly in intensity. "Still, we will give them a chance. We will offer them the opportunity to surrender. Then we can purge all imperialists from their world and proceed with the confederation.

"After we execute Danellan Lancaster and any of his people who were involved in this betrayal, that is."

Callisto's stomach tightened. *He's past reason. He's running on pure rage.*

"Perhaps if you were to speak with their prime minister . . . or a delegation of their senior senators?"

"More talk? Have we not negotiated with them in good faith already? Is there wisdom in allowing a liar another chance to deceive?"

"No, sir. Of course not. But there must be another way."

The anger in Lucerne's eyes faded away, replaced by a deep sadness. "Why, General? Why must there be another way? Because we desire it? Because we wish to avoid bloodshed and destruction? Was there another way on Celtiboria? Did we not treat with the warlords again and again, bribing them with promises of position and wealth, practically begging them to join with us? What did all our negotiations accomplish? In the end we had to destroy them all, and it took three decades of bloody war to do it. We ache for the carnage to end, General, pray to whatever unseen powers rule the universe, but they do not answer. They leave us to wash away our own sins . . . in blood."

Callisto held back a sigh. Lucerne wasn't going to back down—and Callisto wasn't even sure he should. If Antilles was truly in league with the empire, it was a far more powerful base of operations than Galvanus Prime. And imperial resources dwarfed those of the Far Stars. Perhaps there was no choice but war, unless this show of force proved to be enough.

Callisto felt a brief surge of hope, but it vanished as quickly as it had come. Allied with the empire or not, he knew a proud and powerful world like Antilles would never surrender. They would fight. And they would lose, but not before millions had died and great cities had burned. Apocalypse was looming over the Far Stars, threatening to destroy everything Lucerne had built. And Arias Callisto had no idea how to stop it. Or if he should even try.

"Approaching Antilles's system, Captain. Estimate ten minutes until we enter normal space." Lucas was sitting at his controls, monitoring the *Claw*'s position in hyperspace. Most of the systems were down, and he'd had little to do but sit and think about his pending reunion.

The last time he'd seen his father had been six years before, when the Lancaster patriarch had banished his wayward son from the family estate, indeed from all dealings with the Lancaster clan. Lucas had been a world-class fuckup, he couldn't argue that. But Blackhawk's tough love had brought him back from the brink of self-destruction, and he wondered why a wayward adventurer cared enough to make that effort when his own father didn't.

Lucas had embarrassed the family many times, no doubt. And his last scandal, involving the sequential seductions of a powerful senator's wife and then his daughter, had been a difficult one to clean up after, even for a man as wealthy as Danellan Lancaster. Preserving the family's political influence had required sacrificing his only son, and Lucas would never forget—or forgive—his father's choice.

"You okay, Lucas?" Blackhawk asked quietly.

"Yeah, Skip. I'm fine." He was lying, and he knew Blackhawk knew it. But just knowing the captain was there gave him strength. Lucas had been clean for a long time—not so much as a drink stronger than fruit juice had passed his lips in more than five years. But thinking about his reunion with his father was bringing back the old urges. He pushed the thoughts away, but he could feel them tugging at him.

But he knew drugs and alcohol would do nothing to change the facts of this bloodline. Yes, Lucas Lancaster was the rightful heir to one of the biggest fortunes in the Far Stars, but he wanted nothing to do with it. To him, the Lancaster clan, the massive family business, the constant jockeying for power and position—they were all toxic. More than once he felt the urge to reach down, change the ship's course, go to some faraway planet on another crazy mission, and forget all about Antilles and his father. But that wasn't possible. Whatever stress he felt, however much it threatened to break him down, turn him back into what he had been, he had to see this through. Too many lives were depending on it.

"Bring us in as close to the planet as you can, Lucas. The less time we have to spend dealing with their naval patrols, the better." Antilles was no fringe world shithole like Kalishar or Saragossa. The planet had a serious navy, and traffic coming in and out was strictly controlled. Blackhawk couldn't just bring the *Claw* down in the wilderness outside a city and sneak in overland.

"Got it, Skip." Lancaster was working through the checklist, preparing for the transition from hyperspace. He was enormously grateful to have something to occupy his thoughts.

"Sam, are you ready?" Blackhawk leaned over the comm unit.

"I'm ready, Captain. I'll get started as soon as my circuits power back up." Very few ship's systems functioned in hyperspace, and it usually took at least a few minutes for things to recover when a ship jumped back to normal space.

"Remember, we need to look damaged. We have to convince them to override normal landing protocols and bring us in as an emergency case."

"Got it, Cap. They'll think we're close to death's door. I can promise you that."

"Just no radiation leaks, Sam. They have to think our reactor is solid." The Antilleans would never let a ship land with an unstable reactor.

"No leaks, Skip. Got it."

"Whenever you are ready, Lucas," Blackhawk said.

The pilot nodded and stared down at his readouts. "Entering normal space in ten seconds."

Blackhawk leaned back in his seat and closed his eyes, waiting for the feeling of the transition.

"Five." Lucas's voice was firm. He knew Blackhawk was going over again in his mind what he was going to say. They had discussed options for getting around Antilles's lengthy landing approval and customs procedures. It had been Lucas's idea to feign mechanical problems. He knew Antillean shipping law from his days at the Antilles Naval Academy, and vessels with dangerous damage or malfunctions were always given landing priority.

"Transitioning . . . now."

The *Claw* shook briefly. A few seconds later, the main screen came on, staticky and unstable at first, then stabilizing. It displayed the planet Antilles, less than forty thousand kilometers away, recklessly dangerous proximity for a transit.

"Amazing, Lucas. Talk about threading a needle." Blackhawk flipped his comm frequency to the Antillean channels. "Antilles Control, this is the vessel *Wolf's Claw*. We have a severe life support malfunction and request immediate permission to land so we may conduct repairs."

Lucas smiled. Blackhawk was perfect, just enough panic in his voice to make it believable. He knew Sam was down in engineering, ejecting fluids and gases from the ship, confirming to the Antillean scanning net that the *Claw* was, in fact, a ship in distress.

"Vessel *Wolf's Claw*, this is Antilles Control. We have scanned and confirmed your damaged systems. You are cleared to land immediately at Bay 11 in the Charonea spaceport. We are transmitting your landing instructions now. Please do not deviate from this flight plan."

Blackhawk smiled. "Thank you, Antilles Control. *Wolf's Claw* out." He turned toward Lucas. "And that, my young friend, is how it's done." He paused then added, "Thank Chrono we've managed to avoid killing or kidnapping anybody on Antilles. It's one of the few places we're still welcome."

"Hopefully that will still be true in a few hours." Lucas smiled, and he managed to push the thoughts of his father away, at least for a few minutes. But he couldn't avoid it for long. He was home, back where all his demons lived.

"Get the scanners up, now." Cedric Kandros was barking orders into his comm unit before the system had even rebooted. *Iron Wind* had just emerged from hyperspace, and the crew was still scrambling to bring its systems back online. But Kandros didn't have Lucas Lancaster at the helm or Sam Sparks in engineering. Which meant that once again *Wolf's Claw* had the advantage while Kandros impatiently waited to reestablish contact with Blackhawk's ship. "How much longer?"

"Just getting scanning power now, Captain." Quintus was staring into the scope. "The tracer's holding." A short pause then: "Chrono's stinking hide, they transited right on top of the planet." He turned and looked back at Kandros. "I brought us in as close as I could manage, but they emerged less than fifty thousand kilometers out." There was surprise in his voice, almost outright shock. "I've never seen a ship transit so close to a planet before."

Fucking Lucas Lancaster, Kandros thought. "Well, bring us in on a normal approach. It's the best we can do." He sat in his chair, shaking his head.

"Captain, *Wolf's Claw* is bypassing the entry queue and moving into a final approach pattern." He turned to face Kandros. "How could they get priority landing authorization?"

"I don't know how Arkarin Blackhawk does half what he manages, Starn." *I'd steer clear of the dangerous son of a bitch if it wasn't for that million crowns.* "Contact Antilles Control right away and request permission to land as soon as possible. At least we've done some jobs for clients on Antilles. We're in their data system, so we should get visitation visas without too much trouble."

"Yes, Captain."

Kandros looked at the screen displaying a magnified shot of Antilles. *Why here, Blackhawk? You couldn't just go to some shithole fringe world like you usually do? Someplace we could have blown you away in a saloon and walked out the door?*

Now he'd have to find just the right moment to strike, and until he knew more about what Blackhawk was doing, that was going to be tough. But he swore one thing: whatever happened, Arkarin Blackhawk was not getting off Antilles alive.

He had a million reasons to ensure that.

"Antilles? Why would they go to Antilles?" Astra turned and looked at Lys. The yacht's AI and scanning suite had just come back online. It hadn't taken long to confirm where they were. Astra had expected to chase the unidentified ship—and by proxy, *Wolf's Claw*—to some fringe world on the edge of the Far Stars, the kind of dusty and disreputable hole in the ground Blackhawk tended to favor. Antilles was just about the last place she'd have expected him to go. The planet was one of the Primes, cosmopolitan and highly developed. The *Claw* might stop there occasionally for R&R or to resupply, but she had no idea why Blackhawk would take off like a bat out of hell for the place.

"I don't even have a guess. We're assuming this ship was following *Wolf's Claw*, but we don't know for sure. It's possible they gave up chasing the *Claw*. Maybe these guys live here and going after them was a waste of time."

"I don't buy that." Astra made a face. "You think they took the risk of sneaking a tracer past Ark's people so they could ignore it and go home?"

"No, of course not," Lys replied. "But I have no idea why *Wolf's Claw* would go to Antilles either."

"I don't like this, not one bit. We need to get down there and find Ark."

Lys nodded. "I will contact Antilles Control and request a landing assignment."

Astra smiled. "Screw that. Look at that queue. Way too slow. It's time to leapfrog some of these ships." She punched at the comm board. "Antilles Control, this is the Celtiborian courier vessel *Iridan*. I am Astra Lucerne, on an urgent diplomatic mission, and I request immediate landing authorization."

"Celtiborian vessel *Iridan*, stand by."

Half a minute later, the comm crackled to life. "Celtiborian diplomatic vessel *Iridan,* you are clear for immediate landing at the Charonea spaceport, Gold Sector, Bay 03. Welcome to Antilles."

Astra flashed a smile across the cramped cockpit. "Message received, Antilles Control. We thank you for your prompt courtesy."

She held her smile, and then she winked at Lys. "I hate to play the Lucerne card, but I have to admit . . . it always works." She paused and took a breath. "Now let's get down there and make sure Ark knows he's got a tail."

CHAPTER 27

"GO, LUCAS. I'LL GET AUTHORIZATION FOR THE REST OF US TO leave here as quickly as I can, but you're an Antillean national. Your DNA records are still in the system, so they'll let you right through." They were in the restricted holding area of the Charonea spaceport, where new arrivals were detained until their entry visas could be cleared.

Blackhawk stared at his pilot for a few seconds. "I know this will be hard for you, Lucas, especially alone. But we don't know how much time we have. Probably not much. When the Celtiborian war fleet transits out into this system, we're going to be staring at the biggest fight in the history of the Far Stars." He paused again and put his hands on Lucas's shoulders. "We can't wait. We need to know if Marshal Lucerne's suspicions about your father are correct. You can do this."

Lucas nodded slowly. His stomach felt like two hands had grabbed it and squeezed. He hadn't set foot on Antilles since the day Blackhawk had saved him from getting the worst beating of his life and took him back to *Wolf's Claw;* if Lucas had had his way, he'd have never seen the place again. Even the couple times the *Claw* landed on the planet during those years, Lucas had stayed aboard, without so much as tuning in to the Antillean broadcast nets for old time's sake.

And now I'm going to walk directly into the heart of the society I hate.

"I will contact you as soon as I manage to see him." Lucas forced a smile on his face, then he turned and walked toward a different line, much shorter than the one his friends were on. In a few minutes he was in front of a desk, standing under a sign that read ANTILLEAN CITIZENS.

"Name?" The attendant seemed bored, and she spoke in a deadpan voice.

"Lucas Lancaster."

There was a pause. "Lancaster?" Not everyone on Antilles with that surname were members of the same family, but the Lancasters were legendary on a planet dedicated almost religiously to economic prosperity. They were also extremely numerous, and Lucas had hundreds of cousins, born further from the seat of power than he had been, but enormously wealthy nevertheless.

"Yes, I'm afraid I'm one of *those* Lancasters. Danellan Lancaster is my father."

The attendant cleared her throat and smiled. "We never get anyone of your stature here, Mr. Lancaster." Her eyes were wide, her expression almost one of shock. She didn't sound bored anymore.

Lucas sighed. Of course not. There was a separate area for yachts and other craft carrying the privileged elite of Antilles. He almost laughed imagining his father, or any of his arrogant and spoiled relatives, standing in a line at the spaceport.

"Yes, well," he said softly, "I'm sort of the family's black sheep, I'm afraid. I've been away on a bit of an adventure, and I caught a ride home on a small ship that was heading this way." He looked back at her with a pleasant smile. "I am anxious to get back and see my family, so I'd be grateful if you could get me through here as quickly as possible."

"Of course, Mr. Lancaster." She glanced down at a glass plate on top of a small reader. "If you'll just place your hand on the DNA scanner, I will get you out of here in half a minute."

Lucas reached out and laid his hand on the plate. He had a rush of irrational fear, a strange feeling that the scanner wouldn't recognize him, but it was only a second before the attendant's smile grew even wider—and more repulsive to him. He was still *that* Lucas Lancaster, however much he found the whole concept repellent.

"Very well, Mr. Lancaster. Your ID checks out. Again, welcome home. If there is anything I can do for you, please do not hesitate to ask."

He felt a wave of nausea at the obsequious response his identity had provoked. She was a bored civil servant, with more than a touch of her own institutional arrogance, he guessed. She was ready to provide lackluster service to Antillean bookkeepers or engineers returning exhausted from long trips. Normal citizens standing in line spurred no urgency in her, but at the first hint of his identity she'd turned sickly sweet and rushed him through check-in.

To be fair, though, it's exactly what he'd hoped would happen. Still, he was once again reminded how much he loathed this place.

"Thank you," he replied as he walked past her station and the two guards flanking the door beyond. The sentries had been standing stone still the entire time he'd been on line, but now they jumped at his approach and opened the door for him.

Lucas nodded his thanks, and he felt a sudden urge to get back to the *Claw*, to run away from politics and influence and all the corruption of his home world. He could feel the heaviness of his old life closing in on him, and he remembered the urges that drove him to his pipes and needles, and the escapism he had so often found at the bottom of a bottle.

He realized just how much he preferred the honesty of a straight-up fight, the physical exhilaration of sitting at the controls of the *Claw*, desperately trying to escape a whole pack of enemies in pursuit. It didn't make sense, at least not entirely. But at least in action, Lucas felt accomplishment, a value he brought to his crewmates that had nothing to do with twenty generations of rapacious ancestors.

He considered the real loyalty and affection he felt for the *Claw*'s crew. He thought of Ace, who never seemed to tire of giving him shit about something, but who also would stand by his side and fight to the death before abandoning him. He compared that to the spaceport attendant, and the fawning way she had dealt with him as soon as she found out who he was, and was again reminded that wasn't real, like Ace's loyalty or Blackhawk's respect. It was bullshit. Just like everything else on the world of his birth.

He walked out of the terminal and into the bright sun. Antilles had produced a lovely spring day for his homecoming, at least. Though he imagined a few storm clouds would be more appropriate.

He walked past the monorail station to a waiting line of cabs. There was a long queue, with a man directing the operation. Lucas sighed and turned to walk to the back when he heard a voice behind him.

"Mr. Lancaster, allow me to introduce myself. I am Heinrich Klous, the assistant director of the spaceport. Miss Felter at the check-in desk notified me that you had just come through."

Of course she did. But he simply said, "Thank you." Lucas wasn't in the mood for another round of Lancaster worship, and he turned slowly back the way he'd been facing.

The new arrival waved his hands at the attendant directing the cabs. "I am sorry you did not advise us of your impending arrival. We would have made an effort to move you more swiftly through the spaceport." He waved toward the front of the row of cabs. "In any event, there is no need for you to stand in the line, Mr. Lancaster." He gestured to the lead vehicle. "Please, sir, enjoy your trip to your destination and, again, welcome home."

Lucas sighed. "Thank you, Mr. . . . Klous was it?" He walked toward the cab, but the attendant got there first and opened the door.

"Thank you," Lucas said again, as he slipped inside the vehicle. He glanced back at the line and shook his head. Those people had all been on long trips. They were tired, and they missed friends and family. But he'd cut right in front of them, as if they weren't there. He imagined they were supposed to consider themselves fortunate, blessed even, to catch sight of one of the mighty Lancasters. But he suspected there were other emotions there too, less attractive ones.

Well, let them be angry at me. They deserve to be. If it helps any-thing, though, I am here to stop a war . . .

"Lancaster Tower," Lucas growled to the driver. *Let's get this over with. I want to get the hell out of here as soon as possible.*

"ETA to Antilles, six hours, sir." The bridge officer spoke in a stilted tone. Reporting directly to Marshal Augustin Lucerne was well above his normal pay grade.

"Thank you, Lieutenant." Lucerne was standing on *Glorianus*'s flag bridge next to Admiral Desaix. The crew was sitting around nervously. With most of the systems down in hyperspace, they didn't have anything to do but think about the fact that the marshal was standing a few meters away. And they were a few hours from what might become the hardest war they'd yet faced.

"Admiral, the fleet will transit into the outer system. As soon as all units have recovered and are fully operational, we will adopt battle formation and set a course for Antilles." The red-hot anger was gone from Lucerne's voice, replaced by the sound of resignation.

"Very well, sir." Desaix's tone was somber. It was clear he wasn't happy about recent events. He paused for a few seconds. "Marshal, are you . . ."

"I am certain, Admiral. I appreciate your concerns, and I share them myself, but if Antilles is in league with the empire, we must move without delay . . . and we must strike hard. Time will only make things worse." Lucerne turned and stared at his fleet commander. "You know this as well as I do, Emile. We cannot ignore a fact simply because it is a terrible one to believe." The fatigue in his voice was overwhelming. "I will not stand aside while the Far Stars is sold into slavery. I traded away my principles, strove to great lengths to make Antilles an ally. If she chooses to be an enemy instead, so be it. She will learn what that means. But there is no solution in wishing for things to be different than they are."

Lucerne held the admiral's gaze for a few seconds before turning and walking toward the hatch. "I will be in my quarters, Admiral. I have considerable work to do. Come and get me before we emerge."

"Yes, sir." Desaix nodded. "I understand, Marshal," he added, belatedly responding to the Lucerne's previous comments.

Lucerne walked to the door, waving off the guard who moved toward the opening mechanism. Only specially insulated circuits functioned in hyperspace, and powered doors didn't make the cut as necessary systems. But Lucerne wasn't above opening a door for himself, though he sometimes wondered if anyone else realized that.

He pulled the manual latch and slid the hatch open, slipping through and closing it behind him. He walked slowly down the corridor. He didn't have work, not really. He couldn't begin planning the battle for Antilles until he had some scanning results from the system.

He just needed to be alone for a while. He knew he couldn't have more than a few moments. His people needed him now. They were shocked at the prospect of war against Antilles, so recently proclaimed their newest ally, and they needed to draw strength from Lucerne, from the image of the great man they themselves had created.

Lucerne was disappointed, but not surprised, at least not significantly so. A lifetime of war had taught him to expect treachery above all things. But Danellan Lancaster's betrayal would dwarf all the others in cost. Lucerne knew what he had to do, but now he wondered if he had the strength to carry through to the end—to give the orders that would kill millions. *How much blood can one man's soul bear, regardless of whether his quest be a just one or not?*

"Mr. Lancaster . . ." The assistant spoke into the comm unit. Her eyes were moving back and forth from her desk and the visitor standing in front of her.

"Not now, Jasinda. I don't want to be disturbed."

The response over the comm unit was tinny, but Lucas knew the voice immediately. He wanted to heed the dismissal and turn and leave the building before he had to look once again into his father's disapproving eyes. But this was too important. And he'd promised Ark.

Lucas's DNA had gotten him through every checkpoint in the high-security building except this one. No one was admitted to Danellan Lancaster's office without his express permission, at least not by any assistant who wanted to continue working—at Lancaster Interests, or anywhere else on Antilles.

Jasinda's face was twisted into a strange expression. She'd been one of the executive assistants in his father's office for years, and she had recognized Lucas Lancaster immediately. They'd all believed the young heir to be dead, the victim of his many vices.

Lucas pushed aside his doubts and fears. "Don't worry about it, Jasinda. I will handle this." He reached around and pressed the button behind the desk that unlocked the door.

"Mr. Lucas, you can't just . . ."

Lucas raised his hand. "Don't worry about it, Jasinda."

"What the hell is going on out there? I said . . ." The voice from inside the office was angry, but there was something else there too. Something Lucas hadn't expected. Fear. He didn't know if anyone else recognized it, but he was sure. Something had his father in a near panic.

"Me," Lucas said calmly. "That is what is going on." He walked through the door as he spoke. He stopped just inside, staring at the shocked face of Danellan Lancaster. "Hello, Father."

The elder Lancaster paused, his face a mask of pure shock. Finally, he stood up and said, "Lucas . . . Lucas, my boy, it is really you?" His voice was filled with emotion, although Lucas wasn't quite sure which one. Danellan walked around the desk, moving toward his son.

"Yes, it is me." Unlike his father, there was no emotion in Lucas's voice. He'd wondered for years what he would feel if he ever saw his father again—happiness, sadness, rage? Now he knew.

Nothing. I feel nothing.

His father was coming toward him, extending his arms to hug his son, but Lucas reached out his hand between them. A handshake was all he could offer.

Danellan saw Lucas's expression, and he stopped abruptly, gripping his son's hand. "I didn't dare let myself believe you were alive."

"Yes, I am alive. One might even say well, but that is a story for another day." Lucas looked into his father's eyes. He thought all the old urges would be running wild in him, but he was a different man now, no longer the scared, confused kid who'd almost destroyed himself because of his inability to endure the strain of being Danellan Lancaster's son.

That didn't mean that standing in the room with his father wasn't the most difficult thing he'd had to do in the years since Blackhawk had taken him in, but he suddenly realized he could do it. He was far stronger than he'd been, more confident. And he wasn't alone, the way he'd always been among the throngs of Lancaster relatives and retainers. He was part of something in a way he'd never been in those days. He had left Antilles a scared and lost boy, but now he had returned a man.

"We must go back to the estate," his father was saying. "I will arrange a feast and call the family together. It will be a celebr—"

"No." Lucas's tone was one people rarely used with Danellan Lancaster, and the patriarch stood and stared at his son. "I did not come back here to raise glasses and pretend I am part of this family."

"Son . . ."

"Spare me your pretense at familial concern. You weren't there for me when I needed you, when it was politically inexpedient to stand by me. You made your choice in this long ago, so let us leave it at that and not play at fictions of fathers and sons."

"Lucas, I will not have you address me in that tone of—"

"You will," Lucas said, his voice soft, yet seeming to roar across the palatial office. "I did not come for your approval nor your forgiveness, much less, by Chrono's hide, for whatever passes for love in your twisted mind."

Danellan Lancaster stared back at his son, his expression one of utter shock. "Then why did you come?" he croaked.

"I came to save your life. I came because no matter what I may think of you, you are still my father. And because I will not have millions die because of your greed and folly."

Danellan turned and walked back toward his desk. "I have

no idea what you are talking about. You shirked your responsibilities then, and it is clear you haven't changed."

"But you have changed." Lucas's voice was as cold as space itself. "You were always ruled by insatiable greed, but I never imagined you as a traitor to the Far Stars, as a man who would sell himself to the empire."

Danellan Lancaster stopped walking and froze in place. "I have no idea what you are talking about." His voice was quavering. He turned slowly, facing back toward his son. "I have done no such . . ."

"Stop." There was no anger, only fatigue. "Don't waste your breath on lies. There is little enough left between us without you poisoning that."

Danellan stepped back, leaning against the edge of his desk. He sighed loudly then looked up at Lucas. "You don't understand. I had no choice."

Lucas stared at his father, trying but failing to disguise his contempt. "I have tried very hard to convince myself of that." He took a deep breath. "But none of that matters. Your imperial cooperation ends. Now. If we are lucky, no one will know. Or at least there will be no proof. Have you ever thought about how the people would react to news that Lancaster Interests was in league with the empire? I know you don't spend much time worrying about the masses, but that would change if they were storming the Tower screaming for your blood, wouldn't it?"

"Lucas, you *don't understand*," Danellan said again, strength returning to his words. "I didn't have a choice. They control over 30 percent of our stock. They were threatening a takeover fight."

Lucas stared at his father with utter contempt. "You sold out your people to the empire for *that*? Because they threatened your control of the company?" His body was tense with anger.

"Because you didn't have the guts to fight them? To struggle to maintain control of the company? Or even to lose it without turning traitor? This is the mighty Danellan Lancaster? This gutless thing standing here in front of me?"

"That's enough, Lucas!" His father was livid. "You never understood your duties to the family. You cast them aside, twenty generations of your blood, first for drugs and alcohol-fueled binges and later to play at swashbuckler, or whatever you've been doing while I was here protecting the family legacy."

Lucas paused. Some of his father's assault struck a nerve. He couldn't defend his younger self, and for all the difficulties he'd had with his father, he knew he himself had been to blame for what he'd become. He knew the day he started shifting responsibility to his father or anyone else was the first step on his road back to life as an addict and a lost soul. And he wasn't about to take that step.

"My problems were my fault," he said, his voice a bit shaky but still determined. "I don't lay that at your feet, however miserable a father you were. But where is your precious legacy now? In the hands of the empire."

Danellan stood staring wordlessly at his son.

Lucas shook his head and continued, "I still don't understand how you could even think of dealing with the empire. How could you even believe what they promised you?"

Danellan opened his mouth, but Lucas cut him off with his hand. "Don't even try to explain. I don't want to hear it. But it ends now. Whatever you promised them, forget about it. We will fix this."

"I can't back out. It's too late." His father's voice was defeated, and Lucas was surprised how much it shook him, to see his father—an arrogant tyrant for as long as he could remember—so weakened. "They will take over the company," Danellan said. "The Lancaster family will be destroyed."

Lucas pushed back any sympathy he might have felt, looking at his father with iron firmness. "It is not too late for you to find your resolve, to save the family. With strength, not with craven weakness. I have faced danger from the imperials, too—threats made at gunpoint and in battle, not in the confines of the boardroom. You are my father, and you will always be that. But you are a coward, too, and it is time for you show some courage."

Lucas walked forward, stopping less than a meter from his father and staring at the elder Lancaster with an unrelenting gaze. "And I will make it easier for you to do just that, for what is more effective at finding a gutless man's missing bravery than an even worse threat. Because whatever you fear the imperials might do, you have a much greater problem, Father, and it is almost upon you."

Danellan looked at his son in confusion. "What do you mean?"

"You gave your word to Augustin Lucerne. You accepted what he offered you and pledged your loyalty to his cause. Do you know so little of the man to think he would stand by while you reneged on every agreement you made?" Lucas's voice was deep, foreboding. "He knows, Father. He knows you have betrayed him. And even now he is coming here to take his vengeance."

Danellan Lancaster stared back at his son, his face white as a sheet. "How . . . no, it is not possible." His face was twisted in fear and despair. "He wouldn't dare to invade Antillean space."

Lucas shook his head. "You met Marshal Lucerne. Does he seem like a man to be trifled with? To accept treachery? He knows you purchased Vestron Shipping, that you have been delivering arms to Castilla and Rykara. And Nordlingen. And he is coming for you, even now."

Danellan's eyes widened. "Arms? We delivered no arms." There was a wave of outrage in his tone.

"He has the evidence. From a Vestron convoy captured at Nordlingen. It was all in the data banks. The previous shipments, your approval of all of it."

"But I had nothing to do with that!"

Lucas paused. He knew he had no reason to trust his father, yet he found himself believing the older man's protestations. *Not that it matters now . . .*

"Be that as it may, he still knows you postponed the Senate meeting to ratify the Confederation Treaty. He is coming at the head of his fleet, and he will compel Antilles's compliance with its previous commitments, at whatever cost."

"He is coming . . . he is coming to kill me." Danellan reached out with his hand, steadying himself on the edge of the desk.

"Yes, Father. He is."

CHAPTER 28

"I THANK YOU FOR YOUR HOSPITALITY, SENATOR RÁMES." ASTRA Lucerne smiled sweetly as the Antillean politician leaned down and kissed her hand. Astra came no more naturally to politics than her father, but she was a Lucerne, and she did what was required by the situation. Her knowledge of Antillean politicians was extremely limited, but Rames's reputation—both as a major power broker and a shameless womanizer—had reached all the way to Celtiboria.

"It is my pleasure to receive such a charming ambassador."

If he stares at my breasts one more time, I'm going to show him just how charming I can be. "Indeed, Senator, you are far too kind." She pulled her arms back, pushing her chest up and forward. A Lucerne used whatever weapons she had. Astra would have preferred the sawed-off shotgun with the worn pistol grip, but she hadn't been able to come up with a good reason an ambassador would be so armed, so she'd—reluctantly—left it on the ship.

She leaned in, bringing her lips closer to his ear. "I am afraid, Senator, that I am quite tired. I find space travel extremely exhausting." She smiled again and ran her hand through her hair. "Perhaps we can meet again later . . . and get to know each other better." Flirting with the oily politician was enough to turn a rodent sick, but she was here for a reason, and if letting the dim-witted fool think he had a chance was helpful, then so be it.

"Of course, Lady Lucerne. I have taken the liberty of having quarters prepared for you at the Charonea Grande Hotel." He glanced over at Lys, who was watching impassively from a few meters behind Astra. "And for your companion as well." He paused and smiled at her with an expression that reminded her of the Celtiborian swamp viper. "And tonight, dinner perhaps? At my estate . . . just the two of us? Shall we say ten P.M.?"

"I am most grateful, Senator, and I look forward to dinner."

Rames smiled and bowed. "Until tonight, Lady Lucerne." He gestured to an aide standing behind him. "Cavendish will escort you to your quarters."

"Until tonight, then," Astra said.

She walked away, knowing his eyes were glued to her ass.

Keep staring, idiot. It's the last time you're likely to see it.

Blackhawk looked out through the floor-to-ceiling windows, barely noticing the panoramic vista laid out before him. Danellan Lancaster's office had nearly 360-degree views from its perch atop Charonea's tallest building. To the west lay the New City, the elegant and modern towers of its high-end waterfront quickly giving way to kilometer after kilometer of low-rise workplaces and apartment blocks. The far inland edge of the city was a massive industrial zone, and beyond, a lightly developed band of suburbs before the heavy inland pine forests of Antilles's vast northern continent began.

The view in the other direction was equally magnificent, the glistening Topaz Sea stretching to the horizon, the deep red of the late-day sun reflecting off its rippling waves. Antilles was a beautiful world, and a rich one too. Its development had been managed responsibly, a luxury afforded by the planet's vast wealth and advanced technology. It was a planet of well-planned, prosperous cities, and pristine, untouched wilderness. Antilles was often called the jewel of the Far Stars, and it earned its title in many ways.

That is all over, Blackhawk thought grimly, *unless we can pull this off. If we don't, Antilles is finished. It is strong enough to resist Lucerne for a time, but not powerful enough to defeat him. Its strength will turn a war from an easy conquest into a brutal massacre. The Antilleans will mount a strong defense, and they will bleed Lucerne's forces, triggering more brutality and destruction in response. Two worlds that should be allies will fight the most horrendous war the Far Stars has ever seen. One will be destroyed; the other will be so weakened, it will lack the strength to resist imperial encroachment. Somewhere,* Blackhawk thought bitterly, *the governor is laughing.*

War with Celtiboria would be a disaster for both worlds, but Blackhawk knew it would be the Antilleans who would see their cities burned to the ground, their planet's vaunted industry reduced to rubble. Antilles's wealth would be destroyed, and the survivors of war would know poverty and starvation. Famine and disease would sweep the land, killing millions who had survived the fighting.

Perhaps worse, the effects will ripple across the Far Stars, and the confederation will be stillborn. And there will be nothing left to oppose the empire.

Alone among those standing in Danellan Lancaster's office—indeed of all those who dwelt in the Far Stars, save perhaps the imperial governor on Galvanus Prime—Arkarin Blackhawk had witnessed war waged on such a scale. He'd seen millions killed and whole cities reduced to ash. He'd watched the pitiful bands of refugees, those who'd survived the initial conflagration only to die slowly—of the cold, of hunger, of disease. Even Augustin Lucerne's great struggles to unite Celtiboria fell vastly short of the nightmare his forces would unleash on Antilles.

"You must repudiate the empire publicly and absolutely," he said firmly. "You must declare openly that they attempted to subvert you, and state with no equivocation your determination to resist them at every turn. You must lie and declare that no duress, no threats, could compel you to treat with the empire." Blackhawk turned from the window and stared at the hunched-over form of Danellan Lancaster. "And you must do it immediately."

"But, Captain Blackhawk, what of the imperial threats against my company?" Lancaster's voice was shaky, his fear obvious to anyone listening. "And if I repudiate my agreement with the governor, how can I guarantee the safety of my family?"

Blackhawk looked at the Antillean industrialist, trying to hide his disgust. He couldn't imagine how such a moral coward had produced a son like Lucas. "As for your company, the answer is obvious. You fight. You resist their efforts and counter their aggression with your own."

Blackhawk was trying to rally Lancaster, to awaken whatever courage the man had hidden deep within him.

"The remaining shares are held by trusts and large firms, are they not? Many of these shareholders have done business with your family for centuries. They are dependent on you, and they share business relationships vital to their own interests outside their dividend checks. You must contact them, explain the danger, rally them to your side. If necessary, you threaten to expose them if they treat with the empire . . . let them fear the mobs on their own worlds, the torches and pitchforks that would descend upon them. If you must, you sell and mortgage assets, and you buy more stock yourself." Danellan looked as if he were about to protest, but Blackhawk cut him off.

"Yes—this may mean your plans for the future suffer. I'm almost certain Marshal Lucerne will want to discuss some of those exclusive contracts in light of your recent treachery. But at least you will *have* a future. More important, the confederation will have a future, and you will just have to find other ways to prosper . . . ones that do not sell out the Far Stars in the process."

Blackhawk glared at the wilting Lancaster patriarch. "There are many options for you, but craven cowardice is not one of them. If you refuse to stand up to the empire, you will not live to fulfill the promises you made the governor. Your fear will not save you. Marshal Lucerne will destroy you, long before any of your imperial machinations come to fruition. And he will devastate your planet in the process. Millions will die, all because of your betrayal. Because you are *scared*."

Blackhawk took a deep breath and turned back toward the window. The sight of the terrified Danellan Lancaster was making him sick. "As for your personal safety," he said, "you are one of the wealthiest men in the Far Stars, and Antilles is in the very top tier of worlds. If the governor decides to kill you, he will send assassins, not imperial battleships. You have the capability to defend yourself against such an onslaught. Increase your security, trust only your closest aides, rally the Antillean defense forces. And learn to be a man and accept risks." The last line dripped with naked contempt.

Blackhawk looked over his shoulder at Danellan Lancaster. The industrialist was standing meekly, a shell-shocked look on his face. He was afraid—and confused. It was clear the idea of exposing himself to personal danger was a concept utterly foreign to him.

"If you stand your ground, face up to the imperial threats, I will help you. We will all help you." Blackhawk's voice deepened, his determination clear for all to hear. "If you do not, you sign your own death warrant. Augustin Lucerne is almost here. Have you the courage to face him? For the choice is upon you— will you stand against the imperial governor or against Marshal Lucerne? You must make an enemy of one, and Chrono help you if you dither long enough and fail to make a friend of the other."

Danellan Lancaster looked at Lucas, but there wasn't a hint of support or understanding in his son's eyes. He turned slowly toward Blackhawk, and he spoke, his voice halting. "I will repudiate the empire, Captain Blackhawk. I will stand with you . . . and by my agreement with Marshal Lucerne."

Blackhawk nodded. "Very well. Then I will keep my word and help you." He glanced at Lucas then back to Danellan. "You must come back to *Wolf's Claw* with us. Marshal Lucerne may arrive at any moment, and the Antillean forces will respond to the incursion. If we do not stop this before it begins, it may be too late. War, once begun, is difficult to end."

"Why do you need me to come? You can tell Marshal Lucerne I have agreed to all . . ."

"No." Blackhawk's voice was like ice. "Marshal Lucerne is not a man to be trifled with, and his anger should not be underestimated. You must come. You must present yourself before him, call the rumors of an imperial alliance lies, and convince him of your sincerity. This is no time for half measures. The future of the Far Stars rests on the edge of a knife."

"You are coming, Father." Lucas's voice was without emotion. "And we must leave now."

Danellan Lancaster looked like he might pass out at any moment, but he took a deep breath and turned to face his son. "Very well, Lucas. I will come with you."

"Have you managed to break in yet?" Astra was standing nervously behind Lys. Among other talents, Astra's foster sister and oldest friend was a moderately accomplished hacker or, as Lys preferred to put it, a "specialist in information systems."

Right . . . and Blackhawk is just a "misunderstood freighter captain."

"Yes, just pulling up the data now." She made a face. "I expected Antilles to have better frontline security."

"Can we stick to the point? We've got five hours before I'm supposed to be at dinner with that horned-up Antillean politician. So before I end up having to deliver a diplomatic incident directly to his sack with my foot, let's move along."

"Okay, here it is. The ship is the *Iron Wind*. It's registered as a free trader." Lys glanced back at Astra. *Wolf's Claw* was registered as a free trader, too. It was as good as Far Stars code for an adventurer's or mercenary's ship. "Owner of record, Cedric Kandros. Cross-referencing Celtiborian records." She kept reading. "Looks like he's wanted for smuggling on a dozen worlds . . . he's got a death sentence on at least two."

Astra sighed. Of course that could be misleading. When

she'd pulled up Blackhawk's warrants, she'd almost fallen out of her chair. She loved the grim rogue, but half the Far Stars wanted him—or one of his people—dead.

"Astra . . ." Lys's voice had faded to a dry whisper.

"What is it? You look like you've seen a ghost."

"The last update from the Celtiborian net just downloaded. That's why they're here . . ."

"What? Speak! What is why they are here?"

"There is a price on Blackhawk's head, Astra." Lys turned and looked at her friend. "One million imperial crowns."

Astra's eyes widened, and she stared back silently for a few seconds. "Chrono, Lys! That *is* why that ship is here, why they followed the *Claw*. They're going to kill Ark!"

She spun around. "I have to go warn him. Now!" She looked around aimlessly for a few seconds, as if she expected to find her weapons lying on the bed, ready to go.

"You're not even armed, Astra. You can't just go running out . . ."

"I *have* to, Lys. What if Ark doesn't know? What if they get to him?"

Lys stood up. "Astra . . ."

"Where are they, Lys? Where did they land?"

Lys sighed. She knew Astra well enough to realize no arguments would keep her from running to help Blackhawk. She looked down at her screen. "*Iron Wind* is in Bay 14." A pause while she hit a few keys. "The *Claw* is in Bay 3."

Lys turned again, moving toward Astra. "Let's go."

"No, Lys. You have to stay here in case someone comes looking for me." She reached behind her, grabbing her riotous mass of blond hair and tying it in a tight bun. Waist-length locks were good for flirting with pig senators, but not so much for action.

"What should I say if someone asks for you?" Lys's expression was sour. It was clear she didn't like being left behind while Astra went out alone.

"Tell them I'm in the tub. Or sick. Or locked in the bedroom throwing a wild tantrum. I don't care. Just buy some time. And if I'm not back by ten, tell the senator's people I'm sick." She knew that wasn't going to be very convincing, but it was better than nothing. The arrogant fool had her marked for his bed, but he had more chance of getting a massage from the emperor.

"I'll handle it. Whatever happens." Lys took a breath. "And, Astra, be careful."

"You know me, Lys." She flashed her friend a quick smile, and she was gone.

"Put these on. They cost a fortune in bribes." Kandros was leaning against a pile of crates, pulling his boots off. "We've got three hours, and then the new shift is on. And I don't know anybody in that crew to pay off, so if Blackhawk doesn't come back by then, we're going to have to try something else."

He pointed toward the cargo sleds. "And while we're waiting, you slugs put your backs into unloading these ships. That's part of the deal too. If the cargo doesn't keep moving, someone's going to send a supervisor up here to see what's going on."

He watched his crew move toward the pile of overalls, picking out ones that looked closest to a reasonable fit. He didn't care that they were unhappy at doing manual labor. They'd been called mercenaries, outlaws, even pirates, and Kandros knew they'd take any of those titles before being dockhands. *If they want a part of that million, they'll get over it pretty damn quick.*

"I want two of you on station at the entry to the section. If Blackhawk is coming back, we need to know immediately. And we need to be sure how many of his people are with him. We'll have surprise, but that's it. Don't you get cocky and underestimate any of his crew. We've crossed paths with *Wolf's Claw* before, and you know Blackhawk's people are good. Real good."

"So what's the plan, boss?" Mallock Debarnan was fishing through the pile of work clothes, trying to find anything he had a prayer of stretching across his massive frame. Debarnan was 160 kilos of pure muscle, *Iron Wind's* closest answer to the Twins. "Take out Blackhawk and make a run for it?"

Kandros sighed. Like Blackhawk's Twins, Debarnan wasn't the sharp edge of his crew's wit, and he'd long called the bruiser by a simple and descriptive nickname—Brick. "Do you think we're going to kill Arkarin Blackhawk and leave his whole crew alive to hunt us down?" The loyalty of Blackhawk's people was legendary, at least in the circles that had heard of the adventurer and his followers. "Venturi's got to go, for sure. I can promise you, you don't want to run out of here with her on your tail. She's Sebastiani trained, and one of the best. She'll follow you across the Far Stars. You'll be lucky if the bowl doesn't blow up the next time you take a shit."

Kandros pulled the zipper up on his coveralls. The fit was far from perfect, but it would have to do. "And Tarkus, too. That bitch is fucking crazy. No way we leave while she's still breathing." He turned and looked out over his men, all hopping around in various stages of undress. "And Ace is pretty resourceful. The Twins are a nightmare. . . . No, we take out as many as we can, boys, because the ones we let survive will come after us. You can bet your asses on that."

Kandros slipped his boots back on, pulling the legs of his

coveralls down over them. "Okay, Starn: you, Krieger, and Low-rin start unloading that ship over there. It's on the way from the entry to *Wolf's Claw*. As soon as you see Blackhawk and his people coming, hit the comm unit. Don't worry about anybody picking up the transmission. It won't look like anything but a random signal, and we'll be out of here long before anybody investigates."

"Got it, Captain." Starn turned to the others and waved his hand. "Let's go, boys."

"Mallock, Demetus, you're with me here. This ship is the closest to the *Claw,* so we'll stay put and wait." He turned toward the cluster of his men standing and staring back at him. "The rest of you over there." He pointed to a vessel parked on the other side of the *Claw.* "We'll take them from two sides." His voice deepened. "But be fucking careful when it all hits the fan. Remember, we're over here, too. If I get shot by one of you bastards, you better hope you get killed."

Kandros exhaled hard. "Stay sharp, all of you. These people are fucking dangerous. We take them out immediately, while we've still got surprise on our side, and then we get back to *Iron Wind*." He paused, panning his eyes across his crew. "If we don't . . ."

"Emerging from hyperspace in ten . . . nine . . . eight . . ."

Lucerne sat at one of the workstations on *Glorianus*'s flag bridge. Admiral Desaix had tried to get him to take the command chair, almost begged him, in fact. But Lucerne had declined. That seat was Desaix's, as was command of the fleet. Lucerne would give him orders—very fateful orders, likely—but he would not micromanage the operations of the navy in carrying out those commands. As brilliant a strategic mind as the marshal had, he wasn't going to presume expertise during a naval operation.

"Seven, six, five . . ."

Lucerne looked unemotional, like a statue carved from marble. But inside, he was in turmoil. His rage had driven him to mobilize and order the invasion of Antilles. But he was a measured man, and even the anger at bitter betrayal had quickly given way to reason. The problem was reason was even worse than anger this time. No matter how he considered his options, the conclusion was the same. *There is no way I can allow Antilles to side with the empire, no matter what I have to do to stop it . . . how many people I have to kill. The price of mercy here is ultimate slavery for all the Far Stars. And that is too high a cost, even to save Antilles.*

"Four, three, two . . ."

Lucerne's had been a life of duty, and that had meant doing many things he hadn't wanted to do. Virtually abandoning his dutiful wife, leaving her to live—and ultimately die—lonely and sad in the fortress home where he'd taken her after the arranged marriage that had joined her father's army to his. The countless battles, the brutal and bloody struggles that had left millions dead in his relentless campaign to unite Celtiboria. The cloistered life he'd condemned his daughter to live, always a target, not because of anything she'd done, but simply because of who her father was.

" . . . One. Transitioning to normal space."

Lucerne took a deep breath. He wasn't unduly distressed crossing the barrier that separated normal space from the bizarre alternate universe that made faster-than-light travel possible, but he didn't enjoy it either. His main symptom was a sort of breathless feeling that lasted anywhere from ten seconds to half a minute. It had been alarming the first few times he'd felt it, but now he knew it would pass, and he just stood quietly, as his crew raced to bring the ship's systems back online.

"Reactivating communications and scanning grids." The officer was repeating a report from the main bridge. The flag bridge was Admiral Desaix's domain, and its purpose was fleet command and control. Captain Josiah and his people were more than capable of running *Glorianus* from their own control center.

"Preliminary scanning reports coming in."

Lucerne knew there wouldn't be much in the outer system. Perhaps a patrol ship or two, or a small squadron on picket duty. Antilles had one of the strongest navies in the Far Stars— indeed, it was nearly as large as his own Celtiborian fleet—but most of those ships would be on station closer to the planet, near the massive orbital station or the extensive web of bases on the planet's largest moon.

That didn't mean he could be complacent here, though. The Antilleans would respond quickly to the emergence of a massive invasion fleet, and his people would have a fight on their hands long before they reached the planet. The largest space battle in the history of the Far Stars was about to begin.

"Transmit to all vessels as they hook into the comm net," Admiral Desaix said. "The fleet is to assume battle formation. I want all ships to conduct fire drills and full weapons diagnostics now. Anybody gets caught in action not ready or with an undiagnosed malfunction, the Antilleans are going to be the least of their worries."

Lucerne listened to Desaix snap out his orders. The admiral was a veteran spacer, and a commander not unlike the marshal he served. His men loved him like a father, and they feared him even more. Emile Desaix loved his people, and he mourned every crew member he lost, but when battle was in prospect, those considerations were pushed aside. There was only one way in his mind to end a battle. Victory. There would be time to count the cost later, endless hours for guilt and self-recrimination. But not until the fight was won.

"Admiral, we are receiving a communiqué from the Antillean patrols. They are demanding we decelerate at once and identify ourselves."

Desaix didn't say a word. He just turned and looked over at Lucerne. He would command the fleet, but the orders to start a war had to come from the marshal. "Sir?"

Lucerne sat silently for a few seconds. He could feel the tension on the flag bridge, the eyes boring into him from all directions. He'd ordered the mobilization, directed the fleet to come here. Now, it was time. He dreaded what he had to say, but his resolve was like iron. He had no choice. He had to follow through.

"Open a line, Lieutenant." He stared over at the communications officer, trying to look confident, at least for his people.

"On your line, sir."

Lucerne took a deep breath. Then he activated the comm line. "Antillean vessels, this is Marshal Augustin Lucerne aboard the Celtiborian flagship *Glorianus*." *And I am here to start a war.*

"It has come to my attention that certain segments of the Antillean government have been treating with the imperial governor for the purpose of reneging on the Far Stars Confederation Treaty and establishing an alliance with the empire." His voice was loud and strong. He felt a rush of anger thinking again about Lancaster's treachery, and he channeled it into his words, using the raw emotion to give him the strength he needed. The strength to lead his people into Armageddon.

"I demand the immediate surrender of Danellan Lancaster to forces designated by me. I further require that all Antillean military units stand down at once and allow my fleet to occupy strategic positions around Antilles, preparatory to my dispatching military units to the surface to investigate and apprehend any Antillean citizens involved in this treachery. You have ten hours to agree to these terms."

He took another breath. His words were a declaration of war, and he knew it. No planet as strong and proud as Antilles could possibly agree to such terms. Some colony out on the fringe, maybe, but not the richest world in the sector. They would fight, he knew. They would fight hard. And he would destroy them.

CHAPTER 29

"THE *CLAW* IS A FAST SHIP. WITH ANY LUCK WE CAN GET TO Marshal Lucerne before there is any fighting between his ships and the Antillean fleet." Blackhawk was trying to sound positive, but he knew that a thousand things could go wrong. It was going to be hard enough to cool tensions and rebuild the Celtiborian-Antillean alliance in any event. If blood was drawn, it might very well prove impossible.

"I never intended for things to go this far." Danellan Lancaster was glancing back and forth between Blackhawk and his son as they walked through the spaceport. Lucas and Blackhawk had both taken normal taxis to Lancaster Tower, but they'd flown back in a Lancaster airship, turning a half-hour ride through crowded city streets into a quick five-minute jaunt.

"People rarely do. Things are not as clear when they are happening as they are later, when we look back." Blackhawk was angry at Lancaster for what he had done, but he understood too, and he found himself sympathizing with the industrialist, at least partially. Danellan had been motivated by fear, but Blackhawk knew from experience that under certain circumstances, men would do things they wouldn't normally. And he'd done worse things than Danellan Lancaster had and, in some ways, his reasons were less defensible. Fear wasn't admirable, but it was certainly understandable.

"Don't justify his actions, Ark." Lucas's voice was pure venom. "He sold out Marshal Lucerne, he sold out Antilles . . . all of the Far Stars."

"Lucas . . ."

"Okay, let's stay focused," Blackhawk snapped. He understood Lucas's resentment as well as Danellan's weakness. But now wasn't the time to moderate a family debate. They had to get to the *Claw* and blast off as quickly as possible. If Lucerne's forces arrived before they were in position to intercept them, things were going to go to crap quickly.

Blackhawk walked up to the entry leading to the secure area, and he flashed the temporary ID he'd been given when he cleared check-in. The small light flashed green, and the guard nodded and opened the door. Lucas and his father followed close behind. The guard did a double take when they flashed their Lancaster IDs, but a glare from Danellan kept him silent. Lucas was a member of the planet's elite clan, but his father was the *leader* of that family, known to almost everyone on Antilles, a familiar face on the nightly vidcasts.

"Ark." Shira smiled when she saw them come through the

door. Her eyes moved to Lucas and then to Danellan Lancaster. "Are we still a go?"

"Oh yes, Shira—very much so. Let's get back to the *Claw*." He turned toward Danellan. "I believe Mr. Lancaster can arrange for us to have expedited clearance to launch."

Danellan nodded. "That won't be a problem." He sounded a little shaky, but better than he had.

Katarina was standing next to Shira. "We should be ready to go." She looked at Lucas. "Ace is running your preflight check now so we can launch as soon as we get back." She paused, and a small smile passed her lips. "He insisted on doing something. And with Sam down in engineering and Ark and Lucas out, he was the only left who knows how to fly the *Claw*."

Blackhawk nodded, suppressing his own little smile. He knew damned well Katarina could pilot the ship, at least in an emergency. He also knew how morose Ace got when he felt useless, and he had a pretty good idea why Katarina wasn't back on the *Claw* doing the preflight right then.

"Well, okay, let's get going. We don't have much . . ."

The lights dimmed slightly and red lamps went on all around the landing bay. A loud voice blared through the room's speakers.

"Attention, all personnel. Attention, all personnel. Antilles Defense Control has issued a Code One alert. All incoming and outgoing space traffic is suspended, effective immediately. All foreign visitors are to return to their ships inside the bonded area and await further instructions. All Antillean citizens not engaged in vital activities are to return home as quickly as possible and await further instructions."

Blackhawk stood and listened to the voice on the public

address system, as good an announcement of Lucerne's arrival as a fanfare of trumpets would have been. His heart sank.

"All civilians are instructed to follow any order given by defense personnel. Partial martial law is in effect. A list of restrictions and requirements is available on the main page of the Antilles Information Network, accessible from any public information kiosk. Spaceport personnel are to remain at their posts until further notice. All shifts are extended indefinitely . . ."

"Fuck," Blackhawk muttered. "We need to get back to the *Claw* now. We're out of time." He turned toward Danellan Lancaster. "You're going to have to get us permission to take off."

Lancaster nodded. "I'm sure I can . . ."

"Ark! Look out!" The shout ripped through the air, coming from behind a large pile of crates. Blackhawk's head whipped around. He knew the voice immediately. *Astra? No, it can't be. You're hearing things, you old fool.*

Still, his instincts were on fire. He looked off into the depths of the massive landing area. His eyes caught a shadow, and for an instant, he thought it might be her. Then she yelled his name again—her voice coming from *behind* him—and his mind filled in the blanks. There was an enemy out there . . . and somehow Astra was here to warn him.

His hand went to his waist, but his weapons weren't there. He'd had to leave them behind on the *Claw*. Marching through the streets of Charonea fully armed was a great way to end up in an Antillean jail.

He spun around, ducking, just as he heard a loud crack, and Danellan Lancaster screamed and fell back into him. He reached out and grabbed the stricken Antillean, and he saw Katarina firing just past his head. Shira was a fraction of a second behind, but then the two of them were shooting, raking the area off to the left of the *Claw*.

"Ace, we're under attack." Shira was yelling into the comm unit on her collar. "Send out Sarge and his boys. And the Twins. Now!" She was diving for cover as she spoke. She ended up crouched behind a large shipping container next to Lucas.

Blackhawk had already dropped down, pulling the older Lancaster behind a pile of crates. He was looking around wildly for Astra. Once he might have imagined it was her, but now he knew. She was here. He could hear Shira's fire just behind him, but Katarina's had gone silent. He looked quickly and saw she was gone. She was a predator, not a defender, and he knew she was out on the hunt for their attackers.

"Ark, are you okay?" Astra Lucerne ran up from behind a stack of shipping containers. She was stooped down, staying under cover, and she threw her arms around him. "Thank Chrono I got to you in time. You were followed here by a ship called *Iron Wind*. Have you heard of it before?"

"*Iron Wind?*" Blackhawk couldn't think for a few seconds. His mind was overwhelmed with relief at seeing Astra unhurt. He returned her hug, pulling her closer. "Right . . . that's Cedric Kandros's ship. Kandros's a prick. We've had a few run-ins, but there's no real bad blood between us."

Astra slowly pulled away, looking up at Blackhawk. "There's a contr—"

"Yes, a contract. A million crowns." *And Kandros was just the type of greedy lowlife who would drop everything to try and collect it.*

"You knew?"

"Yes, I knew. But I didn't think anybody would be crazy enough to try to pick me off in the Charonea spaceport." Blackhawk could recall a hundred places he'd been—dung heaps on the edge of human habitation where the idea of law enforcement was one drunken fool with a badge and a creaky old gun. But Antilles? A million crowns was a lot of money, but the Antilleans didn't take kindly to shoot-outs in the streets.

But that was the least of his concerns. He needed to get to Lucerne, and they had enough troubles without a two-bit thug like Kandros trying to collect a bounty.

He turned and stared down at Danellan. There was a growing red stain on his abdomen. They couldn't stay here under cover, not if he wanted to keep Lancaster alive. "Stay with me, Danellan. Stay with me." He knew Danellan Lancaster was the only hope of stopping the unfolding tragedy. *If you die, millions will die with you.*

Kandros was crouched behind a stack of crates, holding his scattergun in his hand. The weapon fired a blast of two hundred flechettes, short ranged but carrying a wide swath of death along its path. It had been intended for Blackhawk, if the bastard managed to get past Quintus and his team, but now Kandros knew he had to cover *Wolf's Claw*. He could hear the fire from the forward position. Whatever surprise he had left would only last a few seconds more. If the rest of Blackhawk's people managed to deploy, it would be all over. They'd be in the middle of a protracted firefight, and by the time either side could gain an advantage, a thousand Antillean troops would be storming into the hold.

The anger and frustration were boiling up inside him. His people had been in position for a perfect ambush, but the alarms had wrecked everything. They had panicked and opened fire—and Blackhawk and that witch Venturi had seen his men just in time.

His head snapped to the left as his eyes caught movement around the *Claw*.

Fuck. Blackhawk's people are coming out. He sat stone still, silent, his eyes focused on the shadows moving around into his field of view.

He watched a swarm of men glide around the ship, fanning out cautiously. *Blackhawk's little group of soldiers.* A huge shadow was looming behind them, and a second later, a pair of hulking giants moved into his field of view. *And his two monster brothers.*

He knew they were all good, really good. He couldn't let them spread out. Even if his men could take on all Blackhawk's muscle—and he doubted that—they'd all end up in some cell, or shot dead by Antillean troops long before the battle was over.

He made a snap decision and lunged out to the side, taking an instant to aim and pulling the trigger. The gun kicked back hard, and he let the momentum push him back, back into cover.

The swath of deadly darts fanned out, taking Blackhawk's people from the side. One of the giants went down hard, and at least two of the soldiers. Then the rest spun around and opened fire, raking the area all around him.

Kandros dove deeper behind cover. He caught a round in the shoulder, a heavy bullet from one of the cannons the giants carried, and then he tumbled down the massive stack of crates, slamming hard into the ground.

He shook off the pain. There was no time. And there was no going back now. He'd shot Blackhawk's people, and he knew enough about the grim adventurer to realize the fight would now be to the finish.

He threw aside the scattergun. It was a one-shot weapon, and he didn't have any reloads. He pulled the assault rifle from his back, wincing at the agony from his shoulder, and he crept around the side of the crates. Hopefully, Blackhawk's people were tending to their wounded. That would give him a little time. It wasn't much of an edge, but it was all he had.

"Sarge is down, boss. And Tarq and Drake." Tarnan was out of breath, his voice a hoarse rasp as he ran up and reported to Blackhawk. His fists were clenched tightly, and Blackhawk could feel the fury radiating from him. "Von and Buck got them back to the ship, and Ringo and I came to find you."

Blackhawk's face was an angry scowl. Three of his people were down, and he didn't know if they were alive or dead. He had a pretty good idea who they were fighting, but he didn't know how many men Kandros had or how they were armed.

He looked around. One last check to make sure Astra was okay. Then he peered around the crates and looked off into the depth of the landing bay. There was a coldness in his gaze, a glare that communicated one thing. Death. Whoever had shot his men . . . they were going to die. Here. Now. In this hangar.

"Lucas, you and Ringo, get your father back to the *Claw*. He needs Doc. Now." His voice was an angry growl. "Take Astra with you . . . and don't let her out of your sight."

"Got it, Ark." The anger toward his father that had been so apparent was gone, replaced by a soft, confused tone. "Come on, Ringo . . . I've got his shoulders. Grab his legs."

"I'm not going anywhere, Arkarin Blackhawk. Not until I know you're safely back in the ship." Astra Lucerne's voice was firm, defiant.

"Astra, I don't have time for this. You're unarmed. You

warned me like you came to do. So please get back to *Wolf's Claw*. Now!" He roared the last word with an intensity that surprised even himself. He'd never yelled at her before, but there was no time to waste. Very few people ignored his commands when he issued them so forcefully, but he had no idea if that applied to Astra Lucerne. To his surprise, she simply nodded.

"Take care of yourself, Ark."

He nodded back. "I will." He wasn't sure if she was really obeying him, or if she was just going to the *Claw* to raid the weapons locker, but he didn't have time to think about it. With any luck, things out here would be wrapped up before she could get back anyway.

He turned his head. "Be careful, Lucas. We have no idea what's out there." Blackhawk whipped back toward Shira and Tarnan. "Give me that pistol." He gestured toward the gun hanging at Tarnan's side.

The giant handed Blackhawk the gun, and he followed up a few seconds later with his sword, too.

"Thanks," Blackhawk grunted, reaching out and taking the massive claymore. Shira only had one assault rifle with her this time, and she had it in her hands, ready. "All right, let's go. Be careful . . . don't blow away any Antilleans. We've got enough trouble here already. But when you're sure it's one of Kandros's people, don't hesitate. Waste 'em."

He knew he didn't have to say that. Tarnan didn't know if his brother was even alive, and Shira was . . . well, Shira. They knew what to do.

Moving forward, Blackhawk crouched low behind a large cargo sled. He took a few silent steps forward, and then he heard a loud crash from behind. He spun around to see that Tarnan had pushed over a five-meter stack of crates on top of at least two enemies. He was climbing over the pile, somehow still holding his autocannon with one hand as he did.

Blackhawk turned and swung around himself. He saw movement below, one of the enemy, trying to extricate himself from the collapsed and broken crates that had almost buried him.

Blackhawk's eyes focused, and his hand raised instinctively, firing two shots. The target's head almost exploded as the heavy slugs impacted. Blackhawk was about to run forward when he heard the deafening roar of the autocannon just to his right.

Tarnan was standing atop the mountain of boxes, blasting away with the enormous gun. The massive projectiles tore through the wood and sheet metal of the crates like they were paper, rendering any cover they provided useless and turning the trapped enemies underneath into strawberry jam.

Blackhawk could see that Tarnan had taken out at least two of the enemy, and he was pretty sure there was nothing else alive under there. "Hold fire," he snapped, as he climbed across the pile of debris. He pulled away chunks of splintered wood and looked all around. There were three bodies—all very dead.

Tarnan turned, looking off in the direction of the *Claw*.

"Tarq is tough," Blackhawk said, noting the concerned look on the giant's face. "You know that better than anyone."

Tarnan nodded, but he still looked uncertain.

"Sam, Ace—I need help in here." Doc's voice was strained, nearly frantic. "Now!"

Ace came down the ladder, grimacing in pain with each step. He was far from recovered himself, but the tone in Doc's voice had been unmistakable. He could see Tarq was in the sick bay bed, and the sides of the cot and the floor all around were covered in blood. His massive frame completely covered the cot and hung off on all sides.

Sarge was lying on the floor on top of a sheet, and Drake was sitting against a support beam, holding a large, blood-soaked rag to the side of his chest.

"What can I do?"

"You think you can handle the fuser?"

"I've watched you use it enough on me. I'll manage. What do you want me to do?"

"See if you can get some of Sarge's wounds closed up. I don't think anything vital was hit, but he took at least half a dozen hits, and he'll bleed out if he just lies there."

"Got it." Ace grabbed the small device, flicking it on with his thumb. "I'll get an anesthetic."

"Don't worry about it." It was a throaty growl coming from the floor. Sarge's head turned slowly. "Just patch 'em closed. I'll be fine."

Ace turned and looked down at Sarge. His body was riddled with gunshots, and half his body was covered in blood. Ace's face had a hesitant look. The fuser was an incredibly useful medical tool, but it met no one's definition of painless.

"Okay, Sarge . . ." Ace was struggling to sound strong and confident, but it was difficult. Sarge looked like hell, and from the quick glimpse he'd gotten, Tarq was even worse. "You want me to try to get these darts out, Doc?"

"No, just leave 'em. I'll go back in and fish them out later. For now, we just need to get him stabilized." Doc looked up from his table for a second, glancing toward Ace. "Thank Chrono General DeMark resupplied us with artificial blood."

Ace knelt down over Sarge. "Okay, you dumb ape, this is gonna hurt some."

Sarge gave Ace a nasty scowl, but he didn't say anything.

Don't say I didn't warn you . . .

"Doc, what can I do?" Sam came running in from the engineering access tube. She looked around the room, and her face went white as a sheet when she saw the blood and three of her friends broken and bleeding.

"Check on Drake," Doc snapped.

"I'm fine, Sam," Drake answered almost immediately. His voice was strained, and it was obvious he was in a lot of pain, but he nodded at her and said, "Go help Doc with Tarq. He's worse off than me."

She ran over toward the cot, catching a glimpse of Ace leaning over Sarge, a quick smell of burning flesh hitting her nostrils as the fuser closed a gaping wound.

Running up to the edge of the cot, Sam looked down. She tried to hold back a gasp as she got her first glimpse of Tarq. He was completely naked, but that wasn't what shocked her. His enormous body was torn open in at least a dozen places. There were four gaping wounds in his midsection, and the floor all around the bed was slick with blood.

She looked across at Doc. He was frantically working, but he seemed lost in the enormity of the task. There were so many wounds, so much blood.

And Tarq was running out of time.

Katarina moved swiftly, silently, like a snake stalking its prey. She'd killed two of the enemy already, but now she was tracking the leader. His plan was in ruins, and if he was smart, he'd be looking to flee and save his life. His crew were all dead or fighting their final battles. He'd made his play to kill Blackhawk, but he'd lost. Escape was his only option . . . unless she caught him first.

She was deep in her Sebastiani mantra, emotions mostly purged from her mind, but she couldn't help but feel a twinge of disgust at her quarry. Her service—and friendship—with Blackhawk had taught her what leadership could be but so often wasn't. Now, the man she was hunting reminded her what most leaders were—and why she'd been able to terminate so many of them in her career without a gram of guilt.

She had a bleak view of mankind, one she knew Blackhawk shared. There were worthy people in the vast universe, she knew, but they were few, and hopelessly scattered. Occasionally, one appeared in a position to truly make a difference. Marshal Lucerne was one of those. His campaigns had been costly and brutal, but through thirty years of war and conquest—and overwhelming victory—he had remained unaffected by the massive power he had accumulated. A moral man was a rare enough creature, but one who remained so once he had grasped the reins of power—that was almost nonexistent.

Yet, now even he is being led by anger and the call of vengeance. And millions of innocents may die because of it.

She brought her mind back to the chase. It wasn't time for such thoughts. Her target was all that mattered, and she focused every thought on the hunt. She could hear him ahead in the distance and followed the trail he had left. Even her enemy's scent became a clue for her to follow.

This mercenary—no, murderer—was out of his depth, she knew, no match for a Sebastiani assassin of the First Circle. She focused all her skills, as her training demanded, but she knew she didn't need them. Her quarry was loud and clumsy, and there wasn't a doubt in her mind she would catch him. If he hadn't tried to kill her friends, she would almost feel sorry for him.

She would find him, but then she was going to deviate from her core training. She wasn't going to kill him, at least not initially. She intended to question him. That meant taking him alive.

He will wish I had killed him before I am finished interrogating him. He will learn what the Sebastiani adepts know of the pain centers in the human brain. He will tell me all he knows. Everything.

She crept around the crates, knife in hand, slipping closer to her prey . . .

"Doc," Blackhawk said, standing over a motionless form lying on the deck, "I need you to help Danellan Lancaster." He looked over toward the *Claw*'s small sick bay, where Doc was working feverishly on Tarq. "Now."

"I can't, Ark." The stress was clear in his voice. "Tarq is in bad shape. I . . . I'm not sure I can . . ." His words trailed off.

"Doc, I need Lancaster alive. At all costs." There was nothing but grim determination in Blackhawk's tone.

"Ark, I can't! Tarq needs me now."

Blackhawk gazed down at Lancaster. The magnate's breathing was ragged, forced. His wounds had been hastily bandaged, but the wrappings were soaked through with blood.

He's going to die if Doc doesn't work on him right now. He looked across the room. *But what about Tarq?* It felt like there was a deep pit in his stomach. Arkarin Blackhawk was a veteran, no stranger to combat and to the difficult decisions it so often required. But he couldn't remember one as gut-wrenching as this one.

He looked up. Everyone in the room except Doc was staring

at him, waiting to see what he would say. He took a deep breath, trying to rationalize what he knew he had to do. But nothing worked. With all his heart he wanted to tell Doc to keep working on Tarq, to do whatever he had to do to save the giant. But he couldn't. Without Danellan Lancaster, he had no chance to stop Lucerne's attack. There were two hundred million people on Antilles—and a lot of them would die in the war that would follow. *And then the empire will just walk in . . . and the billions in the Far Stars will live forever as slaves . . .*

"I need you to save Lancaster, Doc." He paused, his mind reeling as he spoke the unthinkable. "Whatever the cost."

Doc looked up for the first time and fixed his gaze on the captain. "Ark . . . he could die. *Tarq* could die!"

"Just do it, Doc." Blackhawk spoke sadly, but firmly. He straightened up and started walking toward sick bay. "I'll try to help Tarq, Doc. You save Lancaster. Whatever it takes." He could see Doc still hesitating. "Do it," Blackhawk said coldly. "Now."

"Ark . . ." Ace had turned and he was limping toward Blackhawk.

"Not now, Ace." The *Claw*'s captain stared toward sick bay, watching as Doc reluctantly moved to follow his orders. He knew every eye was on him. He could feel the tension, the disapproval of his crew, his family. But Arkarin Blackhawk wouldn't let a holocaust occur, even if he had to risk Tarq's life to do it.

He walked the rest of the way to the sick bay alcove, passing Doc as he did. He glanced down at Tarq. His massive chest heaved up and down, struggling for breath. The floor was soaked with blood.

The blood of my friend.

He took a deep breath. He wasn't a doctor, not even a real

medic. Blackhawk had seen enough battlefields to pick up some first aid skills, but the instant he looked down at Tarq he knew he was in over his head.

He picked up the large fuser . . . and put it back down. He didn't know what he was doing. Blackhawk had a lot of skills, but he was no surgeon. He picked up the tool again and moved it toward a massive laceration. He knew there was tremendous damage to repair, but if he didn't stop some of the hemorrhaging, none of that was going to matter.

Hang on, old friend. Hang on. I'll pull you through this somehow.

But he didn't believe it, not really.

The *Claw*'s makeshift doctor was on his knees, bent over Danellan Lancaster. The industrialist was lying on the deck where Blackhawk had set him down. Doc was moving the fuser slowly across the man's chest, closing up the wound. The bullet that had pierced Lancaster's chest was lying on the floor, a few centimeters away.

"He's going to make it, Ark." Doc didn't look up, didn't hesitate as he spoke. It was obvious he was exhausted—and just as clear he intended to keep going as long as there were injuries on the *Claw* that needed his attention.

Blackhawk didn't respond. He was leaning over Tarq, his hands moving frantically over the big man's still form. His face was covered with sweat, and his gloved hands red with blood.

Doc stood up and walked across the room and stopped half a meter from Blackhawk. His eyes fell on Tarq, and then they moved to the medical display. He hesitated a few seconds then he put his hand on Blackhawk's shoulder.

The *Claw*'s captain ignored him, and he continued what he was doing, struggling to fuse the gaping wounds on Tarq's body. He was ignoring everything else, totally focused on what he was doing.

"Ark . . ." Doc's voice was slow, halting. "He's dead, Ark."

Blackhawk paid no attention to Doc's words, continuing to run the fuser back and forth across one of Tarq's gaping wounds.

"Ark," Doc said loudly. "It's too late. Tarq is dead." He grabbed harder on the captain's shoulders, trying to pull him away.

Blackhawk spun around, pushing Doc hard, almost knocking him to the ground. He stood silently, staring down at his blood-covered hands as they closed into fists. Slowly, he looked up. The room was silent, save for the faint hum of the sick bay life support system, still running, futilely now that the patient was dead.

Blackhawk stared at Doc for a few seconds, but he didn't say anything. He turned and looked back at his crew. Drake was leaning against the wall. He was pale, and he looked exhausted, but he was awake. His eyes were tired slits, and they were fixed on Blackhawk. Sarge was lying in a makeshift bed on the floor next to him. Ace had pulled half the bedding from the ship's cabins to create a comfortable place for the noncom. Doc wanted his patients out in the main deck, where he could keep an eye on them all, and Ace had accommodated him.

Sarge was out, probably unconscious from his own injuries, and certainly from the massive injection of tranquilizer Doc had given him. There was nothing he needed now more than sleep, and Doc had taken no chances with the dosage.

The rest of the crew was standing around the ladder to the bridge. Sam was sobbing softly, her face a mask of tears. Shira was next to her, stone still and silent, staring vacantly into space. Ace was holding on to the ladder, his face red and feverish, the exertion of the last hour clear to see.

Blackhawk looked over at the rest of Sarge's boys. Von, Ringo, Buck . . . they were like statues, staring across the room with barely controlled rage in their eyes. They were focused on Katarina and Lucas, and the sobbing giant they held firmly between them.

Cedric Kandros was bleeding from a dozen cuts, and his left arm was broken, twisted out at an obscene angle. Katarina been far from gentle, but she hadn't killed him either. She'd wanted to. But something had stopped her short of the fatal blow, and she had brought the prisoner back to Blackhawk. Now the wretched creature stood in front of the entire crew, facing his own nightmarish judgment day.

Kandros's people were all dead, lying on the blood-soaked floors of the landing bay. Even the massive Mallock Debarnan was sprawled on the ground just outside the *Claw*, his enormous neck broken in an epic struggle where Tarnan's sheer strength and rage had won the victory.

Blackhawk looked back toward the sick bay station, to the unmoving form lying on the sole cot. He felt sick to his stomach, and his joints tightened with unfocused rage. He knew his people felt the same, that despite having killed all of Kandros's people, their bloodlust still howled for satiety. They faced a desperate struggle still ahead, a race to stop a pointless and tragic war. But they knew, even if they prevailed, there would be no sweetness to their victory. Today they had lost one of their own. Tarq had been a great warrior, a fiercely loyal member of the crew, and he'd saved more than one of their lives.

And I just killed him, Blackhawk thought morosely. *I chose the life of another man, a stranger, a moral coward who had treated with the enemy . . . over my friend.* He tried to tell himself he had chosen the millions on Antilles . . . and the billions in the Far Stars, but even though it was true, it felt hollow, empty. *Tarq is dead, abandoned by the man he trusted most. Me.*

Blackhawk turned away from Tarq's body and walked over toward Kandros, stopping just a few centimeters from the man's face. He stared at the captive, and his eyes held icy death. "Crowns?" he spat. "You did this for crowns? To collect a blood price placed on me by minions of the empire?" His voice was thick with rage, with roiling hatred.

"Your men are dead, Kandros. All of them. Was it worth it? Your greed brought you—and them—to this. And now you will pay the price, as those who followed you already have."

He turned and walked back toward the cot, looking down for a few seconds at Tarq's lifeless form. He felt the fury coursing through his body, the need for blood, the lust for vengeance. He leaned down and grabbed Tarq's belt, lying discarded at the side of the bed in a pool of partially congealed blood.

He held it up, pulling the heavy, notched survival knife from the sheath. His hands were still covered with blood—his friend's blood. He drew his hand across his face, smearing streaks down his cheeks, scarlet warpaint, a silent tribute. For now he would take vengeance for his fallen comrade.

He walked slowly toward Kandros. The mercenary was conscious, his eyes wide with fear. He struggled to free himself, but Tarnan's grip was like a vise. He whimpered as Blackhawk approached, but no words could come forth from the gruesome wreckage of his mouth. Katarina had hit him hard with his own rifle butt, shattering his teeth and turning his face into a bloody mess.

"This is what you have earned, Cedric Kandros," Blackhawk said, every word dripping slowly from his mouth, like venom from a cobra's fang. "Now you die, you piece of garbage, and I will leave your body to rot until even the carrion birds are turned sick at your stench."

He moved right up to Kandros, his eyes just a few centimeters from those of his victim.

He moved the blade forward, slowly, steadily. He felt the resistance of Kandros's skin for an instant, then a small pop as the heavy blade penetrated.

Blackhawk stared into Kandros's eyes as he shoved the blade deeper, pushing slowly, so slowly. His victim whimpered, tried to scream through the broken wreckage of his mouth, spitting out blood and shattered bits of tooth as he did. His eyes looked into Blackhawk's, a silent plea for mercy. But they met only coldness, a frigid stare like the icy depths of space. Kandros's hopelessness and despair only energized Blackhawk, and he twisted the knife harder, drawing the last waves of agony from his dying victim.

Tarnan and Katarina tightened their grip as Kandros began to slide down, his own body surrendering the last of its strength. Blackhawk could see the cloudiness in Kandros's eyes as death began to take him, but his victim still convulsed in pain as he shoved the blade upward, slicing from the abdomen to the chest.

"And now I send you to hell, Cedric Kandros." He shoved the blade hard, again and again, slicing and tearing through the mercenary's body. Blackhawk was covered in blood, but still he kept thrusting, until finally he took a step back and let the blade drop to the floor.

He stood there drenched in blood, staring straight ahead but seeing nothing. *You were a great warrior, Tarq Bjergen, and a loyal companion. Take what solace you can. Your comrades in arms have avenged you.* He paused, struggling to hold back the grief threatening to overwhelm him. *And forgive me, my friend, if you can. Though I doubt I will ever forgive myself.*

Blackhawk remained still, his mind deep in dark places. He'd longed for vengeance, ached to make Kandros pay for what he'd done. He wasn't proud of it, but he knew it was true. Cedric Kandros had deserved no better than he'd gotten, but Blackhawk reminded himself yet again that the darkness he'd run from for two decades was still inside him. He'd felt the savagery, the raw brutality, like a beast released from its cage.

He knew the satisfaction of the kill was a poor substitute for a friend who was now gone, that gruesomely killing Kandros wouldn't bring Tarq back. He'd have chased Kandros to the ends of the Far Stars for vengeance, but in the end it was hollow and empty, as he knew it would be. The pain of loss was still keen, as it always was.

He forced himself back to the present. There was no time for mourning or self-doubt. Those were indulgences that would have to wait.

He knew the entire crew was staring at him, and he could only imagine what they were thinking. The *Claw*'s crew had always been like a family, standing side by side against any danger, and trusting one another without question. That was what Blackhawk had built, and it had been the proudest accomplishment of his life. *And now I've destroyed it.* He didn't know how his people would react to what had happened, but he was sure of one thing. Nothing would ever be the same.

He forced himself to lift his eyes, to look at each of his crew members in turn, returning their stunned stares. All but Tarnan. For all Blackhawk's strength and courage, for the raging darkness deep inside that drove him ceaselessly forward, he couldn't bring himself to face Tarq's brother. Not yet. *Will I ever be ready?*

He forced himself from his introspection. He didn't have time for this now. If they didn't hurry, it would be too late to stop the war. And then his terrible decision would be futile. He'd have killed his friend for nothing.

"Lucas, Sam . . . we have to get out of here. We're out of time."

CHAPTER 30

"ALL ANTILLEAN PERSONNEL, THIS IS THE VESSEL *WOLF'S CLAW*. We are launching in thirty seconds, with or without clearance. We do not wish to injure anyone, so please clear the area around the ship immediately."

Blackhawk sat in his command chair. He'd expected to have Danellan Lancaster on the bridge, arranging launch clearance with one of his government cronies. But Lucas's father was on the lower deck, badly wounded and unconscious. Blackhawk had almost ordered Doc to pump the Antillean full of uppers and get him to the bridge, but he held back. He needed Lancaster awake and alert to deal with Marshal Lucerne, and he wasn't sure just how much the wounded man had left in him, even with Doc's pharmaceutical assistance. After what he'd done to save the industrialist's life, Blackhawk wasn't about to let the bastard die—not until he'd served his purpose. After that, he honestly didn't give a shit.

Blackhawk looked like hell. His clothes were soaked with blood. Some of it was his, some Tarq's, which was still smeared across his face in his own primal tribute to his fallen friend. But most of it was from the men he'd killed, Cedric Kandros and his people. The crew of *Wolf's Claw* had been hurt, and one of them lost forever. But no one from *Iron Wind* had escaped.

"Vessel *Wolf's Claw,* this is Major Pollis of the Antillean Defense Force. You are ordered to power down immediately and surrender. You will not be allowed to leave Antilles. If you do not comply and exit your vessel, we will open fire."

Blackhawk sighed grimly. He'd never liked being told what he was and wasn't *allowed* to do, and he rarely let inconvenient rules interfere with his actions. Besides, it was an empty threat. Pollis's troops had small arms only, nothing that could pierce the *Claw*'s armor. Until they managed to get a tank or some heavy weapons sent in, Blackhawk could just ignore them.

"Lucas, get us out of here. Now." He sighed again. He knew some of the men surrounding his ship would be incinerated when Lucas fired the engines. He had warned them, though, and that was all he could do. If he didn't get the *Claw* off Antilles and close enough to contact Marshal Lucerne, the cost would be incalculable—to everyone, not least the Antilleans themselves.

"Fire a half-second burst. Then wait ten seconds before you fully engage," he added. *Maybe they will run at the first small blast.* It was a chance, at least, to send some soldiers back to their families that night instead of killing them pointlessly.

"Got it, sir." Lucas's voice was strange, distracted. Blackhawk knew the last day had been difficult for all of them. Beyond all they had been through, the pilot's estranged father lay on the lower deck, badly wounded, and despite his repeated protestations about not caring, Blackhawk knew his young pilot's true emotions were vastly more complex and confusing.

The ship shook as Lucas fired a quick pulse from the thrusters. He sat quietly, eyes locked on the timer, waiting to engage the main engines.

Come on, guys. You know you can't stop the takeoff. Run. Get behind cover. Blackhawk nodded to no one in particular. He'd done all he could. There just wasn't any more time.

"Liftoff in three . . . two . . . one . . ."

Wolf's Claw shook hard for a few seconds as the massive output of its engines overcame Antilles's gravity and pushed the ship up from the landing bay.

Blackhawk felt the g-forces pushing him hard into his seat. The dampeners reduced the effect the crew felt inside the ship, but takeoff was still a rough ride by any measure.

"As fast as you can, Lucas." Blackhawk was sure his pilot knew what to do. Giving the order was as much for him as for Lucas. The hardest times for a commander were the ones where there was nothing to do but sit and wait. Blackhawk hated feeling ineffectual.

"Pushing it right to the edge, sir." A short pause. "Altitude five kilometers."

Blackhawk knew the Antillean forces were scrambling to face Lucerne's fleet, rushing strength to meet the threat. Hopefully, that would give the *Claw* a chance to slip away. She was faster than anything in the Antillean fleet, so maybe, just maybe, if enough vessels had already been dispatched to the outer system . . .

"Shira, you better get down to the turrets. We don't want a fight here, but we've *got* to get to Lucerne. At any cost." He paused. "And see if . . . Tarnan is up to manning the other gun."

"Yes, Captain." Shira's voice crackled through his headset. Her tone was stilted, unusually formal.

"No," he heard on the comm, in the distance behind Shira. "I'll go." It was Ace. His voice was weak, and Blackhawk imagined him standing there about to fall over.

"Forget it, Ace. You sound like shit. Get back to bed."

"C'mon, Captain. Listen to me. If we get into it with the Antilleans, we have to disable them, not blow them away. You need your best shots in the turrets. And that's me." He paused. "And then Shira. And you can't send Tarnan. Not now."

Blackhawk stared emotionlessly forward. Ace was right, and he knew it. And their lives were all at stake. *It's not like Ace's life wouldn't be in danger lying in his cot. If we get blown to bits, he dies too.* "All right, Ace, but if you can't manage it, I expect you to tell me straight out."

"I promise, Captain." Blackhawk didn't believe it for a second. He wondered if Ace did.

No—I'll find Ace dead in that chair before he'd tell me he couldn't handle it.

"Fifty kilometers," Lucas said. "Passing lower orbital threshold in twenty seconds."

Blackhawk nodded. "Full thrust as soon as we clear orbit, Lucas. We're on borrowed time here."

"I'm ready, sir." The strain in Lucas's voice was clear. "Should be about four more minu—" His head snapped around. "Bogies, Ark. Multiple contacts in pursuit."

Fuck. "Time until they're in range?"

"Not enough. Two minutes, maybe two and a half."

"Prepare evasive maneuvers." *That will slow us down, but we don't have a choice.*

"Yes, sir."

Blackhawk hit the comm switch. "Shira, Ace, you guys better get a move on. Looks like we've got a shitstorm heading our way."

Two fleets were approaching each other in the emptiness of space. They were among the largest forces of war ever gathered in the Far Stars. Both were on full alert, their crews at their stations, ready for combat. One was in perfect battle formation, arrayed for the fight to come. The other, somewhat smaller, was still gathering, its scattered units rushing to take their places in the battle line.

Deep in the control center of the *Glorianus,* Marshal Augustin Lucerne sat quietly, lost in thought, as the razor-sharp instrument of war he'd spent his life building hurtled toward its greatest test.

This wasn't the war he'd imagined, the righteous struggle he'd prepared so long to fight. The ships his forces approached should be allies, not enemies, but once again betrayal and treachery had destroyed the best-laid plans. The spacers manning those ships were innocent, he knew. At least the vast majority of them. But they would die all the same, their lives forfeit because of the actions of their corrupt and duplicitous leaders.

Many of his own people would be lost too, Lucerne realized. Men who served him loyally, who trusted him to lead them . . . thousands would never return home again, leaving behind broken families and orphaned children. They would die in space, far from home. They would die because faithless men had betrayed their promises.

Lucerne tried to tell himself all that, but he also knew they would die because of *him*, because of his unbreakable, unbendable will. He would pursue his dreams of confederation until they were reality—or until he breathed his last ragged breath. He'd always considered strong will to be a virtue, but now he wondered if too much was as great a sin as too little. Was it arrogance driving him forward so relentlessly? Pride?

"Incoming message . . ." The communications officer looked back at Lucerne, who gestured toward Admiral Desaix. "Incoming message, Admiral," the lieutenant repeated, now staring at the fleet admiral. "We are ordered to leave the system at once and under no circumstances are we to move closer in than three billion kilometers from the primary."

Desaix looked over at Lucerne. The marshal sat completely still, not moving, hardly breathing, staring down at the floor. Finally, he turned toward the admiral and nodded his head. Simple, wordless, but completely understood. It was his authorization to start a war.

"They're coming in from multiple directions now." Lucas Lancaster's voice was frazzled, but still strong with confidence. Blackhawk understood well. Battle was dangerous and deadly— and often wasteful. But it had a way of consuming the mind, and driving away other thoughts and concerns. At this moment, he knew Lucas wasn't a confused scion of a powerful family or the estranged son of a man he wasn't sure if he loved or hated. Or an adventurer mourning the death of a friend and comrade. He was the pilot of *Wolf's Claw* and nothing more. He was undoubtedly afraid, as anyone sane was in battle, but the other emotions that had been tormenting him were gone. Blackhawk knew they'd be back, that his pilot would again face his own personal demons, but right now he didn't think Lucas gave a damn. He had one purpose, to pilot the *Claw* through whatever was coming, and that required everything he had to offer.

"Do your best, Lucas." Blackhawk's hand was on the comm unit, waiting to hit the button and give the order for Shira and Ace to open fire. His hand felt like a block of ice. He knew how good the two of them were. They would try to take out engines, to spare the targets any critical damage. But it was hard enough to hit a ship at all at one hundred thousand kilometers. If the fight went on, his people would kill Antillean spacers. And the disaster that was unfolding throughout the system would get that much worse.

"At least a dozen ships are chasing us now, Ark. They'll trap us sooner or later. And zigzagging around is stopping us from building any decent velocity." Lucas turned his head sharply and looked back at Blackhawk. "Even if we can stay away from these guys, at this rate we're never going to get to the outer system and reach Lucerne."

Blackhawk sighed. The Antilleans were jamming all communications. There was no way to reach the marshal, not across two light-hours of space. And any chance of getting close enough in time was rapidly fading.

"If we can knock out one or two of them, we might be able to blast through the hole before any other ships can come around." Lucas turned again and stared back at the command station. "If we can stay ahead of them on a vector to the deep system, we can . . ."

Blackhawk paused. "No." He fell silent for a few seconds, staring at his screen but seeing nothing. "There's no point. We'll never get to Lucerne in time. And once they start shooting, it will be too late."

"We can't just give up, Ark."

"We're not giving up, Lucas." Blackhawk took a deep breath. "We're going to jump to the outer system." He flipped the comm unit before Lucas could respond, opening a channel to engineering. "Sam, we're going to jump in three minutes. To the outer system."

"What?" she shrieked. "That's impossible."

"She's right," Lucas added. "There's just no way. I don't even have a plot. And that's serious pinpoint navigation you're talking about. If I had half a day to work out the nav, maybe, but . . ."

"Forget plotting. That's the least of our worries. The drive is stone cold." Sam's voice was shrill and loud, even through the speaker. "It won't matter where you plan to go, 'cause we'll blow up the second I feed that much power into the system all at once."

"Enough," Blackhawk said, with a finality that shut both of them up immediately. "We can waste what little time we have arguing about how difficult or dangerous this is, but that won't change a thing. We've got a dozen Antillean naval ships chasing us. These aren't pirates on the fringe, half drunk and shouting wog battle cries. They're Antillean regulars. We're not getting out of this one, even if we start shooting at them and killing innocent spacers. And even if we do that, we still can't get close enough to Lucerne to burn through the jamming, not in normal space. Not in the time we have left. And once they start shooting, everything will go to hell in a hurry."

His volume was moderate, but there was a firmness and an authority in his voice that kept them silent. "You two are the best pilot and engineering team in the Far Stars. If we're all going to bet our lives on someone, there's no one better than you. So, please . . . don't argue with me. Don't give me a list of reasons it can't be done. Just follow my orders. And do the best fucking job you can."

Lucas nodded slowly. "Okay, Ark." He sounded scared, but there was determination in his tone too.

"Sam?" Blackhawk asked softly.

"Fine, Ark. I'll do whatever I can." She paused. "I just hope you understand what a risk this is."

"I understand." He glanced at Lucas then back to the comm unit. "Just do the work. Both of you."

He slapped his hand on the comm unit. "Doc, I need you to get Danellan Lancaster conscious and completely lucid. Now."

"I'll try, Captain." There was doubt in the medic's voice. "I need to be careful how much stimulant I give him. He's still in serious condition."

Blackhawk felt a surge of rage. His mind filled with an image of Tarq lying on the sick bay cot . . . dead so Doc could save Danellan Lancaster. "Listen to me very carefully. I don't care what you have to pump into him. I need him awake and alert now, Doc. I don't care if he dies afterward, but he is going to tell Marshal Lucerne what he must if you have to pump him full of rocket fuel. Do we understand each other?" His voice dripped venom.

"Yes, Captain," came the reply. "I will make sure he is awake."

"The battle line will enter firing range in two minutes." Admiral Desaix spoke calmly, meticulously. He was addressing the entire fleet, the combined might of Celtiboria. For thirty years, Marshal Lucerne's land forces had waged the monumental struggle to unite a world. Now it was the fleet's turn to show its worth.

Desaix turned and looked toward Lucerne.

The marshal nodded, and he put his hand to his collar, activating the comm unit clipped to his lapel. "Attention, all Celtiborian spacers, this is Augustin Lucerne." He paused for a few seconds. "You are part of the finest fighting force the Far Stars has ever known. We are about to enter a combat we did not expect, one we do not want. Yet we know from long and hard experience, we cannot always choose our battles, and often war is forced upon us. Though I wish we did not have to fight here, the brutal truth is that we must, and I know all of you will conduct yourselves with the courage and distinction that have become your hallmarks."

He moved his hand to deactivate the comm unit, but he didn't press it. Instead he continued, saying, "I am here with you, and together we will fight this battle. I know we will win the victory, at whatever cost, and for your steadfastness and your unshakable loyalty, you have my ever-lasting admiration and gratitude. Up, Celtiborians, and to your posts! And fight the battle to come with the ferocity all have come to expect from you."

He finally tapped the comm unit and nodded slowly, painfully to Desaix. "Fight your battle, Admiral," he croaked, and his mind drifted into darkness.

"Ten seconds." Lucas's voice was raw. "Make sure you're strapped in. This is going to be a rough ride."

"All right, Lucas, I'm flooding the hyperdrive on one. Then she's all yours." *If she doesn't blow* was left unsaid, though everybody was thinking it. "Three . . . two . . . one."

The *Claw* was plunged suddenly into blackness, as every watt of power was redirected all at once to the hyperdrive unit. The ship lurched hard, and a shower of sparks exploded through the darkness of the bridge. An instant later, the dim battery-powered lights came on, just as another conduit exploded, illuminating the bridge like daylight for an instant.

Wolf's Claw was being shaken apart. Blackhawk's workstation was down, but he didn't need a data feed to tell him the explosions he heard from the lower deck were bad. The *Claw* was like an extension of his body, and he could feel its pain. He knew his ship was dying. A few more seconds, and she was going to blow.

"Now," Lucas screamed, and the ship spun wildly.

Blackhawk could hear more explosions all around the ship, and for an instant he thought they were all dead. Then the alien feeling of hyperspace took him. For the first time in all his travels, the strange other universe that enabled faster-than-light travel felt like a relief.

They weren't out of the woods yet, though. Lucas was flying the ship by the seat of his pants, and they'd be lucky if he managed to get them back to normal space at all, much less anywhere near where they wanted to be.

"Transitioning again," the pilot said, as much to himself as anyone else.

The ship shook hard again and resumed the out-of-control spin. Blackhawk had been holding his breath, but now he exhaled loudly. He could feel it. They were back in normal space.

Lucas was hunched over his controls, firing the positioning engines, trying to kill the roll and stabilize the ship. The smell of burning circuitry was everywhere, and Blackhawk could hear the crackle of electrical fires burning all around him. He knew his ship was wounded, but he was sure she'd do her duty. Still, his stomach was clenched, waiting to see if the scanners came back online—and if they did, how close Lucas had managed to get them to Lucerne's fleet. If they hadn't cleared the Antillean jamming, the terrible risk had been in vain. All would be lost.

He stared at his display and, suddenly, a wave of relief surged through his body. He saw the flickering light of the plotting screen coming to life. The *Claw* was surrounded by contacts. An instant later the comm unit blared loudly.

"Attention, *Wolf's Claw*. Attention, *Wolf's Claw*. This is the Celtiborian flagship *Glorianus*."

Blackhawk stared down at his screen. *Glorianus* was less than forty thousand kilometers away. Lucas hadn't just hit the bull's-eye. He'd split his own arrow.

"*Glorianus*, this is Arkarin Blackhawk on the *Wolf's Claw*. I need to speak with Marshal Lucerne immediately."

"Marshal Lucerne, I have Danellan Lancaster with me aboard the *Claw*. You are acting on partially inaccurate information. Imperial operatives have attempted to take control of Lancaster Interests in an effort to compel cooperation; however, Mr. Lancaster has rejected these outright." Blackhawk spoke quickly, as close to frantically as Lucerne had ever heard him.

The marshal sat at the workstation to the side of the flag bridge, listening to Blackhawk's transmission. "Ark," he replied grimly, "I understand you want to prevent a battle here, but we have evidence that the Lancasters have been working with the empire to deliver advanced arms to our adversaries—including on Castilla, where you encountered them. It is inconceivable the Antillean Senate was not also involved."

"Marshal, you have to listen to me. You are making a terrible mis—"

"Ark, I appreciate your efforts, but we're engaging in forty-five seconds. I can't take the risk that you're wrong. An imperial-Antillean alliance would be a disaster." He paused. "I just can't take the chance."

There was a brief delay then: "Marshal Lucerne . . ." The voice was weak and throaty. "This is Danellan Lancaster. If you stand down, I will come aboard your flagship immediately. I reaffirm the agreements we made, despite imperial attempts to bully me into repudiating them. It is essential that we stand together, now more than ever."

Lucerne was silent, staring at the comm unit but saying nothing. His mind was racing. He was suspicious of Lancaster. He'd never trusted the Antillean robber baron, and now less than ever. *But what about Ark? Why is he so convinced Lancaster is telling the truth?* He trusted Ark with his life. But that didn't mean Blackhawk couldn't be wrong.

"Augustin, listen to me." It was Blackhawk again. "I know you have reason to doubt anything you hear now, and I understand your concerns about Antillean-imperial intrigues. But if you attack now, you will play into the empire's hands. This is what they want—to sow suspicions among us, to goad us into fighting each other. Please, Augustin. Trust my judgment. *Trust me.*"

Lucerne turned and looked over at Admiral Desaix.

"Twenty seconds, sir." The naval officer stood still, like a statue carved from cold marble. "Should I give the order to attack?"

Lucerne looked down at the comm unit then back up to the admiral. Every bit of his vast military experience told him he should strike now. If he didn't, his fleet would sacrifice the tactical advantage. If the Antilleans attacked first, his losses would escalate rapidly. He could even lose the battle.

"Ten seconds, sir. We need an answer."

Lucerne sighed hard. "All ships stand down. Remain on alert. No one is to fire without my specific order."

Desaix relayed the command to the ships of the fleet, and

Lucerne stared down at his scanner, watching, waiting to see if the Antilleans would back off too. If not, in about ten seconds, thousands of his people were going to die.

Danellan Lancaster looked like hell. He was pale, and Blackhawk thought he might pass out at any moment. But that was okay. Lancaster was a flawed man for sure, but he'd come through and done what he had to do. Not only did he address Marshal Lucerne, he convinced the Antillean commander that the Celtiborians had indeed aborted their planned attack. His life had been saved at enormous cost, and now he'd repaid a portion of that debt. Tarq's life hadn't been lost for nothing. Indeed, millions of lives had been saved, and the Far Stars still stood strong, able to face imperial aggression.

"Lucas, why don't you help your father over to sick bay? I think it would be a good idea if Doc checked him out." Lancaster's wound had been bad, but the medic had done an impressive job. The bullet had done considerable damage, but Lancaster had been strong enough to do what had to be done.

Lucas nodded. "Thanks, Ark. I will." He reached his arm around his father's back and helped him toward the *Claw*'s small med unit.

Blackhawk watched the two moving slowly across the deck. He knew the conflict between Lucas and his father ran deep, but Danellan had followed through on his promise, and he'd played no small part in averting a catastrophic war. That didn't erase years of resentment between the two, but maybe it was a start.

Blackhawk had done what had to be done, as always, but he was still troubled. He didn't like misleading Lucerne. The marshal was his oldest friend, and someone he'd been able to trust with his darkest secrets for decades. But there hadn't been time to explain everything, and Blackhawk had been prepared to say whatever it took to avert disaster. He had deliberately misled Lucerne, presenting a highly edited description of events.

Because the fact was, Danellan Lancaster had been on the verge of betraying the Celtiborians to the empire, and the marshal had a right to know the specifics.

But Blackhawk wasn't going to tell him.

As long as Lucerne believed that Lancaster had been steadfast, that the information he'd received was misleading, a lot of bloodshed could be averted. So Blackhawk was going to let him continue to think that. The truth could accomplish nothing, except to weaken an already shaky alliance. And Celtiboria and Antilles *had* to be allies. The imperial governor was clearly a danger to the entire sector, and Lucerne's Far Stars Confederation was more vital a goal than ever. *And I can't let Tarq's death be for nothing.*

"Wow . . . do you look like hell." Astra's voice pulled him from his thoughts.

Blackhawk turned around. He was overwhelmed with grief and guilt, but he managed a tiny smile for her. He couldn't even imagine what a horror he was to behold. He had at least half a dozen wounds, mostly minor, but still nasty looking. His clothes were in tatters, and he was covered in blood, most of it dried by now.

"I feel like hell too. We do what we must, but that doesn't mean we can live with ourselves."

"Ark," she replied softly, her voice soft, compassionate, "you didn't have a choice. It's been a shock to the crew . . . and to Tarnan. But they all understand . . . they will, at least."

He sighed softly, but he didn't reply. There was no point in discussing it. He would take the guilt for Tarq's death to his grave. He knew why he'd done it, he understood how many lives had hung in the balance. But in the end, none of that mattered. Not to him at least, not in the place where he judged himself, where justification and remorse were of little value.

He stood for a few seconds just looking at Astra. *God, she's beautiful. And capable too. In another time, another place . . .* He didn't know if Kandros's surprise attack would have succeeded if Astra hadn't shown up just in time, but he knew there was a good chance she had saved his life.

"I never thanked you for coming all this way to warn me." He smiled at her. "Or scolded you for taking such a crazy chance."

"I'll always come when you need me, Ark. You should know that."

"Astra . . ." His voice turned dark and serious. "I need to tell you something. In private. Let's go to my quarters."

She looked back at him, a quizzical expression on her face. "If that was a pickup line, I *know* you can do better." She immediately regretted the attempt at humor. She wanted to make him feel better, but now wasn't the time.

He forced a brief smile and gestured for her to follow. When they got to his quarters, he closed the hatch behind them. "This is something I'm going to tell the others too, something I've kept to myself for far too long. But . . . I wanted to tell you first."

She sat on the edge of the bed and motioned for him to sit next to her. "You can tell me anything, Ark. I hope you know that."

He saw her gesture, but he remained standing, facing her from a meter away. "You say that, but that's because you have no idea what I'm going to tell you. No," he said, knowing she was about to protest, "hear me out. Your father knows this, but he's the only one. I don't even know why I told him. It was years ago.

He helped me when I desperately needed it. Maybe I felt I owed it to him. Or I had less to lose then."

She stared at him silently, her eyes soft, warm.

"I am not Arkarin Blackhawk." He just started speaking, blurting it out suddenly. No amount of planning and delay was going to make any of this easier. "At least, that is not the name I was born with. It is one I took from another man. A man I killed."

He tried to keep his face turned toward her, but he felt an almost irresistible urge to look away. He knew what he was going to tell her would change how she thought of him, and he couldn't bear to watch that in her eyes.

"There was an imperial general, Astra. His name was Frigus Umbra. He served the current emperor's father, and he was the iron fist of imperial will. Wherever there was resistance to the empire's rule, Umbra came, and he brought death and destruction on a scale almost unimaginable. He didn't just crush rebels, he left a mark that would last for centuries, a terror so profoundly imprinted on the collective soul of a people that men yet unborn would still feel its effects.

"He was pitiless, merciless, unable even to feel human emotions it was said. Like a computer he was, a creature who existed only for war, only to serve his dark and brutal master. There were rumors about him, stories—speculations. But his origins were a mystery, shrouded in the secrecy of an ancient imperial breeding program. Umbra was conceived in a laboratory, the genetic material cultivated over centuries from the cream of the nobility. He was not the first general to be bred in that laboratory, but he was the newest, and the most capable.

"For years, Umbra was the scourge of the empire, and he brought unspeakable horror to the enemies of the emperor.

And then, one day, he disappeared, and he was never heard from again."

He forced himself to look back into her eyes. He could see the moistness, the tears building up. She knew what he was going to say, but still it took all he had to force the words.

"I am Frigus Umbra." He held her gaze, watching as the tears welled up and slid slowly down her cheeks. He expected her to look away, or to get up and flee the room, but she just sat and looked back at him. And, against all his expectations, he saw in her expression the last thing he'd expected.

Compassion. Urging him to continue. With a shuddering breath, he did.

"I was raised from birth to be the perfect imperial general. I was conditioned for years, indoctrinated into the service of the empire. I knew nothing else but to serve, to root out and destroy any who challenged the power of the imperial dynasty. And for years, that is what I did.

"Then I met Blackhawk. The real Blackhawk. He was a rebel, or at least he had gotten involved in the revolution on Deltara." Memories he'd long fought to suppress were flooding into his mind. "The battle was over, the rebel armies broken. The survivors were fleeing, trying to get families out of the city before we destroyed it."

Astra was sitting silently on the bed. Her face was wet with tears, but she held her gaze on Blackhawk, listening to every word he said.

"I was in my headquarters, directing the . . . completion . . . of the operation. For some reason that is still unclear to me, I walked out of the command post. I ordered my guards to stay behind. I wanted to be alone for a few minutes. I'd only intended to go fifty or a hundred meters, but I wandered deeper into the city, farther from HQ. I turned and walked into a half-wrecked building. There was a man there, and a woman behind him, holding a small child."

Blackhawk fell silent. He was telling Astra things he hadn't allowed himself to think of in twenty years. He felt as if he was tearing open old wounds. He wanted to stop, to turn and run from the room, but he tried to force himself to continue. He couldn't imagine what Astra was thinking, how her love was turning to shock . . . and revulsion.

She stood up slowly and took a single step toward him. "Tell me, Ark," she said softly. "Finish your story." She reached up and put her hand on his cheek. It was smooth and warm, and her touch was gentle.

He took a deep breath. "I had ordered the rebels massacred, Astra. All of them. But in that instant, I couldn't carry out my own directive. I saw this man, crawling through a nightmare of death and destruction, trying only to save his family."

He forced himself to lift his eyes and look back at Astra. "I was going to let him go"—he swallowed hard—"but then he heard me, and he reached for his gun. I didn't want to shoot him, but my reflexes acted on their own, the training, the instinct." His fists were clenched and shaking, but he kept his eyes on Astra's. "I shot him. And I watched him fall to the ground in front of me—in front of his wife and child."

Blackhawk's voice had been thick with emotion, but now it was dead, almost monotone. "I had ordered the slaughter of millions, but now I was horrified at the prospect of this one man's death. I leaped toward him, turning him over. I intended to help him, to take him back to the field hospital, but I could tell immediately the wound was mortal. He looked up at me and told me his name and asked me to let his family go. I had been pitiless my entire life, with layer after layer of psychological conditioning reinforcing my icy coldness. But now the thought of this man dying roused feelings I had never had before.

"He begged me again to spare his wife and child, and I promised him I would just before he died. They were crying and clinging to him, and I pulled them away, told them to flee. My mind was reeling. I didn't understand what I was doing. All I knew was I wanted to save these people. I tore them from his body and thrust them into the street, screaming for them to run, to escape before my soldiers found them."

He held Astra's gaze like a lifeline. He kept looking for the condemnation, the hatred he had expected, but there was nothing there but sadness . . . and sympathy.

"They died, Astra. They didn't make it thirty meters before one of my kill squads gunned them down. I screamed for the soldiers to hold their fire, but it was too late.

"It felt like a sledgehammer came down on me. I couldn't breathe; I didn't know what to do or where to go. The soldiers were just following my orders—Blackhawk's family died because of me. I just turned and ran. I didn't know what was happening to me. I couldn't think, couldn't focus. I just knew I had to get away. I fled the city. I hid for days, without food or water. I was tormented, and it became worse every moment as memories came back, all the terrible things I'd done."

Blackhawk was shaking, his legs wobbling. The wave of recollection was almost more than he could bear. "I'd broken my imperial conditioning, Astra, though I didn't know what was happening then. Something about the shock of watching that man and his family die reached down to me, to the man underneath thirty years of relentless indoctrination. The guilt was overwhelming, not just for Blackhawk or for those killed on

Deltara, but for the millions dead in my campaigns. For the brutality of the regime I'd fought so hard to preserve. It all hit me at once."

He breathed deeply, raggedly. "I kept running. I ran for so long. Aimlessly, hopelessly, until finally I made my way to the Far Stars. I found service with a few smugglers and pirates. I was a mess. Until I ended up on Celtiboria . . . and met your father."

Astra's hand was still on his face, and he put his own on hers. "He helped me to see, to understand. To find my way toward being a good man, or at least acting like one. Blackhawk had broken my conditioning, and I took his name. I have been running from my past ever since."

"Ark, you *are* a good man. You were no less a victim of the evil of the empire than those your soldiers slaughtered. What they did to you, when you were a child—a baby—it is unthinkable. I can't imagine the pain inside you."

Her eyes gazed into his, and she continued, "But I also can't imagine how you could think I would hate you. How could you not understand that I love you? That I always will?"

"I love you, Astra. More than you can imagine. And now you understand why we can never be together."

"I understand no such thing, Ark. I told you I don't care. Whoever you were, whatever they did to you to make you into that, that's not you anymore."

"But it *is* me." Blackhawk's voice was grim. "I still feel it, Astra. In battle, when there is danger. The coldness, the feeling of the predator. It's all still inside me. That is why I cannot join your father and lead armies. The power would destroy me, make me back into what I once was. I would seek to stay true, but the brutality is still there, waiting to get out. I would start as a freedom fighter, but I would become a tyrant."

"Then don't join the battle. You can retire to Celtiboria. You don't need to have an active role in the confederation." Her voice was halting, as if she was trying—and failing—to convince herself of what she was saying, even as the words came from her mouth.

He tried to force a smile, but his sadness overwhelmed it. "That is a pleasant fiction, but we both know it won't work. I am involved *now*, probably more than I should be. Do you really think I could sit by while you face crises every day and do nothing? I would begin by trying to help, but it is still there, Astra, the voices, the old compulsions. I fight them, and I am their master. But they feed on power, and sooner or later, they would wear me down, take control. And you never want to see me like that. And to sit at your side, at the top of the Far Stars Confederation . . . it would destroy me.

"You are your father's daughter, his only child. Your future is to rule, to serve the people of the Far Stars, and carry forward your father's dream. Millions will have better lives because of you. Would you walk away from that? Could you?"

"But, Ark . . ."

"Please, Astra. Don't. What are you going to say? You know what I am telling you is the truth. I can't risk becoming what I was. Not for anything. Not even for you. And what about you? Am I wrong? Or are you no more willing—no more able—to walk away from your duty, even for love?"

She started to say something again, but then she closed her mouth and just looked back at him sadly. Blackhawk returned her gaze, and he knew she had decided. However much she might want to leave her responsibilities behind, to spend her life bouncing around the Far Stars in the *Claw*, it was something she could never do. She had strings pulling her just as he did. Their lives weren't their own; they owed too much to others. Blackhawk was running from a past he might never escape, one that might even claim him in the end. He would die before he became again what he had once been. And Astra's debt was to the future, to make certain her father's dream didn't die.

They stood looking at each other for a long time. Finally, Blackhawk said, "Accepting the truth about me, knowing you still see enough in me to love . . . that is worth more to me than anything else in my life." He pulled her back into a tight hug, and for just an instant he forgot everything and felt her warmth against him.

"But now we all have work to do. The empire is still out there. We may have averted this crisis, but there will be another—more than one . . . and soon." Blackhawk closed his eyes and thought about the softness of her skin, the scent of her hair. He knew better than anyone what was coming, the danger and intensity of the struggle they faced. But that was for tomorrow. For just this brief time he wanted to forget it all, and to pretend Astra could be his, that they could live a normal life together. He felt her face pressed against his chest and her hands gripping his back, clinging to him—and he knew she felt the same way.

EPILOGUE

BLACKHAWK LOOKED OUT OVER HIS CREW. THEY WERE ALL assembled, sitting around the lower deck, watching him with inquisitive eyes. He'd called them together, and they had come. Even Tarnan, who seemed to stumble about vacantly over the last few days, was there now, attentive. Blackhawk's tone, the look in his eyes—they left no doubt this was something serious.

He could feel a difference, however. These people were the closest to him in the universe, indeed save for Marshal Lucerne and Astra, they were the only ones he truly cared for. But now there was a distance, a coldness. He knew he had sacrificed one of them. The alternative was to let millions die and leave the Far Stars defenseless before imperial aggression, but that didn't change the fact of what he had done. He had ordered Doc to help Danellan Lancaster first, and Tarq had died as a result. Blackhawk knew he would never forgive himself, and he didn't expect his crew to feel any different. He didn't know his action had killed Tarq. The giant had been grievously injured, and he might have died despite all Doc could have done. But Blackhawk had taken away that chance.

He didn't know if things could ever be the same on the *Claw*. He knew the crew understood—or at least that they would come to understand once the shock and grief was less fresh. But he wasn't sure it mattered. They might forgive him intellectually, but on some level they would view him differently. They had seen him put a mission above one of their number. He hadn't had a choice, not a conscionable one. But his crew were people, not machines. Logic wasn't the sole dictator of their feelings. Rationality only went so far, and raw emotions still held their sway. They might stay with Blackhawk; they might continue to fight at his side. But there would always be something there that hadn't been before. And the thought of it tore at his insides.

But now it was time for something else—it was time to tell them about his history. He'd hesitated, wondering if it was a good idea, especially so soon after Tarq's death. But this wasn't something he would decide in a calculated way. He owed them this. It was long overdue. And he would make good now on something he should have done years before.

"There are some things I wanted to tell all of you, things about my past . . . who I am. Was. Both."

He took a deep breath. He dreaded this more than any battle he'd fought, any enemy or creature he'd faced in combat. He looked across the room, and he saw Astra standing against the far wall. She was looking at him. There was sadness in her gaze, but love and support too. She stared at him as if to say, *You can do this.*

"I know you have all wondered about me, about my life before we came together, before the *Claw.*"

They were all silent, staring back as he spoke. Sarge was propped up on one of the workstation chairs, surrounded by his somber group. He was still weak, but he'd insisted on sitting up and listening to Blackhawk. Drake was sitting on the floor, heavily bandaged, but awake and alert.

Ace was actually standing, albeit leaning pretty heavily on Katarina. He still looked worn and haggard, but better than he had a few days before.

Okay, just do it. "There is a lot about me none of you know, especially about my past." He looked around the room. "I let that go on for far too long, kept too many secrets. You have shared dangers with me. We have bled together, suffered together . . ." He looked over at Sarge and his people, at Tarnan and the emptiness next to him. "Lost our own in battle."

He took a deep breath. "You have earned a right to know the truth . . . all of it. And if, once you have, you no longer wish to serve on this ship, I will understand. I will shake your hands and wish you well and not try to stop you from doing what you must."

He could see the curiosity. He knew they'd all speculated about his past.

Now you will finally know the truth.

"I was not born in the Far Stars. I came here from the empire almost twenty-five years ago. As a child, I lived in an imperial facility. I never knew my parents. I was trained . . ."

"The empire is an evil from our past, one that has returned to again threaten us. I know this, because imperial agents came here, to Antilles. Came to my *office*. They blackmailed me, sought to suborn me to their cause. They brought us to the brink of war with our friends."

Danellan Lancaster stood at the podium, addressing the assembled Senate. He wore a formal white robe with the red sash of a senator emeritus. Lancaster was a magnate, not a politician, but his family had long held a clutch of hereditary seats in Antilles's ruling body.

"What we almost witnessed the other day was a tragic confrontation between the Grand Fleet of Antilles and the forces of Marshal Lucerne of Celtiboria. This travesty was the result of misinformation supplied to both sides by the imperial governor, and only through the intervention of a brave few was disaster narrowly averted."

Blackhawk sat in the gallery watching Lancaster speak. The industrialist was still weak from his wound, but he had insisted on calling the matter of the Confederation Treaty for an immediate vote. Blackhawk had been nervous about Danellan Lancaster, but now he was pleased to see his support paying off. Lancaster was on planetwide broadcast, speaking to millions. Governor Vos would know that his would-be puppet had chosen resistance over capitulation. Danellan Lancaster had found his courage. He was putting his company—indeed, his very life—at great risk.

Blackhawk's thoughts drifted from the speech. He'd helped Lancaster and Lucerne put the Celtiborian-Antillean alliance back together, and he knew that was a huge success. But he also realized they were far from past the crisis—if anything, recent events were about to precipitate even greater struggles ahead. The Far Stars had grown complacent over the years, as one fool after another was sent to take the governor's seat. But that streak of luck had come to an end, and the man they faced now—Kergen Vos—was not someone to be trifled with. The ambition and scope of his plots showed a mixture of genius and sadism, and while some of those plans had been thwarted, Blackhawk suspected they had barely scratched the surface of imperial scheming. If Vos was set on extending the emperor's rule throughout the Far Stars, there were dark days ahead.

I wonder if we'll be ready.

Blackhawk knew his own people needed rest. Some of them were wounded, the others merely exhausted—and they were all shocked by Tarq's death. It would be some time before they could set out again. He could only guess the condition of the marshal's armies, though he suspected they were as ready as they could be, despite the near war with Antilles.

What didn't need imagination was how *Wolf's Claw* had fared during this last mission—it would be under repair for at least a month. The miraculous cold jump had worked, but not without burning out half the systems in the ship. Danellan Lancaster had insisted on offering the use of the Lancaster shipyards at no cost, a bit of generosity from the old robber baron that had surprised even Blackhawk. Still, even with those resources, it would be some time before they could lift off, and he hoped to have a good idea of where they were going by then.

Happily, he wouldn't be going alone. When the *Claw* was finally ready to launch, she would do so with her full complement. Blackhawk had told his people everything, recounted every horrendous act he'd committed in his years as an imperial general. And to his astonishment, almost as a unit they had affirmed their loyalty and devotion to their friend and leader. They had nominated Ace to speak with him, and he had reassured the *Claw*'s captain that his crew was still with him. Yes,

Ace had told him, Tarq's death had been a shock . . . and it would take a while for that wound to heal. But they knew why he had done what he did.

Only Tarnan was uncertain about staying. The loss of Tarq hit his twin harder than anyone, of course, and he was shaken to his core. Blackhawk had been unable to face him at first, a bit of personal cowardice that only added to his self-loathing. But finally he had gone to see the giant, to look him in the eye and take responsibility for what he had done. Blackhawk never spoke of what the two discussed that day, nor did Tarnan. But the *Claw*'s surviving twin didn't leave either.

Blackhawk wondered if his crew could so easily have forgiven his dark past if it had been *their* families slaughtered, their worlds blasted in radioactive hells. There were millions still living in the empire who had lost loved ones, seen their homes destroyed—all by Blackhawk's actions. But his family on the *Claw* only understood his past in abstract terms. It was one thing to speak of mass murder and apocalyptic destruction and quite another to actually see it, experience it. Blackhawk suspected no one who hadn't been there could truly understand the horror of it the way he—and his victims—did.

He decided it didn't matter. His family had stayed with him, and the burden of secrecy was at last gone. The relief he felt was a weight off his soul. The grief of Tarq's death still hung heavily over him, but they would get past that as well. Raw open wounds would heal with age, replaced by fond remembrance. Tarnan's brother would never be forgotten, not as long as Blackhawk and his people went on.

He looked toward the stage, just as Lancaster was introducing Marshal Lucerne. Blackhawk knew how much his friend hated giving speeches, which made it oddly amusing that he was so good at it. Augustin Lucerne was as inspiring behind a microphone as he was on the battlefield.

"People of Antilles, I come here today to speak with you about a common danger. I am here as a friend, though our mutual enemies have conspired to set us against each other, make us foes rather than allies. Danellan Lancaster's actions helped avert such a tragedy and led us to this auspicious moment. All Antilleans know of Mr. Lancaster as a great industrialist and philanthropist. I now ask that we all recognize him as a patriot and a hero as well."

Blackhawk suppressed a smile. He didn't like politics any more than the marshal did, but he was impressed, as he always was, at just how charming Augustin Lucerne could be . . . especially when he was lying through his teeth.

By all accounts, the vote was a lock. By the end of the day, Antilles and Celtiboria would become the first official members of the Far Stars Confederation. Rykara, Nordlingen, and almost a dozen other worlds would follow almost immediately.

Then the real struggle will begin . . .

"So, Lord Aragona, you have been a captive for some time now. What shall I do with you?"

The miserable Castillan glared at Blackhawk across the small cell, but he didn't answer. The brig on *Glorianus* was much larger than the tiny room on the *Claw*. Aragona had been on Lucerne's flagship for several weeks now. Blackhawk had turned the prisoner over to Lucerne's people on Nordlingen. The prisoner had been told nothing of what his captors planned to do with him.

"The way I see it," Blackhawk continued, "there are three options." His voice was businesslike, but there was a hint of taunting there too. "First, I could take you to Vanderon. I'm sure the bank is annoyed that I have taken so long to complete this job, but I suspect they will pay the bounty anyway.

"Second, I could just chuck you out the airlock. As much as I'd like the bounty, I have a lot to do, and it will be hard to find the time to fly all the way to Vanderon." He glared at the captive. "After all, your guards shot one of my people." He paused, and his voice turned deadly serious. "It is a very good thing for you my friend survived. If he hadn't, we'd be discussing some other options, Aragona . . . extremely unpleasant ones."

Blackhawk had been standing in the doorway, but now he took a few steps into the cell. "And then there is option three," he continued. "You can actually do something worthwhile with your useless existence and help us protect the Far Stars."

Aragona looked up, a confused expression on his face. He stared at his captor, but then another man walked in and stood next to Blackhawk. His eyes darted to the new arrival, who was wearing a gray military uniform and knee-high boots.

"Aragona, this is Marshal Augustin Lucerne. You know who he is, do you not?" Blackhawk glowered at the prisoner.

Aragona looked up, stunned.

"Hello, Lord Aragona," Lucerne said calmly, smiling. "Would I be correct in assuming that you do not know the true source of the weapons you planned to use in your coup?"

"What weapons? What coup? I don't know what you're talking about." Aragona was clearly surprised by Lucerne's question, and he was trying to sound convincing.

"Come now, Lord Aragona. I thought we could discuss this like serious men, but if you plan to waste my time, I will just let Arkarin dispose of you as he sees fit." Lucerne turned and started back toward the door.

"Wait . . ."

Lucerne stopped, but he didn't turn around. "Yes?"

"The weapons . . . I was approached by a man. He said he represented a trade cartel, that he could supply me with advanced arms to seize control of Castilla in return for a monopoly on our imports and exports."

Lucerne turned around and took a step back toward Aragona. "Would it surprise you to find out that you were lied to? That those weapons came not from a trade cartel, but from the imperial governor?"

"The empire?" he asked with genuine shock. "I swear, I had no idea."

"Well, now that you do, I have a question for you. How would you feel about returning to Castilla and launching that coup after all—and setting yourself up as planetary administrator under the new Far Stars Confederation?"

"Is this a joke?"

Lucerne walked over and sat on the bench. "No, I'm afraid not, though I can see the morbid humor in it. The thought of placing someone little better than a gangster in charge does not thrill me, but if I can get Castilla into the confederation without having to invade, I can save the lives of thousands. Your deputies are no doubt still squabbling over your holdings, but I suspect you will have little trouble regaining control. I will provide you a regiment of regulars to assist . . . and to keep an eye on you."

His expression hardened. "You will do as you're told, Aragona, and I'm afraid you will have to keep your illicit plundering down to a minimum. But it is better than the alternative." He glanced at Blackhawk then back to Aragona. "You will still be the ruler of the planet, even if you are answerable to me. An alternative far preferable to any of your other options, I suspect."

Aragona sat quietly for a few seconds. He looked at Lucerne then over at Blackhawk, who was standing there scowling at him. "Okay, I will do it."

"Excellent." Lucerne got up slowly. "Welcome aboard. You will have a chance to atone for your dissolute life, though I suspect that is an inducement that is lost on you at present. Still, you should be pleased. Things could have gone in . . . mmm . . . another direction." Lucerne smiled and walked toward the door. He paused just before he stepped into the hall.

"Oh, and Aragona . . . if you betray me or try to get away with something behind my back, I will find out." He turned and glared at the Castillan with fiery eyes. "And I will come for you. And you will wish I'd given you to Blackhawk."

The masses of soldiers marched across the blasted desert sands in perfect formation. They were clad in the black uniforms of the imperial legions, but these troops had not come from the empire—they had not crossed the vast emptiness of the Void. These warriors were raised and trained in the Far Stars.

They had been scum, the detritus of human society on the fringe, but now they were survivors. They were graduating from a training regimen that had killed almost one of every two participants. Tragonis had continually increased the intensity of the program, condensing more and more training into a shorter time. Vos needed soldiers, and he needed them soon.

Tragonis was more than happy to deliver.

"You have done well, old friend," Vos said. "A bit hard on the trainees perhaps, but there are always more recruits floating around the gutters of the Far Stars ready to take the bounty." Imperial service had a base appeal to many. The discipline was strict, but there were many rewards—if you considered murder, rape, and torture a reward. Vos suspected for those who joined up, it was exactly that.

"Thank you, Governor." Tragonis was sitting in the imperial box with Vos and Wilhelm. And seated next to the governor was Kalishar's ruler. Rax Florin looked out over the proceedings nervously. Tragonis had shown the ka'al complete respect in their dealings—there was nothing to be gained from antagonizing their host. But he couldn't imagine any monarch could watch thousands of troops—even an ally's—march across his world without a bit of pause. Tragonis knew Vos would dispose of Florin the instant his usefulness was exhausted . . . and he suspected the ka'al knew it too.

"This is the first group of ten thousand, but there are over eighty thousand in the second class, and two hundred thousand in the third. In two years, we will have one hundred legions, fully equipped and trained."

Vos nodded and watched the parade move past the box. He hoped these soldiers fought as well as they marched. Having an effective army would allow him to accelerate his plans.

Many of his programs were proceeding well, but the setbacks had been costly—the debacle with Danellan Lancaster and Antilles being the worst. Because despite Vos's meticulous planning, Lancaster had proven to have more courage than he would have thought. Now, not only were Antilles and Celtiboria formally allied as members of the Far Stars Confederation, but Lancaster had publicly declared the empire had tried to suborn him. Lancaster was an influential man, and his word carried weight. Vos had benefited early from the complacency caused by his incompetent predecessors, but now he suspected the fear of the empire would grow again.

The plan was perfect, but it didn't count on one thing.

Arkarin Blackhawk.

Blackhawk was the constant thorn in his side, and he was certainly behind this recent disruption. A million crowns—a massive fortune in the Far Stars—yet no one had managed to kill the bastard. There was obviously more to Arkarin Blackhawk than some rogue mercenary prowling around the Far Stars, and Vos was determined to find out. As soon as he got back to Galvanus Prime, he was going to put a dozen people on it. Every investigation so far had come to a dead end twenty years earlier. He refused to accept that, though. Once and for all, he was going to find out who this mysterious adventurer was—and what he was hiding.

That would take care of one problem, but there was another serious obstacle that was growing larger day by day.

He turned to Wilhelm, a glint in his eye.

"Mak, I have something I want you to handle for me.

"It's time we do something about Marshal Lucerne."

And make sure to read the stunning conclusion in *Funeral Games* in trade paperback and eBook, on sale January 2016.

ABOUT THE AUTHOR

Jay Allan currently lives in New York City and has been reading science fiction and fantasy for just about as long as he's been reading. His tastes are fairly varied and eclectic, but favorites include military and dystopian science fiction, space opera, and epic fantasy—all usually a little bit gritty.

He writes a lot of science fiction with military themes, but also other SF and some fantasy as well. He likes complex characters and lots of backstory and action, but in the end believes world-building is the heart of science fiction and fantasy.

Before becoming a professional writer, Jay has been an investor and real estate developer. When not writing, he enjoys traveling, running, hiking, and—of course—reading.

He also loves hearing from readers and always answer e-mails. You can reach him at jay@jayallanbooks.com, and join his mailing list at http://www.crimsonworlds.com for updates on new releases.

Among other things, he is the author of the bestselling Crimson Worlds series.